# HARDBOILED CTHULHU

Two-Fisted Tales of
Tentacled Terror

PUBLICATION ACKNOWLEDGMENTS

"Pazuzu's Children" was previously published in *Cthulhu Codex* #10 (Eastertide 1997)

"Outside Looking In" was previously published in *Dreaming From R'lyeh* #4 (2005)

"A Change of Life" was previously published in *Book of Dark Wisdom* #3 (Spring 2004)

"The Watcher From the Grave" was previously published in *Classic Pulp Fiction Stories* #58 (March 2000)

This is the first American publication of "The Questioning of the Azathothian Priest," which was previously published in Britain.

All other stories and poems are original to this volume.

FIRST EDITION
10 9 8 7 6 5 4 3 2
Published in May 2006
ISBN: 0-9759229-7-1
Printed in the U.S.A.

Published by Dimensions Books, an imprint of Elder Signs Press, Inc.
P.O. Box 389
Lake Orion, MI 48361-0389
www.eldersignspress.com

# Hardboiled Cthulhu
## Two-Fisted Tales of Tentacled Terror

dimensions

books

2006

# TABLE OF CONTENTS

# Sleeping with the Fishes

## James Ambuehl

I never should have taken that job:
But she looked at me so sweet,
With legs that went on and on,
And a smile that couldn't be beat.

So I went to stake out the pier;
There was something in the air that night.
And though Mama Hazard's boy is tough,
I gripped my .45 tight.

The ship came in on time,
And the gunsels began to unload.
At the orders of a foreman
Who looked like a giant toad.

They unpacked a humongous crate,
And in front of it gathered 'round.
Then began a chanting, answered
By a monstrous bellowing sound!

I drew my gat and came forward;
They all turned and looked at me.
Then the crate, behind me, splintered –
The bellowing horror was free!

My gun barked; the men all fell.
And I ran to the cab of the crane,
And shifted the gears rapidly,
As on and on the monster came!

But I hooked it with the monstrous claw,
And dropped it in the sea.
It fell with a mighty splash,
And then I laughed, quite madly.

But as I sit here writing,
Vain though I know my wish is;
I pray that eldritch horror
Is again sleeping with the fishes!

# THE PISCES CLUB

## James Ambuehl

She had the kind of body that would make a bishop kick out a stained glass window. She had class too, the kind of class you just don't find every day in Kingsport. Believe me, I'd know. I've been working this town for nearly fifteen years now, ever since they kicked me off the force in nearby Arkham for busting up a guy who beat up his wife and kids one too many times . . . but that's another story. And just in case you came in late, the name's Hazard, and I'm a P. I.

I had been killing time in my downtown office late that afternoon, reviewing old case files, cleaning my gun, basically doing anything I could to help keep my mind off of just when my next meal ticket would come along, when she came to see me. She being Jennifer Marlowe, the lady in question from my earlier statements, who could have easily been a stand-in for Greta Garbo or Jean Harlow. I could see right away that she had great gams, and the face of an angel; a face that would light up . . . well, I think you probably get the picture. Anyway, to make a long story short, she asked me to fetch some relic for her — an amulet, which she claimed was her birthright — and for what she was paying me, half in advance yet, I would have scoured the ends of the Earth in search of such a trinket. Yep, I thought to myself as my belly growled at the promise of a fine steak with all the trimmings, I'd even brave the Pisces Club.

The Pisces Club was a sort of gathering hall for an elite organization, which was also known under that singular name. The Club was part social club, part religious order, and all gangster from what I could gather of the rumors flying about from Dunwich to Innsmouth and back again. You don't tangle with the Pisces Club if you want to stay healthy, if you know what I mean. And sucker that I was, I took the job. The gratitude was written all over her beautiful face when I told her. And then she leaned her willowy frame over my desk and kissed me.

And in that deep passionate embrace there was definitely a promise of something more when the job was done.

After she'd left, and I'd got back from treating myself to some long-overdue dinner, I tried to get some routine work done, but it was no use. She was in my thoughts. Here I was, a hard-as-nails lug, acting like a lovesick puppy! Disgusted with myself, I finally curled up on the couch in my office and grabbed some shut-eye.

When I awoke the next morning, I was sweating to beat hell. It was still Spring, but I could feel that Summer was on its way. It felt like one of those days you could fry an egg on the sidewalk. Good thing too, since I was pretty sure I didn't have a skillet anywhere in the office, and I couldn't go back to my apartment. See, there was this little matter of an eviction notice served on me for, yep, you guessed it: busting up another tenant. And if you're thinking he deserved it too, well, you win the Kewpie doll. I peeled my eyes open slowly, the sun an orange glow beating in from the west window. Waitaminnit. The *west* window?

I rolled off the couch and lifted the shade and peered out. The stars were still twinkling in the night sky; the glow was coming from beyond my front door, somewhere down the hall. The office suites connected to mine were on fire!

I palmed my .45 from my top desk drawer and sprinted toward my office door. Peering through the frosted glass, I could see a shape silhouetted in the fiery glow, a big shape, and it was heading directly toward my office. Pocketing the rod, I instead grabbed a two-by-four I kept stashed behind the door — just in case — and slid up against the wall. I raised my club above my head.

The doorknob turned slowly, then the figure stepped inside. As I brought my club down on him again and again he let out a squawk and lay still.

I thought just then that my eyes must have been playing tricks with me. I could have sworn that while I was beating my assailant to a pulp, well, he didn't appear to be *human*. He was . . . *something*. Something strange, and believe me, I've seen strange in my day. This was Kingsport, Massachusetts after all, centered in the heart of the Miskatonic Valley, an environs known for strange with a capital 'S.' And when I went to examine my fallen foe, I felt beneath my hand not the flesh or clothes I expected to find, but *scales*!

I lit a match and held it over his face, in an attempt to gain a closer look-see. I soon wished I hadn't. What I was seeing was more fish than man! But I had to cut my gawking at the mook short, for just then I heard heavy, pounding footfalls coming my way. The galoot's partner must have heard his cry!

Diving behind my heavy oaken desk opposite the door, I drew my .45 from my coat pocket again and waited. He soon stepped just inside the doorway, and he looked even bigger than the last bruiser, if that's at all possible. These mugs easily dwarfed me, and I'm no small fry myself. And I could tell by his outline that he wasn't any more human than the last guy was. He saw me then, and I saw him reach inside his trenchcoat for a piece. But he didn't draw out any rod I recognized, see, but rather a shiny metal disc. A jet of flame leapt from the disc like something out of those *Buck Rogers* serials, and the desk I was crouching under caught fire and began to blaze fitfully. Knowing I was outgunned here, I raised up and fired three shots in rapid succession, then propelled myself backward with all my might.

I felt glass shattering at my back, then the unsettling sensation of falling. Then the hard-packed earth rushed up and knocked the wind out of me. I had jumped from my third-floor window, down into Mrs. Wojnowski's back yard. I raised my head and shook it, the cool night air helping to clear all the cobwebs away, and as I came to my senses I heard a sound to my right. I exchanged my gat in my hand for a pair of brass knuckles nestled deep in my pocket, and I shot my fist out for the skull of my neighbor lady's charging Mastiff hound. It gave with a mighty crack beneath the force of my rabbit-punch blow, and staggering dizzily a moment, the dog quickly collected itself and yelped away into the night. Then I got to my feet and ran through the yard. I made my way down the block a-ways, then turned in the direction of my office. I could tell by the volume of the sirens that the police cars and fire trucks were near now, and I resigned myself to the fact that I'd never get the chance to retrieve anything further than myself from my now brightly-blazing office; the whole building was burning like a Roman candle. I needed a drink, I thought, as I especially lamented the loss of my twelve year-old bottle of scotch which I had kept in the bottom drawer, a bottle which was likely helping to fuel the flames now.

Fish-men and ray-guns? Mama Hazard didn't raise no dummy, and I knew at once that I was out of my element, like a fish out of water. Little did I know just how apt that description might turn out to be. Luckily, I knew just who to see. It was a long drive over to Arkham, and Miskatonic University was just opening for the day when I got there. I wandered over to the Folklore and Mythologies Department, and went to see Professor Phil Craft. "Four-Eyes" Phil was an old school chum from way back in High School, when Phil was the unfortunate victim of a daily Senior extortion ring. He shook like one of those little yapping dogs, and he gave me a look kind of like one of them to boot, when I had approached him at his locker one day. I think he thought I was going to deal him more of the same. But I had lain my own form of extortion on him: I'd take care of the bullies if he'd help save my own failing academic standing. Needless to say — brains and brawn — it was the beginning of a beautiful friendship.

"Albert," he called out, breaking into my thoughts as I rounded the corner to his office door, "what brings you over here to Arkham?"

I was about to growl that nobody but my Mama called me Albert, but I just shrugged it off. Phil was a good egg. He invited me into his office, where we had a generous helping of his own prized bottle of Scotch, which I assured him we'd need for the tale I was going to tell. It was a whopper. Then, I did.

I had to hand it to him. He was a cool customer, and when I'd finished my spiel he began one of his own — something about Man not being the first ruler of Earth and monsters having been there before, but to be honest, I tuned most of it out. Mooks with guns I understand, but what do I know from monsters? I didn't even believe in them . . . until today. Phil went on though, and finally I couldn't hold back any longer.

"Doc, just tell me about these Deep Things, okay?" I fairly screamed.

"Deep *Ones*, Albert," he corrected me, looking at me and blinking like an owl. "Servants of Great Koothooloo. It's the first I've heard of them in Kingsport, though. But I suspect this 'Pisces Club' is an off-shoot of the Esoteric Order of Dagon in Innsmouth." He looked to go on, but the expression on my face made him change his mind. Instead, he quickly sketched something on a piece of notebook paper, wrote a note under the sketch, signed it, folded it, and handed it to me. "Is this the creature you saw?" I could only nod dumbly. Phil Craft could have been a professional artist, for all the lifelike realism he gave the fish-man he had drawn. It was exactly like the one I had seen.

"Yes, Deep Ones, I knew it!" he screamed excitedly, then went on more solemnly. "Listen, Albert, I'd ask you to forget this client and her job, but I know you all too well for that, my friend. I remember all too well your single-minded pursuit of Deborah Channing, the Head Cheerleader — and your winning her too, from that football Captain, Doug Peterson. So with that in mind, infiltration is probably your best move. Here, take this sketch over to the Theatre Department and ask for Conrad Weiss. Tell him I sent you, then hand this to him. He'll help you out. And Albert, I'm sure I don't have to tell you this, but be careful!"

He didn't have to, of course, but I appreciated it all the same.

The Theatre Department wasn't hard to spot — they had a gigantic poster with the details for a play they were to perform next week, called *The Yellow King* — and I was led backstage by a student (pretty, fresh-faced girl, I noted, but then, that was just me), to meet with Weiss. I wasn't sure just what to expect, but Conrad Weiss definitely wasn't it. He smelled better than most of the dames I knew, and by the shade of his eye-shadow it was obvious he knew his way around make-up like a fifty dollar floozy knows her way around a guy's . . . wallet. In fact, the man was creeping me out big-time, almost as bad as those fish-men. But a job was a job, and being *too* cautious didn't put food on the table in my line of work. I swallowed my pride and sat with a heavy sigh in the make-up chair.

"Get to work, Lon Chaney," I called amiably enough, then saw fit to growl, "and no funny business."

"I wouldn't dream of it, handsome . . . well, *dream*, perhaps . . ." he lisped at me with a smile and a flutter of the eyelashes, then got down to work.

I was glad to see that he preferred to work in silence, and left me to my thoughts about what Phil had had to say about the Deep Ones. The fish-men were bad enough, but who or what was Koothooloo? I wasn't so sure I wanted to find out. Getting rousted by coppers, shot at by goons, even getting your car turned into so much Swiss cheese by tommy-guns like my last flivver had been was one thing, but these monsters were entirely something else. What was I getting into here, and how deep was I willing to go?

So ran my thoughts over and over again, for seemingly endless hours, when Weiss finally announced with a flourish that he was finished, and spun my chair around to the light bulb-surrounded mirror before it. I couldn't believe my eyes: With the long, sweeping fins, the gills on the side of my neck, the flabby lips, the bulging eyes, not to mention the greenish color of everything, I was *hideous*!

After Weiss had turned down my offer of a couple of sawbucks for his troubles, and he handed me a free pair of tickets for the upcoming *King in Yellow* show — and letting it be known, incidentally, that if I could not find a date for the affair that I could certainly always sit with him; I told him I would bring Mama Hazard if nothing else . . . but hey, he didn't have to know she was pushing up daisies, right? — I took my leave and headed outside into the sun once more. I scared a wino halfway into sobriety while shambling my way to my DeSoto, and had to ease behind the wheel so that I wouldn't tear the material of my costume. But it was mostly hard rubber and pretty durable anyway, and I really had to hand it to Conrad Weiss. He could have given the special effects I saw in that weird movie last year — *Frankenstein* — a run for their money. I made it back to Kingsport by early evening and parked a block down from the Pisces Club, then eased my seat back and grabbed some more shut-eye.

◆　◆　◆

It was getting near Midnight when I approached on foot, and I saw a small line of people waiting to get into the Club. Resisting the powerful urge to run screaming away into the night, I got in line with some of these fish-men myself. Again, I had to hand it to Weiss. The costume he'd made was as good as any of these I saw here. And I told myself that they were just that — costumes — even though I knew they weren't. And I was relieved when the gorilla at the door waved me in like I belonged there or something. For all he knew, I did.

The crowd was swiftly ushered inside and led through a game-room and past a bar, to a set of double-doors. That double-door was something too, with a filigreed shape upon it looking something like a giant octopus-headed man with wings.

"Ya Koothooloo!" I heard our usher chant, and we were directed to join him. I tripped over the words like a pro; yeah, right. Then the doors swung open and we were led inside, to what looked like the inside of a church chapel. We lined up in the foremost pews, and I was lucky to get the aisle seat in the first one. It would make my escape that much easier, having an open area directly before me, should it come to that.

Taking my seat, I finally took the opportunity to inspect my sur-roundings a bit more clearly. The pews were arranged in a loose semi-circle about a raised dais or stage, upon which sat a large stone table inclined upwards at an angle facing us. A podium stood to the right of this, with a large black book resting upon it. The hall was decorated with large stained-glass windows on its outer walls, and the creatures depicted in them were the shapes of madness. One had the appearance of a blobby cluster of spheres, with something squat and tentacled hiding behind it; another showed a monstrous snake-creature rearing up; a third showed a large black tree covered with sharp-fanged mouths. There were others too, but another figure had taken its place at the podium and the ceremony was starting.

"Praise Day-gon!" the tall, skeletal and somewhat froggy figure I recognized as Septimus Waite, one of the Valley's most elusive crime-bosses, cried aloud. "Praise him in his Father's name, the name of Great Koothooloo! In his image we are formed, and here, safely away from the prying eyes of the Enemy, in his image we shall be!"

The high-priest was droning on, and if I didn't have a photographic memory (an excellent thing to have in my line of work), I never would have doped out what he was saying. But just then a group of robe-wearing acolytes carrying silken pillows entered from the wings behind the altar, and I saw arranged on the pillows various holy relics . . . including what could only be the amulet I had been hired to grab.

Then another pair of fish-men came forth, dragging a naked, struggling form between them. I saw what appeared to be a young girl of roughly 13 or 14, and as the high-priest left off his litany they brought the girl to the altar and chained her hand-and-foot to its reddish surface. And I just knew those stains wouldn't turn out to be tomato paste.

The high-priest resumed his chant, and at the utterance of the name "Dagon" (which I found was the correct spelling, when I looked it up later at good ole M.U. in Arkham; and the other guy was called "Cthulhu," of course), a section of floor before the altar began to slide away, revealing a monstrous pit. Sickening slurping and squelching sounds came from its depths, steadily growing louder as the girl stared down bug-eyed and began to scream.

I could sit still no longer, and I jumped to my feet and leaped upon the stage, my hammering fists battering my way through the confused creatures surrounding me. I bee-lined my way toward the robed acolytes. Seeing me coming straight on, like an onrushing freight train, they threw down the pillows and fled. I stopped only to scoop up the amulet and stuff it deep down inside my fish-suit, then grabbed the end of the trident of one of the creatures rushing on me and hauled back on it, flipping him head-over-heels over me. Another swiped at me with a sickle-shaped blade, bellowing something like (courtesy of that photographic memory again): "Fun-gluey muggle-noff Koothooloo Rulay woggle-noggle."

"Betcha can't say that three times fast, fish-face!" I taunted with a false bravado, then drew my .45 from a cloth-lined fold in the fish-man costume I'd had Weiss put in there — just in case — and plugged him three times. Then, pocketing the gat and grabbing the trident again, I prepared to hurl it at the high-priest. But as I turned to do so, I saw out of the corner of my eye that the poor girl was nearly mad with fright now, and a knot of questing tentacles as big-around as my leg was trailing from the pit and clustering at her bound feet.

Uttering a barely-coherent prayer for her, I hurled the trident through her mid-section. Better that than the nauseating death that awaited her below. Then grabbing my piece again and firing my last three rounds into Septimus Waite at point-blank range, I turned and sprinted for the nearest stained-glass window — the one with the spheres and the tentacled creature — and dove headlong through it.

If I expected to feel the glass breaking and the sensation of falling again, then I was sadly disappointed. Instead, I felt a bout of nausea as I was torn by shrieking winds, and then I felt hard-packed earth again as I became aware that I was in a clearing in the woods somewhere. And it was daylight again.

Gaining my feet and carefully making my way along a twisted path leading out of the woods, I emerged and saw the rounded hills of Dunwich surrounding me. How I had traveled, seemingly in an instant, from the town of Kingsport to the town of Dunwich I really had no idea.

But I was very grateful now that I'd hunted often as a boy in Dunwich, and knew the countryside somewhat. Getting my bearings from a couple of her queer monuments, older than the town itself, I hiked my way over to Dean's Corners, and at Osborn's General Store I was finally able to get a ride from some old-timer in a battered Ford pickup truck back to Kingsport. He seemed to think I had been fishing for some reason, and when he indicated my green "waders," all that remained of my fish costume, I couldn't help laughing. In fact, I laughed and laughed until I ached from the exertion, and when the old man dropped me off downtown, I think he was rather glad to be rid of this chortling madman.

◆　◆　◆

My first instinct (after buying a fresh suit from the thrift shop, of course) was to go back to see Phil at M.U., to try and get him to help me make sense of all this cockamamie jazz (that photographic memory does me no good, see, when I just don't have the good sense to listen!). But I had the amulet now, and I wanted to get rid of it as soon as possible. Not that it was an ugly thing — it was really a beautiful, if alien, work of art. But just holding it kind of gave me the willies. That, and I recalled how Phil was against me getting hold of it in the first place; maybe he'd try to talk me out of giving it to her.

So, I hopped a cab over to the Marlowe Mansion. And mansion was right. The place looked like something out of the movies. Shrugging off my awe, I went to ring the doorbell. With not a servant in sight, Jennifer Marlowe answered the door herself. And she looked wonderful doing it too, dressed in a silken negligee and nothing else.

"Mr. Hazard . . . Al. Did you get the amulet?" I held it up in my hand, probably just then grinning like a monkey.

"Good," she purred, and came forth to embrace me. Her lips tasted like honey. "Let's adjourn to the bedroom," she breathed in my ear.

I followed her up that winding staircase without a care in the world. Leading me to her bed, she sat me down upon it, then rose and held out her hand for the amulet. I gave it to her, gladly. She crossed gracefully to her bureau and sat down and began to brush her long, luxurious hair.

"I am grateful to you for bringing it to me, you know. It's my birthright. And there is the little matter of your balance of payment," she said huskily, rising and dropping her shoulder straps and stepping out of her negligee. Then, lovely chiseled back still to me, she added: "I can't wait to use my amulet again. It will restore my age-old powers. With this I will be able to re-assume my *true* form."

My world went spinning away with those final words. With nerveless fingers I began to fumble for my gun in the pocket of my coat lying on the bed, even as she turned toward me, fastening the amulet behind her neck. I watched those formerly lovely pale arms come down a wattled, scaly brown, even as I struggled to load the clip. I raised the .45 to her. The gat barked again and again as she fell to the floor. I could not even bear to look her in what was formerly a lovely face. I just pointed the gun and fired blindly.

I donned my coat again and made my way downstairs, to the liquor cabinet. I sat there in the dark for hours, drowning my sorrows. I didn't leave until every bottle in that place was drained dry.

Yet, life goes on in Kingsport. Life always goes on as usual. Then again, maybe not.

# A CHANGE OF LIFE

## William Jones

I watched as Hannah glided down the flagstone path that twisted through the Trinity Church cemetery. She had the grace of a majestic bird in flight, and somehow managed to appear furtive as a mouse who had just spied the shadow of a hawk flying overhead.

Early spring has always been one of my favorite seasons. And New York City in early spring was a delightful place to visit. Even in 1929, when the financial district was booming, its streets swarming with people, and a vista of dizzying skyscrapers surrounding the district, it somehow still seemed welcoming. So, I was pleased to find myself sitting on the stone bench at the Trinity Church Cemetery — although the majority of my company were less lively than I was accustomed to; even the living ones were stern-faced bankers and brokers on their lunch break. Nonetheless it was pleasant. *Serene.* Yes.

As Hannah approached, a tight, nervous smile flitted across her face. She was clad in a high-collared jacket and pleated skirt, both of a deep red hue. Her hair was silky black and cropped short, with a defiant cowlick that could only exist south of Chelsea.

Her apprehensive glimpses around the blossoming trees and lush grass of the cemetery were not directed toward the other *living* occupants. No, she was looking for someone less obvious.

The city had grown taller since my last visit. I marveled at the numerous buildings reaching toward the heavens, and the number still under construction, each trying to soar higher than the next. I wondered what *thing* drove such marvelous creations. What tortured lives humanity must live that they needed to construct such marvels.

When Hannah reached me, she stood a moment without speaking; she simply gazed at me as though she wasn't sure she recognized me now that she was closer. In the background, traffic growled along Broadway.

"Hello, Mickey," Hannah eventually said. Looking toward the

sharp blue sky and the fiery visage hanging directly above, she added, "It is a nice day for a trip."

"It is," I replied. "Most certainly."

Realizing a brown paper bag was perched alongside me on the bench — I assumed it was my lunch — I snatched it up, clearing a spot for her. The paper crackled — it seemed unusually heavy for a lunch.

Hannah lowered herself onto the bench. "So what do we do next?"

I thought about the question a moment, letting memories slowly float to the surface. It was a good question.

"We need to get you to Penn Station," I said.

"Are you feeling all right, Mickey?" Hannah asked, placing one of her delicate hands upon my shoulder. "You don't look like your usual self. You're . . . quiet and still."

I could tell she longed for a better word than "still," but apparently it eluded her.

She was correct. I did recall being a little more energetic, and much more boisterous. And no, I didn't feel altogether myself, but I knew that would pass. It always did.

"I'm fine," I said. "I'm just not feeling myself today."

Again a cautious expression flashed across her face, but she quickly regained her composure. But now her voice was no longer smooth. There was a slight edge to it.

"I thought we were going to take the ferry to New Jersey," she said. "Why have you changed your mind?"

I shrugged. "Instinct, I guess. Besides, Penn Station is crowded. It's a better place. From there you can head south."

Hannah knotted her hands together, turning to face the stony church. "Maybe I shouldn't do this, Mickey. I mean Dutch has been good to me. Maybe I can just explain it. Apologize. He'll forgive me."

Even through the tension in her voice, I could hear its beauty, its melodious nature. The voice of a singer, an artist. Then I recalled her singing in one of Dutch's smoky speakeasies.

Memories began to shift inside my mind. I was feeling more like my old self. "You know better than that, Hannah," I said. "No one nabs fifty long ones from Dutch Schultz and walks away. Sure, Dutch will smile and say it is all right, but then he'll send someone for you."

I wondered if my vernacular was hyperbolic. I always had the greatest difficulty adjusting to human slang. It was a slippery element of the language, always changing like the seasons. I found it inefficient. There were too many possibilities for spurious interpretations.

Her deep green eyes cast toward me. There was a question in them. At first I thought I had uttered something that gave me away. But then I caught her eye darting at the brown paper bag in my lap. I recalled why the bag was so heavy.

"It's not me," I said. "Well, it *was*. But it ain't no more. Dutch sent me to do the job. But I ain't." Like a new glove, it sometimes took a while to break it in. I was slowly getting the feel for Mickey: how he moved, how he talked. It was all coming back.

She smiled. Her countenance softened; her eyes began to well with tears. "I was so afraid it was you," she said. When I saw you, something seemed different. For a moment you weren't the Mickey I knew."

Even for the greatest artist, manipulating human hosts can be risky. From her reaction, it appeared I had overcome the initial unstable period.

I hefted the paper bag in my lap, feeling the weight of a handgun. My returning memories told me it was a .38 revolver. Clean and simple. Shoot Hannah here, leave, and somewhere along the way ditch the paper bag. No prints, no witnesses to see me with the weapon. Nice, clean and simple. That was how Mickey liked things done. And I was Mickey.

Mickey Guinn, or more affectionately known among the criminal elements of New York City: Mickey "The Gun" Guinn. "The Gun" had been attached to my host's name because of his habit of never carrying a gun on his person. Instead, he toted his instruments of the trade in creative fashions. Today it was a lunch bag, since the church cemetery was a popular lunch spot in the district. I believed that by not concealing a weapon on me, the cops couldn't nab me for a job. Rather, my host believed that. Sometimes in the early stages of transference, personas blended and overlapped. I had inhabited Mickey previously, and knew that there was no part of his personality I wanted blended with my essence. So I decided to be very cautious to prevent bleed over.

"I'm still not the Mickey you knew," I said. "But I am the guy you can trust. And right now you need to get to Penn Station in a snap."

The tears continued to well until they overflowed. Hannah leaned over, wrapping her slender arms around my bulky frame. "Thank you," she said, softly. "I knew I could count on you."

On me, but certainly not Mickey Guinn.

I sometimes found it entertaining how human lives transpired. Unlike my species, humans are corporeal beings, temporally fixed into a solitary biochemical construct that is locked into a social and political superstructure that dominates and controls their lives. Or as Mickey would be tempted to put it, "Some people get stuck with rotten luck." Hannah was one of those people.

Like me, she was an artist, a being of talent. But unlike me, she was unable to practice her art to its fullest extent. She had "rotten luck." Her life was to be played-out singing in the speakeasies of a degenerate Brooklyn bootlegger who was fond of killing other humans for entertainment.

The opposite occurred in human society as well. Despicable, loathsome men, such as Dutch Schultz, were living lives that circumstance has delivered to them. When I considered it, I rarely came across a human who lived the life he or she deserved. A pitiable species.

"Let's get moving," I said, wiggling from Hannah's embrace. "When I don't return, Dutch will get suspicious."

We worked our way up Broadway, walking against a stream of men in suits going about their daily business. Finding satisfied looks wasn't difficult. The human pastime called "economy" was exceedingly profitable in the spring of 1929. But, that was soon to change. Before the end of the year an economic crash would cast the entire nation into turmoil. This was just one *intervention* arranged by the Great Race; one that would reawaken a conflict that humanity had thought to be over. This was typical human folly. Since the Armistice of the Great War, the wounds of the world had not healed; they had scabbed over, and were merely festering. The Great Race knew that the collapse of one of humanity's reigning economic powers would help infect this old wound, spurring a fevered conflict the likes that human history had never seen before. This second global war would bring humanity into the atomic age far too early in their development as a species.

Outright genocide was unthinkable by the Great Race. Aeons ago we'd overcome such temptations. Subtlety and power were our tools. There was no need to directly bring about the destruction of humanity; humanity was too desperate to accomplish this task on its own. They just needed proper guidance. And the Great Race of Yith would gladly provide such guidance. The Earth would someday belong to us.

From Broadway we made our way to Park Row, cutting across City Hall Park, another one of Manhattan's verdant oases. *I do so have a fondness of greenery; it has long been destroyed in the Earth's future. A necessary intervention.*

Hurriedly I urged Hannah to the Hudson Terminal. I knew Dutch anticipated her taking the ferry across the bay, so I figured I could buy her some time by heading to Penn Station. The route was circuitous in an attempt to keep any of Dutch's other toughs off our tails.

*Intermingling of memories must be avoided.*

As we entered the steeple-roofed transit terminal, it too, like so many of the city's other structures, was infested with humans. Each one rushing about, anxious to depart from one location and to arrive at another.

"Mickey," Hannah said in a hushed voice as we climbed aboard a subway car. "I have enough for the both of us." She looked at me sheepishly, the slightest glimmer of a blush on her face. "I . . . I don't mean *we* — us as a thing, that is. I mean I can repay you for your help. You can come with me."

I smiled at the offer. She was a gentle human, very much unlike the host I occupied. "You know I can't do that, Hannah," I said. "I'm in. Always will be."

She nodded quickly, then looked away as the subway car began to rattle and shake into motion. Through the windows I watched her sad reflection as the Hudson terminal slide past my eyes. But in my mind's eye I saw the past and future of the terminal swirling together. A thick forest sprawled outward, a place where humans of different skin pigmentation battled and killed one another. Flames and fire appeared as colossal buildings collapsed, spewing forth roiling clouds of smoke and debris, killing thousands of humans. This spot, like nearly every spot I visited upon this world, was replete, sated and bloodied with the past and future histories of human conflict. It would be a mercy to these creatures when my species dominated this world. Yet, even without the machinations of the Great Race, and the ingenious plans and interventions calculated to direct and alter future human history, it seemed clear that these peculiar creatures would eventually destroy themselves.

Soon we rolled into Penn Station. Waiting for us were more travelers, each pushing and squeezing through the congested station, all in a race to catch a train out of the city or to hurry into it.

With the money my host carried, I purchased Hannah a ticket to Richmond, Virginia. I thought it was the least my host could do after having planned to betray her.

As we approached the train platform, I noticed Hannah stiffen. During our trip across town, she'd been anxious, but having earned her trust, she had gradually relaxed. Now her wariness returned. I scanned the crowd, looking for the source of her anxiety. Although humans did not have collective minds, I've found their physical reactions often betrayed their thoughts. Over the centuries of occupying hosts, I have become an excellent reader of the physical human text.

As my eyes skipped across the throng of jelly-faced beings inside the train station, my host's body reacted to one in particular. Being non-corporeal, I found the most difficult part of inhabiting humans was adjusting to the chemical surges produced by their bodies. Everything was stimulated and activated by chemical and electrical impulses. To successfully inhabit a host required true mastery and artistry. I sometimes lamented the inevitable loss of their kind because of my extreme talent to manipulate them. But, it was better that humanity be destroyed and the Great Race survive at the sacrifice of my gift. It was a sacrifice that I knew I must burden.

Within a moment I was able to pull forth the memories connected to the face that had triggered the biochemical reaction. I recognized the human known as "Dazzy." He worked for Dutch, and from probing my host's mind, I comprehended that we were associates, although much distrust and animosity throve in our relationship.

He stood in the crowd, motionless. People flowed around him as though he were a large stone in a swift moving stream. A broad-brimmed hat adorned his head, and a gray, pinstriped suit hung over his narrow frame. His eyes almost seemed reptilian, and I detected the slightest squint in them when he saw me.

The text of the human body was a complex book. Reading it was difficult and often susceptible to errors. But, some texts are easier to read than others. And Dazzy was one of the simplest texts I had encountered. From the twitch of his hand to the straightening of his shoulders I understood his intentions.

Somewhere during one of my previous inhabitations of my host's body, someone who had worked for Dutch, or maybe Dutch himself, must have detected my affection for Hannah, which is why Dazzy was here. Dutch didn't completely trust my host.

"What do we do, Mickey?" Hannah asked, her voice beginning to tremble.

"You board the train. I'll speak with Dazzy."

Hannah hesitated for a moment, apparently unsure about the plausibility of my suggestion.

"Do it, Han!" I yelled.

Dazzy shook his head as though reprimanding me; then he slowly shifted closer.

Even to the dullest of the humans in the station, it was obvious that this was not a safe location.

A hush washed over the thinning crowd. People backed away. At first their movement was sluggish, uncertain. Then as they realized what was unfolding, they began to scurry away.

Being a master of the study of human psychology, I was certain that in Dazzy's mind time had slowed. Or more accurately stated, Dazzy *believed* time had slowed down. This, of course, was nothing more than a misperception. The Great Race were the masters of time and physics. Humanity had only the faintest concepts of these matters, and even then it was the Great Race who had implanted those limited notions into the minds of mankind's greatest scientists in order that they might develop atomic weapons and bring about self-destruction. *Infants with toys.*

Time held no sway over me. This left Dazzy at a manifest disadvantage in the game he was about to play, or had already played, depending from which perspective I decided to view it.

But Dazzy didn't see the awe-inspiring presence of a member of the Great Race. He saw the fleshy body of Mickey "The Gun" Guinn.

From the corner of my eye, I glimpsed Hannah. She was half on the train, torn between leaving and staying to help me.

"Go," I said to her sternly. "Don't even think it. This host — *I'm* not worth it."

My words didn't budge her. She stood her ground, grasping the handrail along the inside of the train car entrance.

From some place distant, I heard a voice call "All aboard!"

I knew it wouldn't be long before someone would stumble upon this unfolding play; someone who wouldn't try to avoid the situation, but who would call the police. Even for a member of the Great Race time can be inconvenient.

There we stood, Dazzy and I, each watching the other, waiting for the first to make a move. Dazzy was tall, and stood erect in his finely-pressed suit, with a revolver undoubtedly tucked away in a shoulder holster beneath his flashy clothing.

I, or rather Mickey, looked his usual dumpy self, with an ill-fitting suit, and as Dazzy undoubtedly assumed, weaponless. But Dazzy had overlooked the crumpled paper bag. I held the top firmly with one hand, and felt the revolver inside with my other. Dazzy was so intent upon presenting an intimidating façade that he had yet to notice Mickey's *lunch.*

I settled my finger on the trigger. The bag rattled.

"Dazzy!" Hannah called. "Don't do it. It wasn't Mickey's idea. It was mine. I'll return the money."

Dazzy's smile broadened. He definitely had a reptilian look about him. I couldn't help but wonder if he were descended from the race of reptiles that had once dominated the Earth several million years ago, another species humanity was oblivious to.

"Now you're talkin' kid," Dazzy said. "Forget all this and come back. Dutch will forget it all. He'll let bygones be bygones."

*Right,* I thought. That was as likely as humanity's survival.

Dutch Schultz was another human who had a life he didn't deserve. Except, unlike Hannah, his was far better than it should have been. I admit, I have peeked into his future. As one might expect, his death was painful and protracted. It doesn't come until 1935, but when it occurs, he lingers for several days in the hospital, rambling incoherently. Actually, what he says does make sense to a member of the Great Race. He was inhabited prior to his death, and his memories were not properly eradicated. The irony was quite pleasant. Instead of comprehending the true nature of the Great Race, his limited mind was temporally-confused, blending human myths of devils and angels to explain his *possession* by the Great Race. His dying words were so unsettling to humanity that there are those who struggled for decades to comprehend them.

For me, Hannah represented something of a problem. I understood her. She was an artist like me. But she couldn't pick her life, unlike me. This produced an emotion in me that was difficult to reconcile. While I loathed humanity, and longed for their inevitable demise so my species could dominate the world in the future, I pitied humans at the same time. The path I was about to take was forbidden to me. I was not permitted to *tinker* with the Great Plan. But I was an artist, and I had a need to satisfy my personal sense of aesthetics. By helping Hannah escape her present life and give her a new one, one without the likes of Dutch Schultz, seemed . . . pleasing. *Satisfying.* It appeased *my* higher sense of aesthetics.

"You can walk away from this, Mickey," Dazzy said. "Both of you can turn it around now. Just come back and talk to Dutch. He wants to work it out. Give him the fifty G's and he'll forgive and forget."

Dazzy was beginning to repeat himself. I suspected he'd reached the limit of his negotiating abilities.

Both my host and I truly disliked Dazzy. All his offer did was to rouse the suppressed persona of my host-body, causing me to force it deeper into the unconscious portion of the host-brain. Humans are such nosey beings. Even when they've been subjugated to an unconscious region of their own mind they still listen to others' conversations. I am quite put off by the human unconscious and its bizarre abilities. I will be earnestly pleased to rid the world of these creatures. Even when you try to assist one, all they do is make it difficult.

"Lose yourself, Hannah," I said, determining to end this before the crowd started to return. "Dutch doesn't deal. You know that. He doesn't forgive. You know that too. Get on that train and don't come back. I'll keep Dutch occupied and buy you some time."

Something in my words must have finally broken through her stubborn nature. Quickly, in solemn silence, she vanished onto the train. I also could see that my words had an affect upon Dazzy. I watched as his hand slid inside his pristine suit coat, searching for his gun.

I didn't wait to hear if he had another offer. He was a human. I despised him. My host despised him. Most everyone who'd encountered Dazzy despised him. So I applied pressure to the trigger of the revolver inside the bag.

*Baam!*

Not surprisingly, an astonished look formed on Dazzy's face. He was far from brilliant, and even further from smart.

*Baam! Baam!*

The second shot was to secure his death. The third was to satisfy my sense of aesthetics, and to quell the struggling persona of Mickey. He seemed appeased when Dazzy dropped to the ground with a heavy *thump*.

After shooting Dazzy, I didn't wait around. I dumped the paper bag in the nearest garbage can. I had no illusions that Dutch would come looking for me . . . Mickey. But that was my intention. Shortly after leaving Penn Station, after seeing Hannah's train roll away, I released the host-body, allowing Mickey to return to full consciousness. I did not leave him with all of his memories. The recent memories relating to Hannah I had exorcised from his mind. What I did leave was his encounter with Dazzy, and the knowledge that Dutch would come looking for him. By the time Mickey and Dutch sorted out their differences, mainly by Mickey's dying, I figured Hannah would be long forgotten.

I would have preferred to simply eradicate all memories of Hannah from Dutch. But long-term memories require the use of certain technologies that would attract attention to my indiscretions. This was personal art, so there was no need to pull attention to my dabbling.

I did check on Hannah occasionally, whenever I was in the area . . . time. She had moved to a small town overflowing with greenery — it seemed artists like us shared a passion for greenery. There she lived the remainder of her life, teaching young humans to sing. She had a natural talent. And she finally had a life she deserved.

# ACHE

## David Witteveen

---

I was in O'Malley's coffee shop, lost in the latest Hemingway, when Old Man Leary hobbled in. His face was as grizzled and angry as a priest's.

"Hennessy," he shouted. "Stop reading them daft books. We've got ourselves a problem."

Old Man Leary always shouted. He was going deaf. Plus, he was as mean as a weasel.

I sighed, and folded a page corner to mark my place. "What now?"

"It's the Arkham mob. Trouble with this month's cut."

I hunched over in my chair. O'Malley's is quite a respectable coffee shop, as far as Irish coffee shops in Boston go, and it made me uncomfortable to be talking mobster business in front of all the decent and upright citizens. But Old Man Leary didn't claw his way to the top of the Boston gangsters by being dainty about etiquette.

"O'Shea is always good for it," I whispered. "He wouldn't try to stiff us."

"No," cackled Leary. "The coward wouldn't dare. But he sent one of his wee lads to bring us the money, and now the little bastard has disappeared."

"Fine," I said. "I'll find the lad, and get you the money back. Just tell me his name."

"Tom Kelly."

"Tom Kelly," I repeated. I stood up, and threw down a nickel to pay for my joe. "You're a stupid wee idiot to cross us, Tom Kelly. I hope you've made peace with your God."

◆ ◆ ◆

I had never been to Arkham.

I knew exactly three things about it. One: it was up the coast on the Miskatonic River. Two: there was a University there. And three: several

---

years ago we sent Danny O'Shea up there to snatch the bootlegging trade away from the Italians.

I drove my old Ford up the highway. It was early October, and the trees were all red and orange and gold. Some blond college boys drove past me in their convertible, and jealousy stabbed my heart. I was every bit as smart as them. But they were young, rich and Protestant, while I was a middle-aged Irish thug. Just an accident of birth. And yet that was enough. They got to be carefree and educated, and I got to go break heads.

The drive took two hours. The road climbed over some hills then slunk down into the Miskatonic Valley. As I descended, the light grew dimmer and the trees seemed gnarled and barren. A murder of ravens were pecking at road kill, and exploded into flight as I drove past them.

And so I came to Arkham.

The town hunched down over the river. I passed gambrel roofs and web clogged windows, brick-paved streets, and narrow houses slumped against each other. The whole town looked like it was built a hundred years ago, and hadn't been repaired or cleaned since.

It was so beautiful it made me ache.

Leary had given me an address. I stopped at a gas station to ask directions, then drove over to Harvey Street.

The address was down the bottom of some basement stairs. I knocked on the door, and a large goon slid back the window to peer out.

"Sorry," said the doorman. "Members only."

"I'm a guest of Old Man Leary."

The bouncer blinked, shut the window, and opened the door.

The speakeasy looked as clean and respectable as O'Malley's coffee shop. Two dignified businessmen were nursing teacups full of whiskey over near the stage. The wireless was quietly playing sappy love songs. I wandered over to the bar.

The bartender was a thin little guy with brilliantine red hair and an easy smile. "Hey there," he said. "Ain't seen you around here before."

"I just came up from Boston."

"Boston? That's a long way for a drink." He looked me up and down, and stopped smiling. "Oh."

"Where's O'Shea?"

"Have a drink, I'll fetch him."

He poured me one on the house, then darted out the back. I sipped it slowly. The businessmen eyed me suspiciously, but looked away quickly when I raised my glass to them. Guess they preferred their Irishmen behind the bar rather than slouching against it.

The bartender came back, with O'Shea behind him. He was dressed in a tailored pin-stripe suit, and his tie was pure green silk, but he had the squat, square build of a brawler. He pumped my hand like a water fountain.

"You should have come up tomorrow night," he beamed. "We've got a jazz band from New York."

"And you should have our money."

O'Shea's smile froze. "I've got my best men out looking for Kelly as we speak."

"Your best don't cut the mustard, O'Shea. Otherwise I wouldn't be here."

"Okay, point taken. What can I do to help?"

"Say three Hail Marys, and get me someone who knows the town."

"Of course, of course. I'll get you Bobby Quinn." O'Shea sighed. "Let me tell you how sorry I am about this mess. I thought Tom Kelly was smart, you know? I thought he had more brains than this."

I looked around the joint. It was ritzy, exactly the sort of place that would never let me enter if I didn't work for the men who ran it.

"Never trust a thug with brains, O'Shea. They're the ones who get ideas."

O'Shea took me over to his warehouse, and introduced me to Bobby Quinn. Quinn dressed like a movie star, and smiled like a rottweiler. He wrinkled his nose at my battered old Ford.

"That your car? Let's take mine instead. I got a Lincoln V-8."

"Whichever," I replied. "Just take me to where Kelly liked to hang out."

"We've checked all those places already," complained Quinn.

"And you missed all the clues. So let me do this my way, all right? Or do you want to take it up with Old Man Leary?"

Quinn strutted over to his car. "I ain't afraid of old Leary."

"That's 'cause you never drank coffee with him. Let's drive, pretty boy."

Quinn drove me down to an abandoned brickyard near the river's edge. I could hear a cat yowling even over the Lincoln's huge engine. Quinn parked and nodded at the brickyard.

"This is where the boys hang out," he said.

"Which boys?"

"The local Irish boys. Kelly was a one of them before he started working for us. We get most of our new recruits from these boys."

We jumped the fence and walked through the piles of broken red bricks. The cat howls got louder. And I could hear boys cheering and abusing each other.

The boys had cornered a stray cat in one of the empty offices, and were trying to tie a string of firecrackers to its tail. But every time they got close, it would shred them with its claws.

Quinn rolled his eyes at their incompetence. With one fluid movement, he pulled a switchblade from his pocket, dived, and slashed the cat's throat. It screamed and then choked on its own blood. The boys fell silent, wide-eyed with horror and admiration.

"Stop fecking about," growled Quinn. "This man wants to speak to you all."

It took me a moment. I was still staring at the dying cat.

"Tom Kelly," I said at last. "You lot know of him?"

"Aye," said one of the older boys.

"He used to be one of you, right? Anyone seen him in the last few days?"

"We ain't seen him since he joined up with O'Shea," said the boy. He frowned in resentment. "Kelly always thought he was too good for us lot."

"What do you mean?"

"You know. He was always reading books and that, using fancy words. He thought he was cleverer than us."

I looked around at these boys, with their dirt-smeared hands and hand-me-down clothes and brutish resentment. It wouldn't be hard to be smarter than them.

"Do you know where he lives?"

"With his Ma, down on Sullivan Street."

"Right. Thanks." I turned to Quinn. "Let's go."

Quinn was wiping the blood off his switchblade with a clean linen handkerchief. He gave the boys a menacing smile, then sauntered back to his car with me.

"You could have just asked me that," he said. "I know where Kelly lived."

"Lived?"

"He sure as hell won't be coming back there. Personally, I think the Italian mob did him in. Stole the money and dumped him dead in the river. You can't trust those greasy Wops."

He started the engine, and pulled out onto the road. I could see the river from here. Its water was black, like that poor cat's blood congealing on the brickdust-covered floor.

The cat business bothered me. I had spent my whole life around gangsters, and I'd broken my share of fingers and kneecaps. You had to be hard, to survive in this life. Hoodlums weren't supposed to have feelings. But that poor damn cat. It didn't do anything wrong.

Quinn was still smiling to himself.

I wondered if Kelly had ever taken a life. Somehow I doubted it. He sounded like the sensitive type. Not cut out for a life of crime. What must it have been like, having to work with a monster like Quinn? Was that why he ran away?

If it was, I couldn't blame him.

Quinn drove me over the river to Sullivan Street. The houses were tightly packed and crumbling. The smell of poverty hung in the air like chimney smoke.

"You stay here," I told Quinn. "I want to talk to his Ma alone."

"Fine by me," said Quinn. "The old hag probably has fleas."

I knocked on the door and waited. I could hear children inside. The door opened, and a gaunt old lady peered through the crack.

"Mrs Kelly?" I asked.

She looked me up and down in fear. She wasn't that old, I realized. Probably younger than me. But too many children had made her worn-out and gray.

"Are you with the old man?" she asked.

"Which old man? Old Man Leary?"

"I don't know," quivered the old lady. "He said he was a messenger."

"Look, Mrs Kelly, I'm trying to find Tom."

"Tom's gone away."

"I know, I'm trying to find him. Can I come in?"

The door was only open a crack, and she looked to scared to open it wider. I didn't want to use force on the poor lady. But then she looked out into the street and saw the Lincoln. Quinn was sitting behind the wheel, cleaning his fingernails with his knife.

"Don't hurt me," she quivered, and held the door open.

The house was dark inside, and reeked of mildew. Three sickly young children peered down at me from the staircase.

"Is your husband around?" I asked. I didn't want any surprises.

"No. He's dead. Accident on the docks last year."

"Oh. Sorry to hear that. Can you show me Tom's room?"

She nodded and led me up the stairs, wringing her hands on her apron. "I begged him not to get mixed up with O'Shea, sir. I begged him."

"Too late for that now," I said.

She led me into cramped bedroom. The walls were stained with mold. There was a just the one double bed in there, but enough shoes for four. On top of the dresser was a pile of books.

They had to be Tom's. I picked up the top one and read the title. T. S. Eliot's *The Wasteland and Other Poems*. Not the usual bedtime reading for a poor Irish hoodlum. But neither was Hemingway.

"He's always liked to read," said Mrs Kelly. "He's such a bright boy."

A photograph was placed between the pages as a bookmark. I slid it out to look. It was of a young girl, very modern — matchstick thin with a sleek blond bob and dark, bohemian eyes. A pretty girl. And rich. She wore a necklace of pearls. A faint hint of perfume still clung to the picture.

I held the photograph up for Mrs Kelly. "Do you know this girl?"

"No. Tom never brought any of his friends over."

Of course he didn't. You couldn't bring rich girls home to a dive like this. But where would a poor Irish kid like Tom meet rich girls, anyway? The speakeasy? A bookstore? I flipped through the book to the inside front cover.

MISKATONIC UNIVERSITY LIBRARY, it said.

Of course.

Quinn didn't want to drive up to the college.

"I hate those college fags," he said. "They're so uppity."

"Just drive, Quinn."

I had taken the book with me. Quinn snatched it off me and pulled out the picture. "No way," he hissed venomously. "No way was Kelly seeing a doll like that."

"Quinn, drive!"

Evening was sinking down fast. The low light made the houses seem taller. A hunchbacked old man turned to watch the Lincoln pass, and the shadow on his face looked like the mildew stains on Kelly's bedroom wall.

We crossed the river. The dying sunlight glinted off the water. There were shapes beneath the surface. Primeval towers and labyrinthine streets, drowned now by the poisonous waves. I pressed my face to the window, trying to get a clearer view. Bones floated amongst the black weeds.

And then the waters roiled, and something rose out from the depths. Something vast, and ancient, and hungry.

I jerked awake. Quinn looked over at me and sneered.

"This is an automobile," he said. "Not a damn hotel."

By the time we reached the University, it was dark. Quinn argued with the gateman about where we could park, and then we walked across the campus in the gloom. Tentacles of ivy were wrapped around every building.

The library was still open. Quinn saw the no smoking sign and refused to enter. So I went in alone.

It was hushed inside. The shelves were made from dark oak, and delicate electric lights glimmered over the round tables. I lingered in the foyer for a moment, gazing around me. A yearning welled up inside me, to sit down at these beautiful tables and read these solemn books, and just disappear from my no-good hoodlum life.

Then a gray-haired librarian looked up at me and frowned. I didn't belong here. But I had spent the afternoon with Quinn, and some old bookworm wasn't going to intimidate me.

I searched through the aisles floor by floor until I found the girl. She was up near the Archaeology section, scrabbling through a pile of old books. She looked thinner than in the photograph, frailer and more afraid. And there were dark rings under her pretty eyes.

I threw the book of poems down in front of her, and she jumped like a rabbit.

"I'm looking for Tom," I said.

She tried to run. But I grabbed her wrist, and twisted her arm so that soft pale crook of her elbow was exposed.

There were needle marks there. I raised an eyebrow and she slumped back down into her chair. There isn't a college in America that looks kindly on its co-eds kicking the gong.

"Let's start with your name, shall we?"

"Emily," she whispered. "Emily Hawthorne."

"It's a pleasure to meet you, Miss Hawthorne. How did you know Tom?"

"We shared some interests in common."

"I'm guessing books and dope. Wasn't he a bit working class for a rich doll like you?"

She looked away impatiently, and I realized her fear had nothing to do with me.

"Where is he?" I pressed.

"I don't know. We had a falling out."

"Over what? Money?"

"You wouldn't understand."

"Try me."

She fixed those dark-rimmed eyes on me, and a light glittered in them, alien and cold.

"Very well," she said. "Tom had a vision of Lost Carcosa. He thinks he can open a way there, if only he can find the Yellow Book. I told him it was a trap. The dwellers in the lake are just waiting for a bridge to open. But he wouldn't listen"

"You're right," I nodded slowly. "I didn't understand a word."

"Of course not." She wrung her frail hands. "Tom hates his life. He wants to escape. And he thinks he could be happy there, amongst those ancient towers. But it's all just a trick. Carcosa sank beneath the Lake of Hali eons ago. Nothing lives there now except the foulest evil."

She was, I realized, insane. Too much dope. I'd seen strong men ruined by opium, and she was barely a sliver.

"Just tell me where he is," I said gently.

"I don't know," she cried. Her head sunk in despair. "I don't know."

On impulse, I reached across the table to pat her hand. "It's okay. We'll find him. You said he was after a book?"

"The Yellow Book."

"Where would he find it?"

"The Chinaman on River Street could get it. But he wanted three hundred dollars."

"River Street. Right." My hand gripped closed over hers, and I pulled her to her feet. "Sorry, Miss. But you're coming with us."

She was too dazed to resist, until we walked out the Library doors and saw the sky churning above us. The sun had sunk behind the hills, but the clouds still burned purple and red and black.

"He's started," whimpered Emily, and tried to pull free. "He's opening the way!"

Quinn was smoking a resentful cigarette, and turned when he heard her cry.

"Hey," he said. "That's the doll from the picture. Are we kidnapping her?" He smiled at the idea.

"Just get her to the car before the campus guards stop us," I snapped.

He grinned, snatched her wrist, and dragged her along. No one stopped us. The campus was deserted. Quinn threw Emily into the back seat of the Lincoln and slid into the front.

"Where now?"

"She said the Chinaman on River Street. Mean anything to you?"

"Oh yeah. That creepy chink."

He gunned the engine and drove. Emily lay shivering on the back seat. We crossed back over the bridge, and when she looked down into the water, her eyes went wide with horror.

"This Carcosa place," I asked her. "Where was it?"

"By the shore of Lake Hali," she whispered. "On a cold dead planet circling the distant star Aldebaran."

"Sounds delightful. That's really where Kelly is trying to go?"

"You've never seen it in your dreams. You couldn't hope to understand."

"Quit babbling," said Quinn. "We're here."

He had parked outside a warehouse. The sign simply read HERBS. We left Emily in the car and marched up to the shop. The door was open, but Quinn kicked it anyway.

Inside, the walls were covered in shelves of glass jars. The jars were full of dried leaves, snake skins, something that looked like teeth. And the Chinaman sat on a battered leather chair beneath them, smoking a pipe. Despite the October chill, he was shirtless. Every inch of his skin was covered in tattoos.

"Tom Kelly," hissed Quinn. "Where is the wee bastard?"

The Chinaman blinked, calm as a turtle. "Gone."

"Gone where, you filthy chink?" Quinn flicked open his switchblade.

"Quinn," I yelled. "Quit it!"

Something had caught my eye. An envelope was lying on the counter. The same sort of envelope O'Shea used to send his payments to Old Man Leary.

Quinn stopped. He saw what I was looking at, swooped it up and sliced it open. The money was still inside.

"You're one lucky Chinaman," said Quinn, and started counting the bills.

I knelt down beside the Chinaman. The pipe gave off a thick, heady perfume I recognized as opium.

"You sold Kelly the Yellow Book," I said. "Where did he go then?"

"To open the way," said the Chinaman.

"But where? Where does he do this?"

The Chinaman held my gaze. "There is nothing for you in this world," he said. "No respect. No peace. No beauty."

"Just tell me where Tom went."

"The river," sighed the Chinaman. "Where he used to play."

I grabbed Quinn and dragged him outside.

"You're crazy," he grumbled. "You're mad as the stupid girl."

We reached the car. The back door was open and Emily was gone.

"The brickworks," I said. "Quickly."

The sky was still burning when we reached the old brickworks. Even Quinn had noticed it looked wrong. He tossed me an electric torch, but that hideous purple glow was bright enough to see by. We jumped over the fence and started to search.

The brickworks was quiet. Quinn and I sneaked down toward the water. Then Quinn suddenly held up his hand to stop me.

There was a clear path running right down to the river's edge. And standing ankle-deep in the water was Tom Kelly.

His back was to us. He had a book in his hand, and was reading it aloud, whispering the words to the swirling waters. He seemed lost in a trance.

A sudden smell hit us: mildew and decay. A figure clambered up from the ground, blocking our path to the river. A man, but his back was hunched, and his arms swayed with a horrible boneless motion. He raised his head, and I recognized him — the old man I had seen this afternoon, just before my dream.

He shuffled toward us. And I saw that I had been wrong. The dark patch on his face was not just a shadow. The skin there had been eaten away. Through the hole I caught a glimpse of something slick and black writhing beneath his skin, like a tadpole inside its egg.

Quinn cursed and pulled out his switchblade. He was about to leap when –

"Wait," said a voice behind us. Emily stood there, eerie as a ghost.

"It is a messenger from the dark Lake of Hali," she chanted. "It has come to help open the way."

"Feck that," said Quinn, and charged.

He barrelled into the old man, and slashed him repeatedly with his knife. The hunchback's skin ripped under the sharp blade.

And the thing under the flesh was revealed.

It looked like a fish market left to rot. Scales and gills and slime. Tentacles whipped out, wrapped around Quinn's body, and pulled him into the gelatinous mess. Quinn dropped his knife, and screamed horrible liquid screams.

Emily suddenly cried out and pointed to the river. "The way is open! I can see the dead towers, and the black rolling moons!"

I ran. Down to the river, feet scrabbling on the old broken bricks. The sky writhed above me, casting swirling purple light.

A boat was sailing across the dark water. Long oars pulled it forward. Seven tall figures stood on its decks, wrapped head to toe in red silks. In their hands they held bowls of perfume and tall candles of incense. But dark shadows swam in the boat's wake.

"Kelly!" I yelled.

He turned, still whispering the words from the book, and I saw his eyes. They glittered with longing.

Emily scrabbled up beside me.

"Tom," she cried. "It's a trap! They want you to open the way! It's how they get in to our world!"

Tom faltered in his whispering, and the boat stopped. The shadows in its wake writhed in anger. For a long moment, the two lovers stared into each other's eyes.

And then Tom turned back to the book, and continued reading.

The shadows behind the boat leapt with joy. Emily threw herself at Tom, crying. She tried to pull the book from his hands. A black wave rolled up around her, and suddenly sucked her under. Tom didn't even miss a beat.

I turned around and ran.

There was no sign of Quinn or the monster. But Sill's switchblade still lay on the ground. I grabbed it and raced back to the water.

Tom didn't even turn around. I jerked his head back with one hand, and slit his throat with the other. Blood spurted out, purple in the alien light.

Even with his throat cut, Tom kept trying to recite the words. Blood bubbled out his mouth and choked his tongue. The book fell from his grasp, and then he collapsed.

The boat stopped. The silk-wrapped figures on the decks stood there, the smell of their perfumes and incense wafting across the water to me. It drowned out the smell of blood, the smell of sweat, the smell of my miserable life. They were waiting, I realized. Waiting for me to finish the reading.

The Yellow Book still lay on the shore, covered in Kelly's blood.

What did the Chinaman say? There was nothing for me in this world. No respect. No peace. No beauty.

The book was open. I could make out the words, so exquisite that every phrase made me ache.

I reached down, and cradled the pages to my chest. The figures on the boat raised their hands in anticipation.

And with one swift motion, I plunged the knife through the book's cover and in to my yearning heart.

# A Dangerous High

## E.P. Berglund

When I came to, my head was still throbbing. And it hurt, too! Whoever had done it, knew what he was doing. I had an egg on the back of my head, but the skin hadn't been broken. As I stood up, I noticed no dizziness or change in my eyesight. I wondered what I had done in the past twenty-four hours to rate getting sapped.

My name, by the way, is Morris Bench, Morey to my friends. I'm thirty-one, six-foot-two, keep my black hair cut in a flat-top, and I was sore as hell. If you can't tell, I don't like being sapped.

I used to be a professional soldier. I did three tours in Vietnam. During my first tour I received a battlefield commission as a 2nd Lieutenant and was transferred to the military police in Saigon. When we pulled out of Saigon on April 29, 1975, I was RIFed as a 1st Lieutenant — Reduction in Force, which is a euphemism for "we don't need your services anymore." I was transferred to Ft. Ord, California, where I was mustered out six months later.

I had been raised in Oregon and planned on going back there. But there was no rush, so I decided to see a little of Southern California and Mexico, before I headed north. With my savings over fifteen years of military service and my mustering out pay, I was set for awhile. I bought a black 1958 Thunderbird for transportation.

My first night in Los Angeles, I got myself a motel room, and after eating went to a local bar, called the Tip-Top Club. In the morning I planned on coasting down to Anaheim to see Clyde Jonas, who was working at Disneyland. He used to be one of my MP's.

The bartender had just given me another mug of beer. I raised it up to my lips to take a sip, when someone jostled my elbow, spilling beer out of the mug. I looked to my right to see this beautiful little thing in a tight green dress, that went well with her red hair. She appeared to be well on her way to being soused.

"I know you. I don't remember your name, but you're a private detective in 'Frisco."

"I'm afraid you are mistaking me for someone else."

"No, I'm not. I want you to find my daughter."

She shoved a picture of a strikingly beautiful redhead, a younger version of herself, under my nose. "This is my Cindy Ann."

"I'd like to help you, ma'am, but I'm not a private detective."

"I don't know what your fees are, but would a thousand dollars do?"

That caused me to sit back and think. I had been a military policeman involved in quite a few criminal investigations and I must have read hundreds of private eye novels while I was in Vietnam. I really hadn't thought about what I was going to do now that I was no longer in the army. So I decided that I would give it a try.

"I'm not who you think I am, but I will try and find your daughter. When was the last time you saw her?"

"Night before last. She dropped this on her way out."

She handed me a small rumpled up bag.

"Do you have a pen?"

I handed my pen to her.

She asked me my name and scribbled in on the payee line of a cashier's check issued from her checking account. She handed the pen and check to me.

"Excuse me, I have to go to the bathroom."

She slid off her stool and headed toward the back of the bar.

I put the pen back in my pocket and looked at the check. It was issued from the account of Bonnie Lou Miller at the First National Bank of Los Angeles. The address showed that she was living in Buena Park, California. I put the check in my inside pocket.

I opened up the rumpled paper bag and found a zip-loc bag and a sales receipt inside. The sales receipt was from five days ago when she had paid for a sarsaparilla at the Calico Saloon in Knott's Berry Farm, which is located in Buena Park. There was nothing in the plastic bag, but I unzipped it and smelled. The odor of marijuana was very noticeable, but there was an underlying smell that I couldn't place. There were no labels on the plastic bag, but someone had stamped "Tind'losi Liao" in black ink. I didn't know what "Tind'losi" was, but "Liao" rang some bells, something Corporal Lenner had mentioned while we were in a bunker during a Viet Cong rocket attack. I couldn't remember what he had said, but I knew that he had gotten out of the service after his first tour in Vietnam and had returned to Portland, Oregon.

The bartender came up to me and said, "Last call. We're closing in fifteen minutes."

I looked around the bar, but didn't see Mrs. Miller. Well, I assumed there was a Mr. Miller, since there was a daughter.

"Do you remember the redhead that was sitting here?"

"Yeah."

"She went to the rest room and hasn't come back."

"I'll see if she's still back there. She might have passed out, the way she'd been drinking."

He came back a few minutes later to tell me that she wasn't in the rest room, but that she might have left through the back door. Why would someone give me a thousand dollars to find her daughter, and then not want to give me enough information to start my search? But maybe what was in the rumpled paper bag was the only information she *could* give me.

The next morning I checked out of the motel and drove downtown. I found a First National Bank of Los Angeles and cashed the cashier's check. I also verified the address on the check against her account and found that when she obtained the cashier's check it had dropped her checking account balance to zero.

I stopped in a gun store and purchased a .38 Special, a shoulder rig for the gun, and a hundred rounds, not that I planned on walking into a war zone any time soon. With my luck I would walk into a war zone before the 30-day waiting period was up. I then made my way to the Los Angeles Police Department to obtain a private detective's license and a license to carry a concealed weapon.

As I was leaving the LAPD, I bumped into a police captain in uniform. He turned to give me a dirty look, when his eyebrows raised and his mouth dropped open.

"L-T?" he said. A lot of the men I commanded in the military police referred to me as "L-T," the abbreviation for Lieutenant, unless there was a higher ranking officer around.

"Sam? Sam Anderson?"

Sam Anderson was a military police sergeant when I first met him in Saigon when I took over the platoon he was in. When he left Vietnam, he returned to the US to become a civilian. I never expected to run into him in Los Angeles.

He took me by the arm and hustled me back across the street, where we entered a small café and went to the back before sitting down at a table. The waitress came over and he ordered us coffee. While we waited for the coffee, we reminisced about old times when we were incountry.

When the waitress brought the coffee, Sam shifted gears.

"So, L-T, what brings you to the LAPD?"

I told him about Bonnie Lou Miller hiring me as a private detective to find her daughter, Cindy Ann Miller, age 19. I showed him her picture, and the two items in the rumpled paper bag.

"Did the mother say anything about reporting her daughter as missing?"

"No, in fact, she gave me a cashier's check for a thousand dollars, her daughter's picture, and the stuff in the paper bag. She asked me to find her daughter and then she excused herself to go to the rest room and disappeared."

"So you came here to get your PI license."

"And a license to carry." I held the left side of my jacket open so he could see the .38.

He held the plastic bag up and looked at it.

"Talk about being lucky, L-T. I'm the captain of the Narcotics Division. We've seen this 'Tind'losi Liao' packaging before, but we've never been able to actually get a sample of the marijuana.

"But let's go back across the street and let me check that my information is up-to-date."

We got up, he stopped at the register at the end of the counter and paid for the coffee.

As we left the café, I said, "I thought merchants let the police eat for free."

"They do, especially for patrolmen. It's not really a bribe *per se,* but the merchants feel that if they provide the patrolmen something for free, the patrolman will keep a sharp eye out when he's patrolling near their establishment. Some, but not all, of the detectives still accept freebies. But above the rank of detective, we all pay our way. You won't find anything about this in police directives, L-T."

We entered the police department and made our way up one floor, through several thousand hallways, until we entered a door with "Narcotics Division" on a nameplate. We meandered between the desks until we arrived at a glassed-in office in the back corner. Sam motioned for me to sit on the chair or the couch that faced his desk.

As soon as he sat down behind his desk, he picked up his telephone and made four calls.

"Bonnie Lou Miller's drivers license gives the same address that you have. And she didn't file a missing person report on her daughter Cindy Ann Miller in Orange County. But we did find the missing Bonnie Lou. She was found dead two miles from the Tip-Top Bar on her way back to Buena Park. Sorry. Also sorry that the address that was on her bank account and her drivers license isn't any good. Thought you should know, in case you thought about going to her place and checking it out for clues to her daughter's location. The whole block was torn down about three weeks ago."

He pressed a button on his phone and said, "Ramirez, come in here."

"This is Detective Ramirez, L-T. He's got the lead on the Tind'losi Liao marijuana."

I got up and shook the detective's hand.

"Ramirez, this is Morris Bench. He was my lieutenant when I was in the military police in Vietnam. He's now the newest PI in Orange County." Sam paused, then said, "Have we gotten a sample of the Tind'losi Liao yet?"

"No, we haven't, sir."

"And where do we think the source of the marijuana is coming from?"

"The nearest we can place it is in Buena Park."

"Any word from the users about how this Tind'losi Liao differs from regular marijuana?"

"Yes sir. We arrested a young man last night for possession of drug paraphernalia — he didn't have any of the marijuana, but he did have an empty plastic bag. It seems this Liao is distilled from the black lotus and this distillation is supposed to give one the ability to see the past through the eyes of one's ancestors. And the marijuana opens up the mind so that it can travel in the past, or something like that."

"Thank you, Ramirez."

Knowing that he had just been dismissed, he turned and left Sam's office.

"Once you get your feet wet doing an investigation as a private individual, although licensed by the state, give me a ring and I'll give you some pointers on what you can do and what you can't do. Buena Park is outside our jurisdiction, in a manner of speaking, since it isn't part of Los Angeles. So anything you might have heard here in my office, I know nothing about."

Good ole Sam, covering his ass. "And I have a friend in the Orange County Sheriff's Department that will cover us if we need to go into Buena Park."

"Oh, by the way, Sam," I started as I got up off the couch, "the word 'Liao' seems to ring a bell, but I can't figure in relation to what. You remember Corporal Lenner? I think I heard him mention it. I'll see if I can run him down up in Portland and see if he knows anything about "Tind'losi," and get back with you."

"You can find your way out, L-T?" Sam asked as he gave me a business card with his home phone number on the back.

"Sure thing."

◆　◆　◆

I called Clyde Jonas and he told me to come see him at Disneyland around six PM. He said that I wouldn't be interfering with his job, as he was in maintenance on the "*20,000 Leagues Under the Sea*" ride.

As I was traveling down the Santa Ana Freeway, I passed a sign that said "TURN RIGHT FOR BUENA PARK, HOME OF KNOTT'S BERRY FARM." As long as I had the time, I decided to look around, especially since Cindy Ann had been there six days ago. I swung off the freeway and whipped through Buena Park doing all of twenty miles an hour. It's that small. I followed the signs until I came to the Berry Farm — Amusement Park built by Mr. Knott.

I pulled into the parking lot and parked my powerful little "Bird." I hopped out of the car, smoothed my gabardine coat and trousers, yanked my tie off and threw it in the front seat. I locked my car and headed toward this simulated ghost town. It didn't look like a ghost town to me, though. There were too many people wandering around. I heard a warning whistle and dismissed it from my mind, until this old-time train almost dismissed me.

I picked myself off the ground and was dusting myself off, when this kid walked up to me and said, "What's the matter, Pops? Too old to stand up?"

I looked at him closely. He was around twenty years old and his face was pocked from a bad case of acne. He had steel-grey eyes that seemed to bore right through you. He was high on something, as his pupils were dilated. He stood about four inches shorter than I am, and was so thin it made you wonder if he had a square meal in his whole life.

"Beat it, kid," I said, practically snapping his head off his shoulders.

"Big man, huh? Want to know what they do to 'big men' around here? Go upstairs in the saloon over there." And with that he took off in the direction he had just pointed in.

I walked over to the Calico Saloon and looked it over from the outside. It really looked like it was actually built back in the eighteen-hundreds. Kids (little ones) were running around on the veranda and in and out through the swinging doors. I went in through the swinging doors and headed for the bar, which was right in front of me.

The balding, sixty-ish barkeep said, "What'll you have?"

"What do you recommend?"

"Sarsaparilla."

I had a sarsaparilla (ugh!) and looked around the saloon. It really looked old-fashioned. On either end of the bar were swinging doors. People were sitting at the tables, making the place look populated.

I got the bartender's attention and showed him the picture of Cindy Ann.

"Do you remember this girl coming in here about a week ago?"

"Yeah, sure. She comes in here about every four days or so."

"What does she do when she comes in here?"

"Has a sarsaparilla and goes upstairs," he responded, pointing to the other end of the bar, where I could see the stairs going up to the second floor.

I went up them two at a time, making a left at the landing. There were benches stretching off to my left for about twenty feet. Four men were sitting at a table in the far corner discussing something among themselves. I noticed the kid that I had encountered before, sitting next to them.

Fear sprang into those gray eyes, and I decided to go over and find out why. I made my way down the aisleway between the benches, until I came up to the table, with the heavy-set man on the far side doing all of the talking. All four of them were dressed in loud sports clothes, and the kid had on Levis and a tee-shirt.

"Want something, Mister?" the heavy-set man asked me.

"It seems like everyone wants something from me. What's your line?"

He got a perturbed look on his face and said, "Did I ask you to join our little group? I don't recall doing so!"

I decided I didn't like this character. "This kid said I could find out what happens to 'big men' up here."

His jaw muscles tightened and relaxed in one fast motion, making the excess flesh on his jowls seem to ripple.

"I wouldn't go by anything Jimmy says, though. He likes to make people think he's tough, but he's all bluff. But we're not."

"What's that supposed to mean?"

"Just like it sounded. I wouldn't try anything, because I've got a .38 centered on your belly. Just go back down the stairs and back to wherever you came from and you won't get hurt. Understand?"

Now, mind you, I'm not a coward. I just don't like being threatened. I noticed that the table was one that had three legs. The heavy-set man had one table leg between his two meaty legs, and the other two table legs were to each side. There wasn't anybody sitting right in front of me.

I put both hands on the edge of the table, with my fingers going underneath, and shoved with all of the strength in my shoulders. The other side of the table flipped up and caught the heavy-set man right under the chin. The table leg between his legs came up and caught him in the crotch. He was out for awhile. A trickle of blood ran from the corner of his mouth. I guessed that he had a broken jaw. Too bad.

I pulled the table away from him and took the .38 out of his hand, dropping it in my jacket pocket. The other two guys in sports clothes just sat there, their hands in view so that I wouldn't do something drastic. The kid had fallen off his chair and was cowering in the corner.

I glared at the two men sitting there, turned on my heel, went downstairs and out of the saloon. I made my way to the parking lot, making sure to look both ways before I crossed the train tracks.

I had just finished unlocking my T-Bird, when I started seeing spots and stars. Then everything went black. What had I done in the past twenty-four hours to rate getting sapped?

◆　◆　◆

When I came to, I slowly got off the ground. I probably had a puzzled look on my face, because I had a plastic bag in my hand with "Tind'losi Liao" stamped on it in black ink. At first I thought that I had been mugged. As I searched through my pockets, I realized that I had been mugged. I didn't have fatty's .38 anymore. The plastic bag wasn't the one I had originally; that one was still in the rumpled paper bag in my pocket.

I looked closely at the bag in my hand, opened it and smelled. This one had never been used for its intended purpose. Strange. It must have been dropped by whoever had sapped me.

I decided that I would be around for awhile and could see Clyde Jonas some other time. I'd give him a call and let him know what happened to me.

As I pulled out of the parking lot, I thought about calling Sam and letting him know what happened. I saw a service station up ahead on the right that had a telephone booth near the sidewalk. I pulled into the station and parked next to the phone.

I called long distance information and got the number for Bruce Lenner in Portland, Oregon. I called his number, but he wasn't there. I did get a strange message from his answering machine.

"I'm not home at the present time. Leave your name and number and I'll get back to you as soon as I can. If this is L-T, meet me at the Tip-Top Club at six. And, oh yeah, bring the Sarge with you."

I hung up the phone. How did he know that I was going to call him, and even if he did know I was going to call him, how did he know when I would call? And how did he know that I had hooked up with Sam? I sighed to myself. There wasn't any way that I was going to answer those questions, and having talked quite a bit with Bruce when we were in Vietnam, he wasn't going to volunteer how he knew either. He just did. He saved my butt many a time from getting ambushed by the Viet Cong or VC sympathizers, while in the performance of our duties as military policeman.

I picked the phone back up and called Sam at his home and asked him to meet me at the Tip-Top at six. I had about an hour and a half to get there. It was a good thing that the majority of traffic on the Santa Ana Freeway would all be going away from Los Angeles.

◆　◆　◆

I walked through the front door of the Tip-Top Club at a quarter to six. I had really made good time, without speeding. I got a bottle of beer from the bartender and made my way to a table at the back of the club.

I sat down and relaxed my muscles as I waited.

Sam walked through the door at five 'til. I waved at him, he grabbed a beer from the bar, and made his way back to the table. He slid into the chair across from me, then slid it sideways so that his back wasn't directly toward the front door. Habit, I guess.

"What's up, L-T?"

"Well, Sam, I'm hopin' I'll be able to tell you in five minutes. Otherwise, you've made the trip out here for nothing."

Sam leaned back in his chair and got comfortable.

The five minutes seemed to drag on forever, but eventually, at six, the front door opened and in strolled Bruce Lenner. He saw us and came back to our table without stopping at the bar. As he got to the table, Sam stood up and he and Bruce shook hands and pounded each other on the back. Bruce reached across the table and shook my hand.

"Well, now that the greetings and salutations are completed, can we get on with it? Bruce, how did you know I was going to call?"

"I just knew."

"And I suppose that you knew what I was calling about?"

"Sure. Why wouldn't I?"

"Damn it, Bruce! Can't you ever give a straight answer?"

"Not if I want to stay out of the looney bin."

We all laughed.

"I guess I better start this out," I began. "Bruce, I'm now a private detective and I'm looking for a girl. She has been using marijuana and she ran across some in which 'Tind'losi Liao' was stamped in black ink on the plastic bag. Does 'Tind'losi Liao' mean anything to you?"

"Yeah, it does. Liao is a distillation of the back lotus. Taken in its pure form, the mind can travel through the angles of time. The only problem with traveling through time, is that there are also other creatures traveling through the angles of time. Creatures that think the essence of a human is an utter delicacy. These creatures have been called the Hounds of Tindalos."

"Tindalos? Tind'losi?" I asked.

Bruce hailed the bartender and asked him for a glass of water, before answering. "Tind'losi is the adjective form. Anyway, we first found out about the Tind'losi Hounds when Halpin Chalmers learned of them back in the late 1920's. He had experimented with the Liao and in going back through the angles of time, the Hounds caught his scent. The only way that he could avoid them finding him was to get rid of all the angles in the room he was in. The plaster of paris had not dried by the time the Hounds had located him and they were able to get into the room and destroy him. He was found with his head torn from his body and not a drop of blood anywhere, even in the body."

Sam gasped, but let Bruce continue.

"Chalmers knew that the Hounds could only go through the angles of time, but not the curves of time. If he had thought it through, he would have realized that all he had to do was move and the Hounds wouldn't have been able to follow his scent elsewhere in this dimension."

"Sam," I interjected, "did Bruce's description of Chalmers' demise remind you of something?"

"That was one of the reasons that I agreed to meet you tonight, instead of just telling you over the phone," he answered. "Over the past few days there has been a rash of murders from Los Angeles to Anaheim, with the majority being in the Buena Park area. The bodies were bloodless. Some were completely torn apart, some just had the head torn off, and some didn't appear to have been touched at all, except for the missing blood."

"What about the Tind'losi Liao?" Sam asked.

Bruce smiled. "From what the L-T has said, it appears that someone has taken the Liao distillate and laced marijuana with it. Since the Liao would have been breathed in with the marijuana smoke, it wouldn't be at full strength. A German scientist actually experimented with this about twenty years ago. He noted that when the Liao is ingested in the form of smoke, the effects on the human mind are a lot different. The mind cannot just travel where it wants to in time, but can only go to the time of a direct ancestor of the ingestee. And, as such, it's much harder for the Hounds to trace the human scent, plus the fact that the human mind is not traveling in time for a very long period — five or ten minutes. So, if the Hounds picked up the scent, they would have to wait for the laced marijuana to be smoked again before they could take up the trail."

"And the Tind'losi?"

"Someone found out about the Liao, that it actually exists, if you know how to get it. This someone apparently read a story that was published back in 1929 about the Hounds and that the Liao was only used to travel in time. He had a sense of humor when he named his laced marijuana 'Tind'losi Liao.' But I doubt if he actually believed in the existence of the Hounds, since the story published in 1929 was a fictional story."

Bruce turned in his chair and waved at the bartender. He came over and Bruce asked for some more water. He then turned back to Sam and I and took a swallow from his near-empty water glass.

"So, it appears, Sam, that your rash of murders may be related to the Hounds. As long as your marijuana dealer keeps selling, you're going to have more deaths."

"Sam," I injected, "what about Cindy Ann?"

"Well, it seems like we have to find the dealer. If we can find him, confiscate what he has left, then the only ones that will be in danger are those that have most recently bought from him. But we don't know who this dealer is." He took a generous sip of his second water glass. "We have one individual in Buena Park under surveillance, but we haven't seen him doing anything except going from his house to Knott's Berry Farm and back."

"Knott's Berry Farm?" I asked.

"Yeah, why?"

"He wouldn't happen to be a heavy-set man around our age or a little older, and always wearing loud sports clothes?"

"As a matter of fact, that is him."

I proceeded to tell Sam about my experience at Knott's Berry Farm, to include obtaining another of the plastic bags.

"So the guy that sapped you is probably one of the other two guys you met. The heavy-set guy is Rufe Amundsen. Maybe we should pay him a visit. We'll go in my car, since it has lights and a siren."

We all left the club and piled into Sam's car. He pulled out of the parking lot and headed for the Santa Ana Freeway.

It was dark by the time we reached Buena Park. Sam made turns left and right, as if he had lived here all his life. He finally entered a subdivision that I recognized as being right next to Knott's Berry Farm. After the third turn, he slowed down, turned out the headlights, and coasted to a stop at the curb at the third house on the right.

As I slid from the middle of the back set over to the door, Sam passed me his back up gun, a .38, in case I should need it. I slid it into my pocket of my jacket.

As I got out of the car, I looked back the way we had come. There was a female coming toward us and as she passed under the streetlight, I recognized her. It was Cindy Ann.

"Sam!" I hissed, getting his attention. I pointed back down the street. "It's the girl. I'm going to get her."

Sam signalled an OK and he and Bruce went up to the one-story house and leaned on the doorbell. As they waited, Sam pulled his .38 Police Special and cocked it. I turned and started walking toward Cindy Ann. As I drew close to her I looked right at her.

"Cindy Ann?"

"Who . . . who are you?"

"Your mother sent me to find you."

"How do you know my mother? What's her name?"

"Bonnie Lou."

Cindy Ann gasped and started to fall. I caught her before she could hurt herself. I picked her up and started carrying her back to the car.

It was then that the screams started. I had never heard screams like that before, even in Vietnam. They came from the house that Sam and Bruce were at. I looked toward the house to see Sam breaking the door in and they both disappeared into the house.

I opened the back door to Sam's car and laid Cindy Ann on the back seat. I noticed that there were no door handles on the inside of the back doors and a screen ran across the back of the front seat. So if she came to, she wouldn't be going any place.

I shut the car door and ran for the house. The screams still emanated from the house, but they were becoming quieter until I couldn't hear them anymore.

As I entered the front door, I slammed right into one of the guys from the Calico Saloon. He didn't go down, so I let him have a hard punch in the breadbasket. He went to his knees and started puking his guts out.

I pulled my .38 out and started moving toward the back of the house, where I could hear Sam and Bruce trying to break down a door. I entered the hallway and just as they broke through the door, the other guy from the saloon slipped out of a doorway and started toward me. He stopped when he saw me and went for what I assumed was a gun. I raised mine and shot him in the right shoulder. I lucked out as I heard the dull thud of his gun hitting the carpeting. I then grabbed him and pushed him into a sitting position against the wall.

"Don't move, asshole!"

I stepped inside the bedroom that Sam and Bruce were standing in. I didn't really know what I was looking at. It looked like dried up grass was scattered all over the floor, with pieces of plastic bags — one piece which still said "Tind'losi Liao" — and pieces of pink material, from the floor, up the walls, and across the ceiling.

Sam saw the questioning look on my face.

"The grass is the marijuana and the pieces of plastic was what it was in. The pink material . . . well, I think that is the late Rufe Amundsen."

"How can you tell?"

"His wallet was the only thing in one piece."

I snickered. "A Tind'losi Hound?"

"That's what Bruce thinks."

"I guess ole Rufe sampled too much of his own product."

"Hey, Sam!" We heard Bruce's voice from the other room.

We turned and left the bedroom and entered the other one. Bruce was holding a gallon jar filled with a dark liquid.

"I think this is the Liao."

"Bruce," began Sam, "you seem to know more about this stuff than I do. How about you take my car keys and put that in my trunk. I shouldn't say this, but I would appreciate it if you made that jar disappear completely when we get back to the Tip-Top. I trust your judgment to do what's right."

"No problem."

Sam went over to the bed and picked up the phone.

"Ramirez, get two squad cars over here now," he said, finishing with the address.

He came back over to me and said, "L-T, I guess you solved your missing person case. Plus you earned your fee."

"Yeah, I guess so. But why don't I feel happy? The mother's dead, I don't know if there is a father any place, and the girl should go to rehab to get cleaned up."

"I'll take care of the girl and make sure she gets into rehab. So what are you gonna do now, L-T?"

"Well, I do have my PI license. And a thousand dollars that could be used to rent up an office. And from my own money, I could splurge for some advertising. But I'll probably take all of that out of my money. I don't know of any PI that gets a thousand dollars for two days work. Let me know when Cindy Ann is due out of rehab and I'll pick her up and give her her mother's refund."

"Sounds like you're getting soft, L-T."

"Yeah?" I growled. "How about asking those other two guys if I'm getting soft."

# A Little Job in Arkham

## John Sunseri

Milton Trent cautiously — ever so cautiously — pulled the handle on the suction cup. The glass circle whispered almost inaudibly and came free, and Trent placed it atop the handkerchief he'd laid down for that purpose. He raised his empty hand, reached through the hole in the case and paused for a second. If there were any alarms he'd missed, this would be when they went off.

Nothing. Silence.

A bead of sweat rolled down the back of his neck into his shirt, but he ignored it. He focused again on the cameo in the case, his black-gloved hand hovering motionless an inch above it, his eyes locked like lasers on the prize while his ears strained to hear anything unusual. The tick of the grandfather clock (a splendid William Hasler of Chatham, worth maybe ten thousand bucks) plunked quietly in the corner, a creak of a floorboard from the kitchen as the house cooled, and from outside the mournful chorus of frogs in the water garden. Nothing to worry about.

He took the cameo.

He could feel the fine carving through the thin fabric of the glove, could sense the bumps of the diamonds, nine total, could almost imagine the cool feel of the gold setting, but he wasted no time fondling the thing. In a quick motion the cameo was through the glass hole and into Trent's pouch, and he picked up the plunger and the round piece of glass, secreted them as well. He stood, not sparing a backward glance, and moved quickly and surely through the dark room toward the window.

"Very nicely done," came a voice from the easy-chair by the fire-place.

This is not to say that Trent stood there and listened to the sentence for the whole second and a half it took the invisible speaker to say it. No, at the first vibration of the 'V' in 'very', he had gone from a quick

A Little Job in Arkham

walk to a bound toward the window that would have shamed a jack-rabbit. By the time the word 'nicely' started, he had skidded to a halt, his rubber soles squelching on the hardwood as he noticed a bulky, bodyguard-shaped silhouette outside the glass. He'd spun toward the kitchen by the time the 'ly' came, and had taken a fast step toward the back of the house, and was well on his way to sprinting when the lights came on, just in time for the final thud of 'done.'

The study was a lot nicer in the light — he could see the magnificent oriental rugs, the breathtaking tapestries and glassed-in shelves with the huge antique tomes and folios, the ornately-framed Whistler, the less-ornately-framed Gainsborough, a Pickman sketch in its own corner. And a man sitting comfortably in the chair, remote control in his hand, looking amusedly on as Trent turned his head this way and that.

"The kitchen blocked as well?" Trent asked, stopping and casually turning toward him.

"Indeed," said the man. "Your reflexes are very good."

"They've had to be," said Trent. "But apparently I'm slowing down."

"Nonsense," said the man. "You're exactly what I've been looking for. I am Cornelius Bowen, the owner of this house — and, I might add, of that antique cameo in your pocket."

"They say possession is nine-tenths of the law," said Trent.

"If we go by that logic," smiled Bowen, "we could argue that since you're in my home, I own *you*."

Trent took the cameo out of his pouch, reached over, set it down on the table next to him. He then crossed his arms, let himself relax, and looked at his host.

"So," he said, "what next? The cops?"

"An offer," said Bowen. He stood, put down the control for the lights and moved over to the sideboard. "Brandy?"

"An offer," repeated Trent.

"Yes," said Bowen, reaching for a bottle. "I have need of a thief. A great thief. I need you to do a job for me. Would you like a glass? It's 'Old Havana', from Germain-Robin in California."

"Not France?" Trent asked.

"I dislike the French," replied Bowen. "A Frenchman once double-crossed me."

"What happened to him?" Trent asked, taking a few steps toward the old man.

"He died," said Bowen simply, extending a glass. "Here."

"I don't drink on the job," said Trent. "And when I *do* drink, it's usually beer. Cheap beer."

"What do you spend your money on, then?" asked Bowen, taking a sip from the snifter and smiling in appreciation of the taste. "You live simply, drive old cars, you don't have a drug habit. You reside in one of the seedier parts of Boston. You don't frequent whores . . ."

"Whoa, whoa," said Trent, his eyes widening. "How do you . . .?"

"I've been doing my research, Mr. Trent," said Bowen, setting down the goblet. "I needed the best thief on the East Coast, and it turned out he lived in my very own city. I could have saved some money had I known that in the first place."

"Good people have been looking for me for ten years," said Trent. "Entire police departments. Interpol. And you just found me? Just like that?"

"I have certain advantages that most lack," replied the old man. "But once I obtained your name, I monitored you on two of your jobs. Again, you have my compliments — the theft of the kylix from the design museum in Providence was brilliant."

Trent looked steadily at the man, but inside he quailed. How the hell had the guy known that he was involved in the theft of the ancient drinking cup? He'd used his usual string, of course, but he was a hundred percent sure that none of his partners would have ratted him out.

If they had, he'd be in the deepest cell at 200 Nashua Street right now instead of here watching Cornelius Bowen drink expensive brandy.

"May I ask," said Bowen, "what you did with the kylix?"

"No," said Trent.

"Very well," said the older man, a slight smile on his face. "Now, to business. I need a book stolen, and I need you to steal it."

"What book?" asked Trent.

"It's called the *Necronomicon*," began Bowen, but Trent interrupted.

"Up in Arkham," he said. "At the University."

"Exactly," said Bowen, his eyebrows lifting. "You've heard of it?"

"I make it my business to hear of everything valuable and easily portable," said Trent, arms still crossed before him. He wanted to put them into his pockets, but he didn't want to scare the old man. He'd seen one bodyguard already, imagined several more, and didn't need a beating. "And that's a doozy of a profit, that book."

"You've looked into stealing it?" asked Bowen, eyes narrowing.

"I've looked at it," said Trent. "It's impossible."

"Nonsense," said Bowen. "Anyone can steal anything."

"All right, let me amend that," said Trent. "It's impossible for *me*. Maybe if I had three months planning, unlimited funds, and access to a whole lot of hard-to-find information *and* if I had a man on the inside I *might* be able to pull it off. But that thing is locked down tighter than the United States Constitution."

"I can get you whatever cash you need," said Bowen quietly. "And whatever information you need. You'll have to find your own inside man and you'll need to do it quick. I need the book by the end of the month."

Trent laughed. "I guess I'm going to jail, then. I told you, Mr. Bowen, that it's impossible."

"And at the end of the whole affair, when I have the book in my hands," continued Bowen, ignoring the thief's protests, "I will give you a million dollars each, you and your team."

"I . . ." began Trent, then stopped. "Four million dollars?"

"*Five* million, Mr. Trent," smiled Bowen. "Though it was a nice test — but, yes, I'm aware that you use four helpers on your bigger jobs. Shame you didn't bring them along tonight, or I would have talked to you all at once."

"It's a good thing I didn't," said Trent. "I'm a peace-loving man — a thief, not a fighter — but if you cornered Buddy Bang like you did me tonight, one of you would've ended up dead."

"I did research on Mr. Bangatowski as well, Mr. Trent. I assure you, he wouldn't be allowed to be as close to me as you are right now."

"Humph," grunted Trent. He *had* been testing the old man a little bit, but he'd come through with flying colors — if he knew about Buddy, he knew about all of them. And that was scary.

"Why do you need it by the end of the month?" he hazarded, trying to buy a little time.

"That's not your concern, Mr. Trent," said Bowen coldly. "Suffice it to say that I've found myself in a position where I need to buy your services. If you decide that you will not do this thing for me, I assure you that you'll wish you'd never broken in here to steal the Waterston Cameo."

"Mister," said Trent, "I was there five minutes ago."

"You agreed to *what?*" asked Theresa, incredulous.

"I know," said Trent, lighting a Marlboro. They sat in Cloot's, back in their normal corner, 20-oz pints in front of them. "But I didn't have much of a choice, did I?"

"The book's impossible," she said, leaning back and picking up her beer. "We looked at it last year, remember? Drove all the way up there . . ."

"Things are different now," said Trent. Buddy Bang sat way back in the corner, sunglasses on, but Trent felt the man's eyes on him through the cheap plastic lenses. On either side of Theresa were Mike and Willem, and they both stared at him too, wondering how things had gotten to this point — how someone had found them all, found their names and addresses.

Wondering which of them had sold them out.

"Look," said Trent, "we're gonna have to do this thing. Either that, or you'll all have to go on the run. I don't know how this guy got his information, but he's got us all cold — from the stuff he knows, he could send us all to prison for a long, long time."

"Makes you wonder," said Buddy, the lights from the bar glinting on his knockoff Vuarnets.

"Yes it does," said Trent, picking up his glass, raising it to his lips. He took a long sip, set the pint back down, wiped his lips. "I've been wondering some of the same things myself, Bang, and you know what I came up with?"

"What?" asked Willem, elbows on the scarred oak table, Camel hanging from the corner of his mouth.

"I figured that, if any of you had sold us out, we wouldn't be here right now," said Trent.

"Bullshit," said Buddy. "We got a rat amongst us, and said rat is setting us up for something."

"Setting us up for what?" asked Trent. "Even if one of you is a traitor, the only thing we're being forced to do is steal the *Necronomicon*, and that's not some kind of set-up. Bowen really, really wants this book, folks, and he wants us to get it for him."

"I don't buy it," said Buddy. "There's something else going on here."

"Then we're gonna have to be real careful, aren't we?" asked Trent. He finished his beer, set the empty glass back on the table, then sighed.

"I'm going up there tomorrow morning to case the place," he said finally. "Who's in?"

"For a million bucks?" asked Mike. "Versus having that creepy old guy coming after us? What time do we leave?"

"It's impossible," said Theresa.

"I've been saying that," agreed Trent gloomily. They were in a cheap room in Arkham's Holiday Inn, the four of them uncomfortably sitting wherever they could while Willem was out getting food. "Tell me again about the security systems."

"Two guards at the front desk — *armed* guards — and they're pros, not your normal campus cops. During library hours the book is inaccessible unless by appointment — it's in the far-back room in a sealed glass case, surrounded by infrared beams and pressure pads on the floor, and at any intrusion the steel gates slam down in front of the door and the room fills with knockout gas."

"Any way to get around the pressure pads?" asked Mike.

"You could fly," suggested Theresa. "Assuming, that is, that you could also avoid the beams — the projectors are actually set into the walls behind bulletproof glass."

"How about cutting the power?" asked Buddy. "Knock out the electricity . . ."

"They've got two backup generators in the basement," said Trent, looking over the blueprints Bowen had gotten them. "Both are self-contained and also defended. And that's where they keep the dogs."

"What kind of school library has freaking *guard dogs*?" asked Mike.

"It's a tradition," said Trent. "Apparently, they came in handy one time — there was some yokel tried to steal the *Necronomicon* a hundred years ago, and the dogs took him out."

"Nice," said Buddy. "They run through the place at night, shit everywhere?"

"I don't know about the shitting," said Trent. "Maybe they're trained not to. But, yeah, they've got the run of the place after the library closes. And then the library's got all those *weird* defenses — the things all over the walls . . ."

Two knocks came at the door and everyone tensed, Buddy reaching down and grabbing his pistol — and then two more knocks and Trent nodded. "Come," he said.

Willem entered, three pizza boxes piled up in his hands. He kicked the door shut behind him, set the food down on the table next to the Gideon Bible and shrugged his shoulders. "Cold out there," he said.

"You get combination?" asked Theresa, moving over to the pies.

"Two large combos and one plain cheese for Mr. I Don't Eat Meat," said Willem.

"Fuck you," said Buddy, grabbing his box and returning to the bed. He opened it and steam escaped into the air. "I take *care* of my body, lard-ass."

"Meat is *good* for you," protested Willem, shooting a quick look down at his gut. It *was* pretty big.

"How about digging from underneath?" asked Mike, taking a can of Coke from the minibar.

"It'd take a month to tunnel under where we need to go," said Trent, "and we don't have a month. Even if we could get underneath, we'd have the problem of escape."

"Yeah, what about escape?" asked Theresa. "You go to the cop shop today?"

"The police station's on the other side of town, which is nice," said Trent, moving over to the window and looking down at the parking lot. "But they patrol. If we time it right, it'll take 'em ten minutes to respond. If we don't, they'll have a car there in a minute or two."

"I've got routes all drawn up," said Theresa, "and we can get a fast car from the Bruno brothers."

"The problem is getting that damned book out of the safe room," said Trent. "How about we just make an appointment to work with the book — say we're doing research, do a switcheroo . . ."

"Never work," said Theresa. "First thing I thought of, so I made inquiries. Turns out they only let you use the *Necco . . . Neconimo . . .* whatever the hell it's called, if you're internationally well-known in your field and they've got you on some kind of list. And even then they set you up with two special guards and one librarian standing watch over you while you work. No chance to make a switch, even if you've got a copy to switch — the thing's distinctive-looking."

"We could make a copy," mused Willem. "Polish Rob is real good at that kind of shit — you've seen his work."

"He's real good at driver's licenses," said Trent. "This might be a little much for him."

"No, really," insisted Willem. "One time, he made an imitation Shakespeare first folio for some guy from New York wanted to switch it out with the one at Yale."

"What happened?" asked Buddy, interested.

"Didn't work out," said Willem, sipping a 7-Up. "Guy made some bonehead mistake, pretended to be a professor from Wales or somewhere, and ran into a Welsh librarian who wanted to talk with him. Far as I know, he's still in jail in New Haven. But the forgery sure looked good."

"Amateurs," muttered Trent. "Goddammit, though — how are we going to do this thing?"

"I've got an idea," said Buddy. They all looked at him.

"We're not going to use machine guns," said Theresa. "We're not going to take hostages or kidnap the librarian's wife and kids . . ."

"Hey," said Buddy, wounded, "what kind of guy do you think I am? I'm a gentleman burglar!"

"You're a semi-civilized thug," said Theresa. "But that's okay — we love you anyway. What's your idea?"

An hour later, Trent nodded.

"That might work," he said. "But we've got a lot of stuff to set up. Theresa, can you get hold of the Brunos and get what we need?"

"Easy," she said. "I imagine this'll be right up their alley. They grew up in the construction business, you know."

"I'm amazed they grew up at all," said Trent. "New Jersey wiseguys don't usually last that long. Willem, call Polish Rob. Bring him all the pictures we have of the book. Buddy, I'm gonna need you to do the research on the cops — find out when they patrol and where, give us the biggest window we can get when this goes down."

"And me?" asked Mike.

"You're the point-man," smiled Trent. "You're the only one hasn't been on campus, so they won't have your picture."

"Great," said Mike, grimacing. "How about you?"

"I've got a little more research to do," said Trent, "and I've got to use the school library to do it."

October 24 — a full week before the deadline Bowen had set — was a bright, crisp day in Arkham. It had rained the night before and the cobbled paths in the quad still shone wetly, water slowly dripped from the maples and elms onto the carpet of leaves beneath, and students wore wool jackets and gloves on their way to class.

Richard LePlante, head librarian at Miskatonic's Curwen Rare Books Library spent a few moments talking with the guards on duty before his shift started, the three of them drinking coffee he'd brought from the Starbucks at the Student Union. They chatted about inconsequential things as the first few research students of the day entered, went through the check-in procedure and the metal detector and began negotiating with the assistant librarians for access to their thesis materials. LePlante finished his chat, nodded at the door guards and went to his office.

It was quiet for the first half-hour, and he got a fair amount of work done on his correspondence — Professor El-Ibrahim from Cairo University wanted to stop by on his visit to Harvard and look at the cuneiform holdings, and a team of archaeological researchers digging in Arizona wanted him to check a few strange coincidences they had discovered in the Native artifacts they had dug up — he responded in the affirmative to the Egyptian, made a note to look up the symbols for the diggers, then sighed and reached for the stack of acquisition forms. He hated this part of the job — acquiring new works, vitally important though it was, kept him from dealing with the already-rich collection they *had*, and he wished he could delegate the buying decisions to someone else. But the trustees counted on his judgment and his alone, so he was forced to wade through catalogs of ancient books every week, searching for gems . . .

"If it were done when 'tis done," he sighed, "then 'twere well it were done quickly." Shakespeare was his passion, and his frequent use of the Bard's quotations often annoyed his wife — but in the solitude of his office, he let fly.

But today, just as he took the top sheet of paper from the stack his secretary had left for him, all thoughts of classical language and iambic pentameter were driven from his head.

The sound was so loud and sudden, so explosive, that LePlante's first thought was that a gas line had blown and that the ceiling was coming down. He dove for the floor under his desk and squinched his eyes shut, waiting for the masonry to crush him like a roach.

More grinding, rumbling sounds, and he realized they were coming from outside his office, from somewhere back in the stacks.

From the rare book area.

He got to his feet, papers flying everywhere, and sprinted for the door. He threw it wide, darted out into the hall where students were milling in panic and confusion, and looked back through the main room — where a cloud of stone dust billowed through the stacks and carrels from the rear of the building.

"Oh, shit," he said, and started running. The guards from the front door followed, and they sped past the small knots of seniors and grad students toward the Rare Book Room.

As they did, the alarms started, wailing like banshees in the cavernous library.

The bulldozer had worked just fine, Mike Mulligan thought as he unbuckled himself and watched as light poured into the dark room through the hole he'd knocked in the wall. The gas was already starting to billow into the chamber and he again checked the seals on his mask and goggles, nervously wondering how powerful the stuff was — it couldn't be *too* powerful, he reassured himself; otherwise, it would damage the books it was supposed to protect.

The steel gate had dropped instantly as he'd breached the wall, but he could sense motion from beyond it as he hopped to the ground, avoiding chunks of broken stone and masonry. That would be the library guards, and it would take them a moment or two to figure out that they'd have to go around.

Mike reached back up into the cab of the 'dozer and grabbed the sledgehammer. He waded through the cloud of dust and smoke, raised the thing and swung it as hard as he could at the glass case in the center of the room, thankfully undamaged by the flying, falling hunks of marble and granite.

The glass shattered and he dropped the hammer, conscious of the red beams of the security system shining through the haze, playing across him. He reached in, grabbed the book and shoved it into his jacket. Then, not even looking at the men screaming at him through the bars of the security door, he picked his way back outside.

Where two cops waited, guns drawn and aimed at him.

City cops.

"Thank God," said LePlante, huffing and wheezing from his sprint through and around the building. "Where's the book?"

"It's safe, sir," said the older cop. "We're bagging it and the other one for evidence, and we'll take it over to the station . . ."

"Other one?" LePlante asked, confused. "What else did he take?"

"Just the big one from the glass case, sir," said Officer — LePlante squinted through the haze at the man's badge — Officer Robie. "But he had a duplicate on him. Probably meant to drop it somewhere, slow down the pursuit."

"How was he going to get away?" asked the librarian, frantically looking around at the scene. The cops had already shoved the would-be thief into the back of the Arkham PD patrol car, and it looked as though they hadn't been gentle about it; the man was bleeding from a wound on his scalp and struggling frantically to get out of his cuffs. The other officer was gently shoving both copies of the *Necronomicon* into large plastic bags near the hood of the car.

"We got a witness says a sports car parked about a hundred yards that way" he gestured with his pen down the access road "tore off as soon as they saw us. Had a good-looking woman driving . . ."

"Oh my God," said LePlante. "There was a blond woman here a couple of days ago, asking to be allowed to examine the book . . ."

"Good thing you didn't let her," said the cop, smiling. "I guess they figured, they couldn't do it the easy way, they'd just try a little harder."

"You can't take the book, Officer," said LePlante, turning his attention back to the policeman. "It's fragile, it's been through physical trauma today and it's valuable beyond belief. It must stay here."

"It's evidence, sir — sorry," said the cop, still writing in his notebook. "Don't worry — we'll take care of it for you and you'll get it back just like it is now . . ."

"Officer," LePlante said, drawing himself up and staring at the man with the full authority he was capable of, "I understand your rules, but they simply cannot be allowed to apply in this situation. This is a serious attempt at theft, and for all I know you're part of the team of burglars."

Officer Robie looked at LePlante and frowned. "Sir, I'm gonna forgive your slur on my professionalism and that of my partner. I'm gonna put aside for the moment that I've been protecting this burg for fifteen years and I've been decorated for bravery twice, because there's no way for you to know all that. But what I'm *not* gonna do is let some pantywaist librarian dictate police policy to me."

LePlante took a step back, feeling the sheer anger of the cop radiate through his bulky body, though his voice and manner remained outwardly placid and professional - he felt as if he were confronting a wolf in human guise. But he refused to give in to his atavistic fear, and instead forced himself to respond firmly and forcefully.

"Regardless," he said, his voice steady, "you cannot be allowed to take that book. I want to talk to your superior — hell, I want to talk to the chief." And he began moving toward the other cop, who was just beginning to open the door of the squad car and put the plastic-wrapped books into the front seat.

"I'll take those," said LePlante, holding out his hands expectantly and hugely grateful that a crowd of people had gathered, undergraduates mixing with professors and grad students, and that the two security officers from the library had followed him and stood just feet away, hands resting lightly on their pistols.

The cop with the books — Officer Raffles, according to his badge — looked at his partner quizzically.

"Guy wants to talk to the chief about avoiding procedure," said the first cop. "Doesn't want us to take the books."

"Well, tough shit," said the second policeman. "I don't particularly want to argue about it. Regs say that . . ."

"Oh, Christ," said Robie, looking around. "We got people filming us." They all looked around and, indeed, a couple of the students had brought out digital cameras and were recording the scene.

"Remember Rodney King, Officer," said LePlante a bit smugly. That was probably a bit unfair, considering these guys weren't beating on him with their nightsticks — but boy, did they look like they wanted to.

And now the security guards were getting into it. "Say," said one of them, hand still on his gun. "Why don't we just put the books aside for a few minutes and call up the Chief of Police. He can come down here, we can call up the University's lawyers, maybe come up with some kind of compromise . . ."

"Why don't the rent-a-cops just shut their fucking pieholes and let the professionals do their job?" snarled the first cop. You could tell — he wanted to reach for his own pistol — but then he looked around again, saw the students with their cameras again, and shook his head. "Aw, fuck it. Give these assholes the books, Charlie."

"You sure, John?" asked the other cop, confused. "I mean — regulations say . . ."

"Go ahead," said Robie. "We got more important things to do, anyway, like getting this scumbag in the back to the station."

The other policeman shrugged and handed LePlante the books, both of them sealed in plastic.

"Now," said LePlante, "let's call the chief . . ."

"You call the chief," said the big cop, scowling. "We're outta here."

"Oh no," said the security guard. "I think we should all just wait around for a while . . ."

But instantly, quick as cats, both cops — fake cops — dove into the car. While the security guard hastily yanked out his firearm, the cruiser started up with a roar as the engine caught, and in less than a second it dashed onto the road, tires squealing.

The guard managed to get a couple shots off, missing completely with the first one but shattering the rear windshield with his second, and then the car was gone, disappearing into the woods as the road curved.

"Goddammit!" roared the security guard. "Ralph, get 911 *right now!*"

"On it," said the other, reaching for his cell phone.

LePlante stood for a moment in shock, the weight of the *Necronomicon* and its double heavy in his hands, watching as the guards sprang into action, feeling a sense of relief spread through him.

They had failed. It had been a complicated, devious plan, but the thieves had failed.

He staggered back inside through the hole in the wall and set the package down, waving slightly to dissipate whatever gas was still in the air. He spent thirty seconds ripping open the tape on the bag, then with trembling hands drew out the first book. It *looked* like the *Necronomicon*, with the ancient hide cover, but when he cautiously opened it he was faced with blank pages.

So he took out the other one.

"Guy had guts," said Buddy, removing the plugs from his cheeks, ripping off the false mustache.

"Yeah," said Willem, stretching, leaving on the toupee for the moment. They walked briskly away from the damaged police car toward the panel truck Theresa had stashed for them in the copse of trees. They both wished she could be driving — the woman was flat-out the best wheelman they'd ever come across in their lifetimes of larceny — but she'd been busy setting up a fire in an abandoned building way the hell on the other side of town that would keep the patrol cops busy while they pulled off their heist.

"And the Pole did a good job on the books," said Buddy, casually reaching in to his cop jacket and pulling out the real *Necronomicon*, sliding it onto the dash of the truck while he climbed in. "A *hell* of a job in just a couple days."

"I told you he was good," said Willem. "Expensive, but good."

"I hope the old man's not counting on us paying for all this shit out of our take," grumbled Buddy. "The bulldozer, this truck, the cop car, the uniforms and the copies of the book — they should all go on expenses."

"I'm with you pal," said Mike, coming out of the bushes where he'd thrown the gas mask, his latex gloves, the goggles and the clothes he'd worn for the job. "But let's talk about it on the road, huh? They'll set up roadblocks real soon."

"They've got fifteen cops in this town," said Buddy, scornful. "And thirty roads out. Theresa's got us maps, and we'll be just fine."

"Just saying," said Mike, sliding into the seat. "You gonna leave the book up there?"

"Naw," said Buddy. "Throw it in the glove box."

"Welcome back, Mr. Trent," said Bowen. "And congratulations."

"Thank you," said Trent, the bulky box in his hands. "You got our money?"

"Is that the book?"

"Money first," said the thief. He looked out the window, saw the shapes of his team and the gigantic forms of Bowen's bodyguards out there, silently waiting for the business to be concluded. Watching the frogs, maybe.

"Show me the book first," commanded Bowen.

"I flipped through it," said Trent, beginning to fiddle with the latches on the lead box. "Some creepy stuff in there, man. I've been having nightmares all week."

"The uninitiated should not view the work of the Arab," whispered Bowen, his eyes avidly watching Trent's hands. "It can be . . . dangerous."

"That's what I hear," said Trent. "But I imagine *you* won't have any problems with it, will you? All these spells and incantations and such — I bet they're right up your alley."

"Hurry, man," urged Bowen. His hunger, his *need* for the *Necronomicon* was almost palpable.

Trent stopped what he was doing for a moment, looked over at the older man. "So why do you need the book by tomorrow, Mr. Bowen? Something important going on on Halloween night?"

"That is none of your concern, Mr. Trent," said Bowen.

"I did a little research," said Trent, ignoring the older man. "See, I was wondering a couple of things about this whole mess. First of all, how had you found me in the first place? That little trap you set, with the Waterston cameo, was brilliant, and you knew I'd come for it. But how?"

"Psychology," said Bowen, smiling thinly.

"I don't think so," said Trent. "It's more like you'd been watching me, watching my methods and techniques. But that's impossible."

"Obviously it wasn't," said Bowen. "Like I told you before — I have resources the police don't have . . ."

"And when I broke in here, you somehow managed to sneak into the room while I was working and plant yourself in that chair, there," continued Trent. "Which is *also* impossible. There's no — I repeat, *no* - way you could've done that without me hearing or sensing you."

"So how did I do it?" asked Bowen.

"Magic," said Trent.

The two men looked at each other for a moment, then Bowen smiled again, a toothy smile full of menace.

"Magic," he repeated.

"Yep," said Trent, beginning again to fool with the latches on the big leaden box. "Magic. I'm kind of a hard-edged realist, Mr. Bowen, but I'm not stupid. If I have to accept that magic exists, I'll do so. And the more I looked at the *Necronomicon*, the more I realized that, yeah, this stuff might be for real."

"That's very . . . broad-minded of you," said Bowen.

"Thank you," nodded Trent. "And once I accepted the possibility that you were some kind of magician, it answered another question for me. See, if you could do all sorts of mystical stuff, why couldn't you just go get the book yourself? Seems like that'd be fairly easy for a wizard or whatever the hell you are."

"Seems that way," said Bowen, his eyes again locked on the box in Trent's lap. "So, why couldn't I?"

"We got through all the defenses and alarms and poison gas at the library," said Trent, clicking the locks open. He didn't raise the lid, though — he just looked at Bowen while he spoke. "But Miskatonic also had all these doohickeys all over the place, on the walls, embedded into the floor, things looked like hieroglyphics. So while we were waiting to pull off the caper, I did some more research in some of the other books in the library. Turns out, they're *mystical* protection. According to the books, you can't do magic around these Signs."

Bowen shook his head, as if dislodging a fly. "And your point?" he said.

"My point?" repeated Trent, now smiling himself. "I don't really have one. But I do have an experiment I'd like to try . . ."

And he opened the lid, turned the box around so that Bowen could see inside.

There was no book. Inside, resting on a cushion of red velvet, was a stone carving — one of the Signs.

"We took a few of these things while we were in there," said Trent. "Just in case. Seemed the prudent thing to do . . ."

Bowen snarled and shrunk back in his seat, his eyes widening, his lips curling. He threw up his hands, gnarled like claws, and hissed like a pissed-off snake. "Put it away!" he choked finally. "Close the lid!"

"Now, see," said Trent, nodding, "this was the other possibility I discovered. If you were just a wizard, this wouldn't hurt you or anything — just keep you from casting a spell on me. But looking at the way you're reacting . . ."

Bowen started kicking his feet on the floor, moving the chair backwards, but Trent got to his feet, pulled out the carving and took a couple of steps forward, toward the frantic, wriggling form of the old man.

". . . I don't think you're human at all," he said. And thrust the Sign forward, directly into Bowen's face.

The wizard keened loudly, his voice as high-pitched as a tea-kettle, and fell backwards, the chair collapsing under the spasmodic thrashing of its inhabitant. Trent was just as quick, however, and leapt over the fallen chair to keep the ancient sigil trained only inches from the face of the man.

But it was no longer a man — the skin had started to stretch and peel over Bowen's skull, and blood oozed slowly from a dozen splits in the flesh. The thing's hands thrust up, claws forcing themselves through the false meat of the man suit, and Bowen's whole body convulsed and ratcheted itself into new, impossible configurations. Trent fought the impulse to step back, to get away from the monstrosity, and instead moved even closer, inch-by-inch, until the stone actually touched the writhing, gibbering mass of alien flesh and *faux* humanity.

The thing had been loud before, but now it let out such an air-raid siren of a scream that Trent could feel his eardrums compressing. He wanted to drop the totem, throw his hands to his violated ears, but forced himself to keep going, to keep moving with the scuttling insectile horror around the room, to ignore the flailings of the thing's arms and tentacles, to ignore the gobbets of Bowen-flesh that it sloughed off as it crawled along the floor, to ignore the madness his eyes refused to accept, and to keep the stone sigil touching the creature.

And, suddenly, with one last inhuman alien wail that sounded like a star exploding, the thing finally fell — collapsed loosely inside the bloody dressing gown it had been wearing — bubbled like pancake batter on a hot grill — melted down into the floor — and the last thing Trent saw before he threw the Sign onto the roiling mass of decomposing plasma were the being's eyes, red and violet, multi-faceted like a mantis's, glaring enragedly at him with a hatred more intense than nuclear fire . . .

And then the doors to the patio burst open and Willem and Buddy and Theresa and Mike poured into the room, gabbling in excitement and terror.

"Jesus," yelled Willem. "The bodyguards — they just fucking *melted.*"

"Oh," said Buddy, the only cool one in the group. "I see your plan worked."

"So where's the five mil?" asked Theresa, still staring at the mess on the floor.

"There never was five million," said Trent, taking a big gulp of Bowen's cognac. "We were supposed to die here tonight."

"There's some pretty good stuff in the house, though," said Willem, looking around at the paintings and artworks.

"Yeah, we'll take everything when we go," said Trent. "You all still have your Signs?"

"You kidding me?" said Theresa, pulling on the chain around her neck, tugging the stone sigil into view. "From now on, this thing sleeps with me, bathes with me . . ."

"Sounds fun," smiled Mike, leering at her. But Trent saw him fingering his own Sign and nodded.

"So how about the *Necronomicon*?" asked Buddy. "It's worth a lot of money — what're we gonna do with it?"

"Miskatonic's offering half a million for its return," said Trent, poking at the bubbling mess that had been Bowen with his boot, and grimacing. "I say we take it."

"We could get a lot more," complained Buddy.

"Yeah, we could," said Trent. "But then we'd have to worry about who actually had the thing in their possession. Can you imagine one of these things" — pointing down at the pool of ichor — "getting its claws on the book? God knows what would happen to the world."

"Yeah," sighed Buddy. "I get your point."

# Day of Iniquity

## Steven L. Shrewsbury

Who has permitted you to hate, murder, and rape? Judgment shall overtake you sinners. The remedy being far removed from you because of such sins. Your Creator will rejoice at your destruction.

–FRAGMENT XXVIII,
*Daemonolateria*

## Act I — Deal With the Nephilum

"You throw down the body of an olden woman in front of the Son of God himself, and expect information?" the deep voice asked before stopping to chuckle. "You truly are from the barbarian lands of the north, Jarek."

Steely fingers held the writhing body of the aged woman on the slab. These weathered digits were attached to the thick, muscled arms of an enormous man. Beneath his heavy mustache, his lips curled back and he grunted, "It is you who sets the price of accurate tidings, Neurath. Besides, what makes you so special? There are many sons of the gods running across this planet."

The flickering firelight in the dank cavern only showed the massive outline of the son of god as he leaned forward. From these shadows came the sound of nostrils flaring and the wet scrape of steel on stone. Though Jarek was a giant of a man, he was dwarfed by the figure that stood up. The air gasped as a heavy blade passed through it. Jarek never flinched as the Nephilum Neurath dropped the axe head the size of a man's chest on the stone slab. The naked woman wheezed and then gave out an ear-splitting cry before her sobs exploded into insane squeals. Neurath clumsily dropped the axe beside the block. He reached down, picked up the skinny leg freed up from the body, and put the bloody tip to his huge mouth.

"Good enough?" Jarek asked, still holding the woman firm, eyes trying to avoid the bizarre grooves that ran over Neurath's skin. His flesh appeared completely tattooed or engraved with images of unnamed creatures and bizarre events only captured by the mind of a man or god insane.

The son of god sighed, showing his boredom. "It will do for starters." Neurath seized the tiny figure on the stone as Jarek released her. As the behemoth turned, he hung her on metal hooks. These applications to the cave wall pierced the screaming woman through the back, protruding out from under her collarbones. Neurath asked, "So, savage, what is it you require of me?"

"What no one else can give," Jarek replied, a hand on the grip of a short-sword at his waist. "I need to know where the cult of Ensibzianna hides. It's said the malevolent son, Alagar, leads these folk at the moment."

Neurath sat back, still chewing his food, and said through crimson teeth, "You come to a Nephilum for such a boon? You have stones in those russet trousers, I will grant you that, savage." Swallowing, he gestured with the leg and muttered, "Alagar, curse me running, that damnable imbecile."

"I know the charge of one who thinks he is descended of the gods," Jarek stated and motioned to the cave entrance. Two husky men, nearly copies of Jarek in large build and hirsute body, carried in a struggling figure. This time, it was an old man. They stripped him of his scarlet cote-hardie, then his gypon and again, Jarek held his offering down on the granite wedge.

Neurath arched an already serrated mono-brow and said, "You came prepared. So the primitives from the Caucausia Mountains are learning, eh?"

"I'd never travel this close to Shynar unless it was vital to me or my kindred," Jarek said as he maintained his pinning clutch.

With a single nod, Neurath scooped up his axe and reared back. The old woman hanging behind him screeched louder and passed out at last. The blade fell and this time the giant extracted a left forearm from the stone block. Sampling this meat and wearing a more appreciative look, Neurath ignored the elderly man's shouts and said, "Very good, barbarian. He is from afar, excellent vintage, too." Neurath then hung this old man on a set of hooks near to the drooping woman. The tongue of the aged man screamed curses unto the barbarians, their mothers and the sons of god.

Jarek waited patiently, never speaking.

Neurath noted Jarek's patience. The reclining giant gnawed on raw tissue and said, "I admire you, primitive human. You hold your tongue." He wiped his ruddy-skinned forearm over a bloody maw and asked, "You knew the price was blood and provender?"

"As is the cost with anything," Jarek replied with a calm voice. "All matters come down to blood."

Gulping with a stiff grunt, Neurath sucked on the forearm and wore a reflective expression. He then said, "Ensibzianna, aye? A cult indeed worships my half-brother Alagar from the heavens. His ego is overloading his ass, truth be told." He fanned himself with the bone and licked marrow from his upper lip. "I know where he awaits oblations from his foolish admirers."

Since the pause was so long, Jarek sighed and turned to his men. They exited the cave and returned with another screaming contribution. Again, this woman was older, but not as ancient as the first one Jarek lay down before Neurath.

Neurath's hawkish nose twitched. "You keep the fatter ones for later? You are wise," he snorted, watching the men place her under Jarek's hold.

This woman did not cry, but cursed Jarek and Neurath. "I invoke the names of Asmodeous and Azathoth to burn out your eyes!" she yelled with enormous malediction. "May Tiphereth mate with your mother! May Belial pass water in the face of your sister and all of her children fall from her belly before it is time!"

Neurath gave a bored groan as he picked up the axe. "Mouthy one, no?"

Jarek held her with great difficulty as she made signals with her fingers, blaspheming heavily. Frowning, Jarek said, "I will throw in a few more if you cut off her head."

With a slight chuckle, Neurath chopped and she yelped. He took her left foot off and promptly placed the woman on the wall. Though wailing in agony, she still uttered profanity and further curses at them. The old man next to her had fallen unconscious. The giant eyed her and then Jarek. "Maybe you are correct." He then picked up the foot and started to pick at his teeth with the little toe of the appendage. "This cult is located in the ruins of Larak at the edge of the desert of Dundayin. This is most certainly true."

Jarek nodded and started to turn away.

"Tell me," Neurath mused, chewing on the cold toes amid the ear-piercing curses of the woman. "Amuse me, savage, for my life is very monotonous. Why does the cult of Ensibzianna enrage you enough to bring sacrifice unto a son of god that is not of your faith?"

"I am of the Keltos folk and my god is Wodan," Jarek responded with assurance. "He gives strength the moment one is planted in your mother's belly and watches us to see if we will stray from the good course. If I were not smart enough to find my lost blood amongst the cult, Wodan would not show his favor to me."

Neurath nodded, as if lost in thought. He then supposed, "And yet you had no trepidation of bringing these ones in for me? You fear not their powers? They are all necromancers and witches, as it were."

Jarek shrugged. "Why should I be afraid? I don't believe in their gods."

The cackling laughter of Neurath echoed out of the cavern as Jarek exited.

Just outside the cave, the acolytes of Neurath frowned at the Keltos men. The three women were tall, quite plump and dressed in green samite robes. The youngest one stepped forward, her black tresses shaking, and said to Jarek, "You fancy yourselves real men? You do not know what it is to be a true man."

Jarek did not reply, but one of his men, Garton, dismissed her and told her, "You have courage because you can take in a giant? Wodan craps knives on you and so do the rest of the Elder Gods."

As they climbed on their horses, the woman persisted, wishing blight on Jarek. Looking down, Jarek retorted, "What kind of woman lays down with what is not human?"

She snapped back, "What kind of man brings in old ladies to sacrifice for his desires?"

Hair across his face in the wind, Jarek's frown was still visible. "They were just witches. They had said they could tell me where my true love was located." He then smiled wolfishly. "They lied. Take care that I find my love at Larak as Neurath says, or we shall be back."

The other fleshy acolyte put her arm around the cussing girl and said to Jarek, "She is young."

Garton pulled on his face-wrap to ward off the trail dust and muttered, "She may not get much older."

The young woman said, "To give up lives for meat, just for your love, that is barbaric!"

Jarek and his kindred laughed. "We are barbarians," Jarek informed her as they left.

## Act II — Watering Hole Watcher

A grizzled man, ancient of years, opened the door to his home. The small abode, made of mud bricks, was the lone structure aside from a grain storage bin at the oasis. Several palm trees and a long pool of bubbling water made the oasis unique on the edge of the vast desert of Dundayin. Wobbling, using a withered branch for support, the old man was the only one there to face the barbarian horde.

"Good day, men," the old one said, shielding his eyes to the sun.

The watcher then saw several women dismount from amongst the great force. Not much smaller than the men, these females were sturdy-built and armed with swords, too. He lost count of how many there were in the pack.

The host of hairy men climbed off their horses and led them to the water. There were so many of the barbarians that they refreshed their horses and themselves in shifts.

From out of these strangers emerged two blue-eyed men. Removing the dark cloth from their faces, they nodded at the watcher and shook off the dust.

"I am Jarek and this is Garton. We shall use your water."

Looking back the way they came, the watcher said, "Far from home, I see."

Jarek went to the bubbling spring and buried his face in the water. Emerging with a wild gleam in his eye, he looked at the elderly man and then directed his eyes south of the oasis. "Larak is not far from here. I can see the ruins in the distance."

The watcher grunted in agreement and then sat in a crudely-made wooden chair. "Not much there, young man."

Never taking his eyes from the distant site, Jarek murmured, "All that matters is there, oldster." He then gestured to his men. They unloaded a few long rolls of cloth and lay them at the door of the watcher. "There is dried meat and nuts in there. We remember who honors us."

"I thank you for that and my life."

Jarek still never looked at him, but replied, "No use killing an aged watchman, is there?"

"I suppose not."

"Previous owners of the food have no more use for it. Call it a gift from Wodan."

The watcher looked back to the North. "Wodan? My, you are far from home. By your fair hair and blue eyes, I'd guess you were of the tribes beyond the Caucaus Mountains."

"You would guess correctly."

The old man fell silent. He took a few breaths and then looked toward Larak.

Jarek gestured for the women to refill the skins of water and at last looked at the watcher. "And you wonder why we are here, so far south?"

Shrugging, the watchman said, "I'd deduce it has to do with the faction of Ensibzianna in Larak. They absorb many followers and hold up in the ruins. There certainly isn't anything to rob or rape in the remains of Larak."

Jarek's huge hands curled into fists. "That is not why I . . . we are here." He bent over and leered at the watcher. "Why are you out here at the edge of the desert?"

"My father before me lived and tended this oasis. It's my life. This is where I live and belong. I do as I was taught. Surely, even you folk of the north know to honor your father and his wishes."

"We know of blood, old man," Jarek nodded and walked to his horse. "My niece here is twice the fighter most men are, and worth dying for."

The aged watcher eyed the stout, blonde girl covered in heavy furs and cloaks. "Take care. There is a gang of fighters in Larak."

Jarek smiled. "That's all right. I brought my own."

With a snicker, the watcher wished, "Be of fine fortune then, even if you meet your death. If you seek after your kin, I hope you find them."

"I will," Jarek promised. "If they send my Keltos ass back to Caucausia, they won't send it back alive. The fools in Larak plan a sacrifice tomorrow, a grand hecatomb of children and infants. I know through their by-laws and their slavery to the shifts in the lights of the sky. If anything, these religious dolts are dogmatic and prisoners to their rules. We will take them all to Hell before any of my kin falls."

"God be with you," the watcher wished him.

"God loves men like me," Jarek said, half-jovial.

"Why is that?"

Jarek shrugged. "He just does."

As the barbarian leader walked away, the other blonde man, Garton, looked at the watcher and proclaimed, "God has balls. So does Jarek. God respects that."

## Act III — Bloodbath at Larak

Stopping a fair distance from the ruins of Larak, Jarek surveyed the scene. He saw heavy-set men and boys, sorry excuses for pickets and guards, scurrying to tell that a massive force was at the doorway to the despoiled city. That did not concern Jarek at all. "They need to keep what I want alive," he muttered to no one.

The city of Larak was once a great spectacle, Jarek heard tell, but it was destroyed long before he drew a breath in life. Previously, his warrior grandfather, Rogan the Kelt, told him, the desert of Dundayin was once a raging sea. Off to their left, all the barbarian horde could see was an endless wasteland hemmed by a more fertile ground.

One of the warriors said to Jarek, "Looks as if that land over yonder is the piss bucket of the gods!"

After the laughter subsided, Jarek said gesturing toward the ruins ahead, "My grandfather told me that Larak was destroyed and he didn't lie. But what sort of creatures could have done that?"

While rows of obelisks remained, several blocks of these phallic stones were knocked every way as if a child destroyed a playground sand-sculpture. Numerous high stone walls slumped over, some broken and jagged, others still forming corners. The ceilings of many of these buildings — which Jarek guessed were temples — were caved in, spilling light and sand through the breeches. Grim, chaotic visions swam in the primitive skulls of the foreigners to the desert. Jarek's heart started to beat faster, but he never would have admitted to such a fact. It was as if the structures were toppled in a pattern, he thought.

"What vanity," Jarek declared, pondering the configurations not leveled by human hands. "To build up marble houses for their gods to live in — huh — looks like one of them grew angry enough to knock down the habitation."

"Shall we send them to their gods?" Garton asked, causing a cheer to arise from the multitude.

Calmly, Jarek gripped the handle of a sword on his back and said, "Yes. Grandfather said Asmodeus grew angry and took the sea with him. I would see them all drown in their own blood."

Whichever riders rode two at a time let their spare dismount. As these lines of footmen assembled behind the line of horsemen, those inhabiting the ruins of Larak scuttled like disturbed rats. Unorganized and half-dressed, these residents created unity only in their communal fear . . . at the shout of the Northern barbarians, heralding their berserk charge.

Shouting with insane vehemence, the Keltos folk moved *en masse* toward the broken granite carcass of Larak. Jarek felt his blood leap in his veins as the thunder in his ears was drowned out by the cacophony of hooves.

A few dozen valiant souls actually stepped forward to fight. This force of cultists swiftly retreated when they realized the size of the tide of livid humanity bearing down on them.

Swinging broadswords, bludgeons, and stabbing spears, the multitude rode into the crumbling streets, slaying whomever they encountered. Jarek led them in first, removing the skullcap of a bald-headed man with his great sword. This man swung a curved footman's axe at him and missed badly. After one swipe from Jarek, the slop of brains painted the nearest fallen obelisk. The ancient mosaic of creatures half-man and half-squid was further obscured by the gray gruel.

There was no organized resistance from the cult of Ensibzianna. Since the attack was also lacking in order, they made the melee additionally turbulent. Most of the Keltos host leapt from their mounts, dragging downward running members of the religious assemblage. Punching, stabbing and slashing, the Keltos folk made rapid work of anyone unlucky enough to be caught.

Jarek and Garton met, gathering their troops behind their backs. In front of them was one of the more complete edifices. Pouring from this cracked structure was an armed, fighting force. These lean men all wore thin chain mail and brandished shields, axes, and short scimitars. Prepared for their deaths, the Keltos screamed for *Wodan* and charged.

Blood spattered the ancient pillars anew and the dust became muddy in the spilled ichor. Jarek looked down at a fallen Ensibzianna cultist. The mouth stretched open too far, crimson sparkling as it ran out fast like vomit. Helmets flew and heads rolled free from them as Jarek's men forced their way forward. Links of chain mail bent or shattered under the strength of their strong blows.

A press of bodies forced Jarek's back to a huge block of stone. While three held him in place, one short-haired man grinned and stepped away from the throng. He held up a flail and spun the metal spiked head around in victory. He gloated too long before delivering the death-blow, for this gave Garton time to make a diagonal slash and remove the head from the short-haired cultist, nearly taking off his shoulder as well. Jarek pushed off one of the cultists and this man landed on the end of Garton's sword. Only impaled through the kidney, the man howled and slipped off the blade. Garton's left hand swung around, now wielding a war hammer. Though the cultist's head did not explode, it did give a loud, wet *pop* sound as the body under it plummeted.

Driving a knee into the groin of the man to his left, Jarek pulled a dirk from his tunic and jabbed it into the belly of the man on his right. Gritting his teeth, he pulled upwards until he struck the man's sternum. The opposite expression of Jarek, this man's mouth hung open as his guts unraveled. Jarek made a downward swipe with his knife, scooping out a section of roping guts, and slapped them across the face of the other man, still holding his groin. When he howled, then gagged in disgust, Garton threw Jarek a spear. Jarek twirled the weapon, struck the disemboweled man in the rump with the base of the spear, causing him to collapse in full atop the screaming man. Jarek then raised the spear and impaled them both at once.

Jarek nodded to Garton and they moved closer to the center of Larak.

Throughout the massive slaughter, the Keltos tribesmen ran amok and prevailed. Shoulder to shoulder, they advanced to the main shelter of the cult of Ensibzianna.

Suddenly, a huge shape stumbled out of the break in the wall. The invaders froze for a moment, but their tension soon passed. Alagar himself entered the fray. However, this giant, twice as tall as even the hulking Jarek, was no fiend incarnate. His muscle tone was gone and his elongated limbs were slack at the biceps. His stomach hung low over the green silken kilt that covered his nakedness.

"He has seen better days," Garton remarked, holding back a smile.

While Alagar staggered, trying to hold up his huge mace to fight, Jarek said, "He was once a lover of great capacity."

Garton affirmed, "Butcher me if I end up as such."

"Agreed," Jarek guaranteed him and waved an arm at the youths in the tribe. These boys, barely in their man-making stage, were along on the trip to complete that particular journey. They launched short spears at the immense Alagar. Many of the lances were stubbled off on Alagar's thick skin, but a few of them held in his flabby belly. This distraction was all the tribe needed to thrust ahead. While Alagar swung down, crushing the spine of one attacker, the Keltos folk swarmed his legs, chopping with great battle axes, taking his toes and ankles out with ease.

Alagar fell to his knees and swiped his mighty arms, shoving several off himself. Jarek and Garton attacked as one, both swinging their swords down at the top of his shoulders. While all of Jarek's overhand broadsword swing removed the left arm of Alagar, Garton's blade delved into the joint of the right shoulder. The giant lowered his brow and thumped Garton to the dirt. His head swayed to Jarek, and with a clumsy impact, caused the Keltos leader to drop his sword. Frantic, needing a weapon, Jarek performed as all barbarians do and fought with what was at hand. He grabbed the wrist of the giant's dismembered arm and shouted a wordless war-cry. Swinging the limb up, he slammed the bloody stump of the arm into Alagar's jaw. As if he were stabbed, the Nephilum grabbed his mouth and blood spurted out. It was an orange fluid. Jarek assumed the giant bit his tongue off from the blow. In moments, Alagar felt the points of a dozen spears in his chest and belly. He slumped back and breathed his last.

"At least he came out and fought," Garton commented, sucking air, winded by the struggle.

"He had courage, perhaps as much as any cornered beast, aye?" said Jarek as he turned and saw further members of the cult streaming out of the pillar-lined streets. Screwing up their audacity, they meant to retaliate.

Rushing forward, the counter-offensive had some teeth to it, at least until they beheld their dead Lord Alagar. At the spectacle of his bloody corpse, they shrieked and fled.

"The day is ours!" Garton rejoiced and many jumped in the air.

Jarek looked into the main shelter. "Almost."

## Act IV — All in the Blood

Drawing near to Jarek, Garton said in a low voice, "Do you think Neurath warned Alagar that we were coming?"

Peering into the lopsided stone structure, Jarek shook his head from side to side. "No. They were ill-prepared for a strong assault. Besides, how could Neurath have done that?"

Garton thought for a second and answered, "Perhaps a power of the brain?"

Jarek gave him a distasteful glance and motioned for him to follow along on inside. "I doubt that. Besides, the Nephilum all hate each other."

"Why is that?"

"Imagine a family where all of the children think they are god."

Grunting a little, Garton looked over the interior of the barren building. "I see. Still, we killed his brother."

"Neurath will not care," Jarek promised as he walked, unarmed, towards the front of the building. "One less sibling to worry about. Neurath would applaud me if I brought Alagar's head to him."

"Will you?"

Jarek looked at him and smirked. "No."

At the echo of their voices, a few people scrambled from behind a crumpled tapestry. These few older men never made it out alive, running into a line of thick-set barbarians. Garton and Jarek never concerned themselves with them. The fallen tapestry revealed a vulgar, decaying stone altar. Once, it was an oversized pair of breasts divided by a phallic symbol. When Jarek walked behind the slab, his smile faded.

"Come on out, dog," Jarek snapped, his mouth forming into a snarl.

The figures popped up so quickly, Garton stepped back and held up his sword. One person was a man of great age. His eyes flared with vitality as his arm easily subdued the woman under his grip. Arm around her neck, his other hand held a curved blade.

The flaring eyes of the man danced as he said, "Come closer and she dies, dirty savage!"

The woman was much taller than the elderly man. Her ginger-colored hair was disheveled and her face grimy. She wore a single-pieced cloak, but this simple cover never hid her advanced state of pregnancy. The look in her eyes was one of terror at the sight of the barbarian warriors.

Jarek scowled at them and his gaze focused on her. Eyes dancing over her appearance, he reached out an arm to Garton and took a short sword.

The man shouted with vigor, "Stop, or I will sever the cow's throat! I will do it as sure as you live. She was one of you and is now one of us. I am a priest of Alagar and ready to die, so back away or I shall cut her from ear to ear."

The blade of the short-sword bounced off Jarek's thigh. He said coldly, "Do as you must."

Confusion reigned in the eyes of the priest as his gaze went from Jarek to Garton. The woman also looked frightened and tears flowed from her bulging eyes.

"I said," the old cleric repeated. "I will kill her!"

"Kill her then," Jarek said as he stepped forward. The priest and woman bumped into the stone slab as Jarek's left hand reached out. However, he never grabbed at the old man nor her arm to pull her free. Instead, he placed his hand lower, on the flat in her middle, below her breast, above her stomach. With an almost elegant thrust, Jarek sliced a crescent wound around the belly of the struggling woman. Stunned, the old man released her and she sprawled on the altar, screaming in horror as Jarek carved the baby out of her mid-section.

Through a splay of screams, spewing crimson fluid and pulpy gray tissue, Jarek performed his duty. Stepping back with the infant, Jarek felt the child contort as more pliable gore fell away. With his pinkie finger, he cleared the tiny mouth and held the baby up. With a scream, the child's tone joined the throng of barbarians now gathered in the temple. With great happiness, they shouted their welcome to their blood. Another cut was made and Jarek turned, showing them all. Quickly, word spread that it was a boy. He handed the child to his niece.

"You . . . bastard . . ." the celebrant of Alagar stammered as he glared at the dying woman, who tried to fix her guts a few times before the agony overtook her.

Jarek watched as his niece removed the upper flap of her chain mail, and then her blouse. With no hesitation, she placed the child to her breast and it fed. Smiling, she then bowed her head to her uncle and said, "Though this is not my daughter who died, I shall raise him as my son."

"Good," Garton said as the crowd applauded. "Then he will not have a mother who sacrificed him to a filthy god for gold."

Laughter rippled through the chamber as the old priest looked at the woman, suffering. He was about to cut her throat in mercy when Jarek slashed at his wrist. The old man dropped the knife as blood gouted from his wrist.

"No compassion for her," Jarek said ruefully. "Let her die as all traitors and the unfaithful must, alone in the dust."

The mass of hirsute humanity started to recede from the temple and the priest shouted, "That is it? You are just going to leave?"

"I have what I came for," Jarek replied, waving at his son, feeding and mewling at his niece's breast.

"You destroyed all of my magnificent plans, all of my dreams of power at the great day of sacrifice," the man screamed, fists hitting the altar and the dying woman's head alternately. "I could have beckoned the demons to give me true power and you slew all of them, all of the other carriers of the seed, for what? For that barbarian bastard?"

Jarek stopped, turned and said, "All that matters is blood. Isn't that what all of you rubbish say? Isn't that what all of your demon lords require for happiness? Hell, isn't that what the one, true God really is supposed to desire for the forgiveness of sins — blood? Yet, you find it so hard to understand that we would do all of this for blood. You have not the right to survive."

Leading the old priest to focus on him, Jarek walked across the room. With a single graceful movement, his niece drew back and threw a dagger. End over end, the blade flew true and struck the priest's throat. Tearing loose his Adam's apple, the old man fell, choking and writhing in the dust.

Turning their backs on the priest, the barbarians left the ruins of Larak.

Before they set out for their mountainous home, they stopped at the oasis to water their horses. Again, the old watcher came out of his hut to see Jarek. This time, the watcher's eyes widened at the sight of the new baby.

"So," the watcher said, pondering the significance of what he saw. "You have your love that was lost in the ruins at Larak?"

"Yes," Jarek said with pride in his voice. "This is my son; the only thing truly conjured in the day of iniquity wrought at Larak." Buoyant laughter traveled through the crowd. "Let that be a lesson to all, old man. If you try to use blood for blood, the wrong thing may come unto you."

The watcher nodded and looked at the child. "How is this one to be named?"

Jarek reached out and his huge hand touched the chest of the boy. Tiny fingers gripped the hand of the warrior, and turned into fists. The blue eyes of the baby blinked and stared up at his father.

"He shall be called Rogan, after my grandfather. The name means, *King of the Bastards*. Born into a world of blood and violence, let him get his mouth full of it. He better get used to it."

The barbarian horde then extolled Wodan to bless Rogan, son of Jarek, with life and strength.

Rogan cried out as well to the clear, afternoon sky. The infant looked at the blood on his hands and years later, Jarek's niece swore unto Wodan that little Rogan *laughed*.

# ELDRITCH-FELLAS

## Tim Curran

## One: The Life

Yeah, sitting there behind the wheel of his Lincoln Continental Coupe — the red convertible, not the black one with the leopard seats — Cthulhu missed the old days. Back when he had a good-sized cult who just did things for him out of respect, out of fear. Now, dammit, he had to work for it. He had to work the streets like any other hood. The life had its ups and downs. He worked for the Outfit, he worked for the Old Man. Extortion, loansharking, gambling, union racketeering, hijacking, sure, the Old Man was sitting on an empire. Cthulhu pushed some junk, ran some books, sold some hot paper, had maybe two-hundred grand in shylock out on the streets at any one time. Did some strongarm stuff, whacked a few guys when they got in the way from time to time.

But, somehow, it wasn't the same.

Guy like him, a made guy, a wiseguy, he had all the broads and booze and drugs he wanted. Lots of money. When he walked into a room, people knew who he was, what he was. He had respect. In fact, he demanded it. If he didn't get, he started busting balls.

Like the other day, Midtown. The Old Man had a piece of all that construction going on up there. Problem was, the owner of that cement company with all the city contracts was late with his payments, his juice. Two weeks. Unacceptable.

The Old Man was pissed. "You go up there, right? You get my money. You gotta throw them motherfuckers a beating, you do it. You do this for me."

So Cthulhu went up there alone. Walked in the office at the site with a length of lead pipe in his hands, found the owner in there shooting a couple hands of five-card with some other guy. Both of 'em went white as spilled sugar. They had some tough, muscle-head with 'em in a yellow hardhat. Cthulhu split that hardhat in two, opened up that mutt's head. After that, he got the money plus interest.

"If I gotta come back here," Cthulhu told the owner, "they'll find your head in a fucking dumpster."

But that was the life. That's how it worked.

Cthulhu snorted a line of coke off the dash and waited for the Mexican. His name was Raymond Gueverez. Owned a string of taco joints, a couple fuck shops where they sold hot books and illegal porn. The little Mex was doing all right, except he had a problem with the horses. He was into the Old Man for $250,000. The juice on that was the standard ten percent, twenty-five G's a week. Except this Mex, he hadn't paid in a month. He'd gone into hiding, declared bankruptcy.

So Cthulhu waited for him.

He sat there and admired his diamond pinkie ring, the sun reflecting off his Ray Ban's and all the gold chains at his throat. There. He saw Gueverez come out of the pool hall, slip into the alley. Before he made his heap, Cthulhu was all over him like a rash.

"Where's the fucking money, you pimp?" he said.

Gueverez fell into a trembling heap. "I ain't got it, I ain't got," he whimpered. "But I can get it, I –"

But Cthulhu got pissed then.

Nothing worse than being lied to. He forgot himself and shed his human skin, pretty soon he was tall as a three-story building. All green and glistening like wet plastic. Tentacles and wings and you name it, just as ugly as a naked leper with a hard-on. He took hold of the little Mex and swallowed him without chewing.

A bum down the alley saw the whole thing, watched it with red-rimmed eyes.

Pretty soon, Cthulhu was just a made guy in an expensive suit again. He wiped his mouth with a silk hankie, looked over at that bum, grinned.

"Human," he said. "The other white meat."

## Two: The Boss of Bosses

In that dank and dismal Arkham neighborhood known as Little Yuggoth, the boss of bosses himself, Yog-Sothoth sat in his office, clouds of pungent cigar smoke drifting lazily from half a dozen blow holes. "It ain't like the old days," he was saying to Nyarlathotep. "Back then, you grabbed yourself a world, took over a few cities, made 'em blasphemous and shit, got some cults going, got some jerk-off to write a book about you. You were set. Even — what? — ten thousand years later, you still had return on your investment. Always some smartass calling you up with that book. You always had a piece of things."

"It's all changed," Nyarlathotep lamented. "The universe's a fucking hole these days. People ain't got no respect."

Yoggy nodded, looking much like a pile of writhing, gelatinous spaghetti. He was all tentacles and squirming ropes and hard, bulging eyes. "I mean, lookit my crew for chrissake. All these guys, shit, they got fucking issues. This one's a hypochondriac, that one's queer, the other one's under therapy. I mean what the fuck happened here? We had a good thing going once, you know?"

"Yeah, we had the world by the balls."

Yoggy slapped the table with a few tentacles, sprayed some juice on the Black Messenger. "We used to be a secret society. Now every mutt and his mother knows who we are, what we are. What the fuck is that about? I mean, hell, those Elder Gods, the EG,I mean they're all over me. They tap my phones, they videotape my soldiers, I can't wipe my wormy ass without them fingerprinting the toilet paper."

Nyarlathotep knew it was all too true. The EG were all over the Outfit these days. Meat-eaters. Slapping 'em with indictments, throwing made guys into the abyss for eternity. It was bullshit. In the old days, the EG was different . . . more corrupt . . . you paid 'em off and they stayed the hell out, let you conduct business.

"We gotta be careful here," the Haunter of the Dark said.

"What are we now?" the boss of bosses said. "You got all these sumbitches out there. They write bad stories about us, comic books, shitty movies. You know what? They even got one of them . . . whatyacallit . . . role-playing games, where all them nerds what can't get laid play pretend instead of pulling their peckers all the time. All this . . . it's *our* thing, you know?"

"It is."

Yoggy said, "And who the fuck started calling our thing the *Cthulhu Mythos*? What the hell is that? I run things here, that guy works for *me.*"

The Faceless One just shook his head, lighting a cigarette. "That was that Derleth. He started that business."

"That motherfucker. Shoulda whacked him out when I had the chance. Ain't bad enough, we had that sumbitch in Providence ratting us out, then we had that Derleth turning our thing into a sideshow." Yog-Sothoth drummed the table with snotty feelers. "And I ain't seeing a dime out of it. Well that's all over with. Now on, the family gets a cut of everything. These mooks don't like that, we whack 'em. We either get a piece of this business or the bodies are gonna be dropping."

Nyarlathotep just nodded; he understood all too well. "I'm worried about that Cthulhu-thing, now you bring it up."

"What Cthulhu-thing?"

"You know, that Cthulhu-thing we were talking about."

"Oh, that thing."

"Yeah, you know," the Crawling Chaos told him, "what we were saying. I'm concerned here. Cthulhu . . . he's a cowboy. He's wild, he's out of control."

Yog-Sothoth looked troubled . . . as troubled as a writhing tentacular mass could look. "He's a good kid though. He's got some balls on him."

"He's getting out of hand."

"Yeah, well . . . if it comes to it . . ."

"We send him over."

## Three: A Deep-Sea Rat Rolls Over

Dagon blew his nose and right away jammed a Vick's Inhaler into his left nostril. "God, I'm all stuffed up. Think I'm getting a cold or something. No wonder, I can't even sleep these days. I need some antibiotics . . . you got any Ceftin? Amoxycillin?"

The EG case agent just sighed. "Dagon, you got to take it easy here, all right? You've got to quit questioning yourself on this. You're doing the right thing."

"Am I?" Dagon scratched nervously at a rash on his neck. Except he had trouble because it kept crawling away on him. "I'm not so sure. I'm a rat. A cheese-eater. You know what that feels like? Informing on your friends?"

"They're not your friends. You know what they're up to just like I do," the case agent said. "Yog-Sothoth is a scumbag and so are the rest. This organized crime façade is just to distract attention from their real plans — world domination. You know they won't be happy until they take over again."

"I don't know . . . I'm confused."

"Sure you are. Just relax."

Carefully, Dagon was fitted with a transmitter that would broadcast the conversations and operations of the Outfit back to the EG. Given time, they'd establish a pattern of cosmic racketeering and indict the whole smelly, writhing bunch.

"God, I'm a rat . . . nothing but a rat. I hope I burn in hell." Dagon blew his nose again. "You sure you don't have any antibiotics? Any anti-itch cream? Jesus, I think I got the worms here or something."

## Four: Extortion, Eldritch-Style

When they were sure they'd cleaned the EG off their tails, Cthulhu pulled his black Lincoln Continental Coupe to the curb. "When we get in there, you let me do the talking. You got that?"

Black Tsathoggua nodded. "Yeah."

Azathoth nodded, too, and the car filled with a gassy, noxious smell.

"You shitting your pants again?" Cthulhu said. "You stinking, smelly pig sonofabitch! Get the fuck out of my car! You burn a hole through my seat cover and I'll bury your rotten ass!"

"I can't help it," Azathoth said. "I got bad digestion."

"Bad digestion, my scaly ass. You stink, plain and simple. Christ, your breath . . . stinks like a dirty diaper full of rotten shrimp."

Azathoth exhaled a cloud of atomic waste. "I got bad digestion, all right? You try being the nuclear chaos for awhile, I got the piles like you wouldn't believe."

Cthulhu just shook his head. "Nuclear chaos. Your asshole is a nuclear chaos. Christ, smells like a burning tire in here."

"Quit busting my balls already," Azathoth said, letting another one rip.

Wearing their human forms, they crossed the sidewalk and went into the building. Up the stairs to the third floor. Place smelled like old kitty litter . . . or maybe it was just Tsathoggua. Guy was real natural and all. Smelled like biker ass under a heat lamp.

Cthulhu said to him, "You know, that soap and water thing, it's not just for breakfast anymore, you dumb shit. And what's with your suit . . . Christ. What you do, pull it out of the fucking hamper?" He paused there, adjusting Tsathoggua's lapels, straightening his tie. He kept shaking his head in disgust at the rumpled garment. Cthulhu only wore tailored Italian suits. Next to the electric blue Armani he had on, Tsathoggua's looked like a welcome mat from a soup kitchen. "We gotta look professional here. Christ, off-the-rack yet. Fits you like a potato sack, Tsath. Everytime you move, looks like two bulldogs fucking under a tarp." He looked over at Azathoth, who was trying to hide the fact that he was flatulent once again. "And you ain't no better . . . oh, Jesus Christ on a stick, would you quit that? I'm gonna have to stick my head in Tsathoggua's crotch for some fresh air here."

They paused before a door and Cthulhu did his bit to the lock — spit on it and it melted into a glob, hit the floor. Pulling on leather driving gloves, they walked right in. There was some fat little guy sitting at a desk, typing on a computer.

"Hey," he said. "You can't –"

"Shut the fuck up," Cthulhu told him. "We got business with you. Ain't that right?"

Black Tsathoggua nodded his head. "Yeah."

Cthulhu reached inside his black overcoat, pulled out a hardcover book with a garish picture of a tentacled monster on it. He tossed it on the desk. "You write this?" he asked the guy.

"Sure . . . you read it?" He looked surprised.

A foul, sewer smell permeated the air suddenly. Stunk like dead rats on a steam tray. Azathoth stood there, grinning, wondering when they'd notice.

"What the fuck?" Cthulhu said, holding his nose. "What's with you? Your ass is one big primal chaos today." He motioned to Tsathoggua. "Open that fucking window, Einstein."

Black Tsathoggua just stared, uncomprehending.

Cthulhu looked at the fat guy. "Is it me?" He sighed, turned to Tsathoggua, making elaborate attempts at sign language with his hands. "The window, shit-fer-brains. Wiiiinnndooowwww. No speakee fucking English?"

Azathoth did it for him. While he was there, he stuck his ass out into the wind, ripped off another one.

The fat guy said, "You read my book?"

"You kidding, he can't read," Azathoth said.

Cthulhu laughed. "Sure I can." He grabbed a book off the desk. "Look, here's one about your dick. *Mysteries of the Worm.*"

"Ha, ha."

"No really," fat boy said. "How'd you hear about my stuff?"

Cthulhu ignored that. "We got business with you, that's why we're here," he told him. He turned to Black Tsathoggua who was scratching his privates. "Make us some coffee, quiz kid."

"Yeah," Black Tsathoggua said, moving off into the little kitchenette. You could hear him in there, dropping things, spilling things, shattering things. He had human hands, but was good with 'em like a concert pianist with hooves.

Cthulhu shook his head. "What a fucking piece of work." His eyes were on the fat guy now. "How much you get paid for writing crap like that?"

The guy was nervous. Looked like maybe he was about to have kittens. "Not much . . . a few hundred, some copies."

"That's it?"

"There's not a real big market."

Cthulhu was disappointed. Had you told him his dick was made of bleu cheese, he couldn't have looked more disappointed. "This is what it's come to? The Old Man has us shaking down welfare cases?"

"I don't understand."

Cthulhu was pissed. "You have any idea who the fuck I am?"

Guy didn't, so Cthulhu showed him. Right away, the guy pissed himself and started hollering for his mama. Cthulhu pulled out a silenced .45 Smith, put two in his head, painting up the walls with his brains and blood.

Black Tsathoggua came lumbering back in with two cups of coffee. Offered Cthulhu one of them. Cthulhu just glared at him, slapped the cups out of his gloved hands. "What're you, a fucking comedian? Do I look like I drink coffee, pimple-dick? What kind of fucking moron are you?" He shoved him toward the door. "You need a bath, you smell like a goddamn pond. Your mother have any kids that lived?"

Black Tsathoggua said, "Yeah."

Cthulhu looked around, Azathoth was gone. But there was an almost violent, palpable stench in the air. He followed the reek into the back room, found Azathoth sitting on the toilet.

"What the fuck are you doing?"

"I'm taking a dump."

"I just whacked a guy and you're taking a dump. I don't believe this shit." He turned away, stomping off. "Well, I guess that's why they call you the fucking idiot-god."


## Five: Dagon on the Couch

Sprawled on his therapist's couch, Dagon was whimpering uncontrollably. He kept shaking his head, staring at the ceiling like he might find the answer to it all up there.

"I just don't fit in with them anymore," he said. "I try . . . but, dammit, it just doesn't *feel* right."

The therapist looked noncommittal. "Maybe you're just looking at it all wrong. Maybe it's *them* and not you. Maybe you've just outgrown them. It happens, you know."

Dagon sighed. "I . . . damn . . . I mean, I love the Mythos, but I'm not *in* love with it. Does that make any sense?"

"Of course it does." The therapist scribbled on her pad.

"Christ, I'm so paranoid these days, I don't even like going out of the house. I get in a crowd and I start freaking out."

"Do you know why that is?"

Dagon shook his head. "It's all too much. I've got too many depending on me. In the south seas, in Innsmouth . . . they all want something. I feel like I'm being pulled in too many directions. They all want me to make decisions and I can't . . ."

"Are you afraid of commitment?"

But that only got Dagon sobbing again.

When he finally stopped he said, "I'm tired of all this scary stuff. Is it wrong of me to just want to make people smile?"

The therapist just watched him, very noncommittal. "Why don't you tell me what this is *really* about?"

But Dagon ignored her. "God . . . I feel like shit all the time. My back hurts, my knees are stiff. I can't beat these headaches. Does it feel warm in here to you?"

"No."

"Oh, I must be coming down with something. My heart's racing . . . God, I think I'm having a heart attack." He sat up, grasping his chest, hyperventilating. "I can't breathe . . . I can't breathe . . ."

The therapist got him a paper bag to breathe in. "You're having a panic attack. That's it, breathe deeply and slowly, deeply and slowly . . ."

## Six: Cthulhu Nights

Cthulhu sat on his leather sofa watching a Lovecraftian movie on TV. He was drinking a glass of Asti Spumante while some tow-headed hooker went down on him. He stared and stared, got more pissed off by the minute.

"Lookit this shit," he said.

The hooker lifted her head up to study the tube and he slapped her back down. "Who the fuck told you to stop?" he said, narrowing his eyes. He sucked down the Asti, thought about all those years he spent dreaming in that sunken city. Thought about what an asshole move that all was.

On the TV, some flopping-looking thing crested a hill. It was supposed to be Yog-Sothoth, but it looked more like a dirty mop. People were running and screaming. Cthulhu started getting real excited about it all. The hooker's head started bobbing real fast.

"The old days," he said. "What the fuck happened to us?"

He pulled a .357 Magnum out from under a pillow and blew the screen out of the TV. Christ, it just wasn't the same anymore. He missed his cult. He missed the maiming and killing. He missed the power.

## Seven: The Mad Arab Social Club

Cthulhu was saying, "So I am all fucked up, right? I mean, I'm wrecked, pissed right to the third gill. I'm leaning up against the bar, coked up and sassy. I'm sucking down the Wild Turkey so fast the gobbler's balls are aching. Then this big dumb EG bull comes by. He knows who I am. So I bump into him on purpose. 'Excuse me,' he says. 'Ain't no fucking excuse for you,' I say. He just turns the other cheek and says, 'Sorry, my mistake.' I just look at him. 'No, that's what your mama should've said when you were born, you mutt. But no hard feelings, right? Hey, I'd buy you a drink but I just gave my last five-bucks to your sister so she'd suck my dick.' He goes livid. Right away, me and this bull are on the floor, punching and kicking. Bing, bang, boom. Finally, I throw that turd off me. 'All right, all right,' I say. 'I was outta line, right? Shouldn't have said that about your sister. That was fucking rude. Accept my apologies. It was your *mother* who sucked my dick.' And then we're at it again, swinging and hitting and you name it."

Everyone was laughing their asses off at Cthulhu's stories like usual. Most of the boys were there, except the Old Man and Nyarlathotep. They were out scheming somewhere. Trying to work the angles on how they were going to bleed this Mythos-thing, get their cut. The crew were sucking up wine and pasta in their absence, carrying on like usual.

Chaugnar Faugn started coughing he was laughing so hard. "You're a funny guy, Cthulhu. You're just so funny."

Cthulhu, picking a speck of lint from his $3000 Armani suit, stopped laughing. Looked around the table. His eyes were like coals in a furnace. "Funny? What do you mean, *funny?*"

Faugn just shrugged. "You know, how you tell a story and all. You kill me. You're funny."

Cthulhu stood up. "Let me understand what you're saying here. Maybe I'm too fucked up or something. What's so funny about me? *What?* Funny how? Funny like a clown? Funny like I fucking amuse you? I make you laugh? Like I'm here to fucking amuse you? How am I so fucking funny? *What in the fuck is so funny about me?*"

Father Yig held his hands up. "Take it easy, Cthulhu, he's just –"

"You shut the fuck up, spaghetti-head. This guy's got a mouth, don't he? He knows what the fuck he said. And he said I'm some kind of fucking clown."

"No, no, I was just saying you're . . . *comical,*" Chaugnar Faugn said, realizing too late it was the wrong thing to say.

"Comical? *Comical?*" Cthulhu said, pulling out a .38 snubnose. "You want comedy, you silly fuck? You want humor, you fucking gay elephant?" Before the others could stop him, he started busting caps into Chaugnar Faugn. He put six holes in his massive head and Faugn fell over, dead on the floor.

"Jesus H. Christ," Shub-Niggurath said, yanking the gun from Cthulhu's fist. "What the hell's wrong with you? What are you? Some kind of goddamn psychopath? Is that what? Is that what you are?"

Cthulhu shrugged her off. "Fuck it. I'm sick of that piss bag. Goddamn elephant-headed freak. Trunk looks like a dick swinging there."

Black Tsathoggua said, "Yeah."

"Who asked for your two cents, you hump?" Cthulhu shoved him away. "Get rid of that fucking mess. Plant it somewhere."

"Yeah," Tsathoggua said, dragging the body off.

Dagon went down on his hands and knees, breathing heavily. "I got pains in my stomach . . . I think it's my appendix . . . oh Jesus . . ."

"Shut the fuck up," Cthulhu told him. "You ain't got no appendix. Like balls, you ain't got none."

There was silence then. It hung thick in that smoky, pungent air. Nobody moved. Nobody said a thing. Cthulhu looked around the table. Nobody would meet his eyes. "Oh, for Chrissake. What gives here? That mutt was bush-league. Shit, even those hacks don't write stories about him. Guy didn't have no bristles on his broom. He didn't even belong at this table."

Shub-Niggurath was not happy. She was trying hard to hold her human form, but it was getting threadbare like an old rug — she kept fuming with a black mist and you could hear her hooves rapping and see squirming appendages flopping around.

"You just can't go around killing people," she finally said, barely able to contain her rage.

"What people?" Cthulhu said. "A fucking human with a goddamn elephant head? And who are you to point a finger at me, you smelly pile of goat-shit?"

"That'll do," Father Yig said.

Dagon was swallowing pills, moaning about his migraines.

"No, let him go on," Shub-Niggurath said in a pouty voice. "Let him hang himself. Maybe the Old Man'll sink him back on that island and we'll be rid of him."

It took a lot of control for Cthulhu not to come right over the table at her. Had he still had his gun, he would've capped her right there. Had he a knife, he would've had a nice shaggy throw-rug come evening. "Listen, you stupid bitch. I'm an earner, you see? While you're tit-feeding all them ass-ugly brats of yours, I'm making money. I'm keeping this fucking family afloat. Any of you doubt that?"

They didn't. Not Father Yig nor Shub-Niggurath nor Azathoth nor Cthugha nor Rhan-Tegoth nor Nyogtha. They didn't say a damn thing. Truth was, they had all lost their edge and they knew it. Problem was, Cthulhu still had his and there was gonna be big trouble. They could all see that.

He was hungry for the old days and that wasn't a good thing.

## Eight: Outer Gods, Men of Respect

"I gotta a couple guys over at that place in Sauk City," Nyarlathotep said to the Old Man, Yog-Sothoth. "They gave us some trouble at first . . . but the hitters I sent changed their minds. We got a piece of that place now."

"Good," Yoggy said. "That's the way it should be. What about that other thing?"

"What thing?"

"You know, that thing we talked about."

"The Kingsport thing?"

"No, no, no," the Old Man said. "That other thing there."

"Oh, the Cthulhu thing?"

"Yeah, that's it. What about that?"

Nyarlathotep lit a cigarette, studied his ash. "I talked to him about this cowboy shit. Told him to settle down. Said he would."

"He's a good kid."

"I told him we'd give him a pass on that Chaugnar Faugn business. Told him he couldn't go around whacking made guys or he'd end up in a barrel at the bottom of the Pacific like before."

The Old Man sucked on his cigar. Havana. Sweet, rich. Didn't do much to cover the odor coming off him, though — like a compost heap at a death camp. "We don't need this kid bringing the heat down on us. He's gotta settle down. Crazy kid . . . whacking guys . . ."

The Black Pharaoh just nodded, flicking the ash from his cigarette into a marble ashtray. "It's the wild, wild West with that kid . . . he's gonna be trouble."

"Fuggetaboutit," the Old Man said.

## Nine: The Saga of the Disfunctional Old Ones

That night, the goodfellas were hanging around the social club, drinking, smoking, gambling, eating sandwiches. Cthulhu wasn't sitting with the others. He was up at the bar, taking the Wild Turkey straight out of the bottle like a baby at its mama's tit. He'd already snorted half of Peru, seasoned it up with some Ecstasy. His head was full of colorful noise and, like a Sumo doing a striptease, he just kept getting uglier by the minute.

Dagon waltzed in, sat at the bar, kept checking his watch. His eyes were red and they could all see that. He pulled a pill case, sorted through what he had in there. Trembling, he swallowed a couple Prozac. Chased 'em with two Darvocet and a shot of Jim Beam Rye.

The guys playing cards — Father Yig, Cthugha, Azathoth, Dark Han — pretended not to notice. They knew things had been rough with Dagon lately. He had issues. They didn't know what; they didn't want to know.

"You're a fucking wreck," Cthulhu told him. "Goddamn hypochondriac."

Dagon gave him a catty stare. "You don't know how bad I got it."

Cthulhu put one hand on his hip, the other flapped in the air limply. "'You don't know how bad I got it,'" he mimicked in a high falsetto.

"Fucking pussy. Why don't you quit this shit? Get some iron in your pants. C'mon, you and me can go bopping, clubbing. Pick up some hookers, get a Medieval clusterfuck going."

"I can't," was all Dagon would say.

"And why not? Gotta stay home and do your fucking nails? Listen to your Liberace CDs? Is that it?"

Dagon started, dumping over the bottle of Beam. "Because I'm impotent, okay? Happy now?"

Cthulhu grimaced, shook his head and turned away. The door opened and Hastur promenaded in, swinging his hips just a little too much for everyone's liking. He'd been hanging out in the leather bars in the Village again, but no one mentioned the fact.

Except Cthulhu. "Well, if it ain't He-Who-Is-Not-To-Be-Fucking Named . . . or is that *She?*" He laughed at that, thought he was a real riot. "Why don't you quit puffing them meat cigars for a while?" He laughed again, swallowed some more Wild Turkey. "Hey? You know what Hastur and a sunken submarine got in common? They're both full of dead semen."

"Oh, eat me, dipshit," Hastur said, adjusting his carefully coifed hair in the mirror behind the bar. "What I do and *who* I do ain't none of your business, honey."

"Goddamn fairy," Cthulhu said. "See, that's why none of these guys write books about you. You're a fucking embarrassment."

Hastur slapped a hand to his ass which was plainly visible in those neon pink leather pants. Then he winked at Cthulhu.

"You motherf –"

"Settle down," Father Yig said. "The both of you."

"What? It's me?" Cthulhu said, anger seeping into him like toxic waste. "This guy's light in the loafers and we all know it."

Black Tsathoggua said, "Yeah."

Cthulhu fixed him with steely eyes. "Hey, shit-fer-brains," he said. "Get your hands out of your shorts and get me a beer, will ya?"

Dagon started to whimper then, and suddenly, began to emit an odd, electronic beeping noise. He went white, patting himself, eyes huge, lips trembling.

Cthulhu knocked Hastur onto his ass and took hold of Dagon's shirt, ripping it open, exposing the transmitter beneath. Dagon backed away, shaking and breathing hard.

"A wire!" Cthulhu roared. "This motherfucker's wearing a wire! He's working for the EG!"

And before anyone could stop him or think of doing so, he pulled out a Browning .45 and put four holes in Dagon's chest. Dagon hit the floor, writhing, pissing blood and some other things that weren't blood at all. Cthulhu stepped over to him and put two in his head.

"Fucking rat," he said.

About that time, a putrid stink wafted into the room. Azathoth came in, shirt untucked, newspaper folded under his arm. "Boy, I wouldn't go in there for awhile," he said.

## Ten: The Night Arkham Died

Finally, it was just too much.

Cthulhu lost it and there was no turning back. Fuck the Old Man and fuck his new order. Cthulhu just couldn't take it. He came off the wagon and he came off hard. In fact, he dove off it, wrecking everything in his path.

Towering over the streets of Arkham, all green and glistening, his tentacles coiling and whipping, his wings pounding like tornadoes, he started taking the downtown apart. Maybe hadn't he been coked-up and full of whiskey and meth, it might not have happened. Maybe. Problem was, this had been building for awhile and nobody — save the screaming populace — was really surprised.

Nyarlathotep showed up, of course, about the time Cthulhu tipped over a row of tenements and squashed anything that ran out. He told Great Cthulhu it wasn't too late. That he could stop this business. They could straighten it all out. Have a sit-down and the Old Man would give him a pass, he was sure of it.

But Cthulhu told him to go fuck his mother and kept destroying and crushing and rending. Buildings came down. Cars were crushed to mangled debris. People were stomped to jelly. The ones he didn't stomp, he ate. He went from house to house to house, tearing off doors and punching through roofs and seizing the treats within. What he wanted here, what he desperately needed, were some virgin sacrifices like the old days. But all he could find were brothels, so he had to take what he could get. He kicked over a tenement and Hastur came running out of the ruins. He was wearing a leather miniskirt, stiletto heels, fishnet stockings, and a blonde wig.

"What do you think you're doing, you big damn idiot?" he wanted to know. "How's a girl supposed to work with all this noise?"

But Cthulhu kicked him/her aside and kept at it. Kept at it for hours, in fact. Finally, downtown Arkham looking like it had been leveled by a nuclear weapon, Cthulhu laid down in the ruins, tired and gassy. Somehow, it hadn't been that satisfying. And that worried him.

"Are you done now?" Nyarlathotep said.

Cthulhu burped. "I thought I told you to go fuck your mother."

## Eleven: Aftermath

It wasn't pretty what came next.

The EG put together a massive racketeering indictment against the Outer Gods. Murder conspiracy, extortion conspiracy, narcotics conspiracy. Everyone was named, including Yog-Sothoth. The EG planned on putting the lot of 'em to bed permanently. Cthulhu was arrested for murder, drug trafficking, assault, and destruction of public property. His lawyer got him out on a $500,000 bail bond.

Dark Han and Father Yig came for him a few hours later.

"The Old Man wants a sit-down with you," Father Yig said.

Cthulhu knew he had to go, so he did. They took him to a warehouse out by the river and Cthulhu walked through a door into an office. 'Course, there was no one in there. It was empty. Before he could say more than, "Oh, shit," Father Yig and Dark Han pulled out 9mm pistols with silencers screwed to the barrels and shot him in the back of the head.

"That's it then," Dark Han said. "Good-riddance."

Cthulhu was packed in a barrel of cement and sunk down into the abyssal ruins of R'lyeh where he would dream away eternity. Everyone was barred from even mentioning his name. This time, the Old Man said, he was sleeping with the fishes for good.

# Outside, Looking In

## David Conyers

I have this dream, whereby I'm looking into the night sky and all I see is this gigantic pulsating disk. It is suspended above the city as if by invisible wires, glowing purple like some sickly form of fungus seen in caves only when there is no other light. The disc is huge, at least a mile across, perhaps more, and so I wonder where the rain comes from.

At least I think this is a dream . . .

One doesn't often consider the dead beautiful, but I did tonight.

Offering a cigarette to the shivering cop standing with me at the Docks, he took it happily. "Poor bastards," I commented. We were both thankful that it was neither of us out on the water recovering the body. For a start we could keep our hands in our pockets while we watched the young men huddled in two rowboats, exhaling white fog from blue lips. The lead patrolman in each rowboat clung to a hooked pole, the barbed ends speared inside the corpse, dragging it through the murky water, while their peers rowed. Oars whispered rather than splashed.

The police had kindly invited me to watch, a little because I'd once been on the force, but mostly because the cadaver was connected to me through a case. I'd done my time recovering the dead from the uncared corners of this world, but today dough came my way via private paying clients. As my business card stated in neat Garamond print, I was a private investigator and glad of it, today especially so.

Finally the rowboats were tied to the Dock. Three unlucky patrolmen were picked to haul the corpse onto the wooden decking, straining their backs as they did. The rest of them appeared relieved, their work done. Perhaps the Superintendent would soon send them home to their beds and the warmth of their wives, now that their hard work was over.

---

Me, I was just interested in the corpse. Alive he would have been embarrassed, but dead he was just shrivelled skin and battered appendages. Flashlights created shadows, a black blanket beneath the clammy flesh. But in the light the various wounds were seen clearly, a whole body of gaping slits. Quickly I realized these weren't random strikes, they formed a pattern, they had depth and not just the physical kind. It was at this moment that I considered the wounds to be beautifully applied.

A junior patrolman spoke, white hands in pockets searching for warmth. "He almost looks . . ."

"Artistic?" I finished for him.

Everyone nodded sagely.

I bent closer, smelling the stench of death. I saw the handiwork of a surgeon, wounds administered delicately and with style as if the killer had created a Picasso. Flaps of skin fell away neatly, perfectly displaying the muscle and bone beneath. I almost said out loud that the corpse didn't belong in a morgue; that this Painted Man should have been hung in a gallery as art.

"You knew this guy?" The Superintendent used past tense. Experience had taught me cops never talked about the dead any other way. But to be honest, I didn't either. Without waiting for an answer, the Superintendent rolled up his sleeves and then slipped on surgeons gloves before he touched the corpse, and I guess he didn't wish to stain his nicely-pressed cuffs. He folded back the skin so that the left cheek was made whole again. At last I saw what I'd come to see; this *was* the man I'd been following for three days now. "That him?" asked the Superintendent.

I hinted a nod. "He was cheating on my client, or that's what my client told me."

"She? An affair?"

I smiled, cat-like. "Or my client is a he, and the dead man owed him money. For someone so nicely-decorated Superintendent, you're jumping to a lot of conclusions."

Perhaps I was being harsh, but I knew the Superintendent's game. He was hoping I'd admit that my client was the dead man's wife. Not that I'd let on, but his suspicions were right. Who else pays twenty-five dollars a day plus expenses to discover if a man is sleeping with another woman, unless that man is your husband?

So like most stories of love and murder, this tale began long before one of the characters became a corpse. The last time I'd seen the Painted Man he'd been breathing, but that didn't say much for the state of his health while he was alive. I'd come close to him once, just before he walked into his Doctor's consulting rooms, scarf wrapped around his face, fedora pulled low, and overcoat drawn tight. Back then his mannerisms suggested that if his clothes were not gripped tight enough he would unravel. I'd put it down to an overactive imagination brought on by too much coffee and too little sleep. Now that I'd seen his corpse, with flesh undone, I could easily imagine him with these wounds while he was alive.

The police had a victim, but I had a suspect. For a moment I considered letting on that I'd added two and two together, coming up with a good candidate for a four, but to do so would conclude the case, at least for me. Better talk to my client first and see what tickled her on the off chance she was still willing to pay for deeper dirt.

"Where you going now?" the Superintendent called as I sauntered away.

"Home, where else would I be going this time of night?"

"It's only early," he jested. I thought he jested.

I waited a moment for him to call me back, but he must have figured I'd answered enough questions for one night. Besides, this was a small town so he'd know where to find me when desperation set in. He knew like I knew; dead bodies cut up like this always had a habit of collecting questions faster than answers, as I was soon to find out . . . again.

Sleep never came easily these days. Through the bedroom window, neon streetlights hummed like flies dying after a fatal ingestion of bug spray. Other illuminations; the headlights beamed from traffic, created an unnatural rhythm of flickering light, manifesting inside as acute headaches. If a pounding forehead wasn't enough to depress, then the endless pelting rain and the constant vagueness of a netherworld wedged halfway between day and night did the job wonderfully. Sleeping was no healthier than if I were to stare into a strobe light all night, which is exactly what I was doing.

But I must have slept, for I dreamed the same dream again, back in the old days when I was a detective. At least I thought I was a detective, because I also remember being a school teacher, and a school teacher was what I'd always wanted to be, not this. I'm getting ahead of myself, this dream was about a time investigating homicide cases except this was like no homicide I ever remembered.

We'd found the body in the messy end of a dark alley. A dead end in a decaying city where refuge was even more prevalent than barred windows, and the rain fell from clogged gutters in sheets rather than droplets direct from heaven. I recalled a couple of snarling Dobermans, savagery in their eyes. Their yaps piercing because they wanted me to know they'd trapped something behind a couple of rusty trashcans, and were eager to kill it.

Whatever it was, one of the Dobermans finally caught the creature in its salivating jaws. Calling the dog off, I ordered him drop his prize; shining the flashlight to see what he'd caught. A rat is what I'd expected, but the dead thing turned out to be a schoolgirl, bloodied, cut up and broken. The Doberman had killed her.

Strangest thing was she was less than an inch in height.

Pocket-sized.

I woke when the telephone rang.

◆　◆　◆

"Yes?"

"You awake?"

"I am now."

"Can I see you?"

"It's very late."

"It's also very early."

"This sounds like *déjà vu.*"

"You were probably dreaming."

"Not of you though."

"That's probably for the best."

"Is this important?"

"I don't call this early for any other reason."

"Okay, can you come round here?'

"I'd prefer . . . with everything that the police just told me."

"Okay, your place then?"

"If you can?"

"Sure. No problem."

◆　◆　◆

In almost every case of adultery I'd ever taken — and I'd taken hundreds — at the end I tend to find that it is the faithful fretting partner at home who gets hurt the most. They're the ones who end up feeling the guilt when the truth is revealed. The spouse who does the cheating, normally they've rationalized their reasons why long ago, based on their perception of what the husband or wife did or didn't do for them, those little annoyances which drove them to have an affair in the first place. *It wasn't their fault, no sir*, they'd say. *If only he or she had done this or that, well then, they wouldn't have needed to find love elsewhere* . . . None of them were ever any more original than this.

But for the faithful one, the victim if you will, they feel stupid when they learn that the wool was pulled over their eyes, because that's what really hurts, the lying. The wool rubs even harder when the one who pulled it down was the one who supposedly loved and cherished them. This aptly described the emotional state of my latest client.

I should also note that I felt we'd known each other from another time, and that she was another school teacher like me. But this must have been pure fantasy when I thought about too much. I'd also like to say that this had nothing to do with any emotional connections I might be making to this case. But who am I kidding? Simply put, I was falling in love with her.

"Past lives," she'd said to explain away my feelings. Only later did I realize that she actually believed this.

But the first time I really met her was when she walked into my office. She was crying, all red around the eyes and cheeks. Bad for her but good for me, because traumatized clients rarely lie, and so I tend to know what I'm getting into before I'm in too deep. When I saw the large diamond ring on the left hand I knew her story before she'd even started. Everything fit the standard model.

She sat down on the visitor's chair, my messy desk separating us. She couldn't stop crying for a whole eight minutes. Enough time to boil an egg. Enough time to appreciate just how badly she'd been hurt.

She was the Singer at the Stonewall Club which I knew only by reputation, a place where lonely men and women sought company from other equally lost patrons, or from a few too many drinks. I'd heard of the joint, but had never been. But seeing the Singer now, it was not hard to imagine her drawing admirers. One was sitting right in front of her.

Soft spots are not something I usually cultivate for my clients. Normally this is easy to do because most clients are professional criminals, or hard in training becoming one. As a result I have a lower-than-low respect for most other human beings that I meet through the course of my work, but with the Singer it was hard not to offer sympathetic, as well as my usual professional, support.

So here I was, on my way to her place and my thoughts were with her again. I was wet and cold in the back of the black cab, driving to a secret rendezvous with the jilted widow.

I wound my watch. The hands said it was four-forty in the morning, a time when even tomcats give up fighting and go to bed. Yet the streets were still crowded with hundreds of shoppers, in their grey suits rushing back and forth between drab outlets, jousting umbrellas and clinging to soaked paper bags containing god knows what kinds of purchases bought in the middle of the night. I never understood the psyche of this town.

The cabbie dropped me at her corner and I paid him his two bucks. Through the rain that always fell straight down, I could see her window light, burning like a lighthouse lost in a pounding storm. She was calling for help, even if she didn't know it yet.

I knocked and she let me in. I shook my overcoat into the hall so I wouldn't drip street grime all over her nice floor.

"Thanks for coming."

She lit a cigarette and offered me one. I accepted even though her only ashtray was three butts away from a fatal collapse. She'd been pacing so hard there were track marks in the carpet.

"I guess you heard?" I asked, not needing an answer. I could see it in those familiar red eyes; she now knew as much as I did. Coward that I was, I'd let the Superintendent deliver the tragic news. "I'm sorry," was all I could offer.

She stood at the window, make-up ruined by tears. Apart from this one temporary blemish, she'd been my most attractive client yet; slim figure, long dark hair, and always dressed in the same grey cashmere business suits worn smart and proper the way I liked. My kind of woman; half her demeanour said *don't mess with me* while the other half screamed *I need to be held!* Looking at her again in the flesh, I could swear I'd known her before.

"You know who did it?" she finally asked. "Who murdered him?"

Shrugging, I considered asking if she'd been told about the unnatural artistry of his death, but details like that would probably just upset her. Instead I stood by her side, sharing the view of the wet streets through the only window, and still she looked to me seeking answers. I wanted to brush a loose strand away from her face to show that I cared, but professionalism stopped me. "I'm sorry, I just don't know yet. I was planning to talk to you later, figuring you might want some time alone."

She scoffed, "Time alone is the last thing I want right now."

Now I wanted to rub her back, sensing that she might like that. "If you want me to keep looking for his lover, I could do with the money." I sounded ruthless preying on an emotionally distraught woman, for that wasn't my intension at all. "Forget the money. I'll do it for nothing."

She smiled for the first time tonight. "I like that you would, but please, this is your livelihood. I'll keep paying."

By the dresser she picked up two of the many empty glasses dotted throughout the room. I could see her disappointment so I went to the fridge and poured us two long-stems of chilled water. She needed it and so did I, but I hadn't expected her to drink the whole glass in a single gulp. Then I noticed hundreds of empty glasses throughout her apartment.

"Did the Doctor do it, the one my husband was seeing?"

I knew for a fact that her husband, the Painted Man, had been secretly seeing someone. The seven roses purchased at the florist, the lying on the phone about where he really was, and the chocolates that left his work but never made it back to this apartment. "I don't know for sure but I have a lead. Your husband was seeing your family Doctor regularly, were you aware of that?"

"No, I wasn't," she took my half-empty glass and finished it just as quickly. Then it was her turn to open the fridge and refill. "I had no idea what he was doing these days, or why. For a time I considered he might be sick." She sobbed when she said, "I've no idea why someone would want to butcher him so."

I finally held her, my feelings too strong to deny them any more. She seemed happy to be held because she hugged me just as tight. While I stroked her hair, while she cried into my newest and nicest starched shirt, I spoke softly. "I know it's hard. I know it's confusing. One day you're mad at him because he's cheating on you, the next he's tortured and murdered and you wonder why everything went so wrong. You hate him and you pity him. You despise him and you love him. Trouble is you may never understand, and that's the worst of it!"

She pulled away to look at me but she didn't let go either. "You know, I remember our wedding day as clear as if it were yesterday. It was a bright day, sunny and full of green trees and singing birds. I remember being happy beyond my wildest dreams, but you know what?"

She left it hanging, so I asked.

"I don't ever remember loving him. I don't even know why we got married. I'm not even sure that I miss him now that he's gone, because I never felt like we shared a life together anyway." She held me close again. "We'd been married five years and yet while I've only known you five days, you are the only one who seems real to me. I wanted to be a school teacher and that never happened, yet . . ."

She stopped talking, and I wasn't sure I wanted her to go on.

"Past lives?" I finally asked.

She nodded, "Something like that."

Like clockwork, fog rolled in from the ocean, and so it was inevitable that the town's claustrophobia grew denser. All I saw in the buildings, in the streetcars, and in the people was the colour grey, broken with occasional darker or lighter shades of further grey. There were blacks too, but blacks in this town means shadows, deep pools of nothingness into which it would be easy to vanish forever. This was not a happy town and these were not happy people. Everyone looked dead here, or as if they should have been, and perhaps I did too. Perhaps we were in hell, and the Devil hadn't yet bothered to put us in the picture.

I walked home partly because I was wide-awake, and partly because I knew exercise would help me sleep later when I needed it. I also knew these streets, knew every corner and alley as surely as I knew that the

Pope was Catholic or that donkeys have four legs. Yet the building before me now was unfamiliar. I certainly didn't remember it yesterday.

The shop signage said SHOE FACTORY in plain, unassuming letters. It was higher, taller than any other building, so high the top of it disappeared into the foggy sky. Stranger still it was all brick from top to bottom, with no windows and no doors. Even if it had been called a chimney it wouldn't have been any less suspicious.

A couple of workmen were busy drilling a hole at the base of the building. Neither spoke a word even though their synchronized actions appeared complicated. Curiosity got the better of me, and so I asked what they were doing. I was told quietly that the Ones on the inside, looking out, were passing cables through.

I asked what kind of cables.

"Cables," they said. "What other kind are there?"

I was reminded of a prison guard I knew back in the old days, because our sons were at the same school. He told me this story which had always stuck in my mind, pertinent now. The guards liked to bully inmates with a form of mental torture, ordering them to dig deep holes in the ground. When a hole was completed many backbreaking hours later, the guards would order that they fill it in again. What kind of holes were these? I might have asked my friends. Holes he might tell me, what other kind are there?

The Doctor's consulting room was in one of the town's older buildings, five stories high with grimy windows and a chimney spitting out smoke so black it suggested that the heating pipes were riddled with cancer. Inside Art Deco walls stained from years of damp were watched over by bronze statues of naked women, breaking their backs to hold up spheres of light illuminating the foyer. The lift was rickety with the dull demeanour of too much rust, and its motor sounded like it wished for a new life as spare parts. I got in and ascended to the fourth floor, but I would have chosen the stairs if I was able to find them.

When I stepped out of the lift four floors later, I was overcome with a peculiar sense of oddness, for all the hairs on my hand and neck stood on end. In my book this meant one of two things; either there was a strong electro-magnetic field generating nearby, or that I should be really, really scared of an unperceived, yet real, threat.

I felt for the .45 revolver heavy on my waist, holstered but itching to be free. Somehow I was sure that those upstanding hairs were sensing vibrations, as if on the molecular level every atom in the building was oscillating near resonant frequencies. No wonder the building spoke that it was ready to fall apart, for it was decaying at the atomic level itself.

But with nothing to see I knocked on the door of Suite 413. It was ten in the morning on a weekday, so after the tenth bashing I had to conclude that whoever was inside must be either indisposed or out. Checking the door anyway, I found it to be unlocked, so not being the shy type I stepped in.

Like most normal people I expect doctor's consulting rooms to be neat, tidy and most importantly hygienic, but I saw none of this. I didn't even see anything inside that looked like it belonged in a doctor's office, not even eye-charts, knee-hammers, stethoscopes, or even a lightboard pinned with x-rays of broken limbs. Truth was I couldn't really see the office at all since there was so much paper in the way. Paper pinned on every surface, corner and piece of office furniture, or scattered about the floor as if lining a gigantic litter tray for an equally gigantic cat. This was artists' paper with sketches drawn to various levels of completion. Those pinned to the walls covered many more drawings pinned behind them, while other fragments that lay scattered upon every horizontal surface seemed to be discarded where they'd been thrown, often torn into twos or threes or crumpled into tiny balls. I was able to spot several wastepaper bins filled to the rims, but you'd need a whole dumpster to clean this place back to respectability.

I made out a painters' easel and a stool, but the more unusual feature was the soaked sheets in the room's center. Once the purest color of whitest snow, they were now stained the crimson-red of the freshest blood. Shoes crunching papers, I walked over, seeing men's clothes hanging over the stool. Presumably these belonged to the model, but I'd also seen those clothes before, fedora, scarf and overcoat. There was no mistaking that they were owned by the Painted Man.

Searching between scattered papers and the mahogany desk I discovered a buried book, the title as plain as day; *Gray's Anatomy*. I looked again at the littered sketches because there was a similarity between those drawings and the illustration on the book cover; cadavers without skin. So the Doctor had been drawing the Painted Man. Considering the volumes of mess, she must have been drawing him for quite some time.

It would have been easy to rationalize this mess as a creation of a very eccentric Doctor who got her kicks drawing naked men and none whatsoever from a little tidying up. Easy to explain that was, except for two big obvious flaws. The first were the large quantities of blood staining the sheets. The second I only appreciated when I checked the sketches more closely, for only then did I notice the important detail I'd been missing. The drawings were of the Painted Man all right, but the anatomical wounds perfectly matched those decorating his corpse when he'd been dragged out of the Docks.

Now the pictures became disturbing, for in them the Painted Man seemed relaxed, calm and unperturbed as if he'd been hanging in pieces while he modelled. Somehow it became easy to imagine that the Doctor wasn't drawing dead cadavers to prepare her own version of *Gray's Anatomy*; she'd had a living, bleeding model posing for her instead. None of this was possible, not in the rational way.

While I was still thinking, I heard a thud, as something heavy fell and remained motionless on the other side of one wall. If there was another room adjoining this office it was hard to tell, as I said, all surfaces were covered in paper. But checking the wall in question, I found as I suspected — a door that would have otherwise been plainly visible. With my .45 in hand I burst in, prepared for anything, or so I thought.

I hadn't expected to find the Doctor like I did, strapped to a chair that had just toppled over. Her eyes and face still appeared to have life in them, as if she'd just been caught unawares, surprised by nothing more than a noise in the next room just as I had. But I knew that she was dead, it was too obvious. Dead bodies are something I've seen with a regularity expected in my profession, so until today I believed that I'd always be hardened to the sight of another murder victim. Not today however, for the top of her skull had been cut clean away and her brain was missing.

So I hastily departed the consulting room, wiping my prints as I did. Only then did I become aware that the vibrations had also departed with the missing brain. I'd sensed this only because the hairs on my hands and neck were no longer standing on end, not because I saw anything. And looking back it was probably a good thing that I had not.

Like all good citizens I figured that the Doctor would own two addresses; one where she worked and the other where she lived. After the initial shock of the brain-scooping had subsided, I planned on calling the Superintendent, telling him what I found, but not before I had a chance to check out the good Doctor's apartment on my own. Two dead in two days, this was stacking up to be a clear case of a classic serial killer, for nothing else made much sense. At least the doctor's death explained the blood on the white sheets, but how could the killer escape so quickly when mine was the only exit from the office?

I'd only walked two blocks before I heard someone calling my name. Then I realized I was in a poorly-lit street and very alone. Only seconds ago it seemed that I was in a crowd, but somehow the crowd had abandoned me.

I heard my name again.

When people I don't know use my name casually, I tend not to like it. Generally this is because such people often have an interest *in* my well-being that may not be the best interest *for* my well-being. But to show this man I wasn't afraid, I could either draw a gun or I could draw a cigarette, and ended up with the latter.

He called again, a voice from the famous city shadows that in my heart I knew consumed everything that didn't belong. Secretly checking that my free hand was warm against my .45 revolver, I stepped closer, searching the darkness more thoroughly until I at last saw the speaker. He was a man as I expected, wearing a rotten tartan jacket infested with what I suspected were flies and maggots. His face was ugly, with missing teeth and white hair that grew in clumps. In a hand absent two fingers was a bottle which smelled of turpentine.

"You're looking for the Doctor?" His larynx sounded in need of a good reconditioning, little more than a whisper.

"Perhaps, who says I do?"

His black beady eyes rolled, "The Fungi from Yuggoth told me. Surely you've heard of the Fungi?"

"Can't say that I have."

"They took the Doctor you know, but you'd disturbed them before they'd finished. You didn't allow them time for cleaning."

I didn't remember being followed, but I was sure that if this guy was on my tail I'd have noticed. His overwhelming scent of excrement would have been warning enough.

"What do you want?" I demanded.

He beckoned me closer with a hand little more than a misshapen claw. I complied, stepping away from the neon streetlights into the darkness of his muddy and toxic world. I felt soiled by his corruption, especially now that I saw his face with disturbing clarity. Those eyes seemed misplaced, as if one was higher in the skull than the other. Then I thought I saw worms crawling through the gums in his mouth.

"She wants to speak to you."

"Who's she then?"

"The Doctor, of course."

I chuckled turning my back, knowing that the Whispering Man had bluffed well until now. But as I walked away he still bothered to call me back.

"They're watching you too, you know."

I was going to ask who, but I already knew what his answer would be.

"They've been watching all of us for a very long time . . ."

I gave up trying to find the Doctor's home, primarily because I couldn't find an address. There was nothing in the phonebooks, nothing from directory. Tired, I quick-stepped back to my apartment to take a shower, only to wake up some time later lying uncomfortably in the tub. Water still falling on me left my skin wrinkled like a Labrador puppy.

I recalled dreams. Vivid images of organic machines, chrome tubes pumping grey spongy mixes, and that putrid-green weapon I'd discovered in the alley. To my back a woman was asking what I saw. I was sure in this dream she was my Wife, not that I've ever been married in the real world. But no matter how hard I tried to catch a glimpse, her face always remained hidden in shadow.

The Dobermans wouldn't shut up, so I aimed the weapon their way, releasing a beam of silvery liquid from what I guessed was the barrel. Simultaneously the gun glowed and I saw chrome-skinned worms crawling through inner tubing. Far more shocking were the dogs, at my feet yapping like puppies now rather than barking, for they were the same miniature size as the dead woman, and confused at how enormous the alley had suddenly become.

It was too much. Quickly before I looked again, I stepped on both dogs as bones crushed and blood squirted from under the soles of my leather shoes.

Behind me my Wife muffled a scream, for she had just seen something I had not. I only sensed the vibrations . . .

And then I woke up.

Out of the shower I dried myself quickly, then found my watch. Either I was losing time, or it really was ten twenty-two at night. How long had I been in the shower asleep? I never sleep that long even when I plan to.

While I was walking past the telephone it rang, as if it knew I was there.

I answered, "Hi."

"Hi."

"She wants to speak to you."

The Singer's voice was unmistakable, the sensual texture struggling against buried pangs of pain.

"Who?"

"The Doctor, she phoned me just a minute ago."

"The Doctor? Not possible."

"What do you mean?"

I didn't want to say that the Doctor was dead, so I lied and said she was out of town and out of reach.

"That's not what she's telling me."

"Are you sure it's her?" The image was too vivid; a face, a head, and a skull empty like a trashcan missing its lid.

"Positive, she's my general practitioner, so of course I know her. Why are you asking?"

I wasn't sure what to say, so I hung on, not saying anything.

"She knew all about your visit this morning . . . in her office. And the paintings."

Suddenly I no longer felt alone in my apartment. Just as the Whispering Man had warned me, I now sensed that I really was being watched. Here was the evidence; how could the Singer know where I'd been and what I had seen, for I'd told no one nor encountered anyone all day who could have reported on my movements? I looked about my apartment, but even here there were too many shadows not to be sure what lurked in all the dark corners.

"Where . . . where do I meet her?"

"She said you'd know where, that you've already been told." Then as an afterthought, "Does this make any sense to you? Any sense at all?"

"I don't know. I'm not sure."

I tried to remember my life, how I came to be here, what decisions I made and the dilemmas I'd confronted to bring me to this point right now, the present. I could remember thousands of events in my past, but nothing on how one event led to the next. My history then was a series of snapshots, with no reasons and no whys or hows. I didn't feel like a hardboiled detective — teaching school children and a family life felt more real . . . No wonder streetlights flickered at me, for this was how I perceived my own life. Scene after scene after scene after scene . . .

This wasn't quite true. Again I remembered that memory I always tried to drive away. The only time I felt real certainty was when I discovered the shrunken schoolgirl and the two miniature dogs, crushed underfoot. But surely that was only a dream? Surely that was a metaphorical interpretation of something troubling to me right now?

The phone had gone dead, so I rang again.

◆　◆　◆

"I'm coming round."

" . . . "

"Are you there?"

"Yeah, I'm here."

"You don't sound here."

"Do you hear that?"

"Hear what?"

"That noise?"

"What noise?"

"That . . . vibration?"

"Get out of there, get out of there now!"

"Where do I go?"

"Um . . . the Riverfront Diner, you know the place?"

"Sure, I know it."

"Go now, go right now and don't even waste time hanging up."

" . . ."

The Riverfront was unusually quiet. The only patrons sat in the dark corners, melding with the shadows. I counted them, three in total; an old couple in their eighties spending the last of their pension on a shared cup of tea, and a sailor with a horrific scar across an empty eye-socket who was flipping through a magazine in which all the faces of the women had been cut away.

I ordered a black coffee, nursed it until was it cool enough to drink. I hadn't counted the Singer amongst the patrons when I arrived, but I didn't have to wait long for her to show up. She was returning from the ladies, her hair tied back in a ponytail brushed through thoroughly so there were no strands. Today she was in a bright red dress matching her glossed lips, immaculately presented and accessorised as usual, but strangely, brightly-colored. She didn't belong in this world. I could only imagine her somewhere sunny and alive.

Sitting next to me, she ordered a glass of water and sipped it fast. Only then did she acknowledge my presence. "I'm so thirsty all the time and I have no idea why."

"You've seen a doctor about it?"

"Yes, the same Doctor my husband was seeing, the one that still wants to see you."

Nothing to say, I said exactly that.

"Have you ever seen anything living in the ocean?"

I shook my head, glad of the change of subject, "Can't say that I have." I told her of a time that I recalled concerning two old men fishing off the pier in the middle of the night. In fact, I remembered seeing the same two guys regularly, always talking in soft tones so as not to frighten fish they never seemed to catch. Oddly, they'd once told me nothing lived in the water, yet I was sure there were always fish in the markets.

"See, this world is crazy, if you think about it too much." She downed another glass. "I think there is something toxic in the water, something unnatural that my body keeps rejecting. It's like I'm not allowed to absorb water just to see how long I can last."

"Last before what?"

"Before it kills me!" she glanced back at the restrooms and turned pale. "It's as if I'm a laboratory rat, testing my resistance to new diseases."

Uncomfortable, I decided to change the subject again.

"Did anything else happen to you between now and when we last spoke?"

"You mean on the phone back then?"

I nodded.

"No, I came straight here like you said."

"Thank god for that."

She smiled and leaned closer. "You were worried about me, weren't you? I think that's nice."

"You're a nice kid, and you've been hurt enough as it is."

She wrapped her arm in mine, transforming this drab scene into something warm and familiar . . . as if we'd both been here before, holding each other as lovers. It was the first good feeling I'd felt since . . .

"Do you know what's going on?" Closer to me now, her tone dropped to a whisper, "because I'll tell you the truth, I'm getting a little scared." She sounded detached, understandable after the bizarre death of her husband. But she also oozed intimacy. Being with her, linking arms, this felt right. She was exactly the kind of girl I would have married if I'd met her first.

So now seemed like the right time to tell her the truth. I told her about the sketches of her husband but left out the gory details so as not to unsettle her. She nodded sagely at each piece of information, as if they were just simple facts and nothing more. It was only when I told her about the Doctor and the missing brain did she show surprise, as the warmth from her body pressed next to me transformed into a sudden chill.

"That's not possible."

"Yeah. Well I've been thinking about that. I've been thinking someone's playing games with us, pretending to be your family Doctor. It has to be, because how else could I have seen her with her head sliced open and . . ."

She frowned. "Please, do you have to be so graphic?"

"Sorry. But you see what I'm saying?"

She finished her third glass. Only a few droplets of water remained, sliding down the transparent interior. I could see our reflections, us seated at the bar. We were outside, looking in, but also inside, looking out of the glass. We were watching ourselves from this strangely-curved angle.

"Are you sure it was the Doctor who called you?"

"Positive. Are you sure it was the Doctor who you discovered dead?"

"For sure," I nodded. "I'd seen her before that, with your husband on several occasions, so there was no mistake."

She unlinked her arm to lean over our bar. "I think you're right, someone is playing an awful game with us."

"These murders are not acts of rage, they're . . ." I was going to say artistic, but I didn't want that kind of image festering in her mind too. The two dead corpses were already too real, yet unreal, for me as it was.

"The Doctor's comments were weird when she phoned. She kept talking about your dreams."

"My dreams?" I couldn't remember telling anyone about my dreams. They had always been too strange, too bizarre to risk sharing with anyone else just in case they revealed something odd about my personality which might suggest insanity.

"She mentioned the shrunken woman."

Now it was my turn to be stunned into silence.

"And the two dogs that you stepped on. Does this make any sense to you?"

This really was too much. So I paid for both of us and we left.

The Whispering Man was easy to find again. His shadow, that window into his dank world, wrapped him like a blanket. "You're lucky," his words spoken through rotting teeth sounded just as decayed. "Very lucky indeed, for the Fungi have not yet returned."

He looked her up and down, in his mind stripping away her clothes as if she was some cheap prostitute. When he finished he pointed, suggesting that we proceed further into the warehouse, further into the realms of the unknown and unlit. Ignoring his obscene ogling, I took her hand, leading the way as we entered the dark ruins. I was relieved when the Whispering Man did not follow.

On the other side, dull light shone through blackened skylights offered the only illumination. The smell suggested damp sawdust and decaying shredded newspaper, once used for the packaging of fragile goods. Wooden supports, now rotting, only just managed to hold the ceiling above our heads.

"Hello," echoed a voice. It was close, too close for us not to have seen the speaker already. It was also a voice unfamiliar to me, like a parrot but punctuated and mechanical. "I'm glad you both made it," each syllable raw as if none of the words belonged in the same sentence.

Switching on my torch I swept the beam between the crumbling columns, just to make sure I hadn't missed anything. I did see something then, not a person but a large shiny cylinder perhaps a foot in height decorated with strange symbols. Connected to the cylinder were rubbery tubes joined to a few odd-shaped attachments. This device was completely alien to the rest of the world we knew. Then my dreams came back to haunt me, for this was the same technology, the same organic design.

"That's right, I'm over here."

Cautiously, together, we stepped up to the alien contraption.

"That's better."

I could see now that the voice originated from one of the attachments.

"Show yourself," I demanded, suspecting a trick.

"I'm right here, right in front of you."

The Singer bent down, taking one of the attachments in her hand. The end nozzle had reminded me of the eye of a squid. Then I recalled that this *was* the eye attachment of the cylinder, and I wondered how I knew such things.

"You're looking at my eye, and I'm now looking at you."

I hadn't realized at first, but my hand on my holster was flicking the revolver's safety on and off, on and off, on and off, on and off . . . There were no vibrations in the room, but I sure as hell thought there should have been. "Who are we talking to?" I asked.

The Singer stood taking my hand. When she answered me she did so with a hint of a smile, "This is the Doctor, alive as I said."

"Are you sure?" It didn't sound at all like a woman's voice, but it didn't sound male either.

"I'm afraid," spoke the mechanical apparatus, "that your friend is right."

"Not possible, I saw you, or what was left of you."

"You saw everything of course, except my brain. Would that be correct?"

I nodded, knowing that the voice was right.

"A brain is all you require to retain your mind and personality, assuming of course you have a life-support system, which is what this cylinder does. It keeps me alive."

I took a closer look at the strange contraption, seeing that it was indeed the right size to contain a single brain, but it still didn't mean that I believed it. "This is some kind of joke right?"

"Perhaps, but we don't have time for this, not before they return to take me away."

"Who returns?"

"They are the Fungi from Yuggoth. This is their place."

"The warehouse?"

"Yes, but more than that, they own everything, including your bodies and your minds."

Scared again and not sure why, I turned to my companion. "We should get out of here, because I smell a trap."

I'd taken her arm but she shook herself free. "Please, wait a moment?" She turned to the cylinder, speaking directly to it. "What did we talk about last time I came to visit?"

The mechanical voice retained its emotionless tone when it said, "We talked about your pregnancy test, that you're not pregnant. In fact you are infertile."

She looked again to me, "It's her. It has to be, for no one else knows that."

Then the cylinder spoke, I assume its words were directed at me, "I know about you too, your secret history."

I had to admit I was curious, "Well, go on then."

And it did, the mechanical voice told me everything.

While it recounted my life with more detail than I'd ever been able to muster on my own, I again remembered my dream. I remembered the shrunken schoolgirl in the jaws of the Doberman and the other mysterious woman lurking in the shadows. As the voice from the cylinder described these visions, the dream became too real, too vivid, until it was this world, our world right here and now, that seemed to be wrong. I knew then beyond a doubt with a sinking feeling in my chest, that my past had been taken away from me, and I'd been 'adjusted' to forget that I'd even had a history.

But it wasn't just me, for I could see the Singer felt the same way. She'd remarked often enough that she had also lost many of her own memories. "We were not the sum of our parts," she'd explained. "We are fragments. Perhaps even a mixing pot of many lives."

When I sensed the vibrations, I knew that we were now being watched. I knew that we were now no longer safe.

But the cylinder still wished to talk, "When I am in this state, a brain without a body, then the Fungi consider that the truth no longer requires obscuration. In this state I remember everything. In a body you only suspect something is amiss, but I know we've been here a long time, a very long time. I know that most of what we see and touch and believe is not real. I've seen reality and it is not something . . ."

I cut the doctor off, "What are you getting at?"

"Get out. Get out now before they return, to snare you so that they will make you forget again. Forget who you really are."

My companion asked the next question, "But what about you?"

"Yes, I called you here because I want you to end it."

"End what?" she asked.

But I knew what the Doctor wanted; she didn't need the emotional context of a real voice for me to understand. The cylinder wished to die, so I drew forth my gun. "Are you sure this is what you want?"

"Yes. If you knew what I knew, you would wish the same upon yourself too."

The Singer turned to me and nodded sadly. She was in agreement. So I emptied all six rounds into the cylinder, enough firepower to crack the metal in two. Yet even though we'd been given enough warning, I was still surprised when a brain did flow free, dying in the growing puddle of the draining nutrient solution.

We ran then, her hand in mine as we escaped the warehouse. Amongst the streetlights and the fog everyone we saw appeared faceless, impatient with unimportant errands; a broken kettle that needed repainting, a blank letter that required urgent delivery, a shoe shiner who only polished new shoes. The world was opening to me now and at last I could see it for what it was; nothing. We, the people of this world, did nothing, we achieved nothing, and worst of all we existed not for ourselves, but for the Fungi. We dug holes for them without question, just as readily as we filled them back in again.

"Where are you taking me'" she asked frantically. Her shoes were not designed for fast getaways, so she clenched her heels tightly in her free hand.

"Here," I said pointing to the Shoe Factory, thankful that there were no workmen guarding the site today.

She read the sign and nodded. The simplicity of the featureless building seemed to be enough for her, and she became calm again. We looked up together, seeing as we expected, the top of the building hidden from our sight, claimed by the night and fog.

"They're in there," I said.

I found the discarded tools of the workmen, neatly arranged in rows from smallest to largest. The most appropriate tool was also a weapon, so I took the sledgehammer and proceeded to pound at the wall. This was hard work and I broke into a sweat, and the noise was loud but pedestrians passing didn't bother to investigate, as if we did not exist. I became ecstatic each time a crack formed between the bricks.

When the hole was large enough I stepped inside. The darkness was the same as the darkness owned by the Whispering Man, but this reached deeper, as if it hid a whole world without light that stretched across the entire face of a planet.

But this world was not infinite, for when I shone my torch I saw stairs, organic and curved, twisting upwards through the center of this chrome-inlaid tower. I couldn't say how high they reached, they too were claimed by darkness and distance, but I knew this was where we had to go.

"Are you coming" I asked, holding out my hand, hoping she'd take it.

"Where are we going"

"I don't know, but I know there is nothing for us if we stay here."

She looked back outside, towards what we had once thought to be a world of familiarity. But now I could see that she saw the interior of the factory as I saw it; a place of nothingness.

With flashlight in hand we climbed together. The stairs spiralled upwards, with each step a treacherous one even though their roughness left little chance of slippage. Yet onwards we marched, a sense of impending victory stronger than our weariness. In no time the darkness also claimed the world below and we were alone. Only our labored breathing and the flashlight with a single miserable beam kept us company, and reminded us that we were alive.

We climbed for what seemed like hours, but we never rested, not even to catch our breath. What had begun now could not be stopped. We needed closure.

Eventually we reached a balcony, but neither of us was prepared for what awaited us.

We saw the city, all of it, forming a large pentagon of city blocks, apartments, buildings, warehouses and shops. Everything was geometric, all corners harsh and foreboding. The town's centre was this tower, rising far higher than any other building or structure. I recalled memories of trees and grass but saw none down there, not in our home. This was a place of machines and industry, and nothing more.

Beyond the city, past the docks and the still water, through the fog and the darkness, unnervingly we understood that our world was contained within a cylinder. The town was an island lost in a sea of inky blackness. I had never known that, never even suspected that we lived on an island. Always our city had been calm, never affected by the weather and I now could see why. Our world was a container.

Those imprisoning walls so far away were of an alien design I could not accurately describe, except to say they were constructed of an alloy unknown to me, appearing to have flown into their current shape rather than welded or riveted together.

On the roof was the biggest surprise of it all, no more than a few dozen feet above us now, I saw thousands of tiny drainage holes, interspersed between fungus growths shining with a sickly purple florescence, the suspended disc of my dreams. At last I could see now why it did rain; drainage holes in the disc were the source. The Singer watched with me with a sense that was either wonder and awe, or fear and trepidation. I knew I only felt the latter.

"When the Doctor told you your dream, I too remembered that I'd had withheld memories. Memories that I'm only now starting to understand," she said as she held my hand. I smiled back, unsure of myself. "I remember being lost in a city, not too dissimilar to this one. I was sure it was a dream, because alien monsters had just invaded the earth. Huge bulbous creatures with heads like squids and wings like bats. Far larger than any building down there, they were eating or crushing any human that crossed their paths, and they demolished everything. A man — very similar in build and dress to you — was holding me, trying to protect me. We were hiding from these monsters, underneath a sheet of fallen iron. He said that the stars had come right, and that our time was at an end. I didn't want to believe him, so he said someone would save us, someone would come soon to take us away — creating a new world for us to live in.

"Meanwhile, the monsters went on killing, and I couldn't bring myself to believe him, although I desperately wished I could. In my dream I don't think we died, for the monsters seemed to have missed us and moved on. We were left alone in a world of rubble that was now dead to us. That man held me, told me that he loved me and that our love was all that was real and all that mattered. After that I only remember waiting."

Her voice trailed away. Disturbingly, I saw myself clearly in the same situation. Was this a shared past life? I knew it was me holding her, telling her make-believe stories so she'd feel better, even though we both knew that the end had come.

"Do you think this place is our salvation" she asked, pointing down at the world below. "Do you think this is the afterlife?"

It didn't look like salvation to me. Again I was reminded of cancer, a living organism feeding on itself to survive, naïvely believing that it could grow stronger by doing so.

"It's a nice dream," I said. "You should share it with everyone you meet. Share the hope."

She turned pale, crystalline breath escaped her gaping mouth. "You know, that's exactly what the man in my dream said."

The stairs continued. I knew we could turn back, even now, and if we did so we probably would have been all right, but could there ever possibly be sanctity, sanity or peace after this? We both wanted to know the truth, for that was all that was left to us now. A laboratory rat is always doomed. Once caged, the moment of death is no longer theirs to decide, no matter how often they run the maze correctly. A rat's only chance is to escape, regardless of how unsafe that outside world might be. At least on the outside, fate is in the rat's hands. That was the path we were now walking.

We climbed again in darkness. Often my flashlight threatened to fail, and I think only hope kept it alight. Without light we knew the stairs would become dangerous, and a fall from this height would be nothing less than fatal.

But it didn't take long before we reached the surface.

We stood upon our container, several miles across. But that wasn't all there was to see for we were suspended by impossibly thick wires hanging from the next container a mile above us. And still this wasn't all, for we saw hundreds of containers disappearing into the darkness. To our left and right, above and below.

Perpendicular to these worlds was an enormous wall, populated with tubing and circuitry the size of motorways. Thick liquids of browns and greens flowed inside transparent tubing alongside cables streaming with multi-colored lights. Everywhere else fungus grew out of control, mushrooms of green and red towering like skyscrapers from perches on the wall, while spores like gigantic whales floated past us, disappearing into the darkness.

We walked for fifteen minutes until we reached the edge of our container, and looked down. The same fluid tubes and circuitry pumped liquid and electricity in and out of our world, just as they did to every other cylinder in this collection. I didn't need to ask what the other cylinders contained, I didn't need to jump to know that the fall would continue forever, and we could both see that there was no means by which to climb down.

I took her into my arms to hold her as tight as I could. "It will be okay," I said with the strongest voice I could muster.

But she just shook her head into my chest. "I no longer believe our dreams are something we just made up"

Once again I sensed the vibrations, the hairs on my body again on end, sensitive to unseen danger. The Fungi from Yuggoth had been alerted to our escape, and they were on their way to return us to our cage.

How long had we been in these micro-worlds? How many times had they erased our past so we'd be readily conditioned for their next round of bizarre experimentation, such as pretending to be a private eye and a singer to gauging our reactions toward a mutilated man posing for an anatomical study? When would I next play the role acted out this time by the Painted Man? When would it be my turn to be the victim of cruel surgery? All I knew was that one day it would be inevitable, for I was sure the Fungi would bring the Painted Man back from the dead just as quickly as they'd return us now. The Doctor or whoever she was had been right; a bullet in the brain would bring it all to an end. But unlike her, I didn't know everything, and so couldn't bring myself to end it now.

Regardless, I checked the revolver, there were no bullets anyway.

For all I knew the Earth really was gone, that humanity had died out long ago and that we were now possibly humanity's only survivors. We'd probably lived thousands of years as laboratory rats, or at least that's what I think my subconscious was trying to tell me.

But those vibrations told me another thing, for they were growing stronger.

She was crying so I smothered her, remembering that we had been

Husband and Wife in the past and that we'd taught at the same school. She was the woman in my dreams, the same woman whose face had been hidden in the shadows, telling me that there will always be someone who loves me, regardless of whatever else might destroy us.

"You want to know what's real, honey? You want to know what's important? It's how I feel about you. I remember you now. It was me with you when those monsters destroyed the Earth. I'm your Husband, and I love you. That's all the reality I'll ever need, to know what my heart tells me."

Far away I could see lights, flashing multi-colored hues like a Christmas tree. Suddenly I was remembering Christmas, that festive season also taken away from us like every other good memory we'd ever known.

"This won't last," she said.

"Of course it will last. You don't have to do anything to love someone. It's just something that you'll feel. It's something that you know will be with you forever."

"Then I love you."

We just held each other knowing that they'd be upon us any second now.

When I finally saw the Fungi, I was most surprised by its enormous size.

I remembered how my dream with the Dobermans, my Wife, and the shrunken girl who was a missing student ended. The Fungi had been the last to arrive. They took away my alien gun and used it to shrink us down to less than an inch in height. Still we managed to escape that time. No wonder we survived the invasion of the bulbous squid creatures that came later, because we were too small to be seen, too small to be worthy meals compared to other, larger humans.

But not small enough for the Fungi from Yuggoth, for they had means to track us down. Captured, tiny enough not to require the removal of our brains for ease of transport from the earth to their world, the fabled world of Yuggoth. We were imprisoned in a cell, this cell, this city, this container. Locked inside what will always be our home.

That dream was a reality, from a time thousands, perhaps even millions of years ago, when the earth was still ours.

# PAZUZU'S CHILDREN

## Jeffrey Thomas

They brought him a few dates and a piece of unleavened bread. His meager repast was not meant as punishment; it was all that could be scrounged, as yet, from the labyrinth's ruins. The man who told him this looked embarrassed as he explained it. This man's role of apologetic host was a curious contrast to his previous role; not an hour ago, the man had repeatedly burned the head of Lieutenant Gavin Hilliard's penis with the head of his cigarette.

Hilliard had read several books about Iraq, and he took his captors to be Yezidi, Devil worshippers. Some of them wore ponytails, and fancy little beards that looked like something actors might wear to look foreign and villainous in bad movies. The Yezidi never uttered any word that started with the sound *sh*, Hilliard remembered, because it was the sound which began the Arabic name of the Devil. He would have to listen for that. But there were things about his captors beyond their appearance that made him consider the possibility.

There was the strange brusque sign language they used as a kind of salute to each other, or to punctuate their speech occasionally. (Maybe in place of *sh* words?) And sometimes they didn't even seem to be speaking Arabic at all, but some tongue even more tangled to Hilliard's ears, who didn't speak Arabic but had at least gotten used to its sound.

And then there were the books. Hilliard's cell in this subterranean complex was carved out of solid rock, rock that had been hidden from the air beneath the sands of the Syrian Desert . . . all but for jutting fangs and talons of stone as if a behemoth had been buried there and fossilized. At first, from his plane, he had taken the natural spires to be the eroded towers of man-made ruins. The rock must be tough to stand up to the hellish blasting desert winds at all; it must have been an arduous process tunneling and building this honeycomb within it. The narrow hall outside his cell was lined in stone blocks, with an arched ceiling. Hilliard could see into it clearly when he was alone and approached the slot of a window in the iron door of his small room. Once he had looked out to see men scurrying down the hall, their arms laden with books. Old books, covered in dust and bits of rock, salvaged from one of the sections of these catacombs that had collapsed under Hilliard's attack.

One of the men transporting this ancient library had seen his eyes in the window, set down his burden, made a weird angry sign with his hand, and slammed shut the panel that covered the window slot. As if the American's eyes were not fit to be gazing at these tomes, even with their covers closed.

And then there was the pendant his host/inquisitor wore. He had worn it when he brought Hilliard the dates and bread, and he wore it now as he returned to the cell. The man brought a friend this time, whose bizarre appearance might help support Hilliard's theory. This new man was weather-eroded as rock himself, entirely bald, his eyes so filmed in cataracts that they were white as cue balls in his skull. Around both eyes were spirals tattooed in blurred dark blue ink, filling the sockets and extending beyond his shaven eyebrows, so that his blind eyes rested at the center of these spirals like the molten centers of twin black galaxies.

The blind man sat down on a chair against the wall. The torturer gestured for Hilliard to sit down on the other chair in the room. He would stand. He was being the polite host again.

He lit a cigarette. Hilliard must have reacted; the man smiled and said, "I know, a nasty habit. I hope I don't have to share my cigarettes with you this visit."

"I told you," Hilliard croaked, his throat feeling coated in the dust of this place. "I don't know anything about why I was sent out here."

The inquisitor was still smiling, drew at his butt; it crackled, glowed brighter like a small glaring eye winking open. "You don't have to play Clint Eastwood, my friend. Your comrades aren't watching. No one will ever know what you tell me." He seemed amused by his own reference to the American film star, explained — though Hilliard didn't ask — "I've been to your country, you know. And England. Elsewhere. Meeting with brothers spread across this world, in dark corners like this." Crackle, ember glow. "I know you were just doing your job. A loyal follower does that, I fully understand. But don't make me do my job, Lieutenant. I have men who take pleasure in it, but it's far too crude for my tastes. I only meet with you myself because I can speak with you. If I deem you no longer worth speaking with, then you'll meet these men of mine I refer to. And we shouldn't let it get to that."

Hilliard sat up straighter, cleared his throat. He tried to appear strong, despite the tears that wound out of his left eye which was swollen nearly shut from a blow by a rifle butt when his captors first found him in the desert. "You can't be torturing me. Even if you don't respect the laws of civilized people, you should at least realize that when my people see me like this it will only make them angrier at your country, and more supportive of Desert Storm."

The inquisitor chuckled, turned his back and began to slowly pace the cell as if he were its restless inhabitant. "You are brave, Lieutenant. But you would have to be, to pilot one of those planes. I myself, abhor flying." He looked over his shoulder. "You have the American arrogance that you'll live forever. That you deserve to live forever. Neither is true." He stopped pacing. "Your people will never see your wounds, Lieutenant, because they will never know that you survived your plane's crash."

The inquisitor went on, "I know; why then cooperate with me? Well, if you do, I promise you there will be no more pain. I will give you a drink. You will go peacefully to sleep like a drunken man. And you will dream forever. But if you are difficult with me . . . if you persist in your pompous American . . . ah, tough guy routine," pause, crackle, glow, "then I will skin you alive. Quite seriously. You will suffer in ways that make man's imaginings of hell seem merciful."

"Look . . . please," Hilliard began. "I . . . I have . . . " A strangled tiny sob cut off his own words and he sagged in his chair.

"Good. That's a good sign, my friend. You're growing humble already. Yes, I know, you have children, a wife, a dog, a little white fence." The inquisitor resumed his pacing. "I mentioned man's visions of hell before you interrupted me. I was going to ask you if you recognized my pendant. Hm? No?" He lifted it from his chest, halted in front of the Navy pilot. "Hm?" he persisted, until Hilliard looked up and wagged his head.

"A demon," he managed.

"This is a representation of Pazuzu. He was the Assyrian devil of the southwest wind. He sowed pestilence, disease . . . just as you bring death from the skies. You see his form is rather like a man's. Man's arrogance is not limited to America, I confess. Men all over have remade the gods in our own image. And also in the image of other life around us. Horns of a goat, snarl of a dog, claws of a bird. The wings are correct, roughly." The grimacing monster that the man wore around his neck had double sets of wings. "The truth is obscured in time, but also hidden purposely, of course. Misdirection. You symbolize one thing by representing it as another. You call it Pazuzu, even when its name is similar but different and infinitely more sacred. You give it the head of a dog because you can't . . . or don't want to . . . imagine it more like the body of a devilfish. But even that description is a human's unimaginative — insufficient — comparison."

Hilliard glanced up at the blind man, who remained silent and seemed to be staring at him but couldn't possibly see through those ruined orbs. Some kind of priest, to give him a final absolution? Or curse?

The inquisitor paced once more, went on, "In the Louvre — I've seen it myself — they have a bronze Pazuzu from the seventh century. There is an inscription which says, 'I am Pazuzu, son of Hanpa; I am the king of the evil spirits of the air who come raging violently from the mountains.' Son of Hanpa; huh. Gods are not 'sons,' though Hlu — though Pazuzu has children. And he is from far beyond earthly mountains. Far beyond this sphere. He is no spirit of earthly winds, but of the winds of *stars.*"

"Did anyone else but me survive?" Hilliard said.

The inquisitor slowly turned his head to regard his captive audience. Suddenly Hilliard regretted his bold interruption. But the Iraqi kept his tone civil. "No. You are the only one, I'm afraid."

There had been five crewmen in each of the two Vikings that had been sent from the carrier *Eisenhower.* Both had delivered their deadly cargo, but once they did so the Vikings had no real means to defend themselves other than their maneuverability. The Vikings had fired flares that were meant to attract ground-to-air missiles away from the planes, but this tactic hadn't worked. Hilliard had never seen where the missiles could have come from, since from the air he had observed nothing at the target site but rocks jutting up from the desert sands. No guns, no structures, no men. Maybe it hadn't been missiles at all, but some devil worshippers' magic, he thought deliriously. All he knew was, his plane had been struck from behind, while the pilot of the other plane screamed something about an arm . . . look out for the arm . . .

"Since you seem eager to return to the subject at hand, let me ask you again," his host continued, still civil. "What did they say you were to bomb out here? What did they tell you about it?"

"Nothing. They gave us coordinates, that's all. They scrambled us fast . . . like they had just found out the information and were acting on it as quickly as possible."

The torturer did an odd thing. He turned to look at the seated blind man, his galaxy eyes unblinking. And the old man nodded once. This seemed to satisfy the inquisitor. He asked Hilliard, "They said nothing to you about what we might be doing here? Nothing about our practices?"

"Nothing. They were very urgent, that's all I know. Bomb the rocks . . . that's all they told us. But we knew it was hush-hush. Something to keep quiet about. They got that across."

Again, the Iraqi looked to his elder. Again, the old one nodded. What, then — was he some human lie detector? Being blind, were his powers of hearing more keen (Hilliard had thought such ideas were a myth), so that he could detect the intonations of falsehood?

"Look," Hilliard said, "I won't say you tortured me. I give you my word of honor on the lives of my kids. I've cooperated with you all along. I don't know anything. Really, it will be better for you if you let me go. If they ever found out you'd killed me . . ."

"Shh." The inquisitor held a finger to his lips. So that sound wasn't forbidden to his sect after all. "You have been in a holy place. Though you do not comprehend them, you have seen things you should not see. You see the Inner Circle."

"But like you say, I don't understand it, so what can I tell people?"

"They must know something of it already," the inquisitor sighed, shrugging. "That's why they sent you. But I wonder if they knew the full scope of things. The full scope of our jihad. They must think this all about silly human politics. That Saddam wants oil, or land, the material things you godless Westerners crave. Saddam is of the Inner Circle, Lieutenant. He is no Moslem. That is a young religion, a religion of mere men. It is his façade, like the name of Pazuzu. Saddam is the Man of the Blue Turban. The Man of the Apocalypse. He is a manifestation of the Faceless One. He is Nyarlathotep."

"I don't understand any of this," Hilliard sobbed abruptly, desperation electrifying his nerves. "I don't *want* to understand it . . . please don't tell me about it! Please just let me go . . ."

"You are very fortunate that I am offering you such a merciful death, Lieutenant. You destroyed many valuable grimoires, important objects . . . and you came very close to slaying one of Pazuzu's children. A being that we were to have unleashed upon your people. A being to make their conceptions of demons seem like fairy tales for children . . ."

A breathless man burst into the room then, and began babbling to the inquisitor incoherently. Hilliard had flinched sharply at the man's dramatic entrance, but grew even more alarmed at the look that came over the inquisitor's face at this news . . . especially when the inquisitor shot a narrow glance Hilliard's way.

The new man left, and the inquisitor bent to whisper in the blind man's ear. The old man nodded, his sightless gaze not wavering from Hilliard until he stood up and shuffled out of the cell, leaving the iron door open behind him.

"Come with me," the inquisitor said gruffly.

"Where are we going?"

"More of your friends are on their way. They'll be here soon. You should be happy, Lieutenant . . . they may have just saved your life. You're going to contact them. Tell them to turn back." The man grinned and flicked his cigarette to the stone floor. "I know you'll do it. I said you were brave, but only superficially. You're a coward with no solid commitment, no real faith, no true loyalty to your God, your country, your kind. You don't understand the glory of true servitude. You will live, Lieutenant. For now. Until those who slumber awaken." He gestured. "Enough chat. Come on; we'd better be quick . . ."

Dazed by the revelation that he would live after having just absorbed the fact that he would die, Hilliard floated unsteadily to his feet. Should he trust this madman, this devil worshipper who believed that demons — more so than chemical, biological or nuclear weapons — were the greatest threats his country had to offer? But what choice did he have? If this place took another bombing he knew the labyrinth would cave in completely. And he would be buried forever amongst these people, his skeleton one day indistinguishable from the rest.

He shuffled out of the cell as wearily as the old man, the inquisitor taking his arm. Together they walked the narrow tunnels of these catacombs, a few times stepping over fallen stones, skirting partially tumbled walls. Dust was still trickling down from the arched ceilings. Men ran past them carrying weapons, supplies, and more of the ancient books.

And then they turned a corner and stopped. A group of nearly a dozen men were ahead of them, blocking an intersection of several tunnels, at least one of these fully caved in. The men were dragging something large and heavy out of one tunnel that looked mostly collapsed, and carrying it toward the mouth of another tunnel.

The object they carried was long as a tree trunk and just as thick, but flaccid, dropping from their arms heavily. At first, Hilliard took the black, slippery-looking object to be the carcass of an immense python. Some pet, living idol, mascot. The tapered forward end he took to be the snake's tail.

But then he saw that along the underside of the glistening black object were rows of suckers, much like those of an octopus . . . except that they were more diamond-shaped than circular, a translucent gray. And, impossibly, they seemed to be moving independently, their edges slowly opening and closing. Could this be the limb of some gigantic cephalopod? Did the men expect to drag the entire creature through these tunnels by just one arm? The entire animal must be impossibly gargantuan. Could this hive connect with some vast subterranean pool, out here in the middle of the desert?

Just then the last man clambered out of the partially collapsed tunnel, bringing up what proved to be — despite the fluctuating suckers — the severed end of the arm. The end was a ruined mess where a falling ceiling had torn it from its body. There was no blood, just a jagged wound in fibrous, stringy flesh, the meat white under the black skin. Dangling from the wound were a number of globe-like bladders or tumors, like obscene clusters of fruit, the largest the size of a beach ball. These globular organs were translucent and covered in webs of black veins. A sloshing sound came from the orbs, and was he imagining that shadowy dark shapes, vaguely human, fetus-like, were contained within them? Was the largest globe actually pulsing with movement, as if its occupant were restless to be born?

Hilliard heard a cry and jerked his head. The man at the front of the great limb had called out in fear as the pointed end wound itself around his neck. Another man moved forward, helped extricate the limb before it could cut off the man's air, held it in both hands as they continued toward the new corridor.

An anus-like pucker the pilot hadn't noticed before at the tip of the tentacle suddenly yawned wide into a straining toothless maw, but the man gripping this end maintained his hold. It was a good thing; the mouth had stretched wide enough to engulf . . .

. . . a man. And suddenly Hilliard understood the globes that hung from the shattered limb. Those figures inside the orbs were not fetuses growing . . . but men being dissolved into grotesque little dolls . . .

"It is a desecration that you see this," said the inquisitor. "A blasphemy that you will live to remember it. But we have no choice. See what you have done to this child of Pazuzu, Lieutenant? But he lives. He will regain his body, in time. But those planes have to be stopped, first." The inquisitor dragged him forward again, and they moved around the back of the great limb and the struggling men.

"My God," Hilliard whispered, glancing back over his shoulder.

"Sorry, it's too late for conversion; I don't think this god would have you. But how quickly one becomes a believer, eh, Lieutenant?"

They would not feed their own men to the creature, would they? Perhaps it was an honor to sacrifice oneself. "The glory of true servitude." Please let it be that, Hilliard thought. Please that . . . and not the other possibility.

That perhaps Hilliard hadn't been the only survivor of the two Vikings after all.

They lost sight of the nightmare spectacle, turned a few more corners and stepped into a fairly large room. Atop a table rested a radio set. Men stood around the room with anxious faces, some gripping assault rifles. One of them was already holding a microphone out to Hilliard.

"Tell them you live," the inquisitor repeated. "You have my oath that you will be freed. No one will believe what you saw. Until the day comes when they see Pazuzu's children for themselves, of course. Whole. And Pazuzu himself, when the stars sit right. But go back to your wife and dog for now, Lieutenant. Tell your friends to turn back."

Hilliard staggered forward a few steps. Hesitated. Lifted his arm slowly, as if under water.

He pictured the Vikings in his mind, soaring on the desert winds. Small, yes, but steel. Angels of death . . . "spirits of the air who come raging violently" . . .

Coward, the inquisitor had called him. No loyalty to his kind . . .

A man wearing headphones gestured wildly, sputtered urgently. The inquisitor snapped, "They're getting nearer. Hurry, now!"

Hilliard accepted the microphone, moved it to his lips. He thumbed on the switch.

"Hello?" he croaked.

"Who is this?" crackled a voice that sounded as though it were filtered through a sand storm.

"Hit them!" Lieutenant Gavin Hilliard cried abruptly, finding his voice. "Hit them with everything you have! Hurry up!"

The inquisitor snarled something in Arabic, and surged toward the American, to tear him away from the radio and speak into it himself. Other men rushed at him. Rifle barrels lifted . . .

And even as their hands found him, he coiled his own hand in the radio cord and with his right wrenched the microphone from the end of it.

And even as the microphone ripped free, Hilliard continued to shout hoarsely into it.

"Hit them!" he screamed. For the love of G –"

# THE DEVIL IN YOU

## Eric J. Millar

---

### 1.

L ou Burma sat at the bar in The Nickel and Dime nursing a piss-warm glass of beer. His wide shoulders were hunched over while his hands fiddled with a coaster, tearing it into little pieces then collecting them up into a pile.

"Put the horses on, Saul. I got some bread riding on the next race." In the dim light Lou's skin looked like tanned leather; his wrinkled face was peppered with pock-marks and the palms of his hands were armored with calluses.

"Where'd you find money to bet on the horses?" The bartender poured himself a shot of whisky.

"C'mon Saul, turn the damn TV on."

"Can't. The tube's on the blink and I don't want to spend the green to get the thing fixed." The bartender slammed the shot back and quivered.

"Get me another beer then. Or are the taps on the blink too?" Lou said.

"Not till your tab's paid off, Lou. The one you got is a pity beer. Next one's gotta be cash up front."

"You know I don't got any cash. If your damn TV worked I could see if I had it coming."

"Well, that's just too damn bad, Lou." The bartender poured himself another whisky when trouble stepped through the doors of the bar wearing a red satin dress, black hose and matching black pumps. She walked swiftly, straight to the bar and put her hand down on the counter. Lou followed her lean arm up with his eyes, past her supple young breasts, and then stared into her bright, green eyes. She gave him a nervous glance then looked to the bartender.

---

HARDBOILED CTHULHU                                                           129

"Do you have a phone in here?" Her voice was like sweetened wine made bitter with panic. Lou stared into his glass of beer and smiled.

"Haven't had a phone in here for five years. Cuts down on the freeloaders." The bartender wiped out a dirty beer mug.

"How about a pay phone?" She looked back and forth between the bartender and Lou. "Anything?"

"Nope. You going to order anything?" The bartender set down the glass he was holding and grabbed another, holding it up to the light to find the filth in it.

She put her hand on Lou's shoulder and grasped with her slim fingers. Lou looked at her slowly as she sat down on the stool next to his, not letting go of him. He took a sip of beer without looking away from her.

"Do you have a car?" she asked.

"Yeah, but I wouldn't count on it for a fast getaway, if that's what you're thinking about." Lou said, his voice like a shoe scraping pavement.

"I need to get out of here right now. I don't care if it's fast or not, I just need to go."

As she finished, the door was flung open and the sleigh bells hanging from the knob let out a violent jingle. Three men walked through, smooth as shadows, and gathered just inside. The lead man's jet-black hair was slicked back, the grease shining under the fluorescent light. He wore a fine black suit with a white tie. He put a cigarillo between his lips and lit it. Two men stood behind him, one by each of his shoulders. They both wore grey derbies and long black coats with their collars pulled up to hide their faces. The man in front smoothed out his pencil-thin mustache with his finger.

"What do you think you're doing here, little sis?" The man hissed, letting two tendrils of grey smoke out between his crooked lips. The woman's grip on Lou's shoulder tightened.

"I thought I'd come in for one last drink," she stammered. "I thought I'd have it with this fine gentleman here."

"Gentleman? Looks more like a trained ape to me," the man said. Lou turned his head and glared him.

The girl glanced into Lou's eyes, silently pleading for help. Quietly she whispered, "Help me," as if the look had not been enough.

"Give me a shot of Jack. Hell, Saul, you better make it two. You never know with groups." Lou stood up from his stool, the woman's hand sliding off his shoulder as he rose.

"You know how you are with drinks, Lou. You get too damn slap-happy." Lou burned through the bartender with his feral eyes. Saul put the two shot-glasses on the bar and poured with reluctance.

"What's that for?" The man in the suit laughed.

"It's for the pain. You never know, with these old joints of mine, how much busting skulls is going to hurt. I have to take care of myself in my old age." He smiled and slammed his right hand into his left, the crack of his knuckles sounding like the trunk of a tree splitting open on a cold night.

The other two men moved forward and began speaking in an unintelligible language. Lou got a glimpse of their faces, seeing something like black oil pulsating and shimmering. He sized up their gloved mitts and saw that they weren't gloves at all, but their actual skin turned to leather and shining the same black as their faces. Any other man might have backed down at these things, but not Lou Burma. Lou moved in closer.

"Not in here!" The bartender shouted, the sound of a fresh shell being pumped into a shotgun echoing through the joint. "I just got this place remodeled after last time you were here, Lou," the bartender pleaded.

The man in the suit threw up his hands and smiled, his two goons backing away slowly behind him. "No need for that, Saully. We're just having a nice conversation." He eyed the girl, "Now, if my sweet sister would just come along nicely, we'll be on our way."

"I think I'll be staying here." The girl wrapped her arm around Lou's and drew her slender body in close to his.

"Just run on home, boy. Your sister's well taken care of here," Lou said.

"Fine, we'll do it this way for now, Pops. You'll be wishing you hadn't but we'll do it this way." The man waved for his men to follow as he left through the door. They peered at Lou and the girl as they walked out.

"Damn it all, Lou. Don't you got any manners?" the bartender said as he tucked the shotgun back into its nest behind the ground coffee.

"Nope." He looked at the girl; she was shivering and staring at the door. "You want me to take you someplace?"

"Your place. Can you take me back to your place?" she said. Her arm was tight around his and her eyes still begged for any kind of help that Lou could give.

"Damn your eyes," Lou said with a long sigh.

Lou waved to the bartender as they slipped through the back entrance. The night air was crisp, bringing goosebumps out on the girl's skin. His black Mustang was parked in the back alley, just behind the dumpsters. He unlocked the doors and opened the girl's before climbing in himself. He revved the engine a moment. The tires squealed as he stepped on the pedal and they disappeared into the night.

# 2.

"So, why don't you tell me what's going on." Lou said. They sat in his dive of an apartment, a tumbler full of Wild Turkey on the coffee table in front of each of them.

"They're after me - my father and brother." She took a quick drink and shivered as it burned its way down her throat.

"That really *was* your brother back in the bar?" Lou asked. He tightened the fingers on his right hand into a fist then released, repeating it again and again as he listened.

"Yeah, they've been chasing me for the past week. I guess they finally caught up."

"So why are they after you? You done something to them? Run away with the family jewels?"

"No. It's really hard to explain why." She took another drink. "Try me."

"You wouldn't believe me. Nobody does. Everyone thinks I'm crazy."

"So I ain't the first then." Lou pulled out a Lucky and lit it. He was getting aggravated; he was thinking maybe the girl was just playing games. Maybe it was a team job, milking gullible saps out of everything they had. Maybe it was his turn as the mark.

"No. I've told the story to plenty of people before you and it hasn't done me any good."

"So why don't you lay this crazy story of yours on me? Maybe I'll think you're crazy but it ain't like I'm going to throw you out. Not a pretty girl like you." Lou smiled and let out a lungful of smoke.

"Okay, okay. They're after me because they need me for a ceremony."

"What kind of ceremony?"

"Nothing that you'd understand. They need me for this ceremony and they're going to sacrifice me." She pulled a thin menthol cigarette from her purse and lit it with a match.

"Sacrifice? What the hell are they going to sacrifice you for? They trying to summon the devil or something?" Lou laughed and ground out his cigarette in the small glass ashtray on the coffee table. The girl didn't need a hero, she needed a shrink, he thought.

"See? I told you that you'd think I was crazy. And it's not the devil; it's something much older and much more powerful than that." She shook her head and stood up, gripping her purse with white knuckles and holding the cigarette tight between her lips. "Everybody thinks I'm crazy. You think I'm crazy."

Lou walked to the girl and put his warm hand on her thin, trembling shoulder. He let out a sigh while his eyes rolled. "I don't think you're crazy. I just think you've had a rough night. You just need some rest and it'll all be good in the morning."

"You're wrong. It won't be good in the morning. They'll still be after me in the morning. They'll still want to kill me in the morning." Her voice became frantic and she put her head against Lou's massive chest. "They'll still want to kill me in the morning." The tears flowed and her breasts heaved with each heavy sob.

"Don't worry. You can stay here tonight and in the morning we'll get you the hell out of Dodge."

"You'll let me stay here tonight?" she cried, her voice muffled by Lou's shirt.

"Yeah, you can stay here tonight. I can't let a pretty girl like you be left all alone. Not with those mooks after you."

"I don't know how to thank you. I really don't." She pushed away from his chest and looked up into his eyes. Her full red lips parted slightly, revealing pearly white teeth.

"As long as you're with me you don't have to worry about them anymore. I'm not going to let anything happen to you. Not a goddamn thing." He pointed toward the open door to the side of the living room. "Just go get some sleep. The bed's in there. It's a bit of a mess, but it'll have to do for now."

"Aren't you coming in there with me?" she smiled, making Lou's heart skip a beat.

"Nope. I'm bunking on the couch tonight." Lou hated himself for the words coming from his mouth. "If you need anything just give me a holler."

"Oh, okay." She looked toward the floor with a shyness that Lou hadn't seen in her before. She walked into the bedroom, turned on the light, and closed the door behind her.

Lou fell onto the empty couch and put one arm behind his head. He pictured the girl in his bedroom getting undressed and curling up, all lonely and cold, in his bed. Then he thought about how young she was.

The light went out in the bedroom. Lou sat up and pulled out another Lucky and lit it, taking the first drag deep into his lungs. He exhaled the cloud of smoke and took the last swig from her glass of Wild Turkey.

He thought of the girl in the bedroom and let the idea of what they could be doing roll through his head. The pretty girls always knew how to push Lou's buttons and they didn't have to push them hard. All it took was one wayward glance or a purse of their lips and Lou was theirs. When Lou took the last puff of his cigarette he dropped the butt into his tumbler; the coals went out with a low hiss in the dribbling of ice and Wild Turkey left in the bottom. He let his head back down onto the pillow. His mind wandered and his eyes began to shut. As Lou fell in love with the girl in his mind, he quietly dozed off.

With blurred vision, Lou's eyes opened to the sound of the bedroom doorknob turning. The rusted hinges squealed as the door slowly opened. He rubbed his eyes and noticed that the lights had been left on when he had fallen asleep. Lou sat up on the couch and scooted his back against the armrest. His hands went to his face as he yawned.

"Is everything alright?" Lou's throat was thick with phlegm and made his already deep voice even deeper. The girl didn't answer. "Hey, is everything okay?"

He heard the sound of footsteps growing closer to the couch. He heard a match strike — the scrape of the head against the box and the hiss of it flaming out was deafening in the quiet apartment. His eyes still were not focused but knew that the girl's matches were in her purse. The purse was still in the living room, sitting next to the chair where she had left it. His neck began to tingle as the person behind him took another step and then stopped.

"You have a nightmare or something?" Lou said cautiously. He was too groggy for a fight and needed to keep the man behind him occupied. Lou figured that if he acted like he still thought it was the girl, they might just keep up the silent act while he got his bearings. He figured wrong.

"My nightmare's over, old man," said the girl's brother. Lou listened to the man's hand rummaging through his pocket. He heard the sound of the blackjack slamming against his skull before he felt it. As the sharp pain at the base of his neck sunk in, his eyes rolled back and he was going out like a light. He heard the man laugh and through the fading light could see his face.

"Your nightmare's just beginning, Pops."

### 3.

"Tag! You're it." Lou stared at the words on his wall and rubbed the lump on the back of his head. The message was sprayed on in bright yellow. The paint was wet, thin yellow streams still crawling down the wall and collecting in puddles at the edge of the floor.

"There goes my deposit," he sighed. The room had been torn apart. White stuffing sat piled on what was left of his chair. The blinds on the living room window had been ripped from the wall and sat in a bundle on the floor, sunlight pouring into the room through the now bare pane. Everything that was made of glass in his kitchen sat shattered on the floor. Lou found his pack of smokes and pulled one out. As he lit it he noticed the knife stabbed into drywall next to the big yellow insult.

A note and a pair of pink panties were stuck to the wall, pierced clean through with the steel blade. He tore the note off and unfolded it.

The note was scribbled in thick black marker; the ink bled into the paper, blurring every letter. Lou got a headache from reading it:

*If you want to tag me back and maybe save the girl, meet me at Roderick's Piers at 11 tonight. I'll be waiting at number 7. I left you a nice little keepsake if you don't feel up to it.*

Lou knew the address; he had worked there once, before it closed down. He crushed the paper in his hand and threw it and his spent cigarette in the ashtray.

Lou staggered into the bedroom and found his mattress split open and tossed on the floor. His clothes lay scattered all over the carpet, white shirts and jeans cut to pieces and left for dead. The girl's red dress sat in a pile on the floor near a broken lamp, its shade twisted and light bulb shattered. He picked the dress up and smelled it. The scent of vanilla and roses filled his nostrils. He held it tight in his hand and walked to the window. They busted in through here, he thought as he inspected it. The glass was still intact but the boards on the outer window frame were splintered and cracked as if someone had taken a crowbar and pried the sliding pane open. Lou took the bottom of the window and closed it, the wood screaming as the boards slid together.

Why didn't she hear it? Lou thought. And if she did, why didn't she say something, or yell out to me? He gripped the dress in his fist and walked back into the living room, kicking through the debris of his destroyed home as he went. He grabbed the knife and pulled it from the wall, pieces of drywall falling away in small chunks. Lou watched the panties tumble to the floor. He looked at the knife blade and saw dried blood crusted on the stainless steel. A great lump of red-hot fury was growing in his gut.

He pictured the man and his two goons dragging that poor, defenseless girl out into the night, naked and frightened. Lou picked up the girl's underwear and rubbed it with his calloused fingertips, feeling the silk and lace as it folded and twisted in his grip. He put them in the hand that held the dress and shook his head.

The girl had trusted him, needed him. She had come to him for help, for protection. He failed her. His mouth opened, a little at first, and a howl formed in his throat. His lips spread wider, the skin stretching beyond the point of pain. A bestial sound filled the apartment as Lou threw his head back and released his anger.

Lou threw the dress and panties at the wall and made a beeline to the bedroom door. His fist closed, his muscles stretching and tightening as his elbow bent and his shoulder hunched. He punched the doorframe with everything he had. The wood exploded, splinters of it flying around like a swarm of wasps. His chest heaved and his shoulders fell. Lightning bolts of pain shot through his knuckles and arm. Lou rubbed his sore hand and was thankful for the pain; it distracted him from the girl and let him focus on what he had to do.

The revolver was still tucked away in his bureau drawer, wrapped with a loose, brown chamois. He opened the chamber and found all six cylinders empty. He pulled out a box of shells, the copper and lead rattling as it moved. Lou found ten bullets, pulling six of them out and loading them one by one into the gun. The four remaining bullets he tucked into his pocket. The gun felt light in his hands, as if he had been born to use it. The wooden grip was cold in Lou's palm as he leveled the gun at the window. He aimed at a pigeon sitting on the fire escape, pulling the hammer back with a trembling thumb. His breath became shallow and his hand was tense, the gun shivering in his grip. He slowly let the hammer back into the safe position and slammed it on top of the bureau.

"You're getting too old for this shit, man," he said to himself. Lou glared at the gun and his head filled with the thought of how insane the whole situation was. He saw the girl's face in his mind, crying and pleading for help. Lou gritted his teeth and stowed the gun in the waist of his pants.

Lou wandered back into the living room and sat down on the couch, his hands holding his knees in a death-grip. The clock on the wall said that it was only noon. He had eleven hours to wait, eleven grueling hours before he had his one last chance to make everything right again. Lou sat on the couch and watched the time tick by, his anger growing with each passing second. At eleven o'clock Lou would be ready for anything. His fingers tightened and he said a silent prayer.

## 4.

The full moon cast strange shadows across the abandoned buildings near the pier. The pavement and the immense brick walls of warehouses looked pale and dead, surrounding him with the loneliness of times gone by. Like the buildings, Lou was old and far past his usefulness. He looked at the flaking mortar and boarded-up windows, hoping that he could do this one last thing and then maybe the world would give him his peace. All he wanted was to be like one of those buildings, ignored and finally getting the rest he deserved.

Lou walked slowly, and watched as the buildings around him became shorter and then disappeared entirely, leaving only the white-capped waves coming to shore and hitting the beach, the water turning to mist and twinkling like the stars in the sky above him. He shivered as a cold wind ripped through his jacket and ran across his skin. He looked at his watch; it was a quarter to eleven. Lou put his hand on the gun in the back of his pants, feeling it and hoping for some strength. When he felt nothing, he pictured the girl's face. His teeth set and he continued walking.

"You made it!" the man yelled, happiness overflowing in his voice. He stood with his legs wide, bright yellow floodlights clicking on behind him and forming a halo around his body. Two goons stood by his sides and began to speak in strange gibberish with low, guttural voices.

"Where's the girl?" Lou stopped, putting his hand in front of his eyes to block some of the light. His other hand lay flat against his thigh and his index finger began to twitch.

"Hell, Pops, not only are you here but you're early to boot!" The man walked toward Lou, his wingtips clicking on the wooden planks with each footstep.

"Answer the goddamn question!" Lou yelled. "Where's the girl?"

"She's fine for now. Right now we get to finish our little game of tag." The man laughed. "I hope you don't mind, but my two friends here want to play."

Lou's hand reached back and gripped the gun tight. "I don't know. You think they know the rules?"

Lou pulled out his rod and fired, aiming it at the man's head. He pulled the trigger two more times and the shots echoed around them like church bells.

"Jesus Christ! What're you trying to do Pops — kill me?" the man yelled as he ducked behind the lights, disappearing into the darkness beyond them. He began to chuckle just then, and Lou thought, he's a lunatic for sure. Lou couldn't get another shot at him, hidden behind the lights as he was, but the other two men were fair game. He looked down along the barrel of the gun, swaying it back and forth, scanning for the two goons. He lowered the gun and started running toward the light, its brightness reaching into his brain and twisting a screw in it. He heard a low chattering beside him and raised his gun. A thick black club knocked it from his hand. One of the goons slithered from the shadows, his shape no longer human. The thing looked like a pile of rotten garbage and smelled twice as bad. It closed in on Lou, who was crouched and ready to attack.

"What the hell are you?" he growled, and pasted it where he thought its face was. It felt like hitting raw hamburger — his hand slapping against the black oily surface and then sinking in. The thing tugged at his arm and Lou stumbled closer. He lashed out with his free hand but it only got further ensnared. Lou heard what he thought was laughter as the creature formed a web around his chest and began to squeeze . . . one of his ribs crackled and then snapped. He groaned in pain and kicked his legs but the thing only gripped tighter. Sweat poured into his eyes, making his vision blur as two more ribs gave under the pressure. His shirt ripped away and got swallowed into the black muck that made up the thing's body.

"*Alive.*" The other goon said as it emerged from the darkness and moved across the dock towards them, its voice a fury of rumbling rocks. It stopped two feet away, its black oily body shimmering in the moonlight. "*Alive,*" it repeated louder. The thing loosened its grip on Lou.

Lou saw his opportunity and took it, tearing his right arm free from the goon and ripping away the web of tendrils around his chest. Adrenaline coursed through Lou's veins as he tore apart each new tentacle that formed to replace the ones that he destroyed. He dropped to the ground with a loud thud and rolled away, free of the inhuman thing. The two creatures changed back into their human shapes and looked at him crookedly.

Lou scrambled to his feet, his broken ribs sending bolts of pain throughout his body. Lou smiled; he liked the pain, it made him feel young. He spotted his gun on the ground nearby and went for it, scooping his hand down and grabbing it. He started running toward the lights. His boots hit the ground like a steady tribal drumbeat as he came closer and closer. He made a blind shot and took out one of the lamps, glass exploding and showering down on the wooden planks. Lou could see a shadow in the distance and took his aim.

There was a crack and a flash, the report of a gun filling the silence. Lou's knee exploded and sent him to the ground. He hit the dock face-first with a wet, bloody slap, his gun coming loose from his hand and skidding away. Lou could feel his ribs clawing away at his insides. He tried to stand but put too much weight on his bad leg, sending him back to the ground. He tried again and finally got to his feet. He heard footsteps behind him and made little hops on his good leg, turning around. He saw a figure walk closer, the clatter of hard-soled shoes getting louder and louder. Lou's fingers closed, forming two tight fists.

"Is that how we're playing this? Can't fight like a real man?" Lou hopped closer with his bad leg hanging lifeless beneath him. His eyes adjusted just as the gun went off again, blowing out his other knee and sending him back to the ground.

"Aww, what fun is that, Big-Boy?" The figure walked into the light. The woman stood over Lou's sprawled body and laughed. Lou gritted his teeth and tears began forming in his eyes. He started getting dizzy from the blood pouring out of his legs.

"W-why?" Lou stared up at her beautiful face. She wore a long black robe that covered her slender figure. If not for her green eyes Lou wouldn't have recognized her. His heart beat faster and his breathing became heavy. The woman crouched beside him and ran the still hot barrel of the gun against his cheek.

"It was all for fun, honey." She motioned to the two goons, who moved quickly to her on either side. "Now, we can't have you petering out on us yet. The real fun's just about to begin."

On either side of him the goons' arms flowered and tendrils spread onto the ground, connecting and forming what looked like a gurney beneath him. They lifted him up effortlessly and moved swiftly toward the light. The girl followed closely behind, her robes billowing in the wind. She lit a cigarette and tossed the still-smoking match on Lou's chest.

"I'll tell you something, Lou. Shoggoths don't make the best of help. They're ugly as sin and none-too-sharp, but they're strong as an ox. These two are going to save your life. At least for now."

Lou's eyes went feral and he glared back at the woman. "You're going to have to kill me, you two-timing little bitch . . . when all of this is over." He coughed and blood oozed from the side of his mouth. "If you don't, I'm going to kill each and every one of you with my bare hands. Hell, even if you do kill me, I might just come back from the grave, just so I can take care of you."

"Now, isn't that thoughtful of you." The girl laughed and put her cigarette out on Lou's arm, the skin sizzling and blistering beneath the hot ash. She looked at the two creatures. "Let's get a move on, we don't have all night."

"I'll kill you all. Each and every one of you." Lou said, his head going limp and turning to the side. He took one last deep breath before blacking out.

# 5.

"Good morning, sunshine," the old man called out cheerfully as he passed smelling salts beneath Lou's nose. Lou's eyes opened and he took a deep breath. He started coughing, each hack working more blood from his lungs. He turned his head and spit some of it out on the ground. He was groggy and hurt all over; the world around him was a blur as his eyes adjusted to the torchlight on the pier. As things began to clear, Lou could see who was standing in front of him.

The old man was a tower, standing nearly seven feet tall, and his long shadow smothered Lou's limp body. He was wide too, and his fat gut filled out the black robe he was wearing. The hood hung behind his neck, giving his aged face a dark halo and accenting his salt-and-pepper hair. His face was like a roadmap of old age, deep canyons resembling wrinkles digging through sun-cooked skin. He spread his dry lips and showed Lou his rotten teeth.

"We've put tourniquets on those legs of yours, son. We don't want you losing any more of those precious bodily fluids," the old man said.

"What's going on?" Lou asked, his head bobbing as he spoke. He found himself sitting up and bound to a rickety chair. Rope dug into the skin of his arms and squeezed the broken bones in his chest. Over the old man's broad shoulders Lou could see a large opal shrine being erected by the shoggoths.

"We're having a party and you're the guest of honor." The old man looked back at his son.

The man with greasy hair nodded and began spreading white grease paint across his naked chest, running his fingers into every crevasse in his chiseled muscles. His face was painted with intricate designs in black that looked like vines creeping through a void of clear sterility.

"Times like this the boy gets downright creepy. He's really into this stuff. I'd have to say he's even more into it than I am." The old man laughed.

"Magic? Devils?" Lou croaked.

"Devils? You kidding me? Those things are child's play compared to the forces we deal with. In the oldest, sickest books you can find the names of things that you can't even begin to comprehend with your little neanderthal brain. Yug-Siturath has more power than God or the Devil! Yug-Siturath is ancient beyond belief, and omnipotent too!" He was fairly screaming now.

"What are you shouting about, Daddy?" The girl walked up to the old man wearing a see-through red nightgown. She stepped around him and sat seductively on his lap. She went in for a kiss and her lips were received by his, their mouths connecting in a way that no father's and daughter's should. Lou turned his head after seeing their tongues whipping at each other like scorpion tails through the openings between their lips.

"Just business, honey," the old man said as they parted, a long string of saliva glistening between their mouths. "So what was I saying?"

"You were talking about Yug-Siturath." The girl smiled and put her hands between her legs, the palms flat against each other.

"Thank you, my dear," the old man said. "They call him The Soul-Consuming Fog. I've used all the years I've been lucky enough to get just studying up on the beast, figuring out how to summon him up and use him, gain certain favors from him. Two years ago I found an old tome that said that drawing the power of Yug-Siturath into yourself will give you eternal youth. Can you believe that? The Soul-Consuming Fog is just like the fountain of goddamn youth!"

"Why the sacrifice?" Lou asked.

"I guess you could call that the catch-22 of the whole deal. To summon up Yug-Siturath you need a sacrifice. I'm not talking about some run-of-the-mill kind of sacrifice either. To get Yug-Siturath to come to us, I need to sacrifice my own flesh and blood, my one and only daughter."

The girl smiled and looked at Lou. "But it's no big deal. According to Daddy's books I get to live forever too."

"So it's really a win-win kind of situation." the old man said with a smile like a jackal.

"Why me?" Lou asked.

"Let me tell him!" The girl squealed with childlike glee. "Let me tell him!"

"Fine, fine. I'll let you tell him," the old man  smiled again.

"We figured that since we're all going to live forever we should have some fun so we made up this game. I went out looking for chivalrous men, just like you, and told them about Daddy's plans. We wanted to see if anyone would be stupid enough to fall for it. My brother got a little too ambitious with the first couple and killed them before they had a chance to see this through. You should consider yourself lucky. We're letting you live long enough to see the end."

Inside his head, Lou was kicking himself. They had played him like a cheap piano.

The old man pulled back the sleeve of his robe and looked at the gold watch around his wrist. "Damn it anyways, time sure flies when you're having fun. Just sit back and enjoy the show."

The old man and the girl walked toward the altar. Once there, the girl climbed on top of it. Her brother strapped her down with thick leather straps and she looked up at him with a smile on her face. The man looked down at her, the paint on his naked skin glistening. He climbed down and took his place next to the old man at the head of the altar. The old man opened a large book bound in black cloth and flipped through the pages. He stopped and placed it on the altar's surface. He began reading aloud.

"*Trg'nthlp-Rgth'blktlp.*" The old man's voice had deepened and no longer sounded human as he read out loud. "*Y'thpsh-plgstrso, plkrslwp'trntlplk, grth-plktrns'plk!*"

The old man grew louder as he read more of the inhuman words from the book. After minutes of chanting he drew a gold-handled dagger from underneath his robe. Reality throbbed and Lou's head throbbed with it. He couldn't take his eyes off the old man, his anger boiling up, and he prayed for the strength to break free.

The old man stopped for a moment and drew the blade across his hand, covering the clean steel blade with his blood. He read another passage and passed the dagger to the young man, who dragged the blade across his hand as well. The young man's eyes were wild and bestial, looking at his bound sister with animal lust. The old man read another passage while the younger one climbed onto the altar and readied his body to thrust the blade into the girl's heart, his arms raised high above his head, both hands gripping the handle tight.

"*Yght-vplstlk! Yug-Siturath! Yug-Siturath! YUG-SITURATH!*"

The young man's arms came down and the blade thrust into the girl's breast. The sky became alive with dark energy and swirled above their heads with great ferocity. Black fog swelled from the sea, swirling around each of them and kissing them with cold darkness. The young man looked at his body and saw the white paint slowly being swallowed by the black. The paint seemed alive and he began thrashing violently and scratching, as if covered by bugs. He yowled and fell to the floor.

"Something's wrong!" the old man yelled through the noise. "Something isn't right!"

He fell silent as the whirlwind of fog enveloped him. Lou watched as the old man's skin peeled away and left only dried bones that dropped to the floor like a puppet with its strings cut.

The girl's back arched and her dead eyes opened; they had turned totally black and shone like marbles in her face. The dagger slowly slid out of her chest and flew off into the shadows. The fog swirled above her, the tornado-like tail focusing at her wound. It began flowing into her lifeless corpse, causing the body to twitch and thrash. More and more of the fog disappeared into her. Lou struggled with the ropes; the pain in his chest no longer mattered to him. The dock began to smolder and Lou could feel it through his shoes.

The dock surged beneath his feet and the area where the altar stood fell into the sea. Lou was thrown onto his back and he stared into the stars, the surf crashing to the shore and the full moon shining in his eyes.

## 6.

The paramedics wrapped bandages around Lou's chest and put splints on his knees. They replaced the tourniquets on his legs and told him how he probably wasn't going to be able to keep them, as if they were just rentals and they were due back in the shop for the next customer. Two kind men and a gentle woman placed him on a gurney. They put an oxygen mask over his mouth and held his hand like a kind mother might do. He would have thanked them if he could, but all that came out of his mouth was gibberish.

"*Yug-Siturath. Yug-Siturath. Yug-Siturath,*" was all that he could say and he repeated it again and again and again.

As they wheeled him to the ambulance a beautiful woman in a red dress approached. She took each step with grace and poise, walking like any good woman should. "What happened, officer? It looks like a bomb went off or something." The woman's voice was sweet like honey. Lou perked up as she spoke to the policeman. "We're not really sure. All we've got is rubble and dead bodies. It could've been a bomb but this don't really look right for it." The policeman took off his hat and scratched his head. "Looks more like an earthquake or some kind of force of nature."

She walked to Lou and put her hand on his shoulder. The policeman blocked Lou's view of the woman. "Who is this unfortunate soul?"

"We're not really sure. He ain't got any ID on him. But I tell you what. He has got to be the luckiest son-of-a-bitch in the world to survive whatever the hell this was."

The woman pushed past the policeman and looked at Lou. He stared at the woman's face and his mouth opened in terror. The woman in red was *the* girl, good as new and looking more beautiful than ever. Lou snapped, lunging for the girl with all the strength he could muster but barely lifted his back from the gurney. He began screaming and the paramedics held him down.

"He sure *is* lucky." She smiled and looked at him with dark eyes, deep and black as the abyss of night.

"You're dead!" Lou screamed. "I saw you dead! This isn't right! It's the devil! You've got the devil in you!"

"Jesus Christ!" The policeman jumped back. "Give him a morphine shot or something."

The paramedics pushed the needle into his arm and he calmed. His eyes closed slowly as he chanted.

"*Yug-Siturath, Yug-Siturath, Yug-Siturath.*"

# THE MOUTH

## William Meikle

---

nd after he killed her he cut out the clitoris."

"Well, that settles it," she said. "It can't have been a man. If it had been, he'd never have found it."

I looked up at her over the top of my drink, but there was no humour in her eyes.

There rarely was.

"I don't know why I'm telling you this," I said. I took a long swig of beer and brushed the foam from my upper lip. "If the boss ever finds out, I'll be knocked back to traffic control. This is all hush-hush. The tabloids haven't even got hold of it yet."

"I should hope not," Jane Woolsey replied. "If they get so much as a whiff that I'm involved, you won't see me for dust."

I didn't blame her. I remembered the last time. She found the body for us, the lurid headlines soon followed, and a media circus set up permanent camp on her doorstep. I would do everything in my power to make sure that didn't happen again.

She played with her hair, twirling the blond tresses around her little finger, a faraway look in her eyes, staring fixedly at something in the far distance that only she could see.

I leaned over and took her hand.

"I'll keep the press out of it, Jane. I really will."

There was a deep resignation in her voice as she replied.

"I know you'll try. But will you succeed?" She sighed and took a long sip from her drink. "Let's just get on with it. I take it you brought something for me? You didn't bring me out here just to hold my hand?"

I realized that I was stroking my index finger along the soft skin between her thumb and forefinger. Suddenly, embarrassed, I let her hand drop.

"Don't worry," she said, and this time there was a sparkle of humour in her eyes. "I won't tell anybody."

---

To cover my discomfort I reached into my inside pocket, but not before checking that no-one in the quiet bar was looking our way.

"The boss doesn't know I've got this. He'll have my guts for garters if he finds out." I handed a handkerchief over the table.

Her pupils dilated as she took the flimsy piece of cloth. Almost immediately her eyes rolled up in their sockets until only white showed beneath her fluttering eyelids. She moaned; a deep bass drone. I thought she might be in pain, but she gasped, just once.

I wanted to reach over, to take her hand, but I knew better than to interrupt. This was a crucial moment.

She screamed, mouth gaping to show twin rows of perfect teeth, nostrils flaring. Her head fell forwards, a swathe of hair obscuring her face, shoulders trembling violently. She flung the piece of cloth away and screamed again, louder this time. The handkerchief floated slowly off the edge of the table, but Jane's body beat it on the way down.

Her head hit the hard wooden floor with a loud thud that echoed in the silence of the small bar.

By the time I got round the table she was shaking, in the throes of a fit. I lifted her by the shoulders and hugged her to my chest, brushing away the barmaid who was hovering beside, half-heartedly offering help.

"No, just leave her — she'll be all right in a minute," I said, stroking Jane's hair. I rocked her softly from side to side. It seemed to calm her.

She opened her eyes and looked up. I was shocked to see tears in her eyes.

"Get me out of here, Dave. Take me home, please."

I lifted her to her feet and she stood, unsteady at first, staring out the customers in the bar until they had all turned back to their drinks. She walked to the door unaided, but as soon as it had shut behind us she leaned on my arm.

"You're going to have to be careful. This one's a bad one."

That was all she would say. She sat, quiet and pale beside me, silent as I tried to find out what she had seen, where she had been. Even as I left her at her door, she refused to speak.

"Not now. Not here in the dark. Come round tomorrow."

She turned away and then seemed to think better of it, looking back at me.

"I meant what I said though. Be very careful."

A chill ran up my spine as I turned back to the car, a chill that stayed with me all the way back to the station. It was still there as I entered the station, but was soon dispersed by Sergeant Briggs and a cup of steaming coffee.

Briggs was an office regular. His wife had long since gone, unable to cope with the unusual hours the police kept. It didn't seem to bother

Briggs . . . he spent all his spare time here anyway, and if anything, he seemed happier now than before. Besides . . . he made great coffee.

"Couldn't sleep again, Sir?" the Sergeant asked, a wide grin on his face. He knew full well that I shared his problem . . . I just couldn't keep from the job.

"Aye, something like that, Sergeant."

The coffee burned away at the roof of my mouth. I sighed loudly as its warmth spread through my stomach.

"Nearly as good as whisky," I said appreciatively, holding my cup up in a mock-salute. "Anything going on?"

Briggs snorted in disgust.

"The Chief is out at another one of his dinners, PC Douglas is plugged into his computer again, the night shift have been called out to a disturbance in the town centre, and I'm trying to make sense of the pathologist's report. Apart from that, everybody else has packed up for the night."

He stopped, and looked so serious that I almost laughed.

"If you don't mind me saying so, Sir, it might be better if you did the same yourself. You look like shit."

This did make me laugh, but my heart wasn't in it.

"Aye — I know, but I've got a bad feeling about this guy. I don't think he's going to stop."

It was only then that the Sergeant's remark about the pathologist's report struck me.

"So what's this about old Swan's report? Don't tell me he cocked it up again?"

"No, he's done a good job. I just don't understand the conclusions. Come through and I'll show you."

Apart from a single angle-poise lamp centre on his desk, Briggs room was cloaked in darkness. The desk itself was strewn with open reports and papers. He had obviously been busy for quite some time.

"Just let me run through it with you, Sir. We'll see if you can make anything of it," he said. He started to talk in that sing-song manner cops do when giving a report.

"Mary Wells, 23, single, no current boyfriend. One ex-lover with a cast-iron alibi. Secretary at a reputable firm of estate agents. She's sitting at home watching television when, round about midnight, someone knocks at her door. We've surmised this from the fact that there are no recorded calls to her house that evening, and from physical evidence found on the doorstep . . . but I'll get on to that later.

"The villain comes in, is he known to her? We don't know, but there are no signs of struggle in the hallway, or on the stairs. It's only when we get to the bedroom that we find any evidence of the intruder at all, and even that doesn't get us very far.

"They may have had sex — but there's no bruising, no scratches, no tissue under the victim's nails — and he kills her — method as yet unknown. He draws a picture on her abdomen — something that looks like a nest of snakes emerging from a giant mouth . . . a pattern that might or might not be significant . . . and takes her eyes, nipples, and part of her genitalia before he's finished. All without leaving any trace of how he did it.

"Or so we thought last night anyway."

He sat back in his chair and sighed, looking more tired than I had ever seen him.

"I've had PC Douglas check up on the pattern. He reckons that it's a representation of Haraffnir — a Celtic water serpent with supernatural power . . . or it may be something older, something that inspired, or frightened, the Celts in the first place . . . if you can believe any of that. Apparently it was famous for carrying off and mutilating young women."

He gave me another long sigh and closed the folders in front of him.

"I'm getting too old for this shit," he said, "Begging your pardon, Sir."

"That's all right," I replied, "most days I know just how you feel. But what's got you so worked up? You haven't told me anything we didn't know yesterday."

The Sergeant picked up a report and slid it across the table.

"Three things," he began. "One . . . the lab report on some earth found on the victim's doorstep, only it's not earth. From the concentration of rotted vegetation they reckon it could only have come from the bottom of the deep sea . . . and recently too."

"So we're looking for a fisherman or a scuba diver then?" I asked hopefully.

"Aye, maybe," Briggs replied. "I hope so, I really do."

He rocked back in his chair and stared at the ceiling. This time I recognised the look on his face . . . it wasn't tiredness this time, it was fear. The Sergeant's voice barely rose above a whisper as he continued.

"The victim's lungs were full of water mixed with brown organic matter. She drowned. And guess what the analysis of the water told us?"

"Don't tell me . . . the deep sea bottom?"

"Right first time. They didn't have sex, but her vagina also carried traces of the same water . . . as did her bath tub."

I sipped the dregs of the coffee as I tried to take in this latest information.

"So where did the water come from? Do you know how far we are from the nearest sea bed? It must be nearly a hundred miles. Did the villain lug the water all the way? And just how much do you need to kill somebody?"

"Now you see what I've been sitting here thinking about. I had the house's system checked out . . . nothing there but standard tap water."

"You said there were three things?" I asked, hoping that more information might shed light on the problem. I was to be disappointed.

"Aye. Three things. The earth on the doorstep, the water in the lungs, and best of all, no prints, no fibers, no physical evidence apart from the water. It's as if he was never there."

I nearly choked on my last mouthful of coffee.

"What? Nothing at all?"

Briggs looked serious. "Not a single hair. I've never seen anything like it. The lab boys are mystified. I've sent them back to get more samples, just in case it's all a huge cock-up. They're over there now.

"They wanted to wait 'til morning but, begging your pardon, Sir — I told them that you'd have their balls in a basket if they tried to file that report. And one last thing just to cheer you up . . . the boys from the press have got whiff of the story. They're already encamped outside the house."

I stood and stretched my spine, palms pressed hard against the flat of my back. I was acutely aware of the layers of fat which I had to press against, and I groaned as my bones resisted any movement.

"I think I'll go over there and take a look around. Maybe I'll see something I missed the last time. You never know, we've got to get lucky sometime. In the meantime, get the ex-boyfriend in for a chat. We should have spent more time on him yesterday . . . maybe you're not the only one that's getting too old for this shit."

I gave Briggs a mock salute, John Wayne style, and headed out into the night.

When I got to the street where the murder had been committed I almost turned back . . . it had been too long a night, I was tired, and looking at a crime scene always depressed me. Only the thought that the perpetrator was still at large kept me going.

In contrast with the rest of the street, number 23 had every light in the house blazing, a beacon in the darkness. Although it was a cold night, the front door was wide open. A succession of white-coated men carried small plastic bags to a van in the driveway.

A huddle of reporters stood in the garden nursing cups of coffee. I hoped that no-one had been stupid enough to talk with them yet. I would have to call a press conference sooner rather than later . . . but not just yet. As I approached the house the reporters noticed me. They came forward with their usual bluster, flash units carried before them like revolvers. It was only when I got to the front door that I managed to shrug them off.

"Just stay there," I said. "I'll tell all of you what we know when I come out."

I hoped that would keep them quiet for a while, but I knew my picture was going to be splashed across the papers in the morning. I just wished I'd combed my hair.

The crime scene was like any other. Whatever it was that had made this house a home had long since gone, leaving only a clinical silence through which white-coated policemen moved slowly and reverentially. I looked down on the dead girl's bed for long seconds, but nothing came to me. My mind was blank and my body was tired. All I wanted to do was lie down on soft pillows and let blackness take me away.

It wasn't to be. I was jolted out of my reverie by someone calling my name. It was only on the second occasion that I recognized the voice, and by then the reporters were on her like a pack of jackals.

I ran down the stairs, almost knocking over a rookie who was too scared, too embarrassed to berate me. I flung open the door and found myself looking straight at Jane. The flashes going off around us lit up the road like a dance floor strobe, but she wasn't in any mood for dancing.

Her eyes were flat and black.

"It's coming for me," she said.

I pushed past several reporters who were almost dropping their notebooks in a rush to get closer to her.

"It knows who I am and it's coming for me."

I put out a hand, whether to comfort or to push her away I'm still not sure, but she interpreted it as a welcome and fell into my arms. The reporters went crazy and I had to lead Jane away. If we'd stayed there we wouldn't just have been on the front page, we'd give them enough to fill the whole paper.

I commandeered a car from one of the forensics boys, and just made it back to the station in front of the chasing pack. Jane didn't say a word, just stared straight ahead, hot and heavy tears running down her cheeks.

Reception was like a war zone. Four young constables were trying, unsuccessfully, to get two very drunk teenagers away from a baying pack of their friends. The arrival of the reporters didn't help matters, and several heads were cracked together and some blood spilled before sanity was finally restored. The reporters were dispatched out onto the pavement, along with the more sober teenagers. The rest were taken down to the cells. All in all it was a good twenty minutes before I was able to get Jane into a quiet room, and by that time she was in deep shock.

I sat her down in a chair and went to get some coffee . . . I had a feeling that the night was nowhere near over.

Before I went back to her I instructed Briggs to keep an ear open for anything that might indicate that our man had done another one, but as yet nothing had come in.

Jane had her head in her hands as I entered the room, and when she looked up at me her eyes were red-rimmed and moist.

"It's coming for me," she said again. I was shocked at the resignation in her voice. "It knows where I am and its coming for me."

"You're safe here, " I said.

She shook her head.

"Not from this I'm not."

The crying started again. I wanted to hold her, to comfort her, but here in the station I was more used to the round of interrogation and recrimination.

I stood quiet and watched her cry — I wasn't proud of it, but I needed whatever information she had.

"Tell me," I said softly. "Please, tell me — we need to get this guy . . . and soon."

"Guy?" She tried to laugh, but didn't quite manage it.

Her voice was weak as she replied.

"I don't know if anything I can tell you will do any good, and I know you won't believe me anyway, but here goes."

She took a long swig of coffee and a deep breath.

"First of all . . . it's old. I get a sense of great age . . . and great evil. Every time I think about it I think of water. Deep, dark, cold water. Second, it's not human."

She must have seen the thought in my eyes.

"I knew you wouldn't believe me, but that doesn't make it any less real to me. There's one other thing, besides the water that is. I get a picture, a pattern. That's important."

Up to now she had been holding herself together, but her resolve failed in the face of my disbelief. She sobbed in great heaving gasps. This time I couldn't ignore her. I took her in my arms and held her tight, until the tears subsided.

When she offered her mouth for a kiss, I couldn't refuse. I fell into it like a drunk going after a bottle.

Sometime later we were interrupted by a discreet cough from the door. I looked over Jane's shoulder into the smiling face of Sergeant Briggs.

"Sorry to interrupt, Sir, but Donnely . . . the victim's ex . . . has just come in. Do you want to talk to him?"

I held Jane at arm's length and looked into her eyes.

"Are you going to be okay?"

She nodded. She didn't exactly smile, but there was a twinkle in her eye that I had never seen before as I left the room.

My good feelings lasted just as long as it took me to get to my office and see the man in my visitor's chair.

He was wrong . . . there was no other word for it. Maybe some of Jane's talent had worn off on me, or maybe it just came from years of sitting across the desk from criminals, but if this guy wasn't guilty of something then I'd retire straight away.

It was in his eyes . . . a deep flicker of madness that he couldn't hide in spite of his slick hairstyle and sharp suit. Then there was the smile. He showed me all of his teeth as I sat down.

"So what's going on, Inspector? I've already told your guys all I know."

"I doubt that," I said, and took delight as that smile slipped . . . just a bit, but enough.

I settled in my chair and lit a cigarette. I refrained from blowing smoke in his face . . . that would have been just too theatrical.

"I need to know about you and Mary," I said, then leaned back and waited for him to speak. He was good, I'll give him that, but nobody has ever managed to psyche me out when I'm sitting in my own chair. Besides, I had a feeling that this one liked to talk.

I was proven right ten seconds later.

"I met her on holiday last year. When I got back I rang her up and we went out a few times. But she wasn't really my type . . . a bit too frigid if you know what I mean?"

I let out a long plume of smoke before I spoke.

"Where did you go?"

"Eh?"

"I said, where did you go? On holiday?"

"The South Pacific," he said. "As far from this shit-hole as I could get."

"Do any scuba diving? See anything unusual? Like a mouth full of snakes for instance?" I asked.

I don't know where that came from, but a policeman's subconscious spends all its time filtering possibilities, so it's no real surprise when you get just the right question. The only surprise to me was the response I got. I had never seen anyone go white as a sheet before. The blood drained from his face, and his eyes went blank.

"Can I have a cigarette, please?" he asked, and before I replied, had leaned across and grabbed the packet on the table. I put my hand out to stop him, my fingers fell on top of his, and the pictures started to unravel in my head like a high quality film show.

We are on a shoreline, among a field of jagged rocks whose shapes look all wrong. There is still over an hour to nightfall but already there is a chill in the air. Dank weed flops in the wind, and occasionally a piece detaches in the swell, to swim in the ripples for a while before softly sinking to join its decaying brothers.

I look over at Mary. She is shivering, goose-bumps have risen across her chest and her pubic hair looks jet-black in the dim light.

The knife feels cold in my hand as I raise it above my head and begin the chant. Far out over the sea the water rises in a hump, something pushing just under the surface, surging forward as it comes for us. The metal of the knife sings as I bring it down. Mary screams and squirms and the knife sinks deep into the ground by her left shoulder. I try to grab her but she wriggles away, still screaming. The last I see of her is the pale white of her buttocks as she stumbles her way across the jagged rocks.

I just have time to turn back towards the sea when there is a surge of blackness and a great wall of water falls over me, taking me down and away into darkness.

I felt the cigarette pack being taken away from my hand and looked up into a pair of jet-black eyes. No pupil, no white, just pools of blackness. When he spoke his voice was harsh and throaty.

"This one awakened me, and showed me where to find that which had been denied me. Now I will rise again."

He jerked, one sudden convulsion, and he tore with his hands at the front of his shirt, buttons popping in sequence as he bared his chest.

The tattoo was a wondrous piece of art.

The snake-like tentacles glowed in blacks and reds and purples, their coils spiralling inwards to a weeping, drooling maw of a mouth which seemed to flow and bulge in time with his breathing.

His chest rose in one great heave, and the tattoo peeled . . . there is no other word for it . . . actually peeled from his chest, uncoiling in one smooth motion, a tentacled blackness rising from his chair. The air got damp, then damper still, the salty tang of the air stinging my nostrils. I pushed my chair back against the wall and half rose as the room went black around me . . . all black apart from a blood-red maw some four feet across . . . and growing.

I strained to breathe. Greyness gathered in front of my eyes.

Suddenly the weight lifted. The room went quiet. I was left alone in the room, staring at Donnely's Cheshire cat grin.

"The girl first, and then it's your turn," he said, just as the screaming started in the hallway beyond. I wanted to smash that grin backward into his face, but the screams grew louder, and this time I recognised them. I was off the chair and out of the room before the first echo died away, almost knocking over Briggs in the hall.

"Don't let Donnely out of the room!" I shouted as I ran past him.

When I entered the incident room I thought it was too late. The walls ran damp with water. Thick black oily water dripped from the roofs to splash in ever-growing puddles. Jane lay on the floor, still and unmoving as black spirals of serpent-like muscle tightened around her. Hovering above her, a huge wet mouth drooled.

It was only then that I realized she was still alive, still fighting.

Her eyes were open and her face frozen in intense concentration. She seemed to be holding the beast at bay by force of will alone.

I moved closer and tried to grab at the black coils, but my hands slid over its surface and came away wet and slippery. No matter how I tried, I was unable to take hold of anything.

"Too late," a voice came from behind me.

I turned to see Donnely in the doorway. His shirt was open and the tattoo on his chest glowed and flowed in a green luminescent light. He held a pair of scissors. Something dark dripped from the blades. Behind him in the corridor lay Briggs, slumped and unmoving in a growing pool of blood.

"Like I said. First the bitch, then you," Donnely whispered, closing the door behind him and moving into the room.

"There's nowhere for you to go," I said. "Why don't you give yourself up?"

He laughed, and I heard the madness in his voice.

"Nowhere to go? But I am the old one. I go where I please and take what I want. And for now, I want you."

He came forward, the scissors held in a knife-fighter's grip. He was six inches taller than me, twenty years younger and a good two stone lighter. What he didn't have were the years on the street. Or the steel-tipped shoes.

My left foot took him in the balls, and as he curled over, my right knee met his face, smashing his nose almost flat. I grinned as the bone broke. He fell sideways, dropping the scissors. I kicked him in the head, one to keep him down and the second for good measure.

I made sure he stayed down and turned back to Jane, half-hoping to see her free from the grip. She was still held tightly, and the huge dribbling mouth struggled to reach her face.

I stabbed down, hard, and the scissors went in amongst the coils. It was like cutting through water. I pulled my hand backward, feeling the tentacles flow around my wrist. The scissors came out and I caught a burst of bright green to my right. I turned just in time to see the glow fade on the tattoo on Donnely's chest. Stabbing again, still watching Donnely, I saw the tattoo flare in a spot approximating the place where I'd stabbed.

I didn't need a second chance. I scrambled across the floor, splashing through an inch of water. Without a second thought I brought the scissors down hard amid the tattoo and cut, stabbed and chopped my way through Donnely's flesh.

The room got suddenly colder . . . colder and wetter. Jane screamed again, but I couldn't pause, couldn't stop as my right hand went up and came down, went up and came down. Donnely's chest was a mass of red, pulpy gore.

I fell back in the water gasping, letting the scissors fall away and taking in deep, sobbing breaths as Jane pushed herself to her feet and sloughed off sheets of water from her body.

There was no sign of the tentacles, or the wet maw of a mouth.

Jane fell into my arms, and for a short while at least, everything felt like it might just be getting better.

Afterwards there was a lot to explain away. Like several hundred gallons of salt water in the interview room and a suspect with his face beaten to a pulp and his chest carved into strips of ham.

Briggs and I managed to concoct a story between us. I don't think anybody believed us, and we both took early retirement soon after, but at least we got our pensions.

Briggs couldn't take to time away from the job. He's working as a security consultant for a chain of warehouses.

As for me, I married Jane. Two years ago now, and everything has been great.

But just lately I've begun to worry. This morning I smelled sea water in our bedroom.

And when Jane came back from work today she told me that she was thinking about getting a tattoo.

# THE QUESTIONING OF THE AZATHOTHIAN PRIEST

## Recorded by Dr. Anton Zarnak
## Transcribed by C.J. Henderson

The judge's pupils rolled, slamming against the upper lids of his eyes with a martyr's force. He groaned loudly, not with sound, but with the twisting of his body, hissing his pain throughout his chambers. Already knowing the dread answer, still he asked;

"You can't be serious?"

"I've never come before you, your honor, when I wasn't serious."

The speaker was a middle-aged man, tall and rough-shaven, regulation length dark wet curls slopping across his head. It was August in New York City, and the weather was draining the life from the planet. Captain Thorner did not like the city when it reached this stage of unmoving heat. He had only felt it once before. He did not care for it then, either.

"A maniac's been *shot,* Captain," the judge moaned. "Murdered. And you want me to dismiss it."

"It's been known to happen."

"And that *man* was known to be in the hands of the city's police department at the time," the judge said, his words set at a distinct tone, as if anyone needed any reminding. "The man was being questioned by police as his lawyer waited in the next room."

The judge closed his eyes for a moment, his left hand to his face. Rubbing at his eyes, more for distraction than anything else, he mused. "It's not bad enough the city fathers look like fools, not ready in any way — Canal Street just buckles — an earthquake, an earthquake in New York City . . . and now you saddle us with this, this . . ."

"I'm aware of what it looks like –"

"Oh, you are? Then tell me, Captain," demanded the judge, his voice trembling with a rage bordering the religious, "what am I supposed to tell that boy's mother?"

"Your honor," interrupted the only other person present. "Before you tell anyone anything, I propose you set aside your biases and read the report."

Silence fell across the room in ripples, fat rolling ones, like layers of caramel folding into a pan. It emanated from the judge, the strength of it sniffing for lies or half-truths, deception of any kind.

"And why would I believe *anything* you have to say, Dr. Zarnak?"

The other man stared at the judge. His visage made him seem a youth, but though his face was unlined, his eyes whispered of un-counted years. He was tall, slender and saturnine, with a fine-boned visage as sallow as antique ivory. His hair was thick and black as night, save for a dramatic silver streak that began at his right temple and zigzagged backward to the base of his skull.

"Because I am a man of honor and I know of things that you cannot imagine."

The sallow mouth moved precisely, spitting words cold and crisp, "You pray that what they say about me isn't true. But, in your locked away heart of hearts, you know it is, and you fear that all your power is just some worthless speck, a puff of nonsense in a mad world."

"Anton," said the Captain softly, his fingers brushing the doctor's arm, auras joining for the moment of contact needed for true conver-sation . . .

The single word worked. Zarnak reeled in his anger — resumed his mask. He could always count on Thorner to remind him not to dwell on any single stupidity in the world around him. It was always those kinds of moments that killed Zarnak's kind, those ridiculous instances of emotion where logical and calm reason were sacrificed in an insane attempt to beat another at his own game. Ego. Mages could not afford such luxuries. Going where he should have in the first place, he set a vibration in his voice that would make the judge more . . . open to suggestion.

"Your honor," a pause was added to allow the moment of respect-given to balance the weight of the coming request, "for everyone's sake, just read the report."

Judge Tyler Reis's head snapped back a quarter of an inch, the sides of it tightening visibly at the ears. His emotions jumbled, his subcon-scious pushed him along the path of least resistance while his momen-tarily scrambled consciousness pulled itself together.

Reis looked down at the document that was suddenly in his hand with shock. It was political suicide to touch a case like this. An honest man, but a careful one, he wanted no part of the nightmare he could see headed for whichever member of the judiciary signed off on this one. Why had he accepted it? He had told himself he would stay out . . .

It did not matter. Reis shrugged with resignation. He had allowed them to make contact, to force his hand. His breath filled with the chill of long dreaded fear, the defeat in it so palpable that it pained him to listen to it. Sitting back in his chair, he decided to just get it over with. Folding back the cover sheet, just a title page concerning certain city-significant numbers, he started with the first paragraph.

My name is Dr. Anton Zarnak. In my capacity as a trained psychiatrist, I was brought in by Capt. Mark Thorner to assist in the interrogation of one Tidril Belbin. The following is a transcription of that account, with commentary by myself at the appropriate junctures.

To begin: I arrived at the station shortly before 9:00PM, the time scheduled for interrogation. I studied the prisoner before hand through the standard two-way glass. It served no purpose. Despite the relative newness of these stations, subject knew he was being observed. More-over, he assumed a stance designed to indicate that he could see through the glass as well, and that he was studying those on the other side.

I note this here since I would expect others to as well, and I wish to strongly point out certain aspects of this interrogation as uniformly disturbing to those in attendance. On more than one occasion during the preliminary observation, Belbin made references which made no sense unless taken in context with what was happening on the other side of the wall, down to and including the rejoinder "Gods bless you" when patrolman Daniels sneezed, and then said "Thank you" to Belbin as he wiped his nose.

Seeing the futility of continuing the "unsuspected observation" we moved inside to confront the suspect. While he was questioned by Captain Thorner I put together the following portfolio on the man.

Belbin could best be described as benevolently arrogant. I see him as a potentially dangerous individual simply because he absolutely believes that existence is futile. If he were to choose to retire from the folly of said futility, he would end his life in a millisecond. I believe if the idea were to come into his head on its own, he might possibly die then and there.

If he were to decide to feel pity toward others, though, he could become the most dangerous of random killers the world has ever seen. There are no simple terms to label such an individual. He is power-ful — within his own mind — to the point of invincibility.

Further: On the question of Rationality: Belbin is the most rational of creatures. He is highly intelligent, ruthlessly logical and exactingly precise.

On the question of Sanity: Belbin would be insane if his belief in himself were misplaced. Since it is not, he must be thought of as –

◆  ◆  ◆

"*Sane?*"

Reis slammed the document against his desk.

"I won't stand for this, Zarnak. Who do you . . . oh, I won't go there again. But, damn you. How am I supposed to explain this to anyone else?"

"You're not, Tyler," said the Captain softly. "You're supposed to understand what actually happened, and then figure out how to explain it all. Any way you can."

"But, what are you asking me to accept here? For God's sake, Thorner, I mean . . . yes . . . what you've brought me in the past — images flashed through Reis's mind – dozens of sailors, slaughtered for their blood; tornadoes caused by "things," as the Captain had called them, "personalities, angels — well, demons really. But, incredibly powerful, Godlike; the winged bodies that had been brought in, burned and slashed; that ape thing –

"This is . . ."

Reis went silent. He knew someone had to read the report. Someone official had to sign off on one of the most terrible murders in the city's colorful history. During the war, people were easier to distract when the insanity hit and Zarnak prowled the streets. But now, with the monster Hitler and the miserable reptile Tojo off the front pages, the newspapers were always looking for some new creature to bleat about to the rest of the sheep.

Tidril Belbin could be that monster.

Judge Tyler Reis turned back to the report. He skimmed over the rest of Zarnak's opening remarks. They mostly concerned things with which the judge was already all too familiar — the circumstances of Belbin's arrest, the young women's bodies found, the mindless carving, blood paintings, the charnel pits. Indeed, what was in the report was old news — there was still information coming in, new discoveries, new terrors to hide being unearthed in Belbin's mansion . . .

Freak palace is more like it, Reis thought, remembering the horrible, horrible photos. Monster — goddamned monster . . .

"It's not a good enough word, anymore," the judge muttered under his breath.

"What isn't?" asked Thorner.

"Monster."

Thorner moved his eyes in a noncommittal gesture. He added his shoulders to the motion. Zarnak sat impassively. Waiting. The judge skimmed the rest of the regular formula of the report, finally getting to page 8, the statement. It's statement. Belbin's words. His justification, his attempt at self-exoneration, absolution, legitimacy . . .

Reis shut down his indignation and his horror and got down to business by reading;

## Explanatory Excerpt 1:

Here within Belbin explains himself in relationship to his deity.

Bel: "You must understand, I am a priest of Azathoth. I do what is expected."

Tho: "Meaning you're thinking of yourself as a member of the clergy? You're thinking this gives you some kind of special rights?"

Bel: [amused] "Meaning, Captain Thorner, friend of Anton Zarnak, that as a priest of Azathoth, I need not really worry about such as you."

Tho: "Really. When you want to leave, you'll what? Snap yourfingers? Snap. Like that? And this Assholethoth, he'll just come and save you?"

Bel: "Hardly. Azathoth pays his followers no mind. Nor does he need to. After all, I am powerful enough to destroy you all with but a moment's concentration. In other words, I have only accompanied you here because it pleases me to do so."

Tho: "You're a tough guy, is that what you're saying?"

Bel: "I am all-powerful, Captain."

Tho: "You? You're the one who's all-powerful. Not this god you shill for?"

Bel: "Azathoth simply is what is. At the center of all time and space, all existence and dreams, all that can be and will be, there exists Azathoth. Greatest of them all.

"What you must realize, of course, is that we do not exist as he exists – we but exist somewhere within the deep and violent crevices of his mind. All of us, Captain Thorner, friend to Anton Zarnak, you and all you know and all you do not know. Azathoth creates fate and destiny, love and chaos. His dreams are our substance. His nightmares, our calamities. He is the absolute, true, pure and only lord of existence."

Tho: "Well, if you won't mind the asking, why would it please such a powerful nabob as yourself to consort with us lowly types?"

Bel: "Please, Captain, what more could I ask for? I plan on placing the city under my control. I've decided mastery of one small planet is something Azathoth can be directed toward. Please understand, his unconscious whims are our reality. There are those of us who have begun to unlock his secrets. Once I've finished my work here, it will be safe for me to proceed with my overall plan."

Tho: "Your work here? And what business do you think you have here outside of answering for your crimes?"

Bel: [smiling] "Captain Thorner, friend of Anton Zarnak, you two individuals are really the only people who could stop me, if, of course, you knew to what extent my powers reach. But, by coming here quietly, I am able to have you both together in one place, not yet prepared to think of me as a menace worthy of your full powers. You consider me a madman, nothing more than a simple psychopath. Your thoughts at present are to do no more than evaluate me."

Tho: "And what are you here for?"

Bel: "I've come to eliminate the two of you."

Reis fanned himself with the report. Though the horrible heat had begun to subside, still it sent the sweat running down his face — neck, chest, everywhere. The fanning turned the rivulets into icy fingers, chilling his body. As he closed his eyes for a moment, a shudder ran through him. His voice a whisper, he asked;

"Why does he say he came to eliminate you? You two? Why would he want to?"

"It's all in the re –"

"Just *tell* me," snapped the judge.

"Belbin thought it was within his reach to take over the world," answered Thorner matter-of-factly. "He felt Anton was the only mystic close at hand who could counteract his abilities. He also claimed to be somewhat worried about me because I was the one member of the force who had consistently been able to deal with things beyond the normal mortal ken. Working as a team, he saw us as, at the least, a formidable nuisance. His plan, therefore, was to get us both in the same place and destroy us."

"And why didn't his plan work?"

"We destroyed him first." Zarnak's cool words brought a rising bile into the judge's throat.

"Yes, that's why we're here in the first place — because you allowed this pathetic lunatic to be . . ."

"Your honor," Zarnak said the title drily, flirting with the idea of finding it humorous, "every minute you spend arguing with us allows this affair to drag on longer — the main thing I believe you wish to avoid. Again I recommend that you . . . read the report."

Once more the doctor set that particular vibration in his voice that bent the judge toward cooperation. Once more the judge turned back to the report. He picked up where he had left off, amazed at the self-assurance of Belbin. Wondering if it came from his faith, Reis skipped to:

## Explanatory Excerpt 14:

Here within Belbin explains Azathoth itself.

Tho: "So when you offered these sacrifices to this . . . Azathoth . . ."

Bel: "Offer sacrifices . . . [amused, distant] . . . I do not offer sacrifices to anyone or anything, Captain."

Tho: "But the women you . . . murdered . . . why did you do it? Weren't they . . . don't you offer sacrifices to this thing of yours?"

Bel: "You are so hopelessly mundane, Captain Thorner, friend of Anton Zarnak, so wonderfully low.

"Azathoth does not accept sacrifice. He does not bestow gifts. A priest of Azathoth is an explorer. A miner. Those who flock to the mindless one do so to gain insights, notions on how best to manipulate the universe."

Tho: "You want to explain yourself?"

Bel: "Through drugs and dreams, I have found my way through the layers of reality and deception on down through to the center of existence. There lies Azathoth, steaming and whirling, mad beyond reason, not maybe even living — not actually alive in the sense that we understand it.

"He is perhaps more of a, a reaction, a contradiction. There is no way to know if, awake, Azathoth would actually be conscious. If he ever does awaken, of course, we will all blink out of existence. Instantly. If he ever remembers us, the planets we stride, the voids in between, we will snap back into existence. And if he remembers us as fiddler crabs, then we will snap back into existence and fiddle our lives out on the bottom of the sea.

"Dr. Zarnak knows this. I have seen him, skulking the high planes, gazing on great Azathoth, watching from afar, afraid to approach closer. I am not afraid.

"I have learned the dreams Azathoth enjoys. I live them to give myself a scent he finds pleasing. I curl within the folds of his immenseness, each time bringing away knowledge and more.

"Azathoth is power. He is power that I mine for myself."

Reis set the report down as his phone clanged on his desk. He took the call, not caring what it might be about. Anything that turned his attention away if for even a moment from the Belbin insanity was welcome. The question on what to do with the new quake victims that were being found proved all too easy to handle.

Before he knew it, the judge was finished with the caller. His mouth dry, neck sweating, he cradled the receiver back on its perch.

I'm getting too old for this, Reis thought sadly. He was, consciously, thinking on his appointment to manage the disaster relief coordination. Subconsciously, however, he was thinking of Belbin. Just too goddamned old.

He breezed over part of the suspect's statement where he confessed to the murders. "Confessed," of course, was not exactly the right word. That implied resistance on Belbin's part, a certain amount of coercion to gain the admission. The priest had needed no prompting to list his dark crimes. He laid out what he had done, to whom he had done it, how often, to what degree, with the thoroughness of a surgeon and the dull precision of a certified public accountant.

The lists of atrocities went on for pages. Kidnapping the victims, drugging them, incarceration, mutilation. All of it was there on the page, Belbin's words recorded in court approved detail, how he had skinned the girls alive, taken tongs to their fingernails, burned out their eyes, used razors on their tongues, on their fingers, their underarms, their ears and breasts and abdomens . . .

Reis read Belbin's descriptions of the things he had already read about in police reports: the bath tub filled with blood, the bloody fingerprints everywhere, the walls and ceilings of the old main room, painted with blood, festooned with organs, the four-poster bed in the center of it all, draped with intestines utilized as curtains . . .

Reis looked up from the report for a long moment. His mind whirled, desperate to find an escape route. He found nothing. He knew Zarnak had somehow tricked him into picking up the report, into accepting the resolving of the Belbin mess.

If only the madman hadn't been appointed an attorney, thought the judge. Hell, he hadn't even wanted one. But, oh no, procedure is all, and so now we have this gadfly buzzing, and the police asking for a cover-up, and this, this . . . he shook the report in his hand with violence . . . and we have *this* to explain it all away.

With a dry and weary sigh, Judge Reis returned to the report, turning to:

## Explanatory Excerpt 23:

Here within Belbin explains his power.

Tho: "So, you think of yourself as what, exactly? Some kind of demon? Or god? What?"

Bel: "I am but a man, like yourself, Captain. I have simply armed myself, as you have armed yourself. My weapons are merely more powerful than yours. As mankind has learned to plunge daggers into the hearts of atoms to split them open, so too have I absorbed the knowledge of this power from great Azathoth. Indeed, to wipe this city from the face of the planet would be simplicity itself."

Tho: "Then why don't you?"

Bel: "As I told you, Captain Thorner, friend of Anton Zarnak, I like this city. It will serve well as my capitol. [highly amused] But I will obliterate some other municipality if you so desire."

Tho: "Yeah, well, maybe later. Right now, why don't you tell me exactly how you're going to eliminate Dr. Zarnak and myself."

Bel: "I have no specific preference. Is there some way you wished to die, Captain? I might be able to oblige you."

Tho: "Oh, well that's swell of you. But perhaps you could just outline any way that comes to mind, strictly for illumination, you see. After all, to us, the way we see it, you're a prisoner. You have no weapons, your hands are cuffed, your legs are shackled . . . it seems like eliminating people should be a bit out of your reach right now."

Bel: "You view the world through such a narrow window, Captain Thorner, friend of Anton Zarnak. But why not? The simplest way to dispose of you both will simply be to think you out of existence. First, though not necessary, I would most likely seek to remove your restraints."

[At this point, Belbin stared at his handcuffs. One by one the links began to disappear. There was a sound akin to escaping steam accompanied by small flashes of light as each one slipped out of existence]

Bel: "At this point, it is all a matter of whim, really. I might collapse the building on you, combust you down to ashes, reinvent you as . . . as maybe fiddler crabs . . . the possibilities are endless."

Tho: "And we're helpless to stop you. You're saying there's simply nothing we could do to stop you?"

Bel: "Quite. Allow me to demonstrate. Captain, please pull your service revolver and shoot me."

[Belbin's cajoling at this point went on for some time. Eventually, not so much to humor him, but more to frighten him into silence, the Captain did attempt to bring forth his weapon. He could not. His limbs were frozen in place, as were my own. I am certain Officer Daniels will report the same sensation]

Bel: "You see, Captain Thorner, friend of Anton Zarnak, I am completely safe. If you try to rise, looking to defend yourself with physical violence, you will find you cannot. My power is infinite at this point, and you are well within the boundaries of my infinity. Your aide, poor Officer Daniels, so less experienced in these matters, I have reduced to a puppet.

"Dr. Zarnak's mind I have entered as well. No spells can he utter. No hand gestures can he make. I set these precautions into motion before you even entered the room."

"You're telling me you actually watched his handcuffs disappear — link by link — right there in front of you?"

"Yes, your honor."

"No sleight of hand, no stage trickery?"

"No, sir."

"And you really did try to pull your weapon?"

"If I could have gotten it out of its holster," said Thorner, "I would have shot him then and there."

The judge stared, unblinking. He could not have imagined such a response coming from the seasoned commander. Thorner was the most highly decorated officer in the city. Reis knew him to be extremely capable and cool under pressure. Without questioning him further, the judge turned back to the report, picking up where he had left off.

Tho: "So, when exactly will all this eliminating take place?"

Bel: "As soon as I have ascertained what exactly your friend, Dr. Zarnak, is up to."

Tho: "What do you mean, Tidril?"

Bel: "Captain, you play the game well, but there is little you can do against one who can read minds. Do not look surprised. Surely you must understand that one who can pierce the veils between dimensions can peer into the thoughts of mortals. Or should I say, most mortals.

"Dr. Zarnak is clever enough to shield his thoughts from me. Even immobilized as he is, it is certain he is trying to find some way past your shared predicament. Aren't you, Anton?"

Zar: "There is no need to."

Bel: "Really?"

Zar: "Yes. I've already taken precautions against you, Tidril. How could

I not? I have observed you, obscenely licking at Azathoth's teat, suckling power. When I was called here to observe you, I knew things would come to a moment like this. You are too careful a being to expose yourself by accident. Any creature that can whisper in Azathoth's ear without bringing about its own end is certainly capable of tip-toeing around the police.

"No, I assumed you wished to be captured. And, considering that you are a creature without remorse, such meant you had something in mind."

Bel: "How amusing. The good doctor lives up to his reputation. And how will you accomplish this?"

Zar: "I will wait until you are distracted with some moment of foolishness, and then I will cause you to cease to exist."

Bel: "I believe you might. And wouldn't that be foolish on my part, to allow you to use my own flamboyance of the moment against me. Very well, Dr. Zarnak, friend of Captain Thorner, perhaps I should put things to an end here and now."

[So saying, Belbin smiled and raised his hands. At this point the building began to shake]

Zar: "Officer Daniels — fetch Mr. Belbin some tea."

[At this point Officer Daniels pulled his service revolver and fired, shooting Tidril Belbin between the eyes. The priest died instantly. The earthquake his summoning began faded as quickly as it had begun]

Reis rubbed at his burning eyes. Looking absently toward the window of his chambers, not focusing on anything, not looking at the others in the room, he asked;

"What did you do, Zarnak?"

"Belbin was correct. I had observed him on Azathoth's plane. It is my duty to watch for such creatures. When I was summoned here, I suspected the possibility Belbin was ready to make some sort of move. Before going into the first observation room, I spoke to Officer Daniels, giving him what you might call a post-hypnotic suggestion. I told him that if I ordered him to get some tea for anyone, he was to pull his weapon and shoot to kill."

Reis closed his eyes. It was all far beyond him. He was a good judge, a good weigher of evidence with a sound talent for gauging the truth in a man's voice. Thorner, Zarnak, Daniels, none of them were lying. As much as he wanted to believe they were, he knew they were not.

"How long will it take for you two to produce an alternate report?"

"Already done, your honor," responded Thorner, his tone level. "Pretty much reads the same. Says at the end that Belbin broke his cuffs, strength of a madman, that kind of thing. Says he turned over the table, got his hands around my throat. Officer Daniels was only doing his duty."

Tears formed in the judge's tired eyes. Such a simple deception. And, it was not as if he had not protected the police in the past. The court appointed lawyer would buy it — surely. The papers, the radio stations, of course they would accept it. It made the perfect end to the story — mad killer forces police to kill him. All neatly tied up.

Reis rubbed his eyes once more. The horrible heat had dropped considerably. It had been building for weeks, every day a few degrees hotter than the one before, less than the day to come. Ever climbing, until, that was, the earthquake.

Earthquake.

The judge's body sagged. Perhaps with the happy ending, with the madman and all his terrible secrets to chatter about, with the earthquake and the still mounting property damage and loss of life, perhaps no one would notice his signature on the case. Perhaps no one would question his ruling, perhaps –

"Zarnak," Reis asked, eyes still closed, ears carefully listening for the answer to come. "Was he really as powerful as he thought he was? I mean, he claimed to . . . to be like a human atom bomb. Was he? Could he? I mean –"

As the judge's voice quavered, Zarnak answered quietly, soothingly;

"He was just a madman, your honor. One the good police of New York City dispatched with their usual aplomb. Really, nothing more should be made of it."

Softly, the report on Tyler Reis's desk was replaced with another. That done, the two men withdrew from the judge's chambers, exiting out into the hall. As they made their way down the hall, Thorner asked;

"Is that what he was going to do, when he started the earthquake runnin'? Was he goin' to Hiroshima the city?"

Zarnak thought for a moment. His friend had seen so much over the years, dealt with so many sinister nightmares. It was true that Thorner was a strong man, and a good one. But Zarnak knew all too well the kind of fear atomic devastation brought to the mind once it was actually understood. Deciding his friend needed distraction more than truth, he offered;

"Perhaps we should just go and get ourselves a little drink."

With a shudder, the Captain nodded, adding;

"Perhaps we should just go and get ourselves a lot of little drinks."

Dr. Zarnak did not argue. Reaching the front door of the court-house, the two stepped out into the waning daylight, the smell of smoke and the howl of sirens still thick in the air.

# Some Thoughts on the Problem of Order
## Simon Bucher-Jones

### 1. In which a question is put to the Ecumenical panel on Religious Outreach.

The H. P. Lovecraft Memorial Symposium was in full swing. The Chairman, a member of the Senate's 'religious' right, had introduced the panelists and was seeking questions from the floor.

"Have you ever considered the problem of Order?" an audience member asked.

The Chairman scowled and moved his hunchbacked body to ease a moment's discomfort. "Something of an old chestnut, surely; in these post-modern days. Still, no doubt it is worth a moment of our time. Ephod Henrickson of the Starry Wisdom Church, how would you respond?"

The narrow-jawed man in black, seated to the left of the Chairman, smiled. "We all agree, I'm sure, whatever our doctrinal differences, that, by definition, Azathoth wills only chaos — and yet from that Ultimate will to chaos, it is clear that some 'order' results. Two and Two does usually equal Four. The Lion does not as a rule mate with the Lamb. Cause and Effect have their common meanings. Thus, some argue, either Azathoth is not wholly Chaotic, or He is not Omnipotent. The former is a blasphemy against His Nature, the latter a blasphemy against His Power. That in a nutshell is the so-called 'problem of order.' But, I believe the problem falls away if it is once seen that the embrace of utter chaos, unstained by any pinch of order would be itself a form of order. Azathoth is, metaphorically, larger than mere chaos and His Glory is seen when His Hand is withheld as profoundly as when it is At One's Throat. Bishop Marsh, would you agree?"

"Most, ah, certainly, mwah, yes." Marsh slumped to the Chairman's right, behind a dozen glasses of water. "Early man, unable to grasp the fact that there can be localized low-entropy events even within a universe that inexorably moves towards a state of maximum entropy, categorized such events as 'orderly' or 'good' and saw in them evidence for a non-existent active force associated with such states. To our ancestors it was natural to ask, if the Gods sleep, who imposed their sleep upon them? But sleep when the stars are wrong is a natural cycle of the Gods. It is not external and imposed, but demanded by the nature of the Godhead, which is to permit those periods of anticipation in which faith is tested and made strong, and in which the, ah, appetite for the living is renewed. The Gods gratify themselves with sleep, that they may be wakened by Their Followers and rejoice. Their High Priest Cthulhu sleeps in imitation of them."

"So you don't accept the possibility that there could be Elder Gods?" the man in the audience insisted. "A force that makes the Gods cower in Their Tombs?" He wore mirrored sunglasses, and a military-cut leather coat like many of the campus posers did, but his face was ruddy rather than fashionably gothick, and he winced as if his eyes hurt under the shades.

Henrickson pinched his nose as at a bad smell. "The Elder Gods made me do it. How banal that sounds. However, I would not want to reject the force of the Elder Gods as a metaphor for humanity's, and other's, failings and intransigences. When we have done less Evil than we should, do we not pray, as with Shakespeare's Malcolm, '*Unmerciful Powers release in me those forces which nature gives way to in repose*' and is it not poetically right that our backwoods associates should continue to chant '*From Nodens and Angels and Heavenly Beasties, Dark Lord deliver Us.*'

"The more I hear of modern preachifying, the less I'm sure I set well with it," the third panelist snapped. Seated to the far left, he seemed almost an afterthought, and it was plain he too felt, and indeed resented the easy answers of the more urbane churchmen. His name tag identified him as Pasteur Hoaeg of the Fourth Reformed Outer Church of Nebraska. "Maybe I don't have the book-learnin' of these gentlemen, and I reckon maybe I was raised one of their backwoods associates. But I ain't a-going to rule out what the Black Book itself teaches, nor what I learned on my mother's knee. The *Necronomicon* says: '*Then Were They Bound By The Sign Of Mnar*', when it speaks of Great Cthulhu an' his kin, and we call that there sign, the Elder Sign in all tradition and faith. That being so, I reckon the Elder Gods do exist, and tremble when they think of the Comin' Day when the Great Old Ones and the Outer Gods will be 'venged 'pon them. Furthermore, until that Dread Day, ain't it our livin' duty to stamp out any such deluded souls as might be drawn into the schemes of the Elder Gods, and do we not play into their hands by suggesting that only human weakness is our enemy?"

"Pasteur Hoaeg takes a more fundamental approach to these matters, and in a very real sense I applaud it," Henrickson said. "But there's every difference in the world between accepting the existence of a folk tradition and demanding that that tradition be in every respect literally true. What matters is that we retain our faith in Our Dread Masters; anything that boisters that faith, be it hatred of the Elder Gods or hunting their supposed human pawns, is in itself worthy. Anything that detracts from that faith, as it might be a false attribution to a stone, or to a supposed Elder God of any real sustainable capacity to stand against the forces from Outside, must be a danger."

"The Chairman nodded, "Well, I think we're broadly in agreement there. What do you feel about the panelists' responses, Mister . . .?"

"I feel they need a demonstration of the existence of the Elder Gods . . ." The man pulled a shotgun from under his long leather coat. "Now this is loaded with pulverized Star-Stones of Mnar. If it's just powdered stone, I guess the panelists are going to get a bit of a stingin'. But if it's blessed by forces equal but opposite to their Gods, then maybe it'll do more than sting." [Cries of 'stop him' and 'Ia Nodens'. A shotgun blasts, twice. There is at least one inhuman howl.]

## 2.In which the police consider the aftermath of the cut and thrust of debate.

Precinct Chief Mendoza had come up the ranks from the Temple District in Red Hook, New York, but he'd never seen anything like this.

"Three important clerics, murdered at a modern university's celebration of a noted religious popularist, Azathoth damn it, it's like something out of C. S. Lewis! Have forensics reported yet?"

Officer Daniels had been on the walkie-talkie to the Dean Halsey Memorial Hospital, where the bodies had been taken. Members of the Hospital faculty and Nathaniel West, the police medical examiner, had been up most of the night, trying to make sense of the wounds. All Daniels could do was recount their findings.

"The bodies have been sort of eaten up from the inside. There's some kind of inorganic crystalline residue, but judging from the effect they're citing everything from anthrax to some sort of radioactive toxin. You don't think there could have been anything in this Nodens Cult, stuff, chief?"

"Lone gunman's the politic line, and the identity of the killer seems to confirm it. He was torn to bits by the crowd of course — the worshippers of three of the most popular Elder Churches don't sit still when the rectors take a whuppin'. The medics saved some bits. Weird eyes, maybe he wasn't taking enough drugs."

Mendoza sniffed. He was no respecter of religion, Daniels knew.

Oh, he paid the normal lip service that holding public office demanded of a man in the Necronomicon Belt of the US, but Daniels doubted that the man had ever attended a single sacrifice. Nevertheless, his men were loyal and would have followed him to R'lyeh and back.

"We still managed to get his wallet mostly intact," Mendoza growled. "According to that, he's an ex-patient of the City Sanitorium, out on release into the community. Just a sicko with a kink in his brain. No conspiracy, nothing to see. No doubt that's how the Churches will want to play it."

Daniels considered, "You mean you *do* think there is something to this Nodens Cult, boss?"

"Ah, who knows? Why do the Thirteenth Tribe Of Israel, and the followers of The Faceless Mullah blow themselves up tussling over the City of the Pillars? I guess if he believed it, then there's something in it, eh, Daniels? So, here's what you're going to do. You're going to get yourself over to the Arkham City Sanitorium and you're going to get yourself committed."

"Holy Cthulhu, chief, on what grounds?"

"You put that amusing '*you don't have to be mad to work here, but it helps*' poster up in the precinct house, didn't you? Well, I guess your witty bluff has just been called. Tell them that you were scared by a vision of night-gaunts as a child. Tell them you've got doubts about Great Cthulhu. Tell them your complexes mean you can't bring yourself to dress up as your mother and knife showering co-eds for all I care, but get yourself into that Asylum!"

## 3. In which Officer Daniels resorts to a prevarication in a good cause.

Doctor Theophobe steepled his fingers and looked at Daniels through horn-rimmed glasses whose lenses seemed made of frost.

"Forgive me, but most people seeking to commit themselves to our care, at least have the common decency to leave a trail of dismembered corpses. I hardly think you're trying. What was it now?" He tapped a bone-white finger on his pencil-scratched notes. "A general feeling of being a bit fragile, yes? A thickening of the skin, and lassitude in the hours of noontide. A certain development of the cranium? Well, you're a trifle old, but maybe this will help." He pushed a leaflet from a greeny-brown pile across the ebony surface of the desk.

'*So You're Going To Change: Life Under The Sea by A. Deep One,*' Daniels read, flushing slightly. "No!" he shouted, "Um, er, not that there's anything *wrong* with, um, you know, all *that*. Very nice, I'm sure, for those that like it, er, are *born* with it, I mean."

He felt the blood surging in his face like a red tide. By the Black Teats of Astarte, he'd have Mendoza for this.

"So what exactly *is* your problem, young man? The Asylum dramatic society is meeting to work on our performance of *1001 Days of Sodom* and I was hoping to get some first-class buggery in before the light goes."

"Right, um." This was it, something outre, something commit-worthy, and yet at the same time something that would let him roam around and talk to the other inmates, without getting him trussed up. "I've been hearing voices."

"Mi-Go, Ghast, Termagant, or Shadmock?"

"I'm not sure."

"Is it electrical with a hint of artificiality, or a booming like a moose bellowing down an infinitely long tube?"

"Er, no, not really."

"Does it whisper an endless stream of obscenities?"

"No."

"Pity, we could all do with a laugh. I take it, it's basically then an uncanny flesh-shredding whistle with occasional overtones suggestive of speech but incapable of being comprehended by mortal ears?"

"No, it's, ah, singing."

"Singing?" The Doctor looked pleased, and reached for what Daniels took to be a standard reference work. Yes, he was right, he could see the gold-leaf title *Chanson De Vermis*, and the authenticating seals of the Outer Church. "Is there, perhaps," the Doctor's fat tongue (black) licked his puffy lips (red), "a sensation of, ah, flute music?"

Daniels nodded.

Theophobe turned to a black-edged page, whose words were writ in gold and silver.

"A feeling of nausea, and of compression, as if a weight that could distend the universe was lowering itself gradually onto your body from all sides? A sound like the cacophonic night-call of a million toads?" There was a glint of something rolling behind the frost now. Eyeballs blue-irised and leering. "And perhaps a faint but unmistakable scent of lavender?"

"What?"

"Ah, so no crossover to the olfactory as yet, good, good. Well, Mr. Metcalfe, I think you should consider yourself very lucky, very lucky indeed. Many people would consider themselves honored to be on the point, the cusp, the very, ah, threshold of the experiences that await you. I will be happy to offer you the run of the halls. You may want to" — he paused, — "interact with the other patients gradually, they're likely to be jealous at such an advanced case." He frowned. "We also have some, well, perversely inclined inmates." His puffy red lips puckered with distaste. "Altruists, atheists, christians. Deluded fools who cannot stand to acknowledge the true reverberant blackness of the abyss of nature."

"Any Nodens cultists?"

Daniels could see he might have overstepped the mark.

Theophobe hunched his white-coated frame forward. He couldn't quite stifle a grimace of disgust. "If that's your, ah, bag, you might want to consider discussing it with our Professor Snipsavour, something of an expert in the viler blasphemies. I can recommend aversion therapy most highly, particularly if you're about to enter the Lavender Zone of the Ghooric Rite. You wouldn't want any nasty, sordid, Nodenic stain on your psyche before going before the Ten Thousand Presences. And now I really must be about my rest period time. All work and no, ah, play makes for a dull life you know, dear boy."

## 4. In which Professor Snipsavour propounds a popular thesis in psychology.

The Professor surprised Daniels in two ways. She was a woman, and she was dressed as a nun of the Catholic Heresy.

The chain-smoking and the whip, he took as normal for a modern psychotherapist, and the gimp-masked and silent men he assumed to be patients, but the perverse icons of a discredited and almost forgotten faith, made him wonder if Arkham Sanitorium's high reputation for being at the forefront of medical science was in any way deserved. It was positively European in its old world decadence.

Her voice and hair were honey. "You saw that old fraud, Theophobe then? What did you tell him?"

Daniels stuttered through his symptoms.

"All lies of course, you bad, bad man. You're no more a pre-initiate of the Ghooric Rite than Rupert there is a good fuck."

One of the gimp-masked men shuffled.

Snipsavour pouted, "Oh, he's sulking now. But he'll never master basic dominance and submission theory with that attitude. He's not coming to grips with it at all. You wouldn't mind fucking him in the mouth for me, would you, just as a step in the right direction? No? At least help me on with this strap-on. The police took a far harder line in my younger days. I blame this rising permissiveness. 'The Elder Gods' indeed, 'Nodens,' I ask you. Before it all ends we'll be 'being nice to people.' It's inhuman." She shuddered. "Life is sex and blood and death. It's self-evident: but the followers of the weakling, failure Gods, deny this and seek to justify their own personal inadequacies in the invented perversions of nature, such as 'marriage,' 'fidelity,' and 'monogamous perversion.' Isn't that so, Rupert?"

"I don't think he can answer you with his mouth full," Daniels said coolly. If the therapists of the Asylum were as concerned about a Nodenic revival as all this, clearly there might be something in it. He unzipped his fly. "Oh, well, while I'm here, I may as well make myself useful."

It was exhausting, if exhilarating work, to assist in the breaking down of unhealthy inhibitions and complexes, and Daniels was beginning to wonder if he hadn't missed a vocation in the psychomedical field in becoming a policeman, but after a while Snipsavour, pulling his earlobe hard so her lips came into contact with it, whispered: "You want the strange old man in Ward X. He's at the core of it. Anyone talks about Nodens here, it's because they've talked to him." She slapped his buttocks playfully, and as Daniels — skittishly — moved to leave, she shouted over the general background noise of the panting, "when he came his eyes were brown!"

## 5. In which an Elderly inmate discloses an unexpected secret.

"You see, it is quite simple. It was all changed, in a twinkling. They turned the tables on us, you know. We simply underestimated their hatred. Oh, it burned."

"Whose hatred?" Daniels probed, trying to cut through the patient's ramblings.

"Oh, all of them. Cthulhu, Hastur, Ithaqua, Akor-Akktu, Nylathatep. It was the effect of the imprisonment, you see. Richard Lovelace was more right than he knew when he wrote: '*Stone walls do not a prison make nor iron bars a cage; mind's innocent and quiet take, them for a hermitage.*' We never understood them, and so we offered them hermitage, and they having minds neither quiet nor innocent perceived only a prison, and so they became, what is the phrase, 'institutionalized.'"

Daniels sighed. So this was the Nodenic creed at its core — the filth that had made a man take a gun and blow away respected Churchmen — a ragged madman with a straggly beard, strapped to a stained bed, talking to him about 'institutionalizing' the Gods. Besides, he'd done some history courses, hadn't the Cavalier poet Lovelace written:

'*Stone walls a perfect prison make, as iron bars a cage, minds innocent therein do break, and know no hermitage; if I have hatred for this show, this world that seems to be, then devils that do toil below, are not so lost as me.*'

Something like that, he was sure.

"So you imprisoned the Gods and they resented it?" He found it hard to keep the sarcasm out of his voice. It was impossible to imagine the Gods, whether he really believed in them or not, locked up by this urine-stained grandfather — still, the notes at the foot of the bed had confirmed what Snipsavour had finally implied. This was the Asylum's prize, 'worst case' Nodenic and unrepentant despite the finest ECT treatment available; the incontinent fountainhead of the killer's warped credo. The one the killer had listened to. Just like Daniels was doing now.

"Yes. They resented it madly, eternally, without respite — for they could not see that they were set aside not in spite but to permit them to learn and grow within themselves. Instead they learned only to hate and to twist and tear, and so when the stars became right for them to join their fellow Elder Gods, they rose up not as the knight arising from his vigil, but as the beast approaching its prey."

"And then what? A dozen angry Gods beat you up and put you in a Sanitorium? You look surprisingly well for it. I'd have thought they'd have ripped your head off."

"They ripped, as you say, our heads off. They ripped our hearts out. They ripped the entire world apart and put it back, built in the image of their own desire." Daniels found the old man's halting voice growing fainter, but it was curiously compelling, so he leaned closer to the bed. "They imprisoned us, they imprisoned even *me*."

The old man's eyes were blue-veined sightless marbles.

"You know me, Daniels."

"I didn't tell you my name!" Daniels protested.

"You tell it with your movement through space-time, you carry it with you from the dark font of your Outer Church. The stain they placed on your soul, identifies you. Do you not see that they *always* intended you for the lion's den?"

Daniels found his hands on the old man's thin cold throat. Choking his ravings into silence. And yet the voice continued in his head, Calm, reasonable, immeasurably old.

"I am I. I am Nodens. I ride the half-shell pulled by white and ethereal horses. This body, this building, this world are the prisons of the Old Ones, built for me in their revolt against the peace I offered them. Do you not see the vileness they have let out of their own veins into the waters of the world's heartsblood? All good in you stands in spite of them. They have built you a world of horror, and mankind has made its heart at home in it, and yet man still builds order, and his true heart cries out for release."

"Yeah, right," Daniels muttered. "I've got your release right here, old man." He jammed his thumbs into the scrawny chicken-neck and pressed harder. Mendoza would be glad to avoid paperwork on this one. When the voice finally stopped, it wasn't until bones had snapped under his hands.

## 6. In which a job well done is justly rewarded.

"What can I say, Daniels? The Outer Churches seem convinced that you've stopped this Nodens Cult in its tracks. I've got three messages of commendation from the Senators for Yog-Sothoth alone, and an invitation to officiate at the Roodmass rites, from the Little Sisters Of The Republic of Shub-Niggurath — you'd best get fit before taking that one up." He winked; Mendoza's voice was full of honest pride; he was too good a cop to resent a rising subordinate.

Daniels just wished his head wasn't splitting. He'd had a pain behind his right eye, since getting out of the Asylum, and he wished he hadn't looked in the mirror. His right eye was shot through with blue veins, and the white of it looked like marble. He wondered if he'd see differently through it when the headaches stopped. Maybe before then, he ought to pluck it out.

# THE WHITE MOUNTAINS

## Johnathan Sharp

"An insidious odor began to penetrate the room. It was vaguely reptilian, musky and nauseating. The disk lifted inexorably, and a little finger of blackness crept out from beneath its edge (came) a great wave of iridescent blackness, neither liquid nor solid, a frightful gelatinous mass."

Henry Kuttner
*–The Salem Horror*

Booze, that's what got me into this mess. The promise of booze and writing off a payback favor. Every now and again I need to step outside the good-guy circle, sometimes it's to dig some dirt, sometimes to fake some dirt. Sometimes you have to bend the rules a little as a private investigator. But hey, I try and stay away from the bad guys if I can, but every now and again, you need to cross that line. Now don't get me wrong, I'm no knight in shining armor, or goody two-shoes. I just know that mixing with made guys can lead you into a whole world of hurt. But that's how I make my living, me — Artie Skipp, Private Investigator.

As it happened, I owed MacLean a favor. In the whole scheme of villains he wasn't a major player, but who and what he didn't know, wasn't worth knowing. I owed him from a few months back; I just hadn't expected him to ask for payback quite like this.

"Skipper, this is where you hide out now?"

It was just after eleven in the morning and I was working on a late breakfast and last night's edition of the *Globe* at the diner opposite my office. I can't say I was glad to see him. Before I could reply he got himself sat down opposite me in the booth.

"Morning Mac." I gave him my poker face.

"Skipper, you don't seem so pleased to see me."

I grunted non-committaly.

"You were plenty pleased when I gave you Oglanby's name."

Yeah, at the time I had been. Oglanby was a real sleazeball grifter, claimed he was some kind of movie producer or casting agent. Scammed a lot of cash and dirty pictures from girls who didn't wonder what a big shot moviemaker was doing this far east. I'd been hired by a set of irate parents who wanted him run out of town with the cops on his tail. Once MacLean got me his name, I made sure Oglanby wouldn't be back in Boston anytime soon.

"Okay, Mac, I owe you. So spit it out, what is it you want?"

"You drive a truck, Skipper?"

"Drive a truck? I'm not being your getaway driver," I growled.

MacLean choked a laugh.

"You see this suit?"

I could sure tell MacLean was dressing better than the last time I saw him. He usually looked like he dressed in hand-me-downs. This was at least a thirty-dollar suit.

"Yeah, Mac, it's not your usual style."

He grinned at me; it wasn't a particularly wholesome grin, not with the missing teeth.

"You know of Eddy Corso, Skipper?"

I knew just about every hood in the city, so that was a loaded question for sure. Corso was big in booze. You wanted hooch in quantity, Corso was your man.

"I told you, Mac, I'm not getting involved in some caper for Corso or any other hoods."

"Look, Skipper, this ain't no trip for biscuits. You still owe me, remember? Do me this favor and we're square."

I was about to interrupt but Mac was in full flow. He dropped his voice a little and carried on.

"Look, Skipper, I've been doing some running for Corso. It's copasetic. The feds got their eyes on his regular guys, but the man has gin mills to water. I've been running up into the White Mountains, there's lots of moonshine up there. You can see the dough is good." He yanked on his lapels to prove the point. "My usual guy gave me some piffle about chasing some skirt. I need a driver for tomorrow. You in? We'll call it quits if you'll bail me out on this one. I'll even throw in some bottles for your own personal."

How hard was it going to be? I figured this was an easy way to clear the debt and earn me some free booze in the bargain.

"Okay, it's a deal, Mac. So where and when?"

"Tomorrow morning, make it seven. The lockup, down on Fosters wharf. And fetch your gat."

That's when I ought to have said no and walked away.

So there I was the next morning. Seven A.M. was not the best time of day for me. Mac was waiting at the lockup, helping another guy load some boxes on the back of a beat-up old truck.

"Skipper, at last. I thought you'd left me holding the bag."

"I don't do early mornings so good." That got a laugh. By now my brain had notched up a gear. "I thought we were going on a mule run, what's on the truck?"

"Nothing for you to worry over."

I wasn't buying that, so I walked around the side to take a closer look. Mac was hauling a tarp over the load. "Wait up, Mac." I wanted to see exactly what I was hauling. I poked open one of the boxes. "Food?" The back was loaded with boxes of food and clothes. "What gives, Mac?"

"I'll fill you in on the way — it's a long ride and we need to get going."

The truck was a real handful. I'd driven worse back in my Army days, but this Ford was a real beat-up old bus. It was hard to keep up any kind of conversation over the engine noise. We stopped late morning at a roadside diner, which Mac said was the last place before we hit the back roads. So I pressed him again about the load we were carrying.

"Where we're going, Skipp, they got no use for dollar bills. Instead of dollars we'll trade the load on the truck for moonshine."

So that was it. I did wonder what kind of people had no use for folding green.

"I got to warn you, Skipp, where we're going is real backwoods. These rubes are a bit, well, a bit odd-looking."

"You done business with them before though?" I asked.

"Uh, well, not exactly, no. Our usual 'shiner couldn't keep up with demand. He put me onto this other clan."

"Clan?" That was a real odd choice of words.

"Yeah, as far as I can make out it's all one family — they sure all got the same looks and they aren't so good. Anyway, I went on up there into the woods and found them. Their hooch is real sweet. I tried to buy some on the spot, but the old man wouldn't have any of it. Told me he wanted to trade, wanted coffee, sugar, all kinds of stuff."

"So we're going out to trade with mountain men?"

"You got it, Skipper. You bring the gat like I asked?"

I patted the snub-nose .38 in my jacket pocket; I never leave home without it.

"What am I then, Mac, your insurance?"

"Let's say you're the muscle. Just let me do the talking and cover my back. They ain't too pretty to look at but don't let that spook you."

To be honest, I was pretty well spooked by the woods. I'm not a countryside kind of guy. I need the city, the smoke, the java and the Janes. I want asphalt and brownstones. It seemed like all there was out here was trees, towering and immense. We'd been following a real bumpy trail for at least an hour. I could tell we were climbing higher into the hills from the way the truck was straining. The woods around here were so thick that they crowded out the sunlight. It felt less like we were riding on a road, and more like driving down an endless tunnel. It didn't feel good to me, other than this track boring through this wilderness like a worm trail, there was nothing else to see but trees. God help anyone that got lost out here.

"What the hell is that?" I stomped on the brakes. There was something lying across the track in front of us.

"Ignore it, Skipp — just drive."

No way. I killed the engine, opened the driver's door and got out. I walked around the front of the truck. This didn't look natural . . . some kind of animal . . . but not all of it. It was kind of hard to tell, but it looked like it could have been a deer at one time. It was roughly the right size but it seemed like it was, well, part dissolved. Like something just sheared half of it off. That's when I noticed the marks on the ground and the way the trees were all broken up on either side of the track. It seemed to me something had come from one side of the woods, across the track, and smashed on through the other side, taking half of the deer with it. That's when it hit me. It was quiet. I mean real quiet. I'm no country boy, but I'd assumed there'd be some kind of noise out here, birds maybe, but certainly something. There was just nothing. No sound and a real sickly, rotten smell.

"Skipp, get back in the truck." MacLean was sounding angry.

"Don't you hear it?" I asked.

"Hear what? I don't hear nothing," he growled. "Now get back in the truck and get us moving!"

"That's what I mean, Mac, there's no sound out here." I climbed back in the cab, feeling pretty uneasy. MacLean was having none of it though.

"Just forget it, Skipp — it's not much further."

"Mac, something took half that deer."

"A bear, that's all."

I wasn't buying that. Sure, a bear could have smashed up the trees, but why leave half of its next meal lying in the track? I was about to hit the gas and get us moving when my foot slipped off the pedal. There was something slimy all over the bottom of my shoes. It didn't seem like mud. And it stunk to high Heaven.

The truck bounced its way down the track for another ten or fifteen minutes. I still couldn't see daylight through the trees, but I could tell we were still climbing. Now, I'm no stranger to skulking about in the dark; it's part of the job. But this was something else. It felt like we'd driven out of one world and into another. The remains of that animal were preying on my mind. There was something out there in the trees that could bring down a deer and take half of it away with no trace. Whatever could do that, I didn't want to run into it.

MacLean had been quiet since we got moving again. He seemed to be a little nervous.

"Skipp, slow down!" he was yelling over the engine noise. "We're almost there. This track is going to fork pretty soon. Go left. It's real hard going, so take it easy."

Jeez, the road was getting worse. Great.

"Listen, Skipp, when we get there, you stay in the truck, okay? You let me do the talking."

That was fine by me. I could see the fork up ahead, so I slowed to an even crawl. It didn't look like where we were going was even wide enough for the truck.

"Mac, we're not going to get this heap through here."

"Don't sweat it Skipp — just take it slow."

I swear the trees all around us were closing in even more. The branches were so low and close together they bounced off the truck's cab and sides. We carried on, fighting our way through this web of undergrowth for another good ten minutes. One particularly hefty branch whacked the front windshield with such force that it cracked it. Spider-webs of glass appeared in front of us.

"Jeez, Mac, you're going to need a new truck by the time we make it back."

MacLean's face was set hard. Suddenly, we burst clear of those damn trees and out into open ground. I'd have been relieved if I hadn't seen the bones everywhere.

MacLean could tell I was spooked.

"Ignore it, Skipp. Just pull up by the shack."

I eased back off the pedals and pulled the truck up to a halt in front of the shack. I took a moment to take a look around. In my game you take in your surroundings fast, since sometimes your life can depend upon it. This was goddamn strange though. We'd pulled into a clearing, the canopy of trees was gone and I could at least see daylight. On this occasion though, that didn't seem to be a plus. I've seen the way the homeless bums in Boston live. Compared to this squalor, they lived it good. There was a whole mess of bones all over the ground; I hoped it was animal bones. The shack itself looked like it was going to collapse with one hefty sneeze. I could see smoke spiralling from a hole in the roof. My eyes dropped back down to the door. There was something hanging from the porch roof just above the front door. It looked like some kind of mess of bones, feathers and twigs.

"What the hell is this place, Mac?"

"Skipp, do like I told you. Stay in the truck." He turned and smiled, a little too uneasily for my liking. "I know you're the man for a tight spot. That's why I got you here. Just stay in the truck while I do the deal. Don't get all in a lather."

I was beginning to doubt Mac ever had anyone else in mind for this little trip, other than me. There probably never was any other guy to drive. But then, I have a suspicious mind.

Mac was out of the truck and walking over to the shack. I scanned round the clearing a little more. That's when I noticed more of those same odd-looking decorations, they looked like misshapen crosses. All around the edge of the clearing these things were hanging from the trees. Little bundles of twigs, bones and feathers. The sun caught one and I saw some kind of flash. The kind you see when something shiny catches the light. I'd been so busy scoping the tree-line I didn't take in the kids. At first I thought they were animals, but no, it was a couple of kids, filthy, and running around on all fours. That's when the two of them came out of the shack. Again, I couldn't decide right off just exactly what I was seeing. The one in front was an older guy, definitely; he was one ugly-looking son of a bitch. Seemed like he was humpbacked, but his face was a real mess. It looked kind of burned all down one side, and he had only one eye. I figured the other was his woman; she was hunched over, her head covered with a filthy shawl. You hear all these wild stories about in-breeding and such. This pair looked they had something other than natural parents.

Mac went over and shook hands with the old man. Rather him than me, I thought. It looked like they were talking, Mac was motioning toward the truck. There looked to be some kind of business going on. My attention switched back over to the kids. They were still playing in the dirt by the side of the shack.

There was a bang on the window. It was MacLean.

"Jeez, Mac, you startled me!" I nearly went for the .38 in my pocket.

"Give me a hand to empty the truck, Skipp."

I climbed out of the cab, waded through the mud and went round the back of the truck. Mac had the tarp pulled back. The ugly old guy was there, checking over what we'd brought. I tried not to look too close; he wasn't such a pretty sight. The smell wasn't no bunch of roses either. He grunted something at Mac and stamped off back towards the shack.

"Deal's done, Skipp. Just unload the boxes and he'll bring the crates of moonshine out."

I was busy hauling the crates off the back of the truck, when I saw someone carrying a crate from the shack. I realized when she got to the truck it was the woman.

"That's okay, Ma'am, you just leave those by the truck and I'll load 'em." I wasn't having a moment of chivalry . . . she just looked so beat that I doubted she could heft one of those crates of moonshine onto the truck.

Mac had walked over to the front porch of the shack and looked like he was trying the wares. Him and the ugly old guy were sharing a drink from a mason jar. I'd got the last couple of boxes off the truck by the time she made it back with another crate of moonshine. She staggered the last few steps toward the truck; I guess she must have lost her footing as she stumbled, almost dropping the crate.

"That's okay, I got it." I grabbed it just before it hit the ground. I heaved the crate of moonshine up onto the back of the truck and turned back around to give her a hand up. I could just make out a smile underneath the shawl as I helped her back onto her feet. I should have known better, I suppose, as that's when things started to go wrong.

"Yaww git away from maa womaaan!" The ugly old guy was stamping angrily towards us. I let go of her hand.

"Look, mister, I was just helping her up . . ." Before I could finish the sentence, he closed the distance and was right by the truck. Before I could react, he swung a fast left hook, laying out the woman with a single punch. I could see Mac was high-tailing it over to the truck at top speed. It was probably none of my business, but I'm not going to stand back and watch a woman get beat on. I rounded on the ugly old cuss and gave him the old one-two. He went down heavy, coughing and spluttering.

"Jeez, Skipp, what in the hell are you doing?" Mac was furious. He went over to help the old guy up. I knelt down beside the woman.

"Are you okay? Let me help you up." I tried to pull the shawl back from her face, but she grabbed at it to stop me.

"Okay, okay. I just wanted to make sure you weren't hurt." She shook her head vigorously. I helped her back on her feet. As I did that, she pulled something from around her neck and pressed it into my hand.

Mac was trying to pacify the old guy. I'd about had it with this whole thing. Without looking, I stuffed what she'd given me into my pocket and pulled out the .38.

"Skipp, for God's sake, put that away." Mac had seen the gun. So had the old guy. He was glaring at me fit to burst.

"Yaww git off'n maaa mountin, yaww git off nawwww. Ahh mayk surtin yaww wonn git off ahliff."

"Skipp, get in the truck and get us out of here now."

The old guy was shouting again . . . I couldn't make it into words . . . it sounded more like he was trying to spit out phlegm than talk, but he kept repeating the same thing and ending with what sounded like: "Nee-ogg-thuh gonna git yaaaa."

I couldn't tell if Mac was mad or scared. He sure looked pale. Keeping hold of the .38, I back-tracked to the truck and climbed in. As I flipped the ignition, Mac got in the other side.

"Get us the hell out of here now!"

I gunned the engine, spun the truck around and headed for the track back through the trees.

I guess I hit the gas a bit too enthusiastically and the truck lurched forward. I just wanted to get the hell away from here. Mac was yelling at the top of his voice over the engine noise. From the language, I could tell he was pissed. I gunned the engine a bit more to drown him out. We were bouncing down the narrow track between the trees; I figured the place where the road forked couldn't be too far away. That's when it seemed like everything happened at once. Despite the cracked front windshield of the truck, I caught sight of some kind of movement in the woods. Then a whole bunch of trees seemed to slide forward. I was so busy trying to make sense of this that I didn't react fast enough with the brake. What seemed like a sideways avalanche was going on all around us. Trees seemed to buckle, bend and finally crack. The effect was like dominoes. From right to left, a whole slew of trees just seemed to tumble and slide over the road right in front of us.

I hit the brake and everything went sideways. For that single split-second everything lurched. The truck plowed straight into this moving pile of trees. There was a terrific crunch as the front of the truck impacted with the woods. The steering wheel was wrenched from my hands and I hit the side door of the truck. Mac hit the windshield. For a moment there was silence, the engine had died. Then there was a sickening grinding noise and the truck lurched again. I could see we'd hit the avalanche of trees and the truck had swerved a good ninety degrees, long-ways on against them. Everything moved again. We were sliding, the trees moved, and so did we.

The driver's side of the truck was impacted against the trees. I tried desperately, but I couldn't force my door. Mac was bleeding, but not stunned.

"Mac! Mac!" I was yelling at him. "The door, bust your door open." He took a moment to register what I was saying, then kicked at the passenger door. We were still sliding, being dragged by the trees. I couldn't figure what was going on. It looked like a mudslide, like some kind of black liquid sludge was propelling the trees. It suddenly surged up over the mass of collapsed trees, dissolving the wood as it flowed over it. Before I could believe what I was seeing, part of it rose up and formed a twisting snake-like appendage. Then another. I was hypnotized. The mudslide seemed to have some kind of life, and it heaved and bubbled with violent malignance.

I turned for a split-second to see if Mac was making any progress with the door. There was a sudden hissing, fizzing sound. I looked back around to see the front of the truck literally dissolve as the sludge bubbled over it.

"Mac, the door — get the door open!" I was yelling now, frantic. The sludge was rising over the hood of the truck . . . in a second it was going to be in the cab. The stench was overpowering, musky and sickly. The metal of the truck was literally dissolving as the noxious, fetid sludge rolled over it.

Mac forced the door open at last and jumped. I followed just as the remains of the windshield buckled and the sludge forced its way into the cab.

I hit the ground on my feet. Mac wasn't so lucky, he went down hard. We were only a few feet from the truck. The avalanche of trees and sludge stopped abruptly. Almost immediately the cab of the truck vanished underneath the wave of the black liquid filth. The sludge seemed to flow and then re-shape itself. I was starting to process a little of what I was seeing here now. This wasn't any mudslide — it was *alive* somehow and it dissolved all that it touched.

I was stumbling backward, trying to get away from this monstrosity. But Mac wasn't fast enough. I've seen people die before in a lot of unpleasant ways, but never anything like this! After holding its shape for a moment, the sludge propelled itself toward Mac. Another long snake-like appendage exploded outwards toward him, while its base flowed across the ground toward his feet.Instinct kicked in and I pulled out the .38. I don't know what I expected, but it was the only weapon I had. The gun barked twice. It was like firing into a bucket of water. The bullets simply sunk into the thing; it just sucked them right into itself. The snake-like thing was wrapping itself around Mac as the rest of it flowed over his feet. Right in front of me I could see it eating through him like a knife going through butter. It had him. As its grip tightened, his body ruptured and dissolved. He didn't even have time to scream.It's then that I must have cracked, 'cause I don't remember anything of what happened next. I guess I must have made a run for it into the woods, and just blacked out. I have no idea how long I was out of it. When I came to, I couldn't tell where I was, but it was getting dark. No sign of the mudslide, or Mac, but at least I was alive.

◆  ◆  ◆

Don't panic. Evaluate the situation. That's what I needed to do. No gun, I'd lost that somewhere. There seemed to be some kind of burn marks down one side of my suit, like something splattered all over me and ate right through my clothing. I seemed to have some cuts on my face and hands, probably from running blindly through the trees.

I tried my pockets to see if I had anything useful. Loose change, a matchbook or two, a couple extra bullets and a necklace. A necklace — *that's* what the woman had stuffed in my hand. I hadn't really paid it any attention before. It was something similar to those things hanging from their shack and all around the edge of the clearing. I looked at it closer; it looked like some kind of misshapen cross on a piece of leather thong. At its top, where you expected to see the top bar of a cross, was a lozenge-shaped jet-black stone with some kind of carving on its face. I wasn't sure, but the carving looked roughly star-shaped, and it seemed to suck what light there was right into it. The stone itself was wrapped tight with another thin leather cord. Wound into the leather were small pieces of bone and feathers. After studying it a moment more, I threw it aside.

It was dark, I had no idea where I was, where the track was, or where that liquid monstrosity was. Okay, calm down, I told myself. Panicking isn't going to do me any good. There's always a way out of a situation, if you can just figure it out.

I was lost. That much was obvious. Mac had to be dead. The truck was gone. That's when the old man's last words came back to me: "Nee-ogg-thuh gonna git yaaaa." Whatever that sluge-thing was, it was alive. It was alive and he set it upon us.

Mac was dead. Mac was dead and I wasn't. That thing had been meant to get us both. It wasn't luck or good shooting on my part, that I was still alive, so why was I?

Take a moment, think.The necklace. The woman gave me the necklace. It was a smaller version of what was hanging from their shack and all around the clearing.

No, it can't be, that's craziness! How can a necklace stop that thing? But what else could it be? From the burns on my clothing I can only assume it had tried to grab at me. But I'd had something that repelled it, something it couldn't dissolve.

So the necklace it had to be. And like a fool, I'd just thrown it away. Frantically, I scrambled to my feet and began searching for it in the dark.There! There it was, lying in the undergrowth, glinting in the low moonlight. I grabbed it. This *had* to be the one thing that had kept me alive.

The only way I was getting out of this was by finding the track we'd been driving on and following it downhill until I got back onto something resembling a highway. It was going to be a damn long walk, that was sure. But what else could I do? It was pointless trying to do anything now. There was little enough light in these woods during the day – blundering around in the dark was liable to cause me a busted ankle at the very least.So, I spent a restless, sleepless night huddled in beside a tree stump. I can't say I actually got any shut-eye, since I was far too jumpy and there were far too many noises I wasn't familiar with. But it felt good to rest a bit anyway.

Come sun up, I was cold and damp, but at least I could see things a little better. Well, at least I could see where I'd blundered through the undergrowth. A blind man could see where I'd been. I could try and backtrack, though it meant going back to where the truck had been. It was a risk, I guess, but what other way was there to find the track? I could stumble through these woods for days and probably never find it. So, I fastened the necklace tight around my throat and set off.I'd never done anything like this before. It's one thing tailing a bad guy all over town, it's another thing entirely trying to follow a trail out here in the wilds. If I hadn't run in such a blind panic, and left such an obvious trail, I'd never have been able to back-track. It took me a couple of hours of hard slog, but I managed to find my way back to the track.I saw the mess of toppled trees first. This was definitely where it had happened. From here on in I figured I needed to be extra-cautious. There was no sign of wildlife and it was deathly quiet. There was that sickening musty smell too. I made my way along the edge of the fallen trees, staying as undercover as best I could. As I got closer I could see they'd blocked the track completely. From here, I could see also what was left of the truck — which wasn't much. The whole front end seemed to be little more than a shell, pitted and corroded by unknown acids, and what was left had collapsed in upon itself. The back portion of the truck was still intact, however. I made my way over to it cautiously. It really beggared belief . . . the truck looked like the deer had, half-corroded away, half-intact. All I could find of any use was a tire-iron. Surprisingly, there were one or two bottles of the moonshine still in one piece, but I darn sure wasn't going to try any of it now!I don't know what I thought I was going to do with the tire-iron, but I took it anyway, feeling better for holding it like a weapon in a solid grip.There was no sign of Mac. I hadn't really expected there would be. That thing must have — No! I wasn't going to think about it. Not while that thing was likely still out here in the woods with me. Mac was gone, but I was getting out of here. I gingerly picked my way over the fallen trees until I was standing on the track with all of it behind me. All I needed to do now was walk, walk until I reached the point where the road forked, and then head back to the nearest town. I couldn't remember the place where we'd stopped at that diner, but I was sure I could find some transport from there. That was my plan. I set off.

I walked cautiously, sticking close to the trees, and trying to keep out of sight while I followed the track. I wasn't sure it was doing any good, but I wanted to make sure I wasn't easy to spot. But the further I got, the more time had passed, the less cautious I got. I had been walking for a couple of hours like this, and by late morning I just hit the middle of the track and picked up the pace. Finally, I could see it front of me, the place where the road forked. I was getting somewhere at last.

A tremendous noise cut through the woods. It was unmistakable, the sound of trees splintering and falling. There it was, to the left and in front of me. I could see it. The forest floor was moving. A viscous sludge was flowing, eating away the bases of the trees as it moved relentlessly towards the track, toward me. It moved incredibly fast — I thought maybe I could outrun it — but the heaving mess moved almost quicker than the eye could follow. A huge slick flowed out over the track right in front of me. It seethed and bubbled. Shapes seemed to form within it, straining to extend themselves from its mass. Prehensile limbs formed and extruded from its mass, only to collapse back in on themselves. Bubbles seethed and burst, forming eyes that dissolved moments later.

I hurled the tire-iron at it in disgust. Like the bullets before, it simply absorbed the hunk of metal. That was it, I had nothing left, only the necklace. The thing in front of me continued to bubble and writhe, but held its overall position, blocking the track in front of me. I backed up a few steps. It flowed forward and stopped. I back-stepped again, it seethed forward again and stopped.

I pulled the necklace out from around my neck and held it out in front of me.

"You want me? You come and get me!" I was yelling at the top of my voice. I took a step forward. Then another. It moved. It moved back, sliding away from me.

Still yelling, I stamped towards the thing. Slowly but surely it began to move, away from me. As it moved, its overall shape seemed to become more and more agitated. All manner of shapes bubbled and

blistered over its black body mass. Snake-like tentacles groped outwards, only to collapse and reform again as it moved.

A few more footsteps and I'd be standing in the middle of it. I shut
my eyes and strode forward, expecting at any moment it would slide
over me — the filthy putrid mass rising up and covering me from head
to foot.

Whatever the stone in the necklace was, it seemed to repel it. The
moment when I would be engulfed never came. It split in two. The two
halves heaved and churned, then flowed apart from the track and into
the brush on either side. I walked forward. I could hardly believe this. It
was dividing itself and letting me pass through. Stumbling, then running, I bolted for the fork in the road. Casting a glance over my shoulder, I saw it flow back together and then slide away into the trees,
collapsing them as it went.

Tired and foot-sore, I walked and walked. Eventually I managed to
get a ride back to civilization on a passing truck. Somehow, I convinced
the driver I'd wrecked my car and needed a ride. I couldn't think of a
better way to explain what I was doing out here, or why I was in such a
beat-up shape.

I try to stay in the city these days, on solid ground. The countryside
and me are never going to get along, and I don't think I ever want to
hear the sound of a falling tree for as long as I live.

Those folks up in the mountains, well, there's been some pieces in
the *Globe* lately after folks went missing up in the White Mountains.
The feds went up there looking for them, didn't find them though . . . at
least, not alive. There's talk of cannibalism, inbreeding, strange rituals.
Once I would have dismissed it as bunk. It's 1931; we have radios, cars,
and movie theatres. It's supposed to be the age of enlightenment. But
believe me, there's things out there, things we don't understand . . . and
maybe it's better that way. To this day I don't know what the hell it was,
that sliding mound of sludge out there in the woods. It was some kind
of creature, of course, but no creature of this Earth!

I still have the necklace though; I keep it for good luck.

# Then Terror Came
## A Tale from the DMA Case Files
# Patrick Thomas

I'm not always crazy about my job, but it's better than the alternative. They pulled me almost literally out of Old Sparky's grasp. I was on death row because I had been possessed by a thing from the pit that used my body to commit the most heinous crimes. The DMA yanked me free because I managed to keep the body count to only double digits, which has apparently never been done before or since with a Seriál demon. That made me mostly innocent, which gave the DMA the excuse to save me. The possession left me with certain aftereffects, which makes me useful in their mission to protect America from mystic threats. It also gave them the motive to mount the rescue mission. I guess I shouldn't complain. I got a new face, a new career, and a pension, assuming I live that long.

It's a big assumption.

Take today's case. Please. I sure as Hades don't want it. I'd say Hell, but it brings back too many bad memories. The victim waiting for the tape outline might already be there, 'cause he sure ain't here. However he is over there. And there. And places I can't even see from where I'm standing. It was going to take a couple of rolls of tape to do the job.

It was taking everything I could muster to not vomit all over the closest cluster of remains. I hid it from the locals, but not my partner. She put a comforting hand on my shoulder.

"You okay?" she asked.

"You already know the answer," I said. Mandi knew how I was feeling. Literally. "How about you?"

"Let's see. Over a dozen people in shouting distance, each somewhere between revulsion, disgust and sick interest. I'm just fine," said Mandi, each word drooling with sarcasm.

"You need the meds?" I asked. Of all the people I've got to deal with in my new life, Mandi's the one I like the most. What's even odder is that she claims she likes me. There's no accounting for taste.

"Nah. This is nowhere near as bad as last minute shopping in the mall on Christmas Eve. The local sheriff thinks somebody threw Mr. Harrison into a wood chipper, then tried to fertilize," said Mandi.

"I can see why he'd think that," I said.

"You don't agree?" she asked with a knowing grin.

"Nope. We wouldn't be here if that were the case. A human can inflict that much damage, but it'd be a lot of work," I said. Mandi knew how I knew and I was grateful she didn't break eye contact. Most of the agents who know my history would have.

"Demon?" said Mandi, not bothering to beat around a bush that had withered and died a long time ago.

"Don't think so. I'm thinking animal or beast of the large, supernatural variety," I said.

"Yep, that's my gut too. I'm just troubled by the lack of foot or paw prints. Might mean we got something that can fly or be partially immaterial."

"You been at this longer. You got any inkling what it might be?" I asked.

"Nope," said Mandi.

"Great. I love a mystery," I lied.

I'm told procedure is the same for a mystical crime as for a mundane one. Inspect the scene, take forensic evidence, interview witnesses and make your best guess.

We took care of number one, the crime scene lab boys and gals did number two, which meant it was time for number three.

I figured it'd be quick as there were no witnesses or if there were, they were probably mixed in with the human meat strewn about the place. Thankfully, it was the forensic lab's job to sort out the pieces.

We headed straight for Sheriff Weeks to see who had been first on the scene.

He was still shaking his head and talking non-stop. It was one way to cope and I couldn't criticize. I tended to shut down.

"I ain't never seen nothing like this in eighteen years," he said. The years seemed about right. You don't see many law enforcement types with more than twenty on the job. They see too much bad, so when the half-pay pension comes at twenty years in, most take it and get out. I'd probably start counting when the number was further away from twenty.

"Let's hope you don't see it again," I said.

"You think whoever did this will strike again?" asked Weeks.

"Unless he turned him, her, or itself in while we were inspecting the crime scene," I answered. "Harrison have any enemies?"

"Not that we've been able to find. He was the quiet type, dealt in artifacts for the Boston museums and some collectors. Been some talk that some of his merchandise is stolen, but as most of it happened overseas, it's a bit out of our jurisdiction. And Boston PD didn't want to be bothered with questions from a small town sheriff in a neighboring state," said the sheriff. I just nodded.

"He been selling anything recently?" asked Mandi.

"We're not sure. We're looking for his business associate now, but other than that he had no family or close friends to tell us if it looks like anything was taken," said the sheriff. The fact that most of the outside of the house was covered in blood and gore would have discouraged even the most helpful of friends anyway. "What do you think did this?"

"Not happy with your wood chipper theory?" I said.

The sheriff shook his head. "No tire treads inside the house or out and a chipper would leave some trace. Still, people are asking questions and I have to tell them something. We haven't even been able to find a single footprint." He looked at us. "We're not going to, are we?"

"It's possible," I admitted. As hard as it was to fathom, it was conceivable that something this brutal might not leave behind any secondary physical traces.

"Some of the men are saying animal, but I'm a hunter. I've seen what a bear or a wolf can do to its prey. This ain't it. I have to admit, I've always thought the Department of Mystic Affairs was a waste of my taxes, mainly because I assumed you always dealt with crackpots and hoaxes, but now..."

"The DMA gets it share of that, but the criminals we deal with are real. They just have different MO's than most police departments are used to handling," explained Mandi. We get that reaction a lot. Unlike fictional agencies, the DMA does not keep its existence a secret nor do we operate clandestinely in the shadows. The criminals do that. We work in the open. Our unofficial motto is *When darkness falls we pick up the pieces.* The problem is nobody tends to believes us. It makes what we have to do even harder because everyone out there, from police to the public, is looking to explain away the darker parts of reality. It's easier than accepting it. I envy them.

"So what are we dealing with here?" Sheriff Weeks asked.

There is a tradition of friction between federal departments and local law enforcement. The DMA has enough trouble being taken seriously, at least until the monster droppings hit the fan, to play things that way. Orders straight from the top are to share all information and theories with the locals, unless they are suspected of complacency. Uncle Sam, the real Uncle Sam, is our bureau's Director and is unbending when it comes to that.

"Supernatural creature," I said.

"Like a werewolf?" asked the sheriff.

"Not a lunamorph," said Mandi.

"A what?" asked the sheriff.

"Classification for werecreatures. Wolves are the most common, but there are over three dozen separate classifications. It's not one of them," said Mandi.

"How can you be sure?" said the sheriff.

"Used to work with one. Tracked a few more. A lunamorph kill doesn't look like it's been shredded," said Mandi. "We're not sure what kind of creature this is."

"Great. What should I tell my people and the reporters? You have a cover story?" asked Sheriff Weeks.

"Truth works as for as I'm concerned," I said.

"Agent Karver, you can't be serious. We do that and we'll have a panic on our hands," said Weeks.

I shrugged. It wasn't worth arguing with this guy. "It's your call."

We got the details Weeks had on the case so far. The only thing resembling a witness was a guy walking his dog. The dog found part of Mr. Harrison early this morning. The crime scene techs think it was his pancreas. The dog walker called 911 on his cell phone. The locals had canvassed the neighborhood and so far had come up with jack and squat.

"We're going to give the inside the once over," said Mandi.

"Okay Agent Cobb."

"Call me Mandi."

The sheriff smiled. Mandi was giving him an emotional tune up. He'd end up stronger and able to deal with this mess easier. And he'll find himself very fond and extremely trusting of my partner. It was against regs for her to be doing it and Sam would have a fit, but I wasn't going to tell.

"Call me John," he said. "What's your first name, Agent Karver?"

"Just Karver," I said.

The sheriff looked perplexed. "Must be rough getting by these days with that name, what with the serial killer that the media nicknamed Karver."

"Bart Andrew  Higgins is dead," I said. "And comparisons don't bother me." The DMA let me choose a new name, as long as it wasn't one of my names. My choice makes sure I will never forget what something did using me as its vessel.

The house was relatively untouched, other than one door smashed in and another smashed out. And an overturned couch. There was no blood or remains inside, which was a blessing. We worked our way through the residence. The guy seemed to decorate in modern clutter. Papers, books and other assorted junk were everywhere, but were organized into neat piles.

"This will take weeks," complained Mandy.

"Not necessarily. Let's start with a couple of assumptions. Ernie Harrison made a living selling presumably stolen artifacts. He may have gotten a hold of something mystic in nature, possibly cursed. And it was probably a new acquisition or he'd have been dead sooner. He'd have kept it somewhere . . ." Walking into a closet, I lifted up a small throw rug, and found a trap door revealing a dial and handle. ". . . safe."

We had the crime scene techs dust for prints and test for blood. There were some minute traces of blood on the throw rug.

"I doubt whatever killed Harrison then went into safe cracking," I said.

Mandi nodded. "It could have ripped it open instead."

We were both thinking someone could have sicced this thing on Harrison.

There was an envelope of pictures on his dresser, recently developed. Most were of artifacts, one in particular. A couple were of Harrison and another man. I recognized Harrison from a printout the sheriff had of his driver's license photo. Of course, we were all aware that the remains might not be Harrison's, but his wallet was found in one pile of shredded corpse. The lab would test the DNA against samples found in the house so we could be more certain of whose murder we were investigating. My next question was who else was in the picture. Before I could voice it, a female deputy came into the room. "The sheriff wants you to see something outside."

We followed. The crime scene techs had bagged some of Harrison's remains, revealing the ground beneath. The sheriff and several of the rest of the locals had lit up cigars. Old cop trick to help block out the stenches associated with a crime scene. He offered us stogies, which we turned down. I was sucking on one of the nastiest menthylated cough drops you can buy. It only helped a little.

"This help?" He pointed to a trio of prints. They looked vaguely canine, if there was a pooch the size of a rhino.

"Maybe," said Mandi. In addition to what the crime scene techs did, we took pictures with our phones and sent them back to DC for analysis. Our equipment was easily the match of theirs.

While the crime scene techs made plaster molds of the prints, I held the picture of the two men up to the sheriff. "Any idea who the other man in the picture is?"

"Yes, that's Mr. Harrison's alleged partner, Don Baker. He's the one I sent a unit to question a while ago. I haven't heard back from them yet."

"You see the necklace in this picture?" I asked.

"It looks like it's made out of jade," said Weeks.

"It could be. You find it anywhere outside or in the house?"

"No. Is it important?" he asked.

"It may be. If you or your people come across it, treat it with extreme caution. Instruct everyone not to touch it until you call us. It may be nothing or it could very well have something to do with this killing." I handed him two of the photos. One showed the front of what looked like a jade amulet. There were some symbols I didn't recognize, but then again it wasn't my specialty. They were around the image of a creature that looked like a cross between a winged dog and the sphinx. It wasn't pretty. The second showed the back which had a skull.

"Will do. What's your next move?" asked Sheriff Weeks.

"We go to talk to Baker."

But Don Baker wasn't at home. We called the office psychics. Luckily, they were having a good day and directed us to a nearby gym. We had to get by a trainer at the door, who demanded to see our membership cards. The ones we showed him weren't what he was expecting, but they worked just as well.

A few well placed questions later, we found Baker toweling himself dry in the locker room. He was relatively well muscled, at least in comparison to his dead friend.

"Miss, I don't think you're allowed in here," said Baker, using his towel to cover his manhood.

Mandi flashed her badge. "Federal agents, Mr. Baker. We'd like to ask you a few questions."

"Normally, I'd be happy to, but I'm kinda naked. Can't this wait a couple of minutes until I get dressed?" he asked.

"I'm afraid it can't. Tell me when is the last time you saw Ernie Harrison?" I said.

"Last night. Why? Did something happen to Ernie?" Baker asked, trying for concerned. I'd say he got more like suspiciously interested.

"I'm afraid Mr. Harrison is dead," said Mandi.

He fell backwards onto the wooden bench, even dropping his towel in the process. He was good, but one look at Mandi's face told me he was faking.

"How did it happen?" Baker asked, absently picking up his towel.

"We were hoping you'd be able to help us come up with an answer for that. Where have you been for the last twenty-four hours?"

"At home alone, except for my visit to Ernie's last night and my trip to the gym today, but I can tell you Ernie was alive when I left him."

I held the picture of the amulet out in front of me. "Have you seen this?"

"Of course. The Jade Hound," said Baker, reaching into his gym bag. "It's right here . . ."

Mandi and I drew our guns so fast I wasn't sure who cleared their holster first.

"Sir, do not move or speak or we will have to shoot you," I said, unsure if the amulet could be activated by incantation. "Drop whatever is in your hand and step away from the bag."

Baker listened. I kept my weapon trained on him while Mandi secured the bag.

"It's here," she said.

I nodded and cuffed him. "Let's go."

"Why? For what?" he asked.

"I think you already know," I said and read him his rights.

"Can't I even get dressed? At least wrap a towel around me," whined Baker.

Mandi held up a wash cloth. "You shouldn't need more than this. Waste not, want not."

I actually helped him into a pair of sweat pants and sneakers and we took him to the local police station. As we left I could hear a distant howling. Baker seemed to hear it too and he looked around nervously.

It didn't go well. He asked for his lawyer right off the bat. The only thing we got out of him was his claim that Harrison had given him the Jade Hound as a gift. Baker was smart. By washing up in a public shower, any blood or genetic evidence we found could never be tied to him beyond a reasonable doubt.

Next we had the usual issue of convincing the local DA that magic means could be used to murder. Unfortunately the ADA was a fundamentalist Christian and was offended by the very thought of magic. Don't get me wrong, I'm not anti-religion. I still go to church on occasion, although I prefer to stay in the back. I figure I need it more than most. The problem is so many people are so blinded by their own beliefs, it shuts them off from seeing reality. He figured we were trying a frame job and wouldn't even agree to hold him for twenty-four hours. I tried to get him to go out to the crime scene with no luck. Even Mandi's propathic persuasions did nothing to change his mind.

In less time than it took us to track him down, Don Baker was back on the street with the Jade Hound amulet in hand. There was definitely something magic about it, like it was charmed to make people want to have it. Never a good sign.

Mandi and I stood on the steps of the jail house as he left. He shot us a jaunty salute, which pissed me off. I marched over and blocked his path.

"Is there a problem, Agent Karver?" asked Baker.

"Yes. You had something to do with your partner's butchering. This ain't over," I said.

"I'm innocent. Even the DA agreed with that," said Baker, with a smirk that made me want to mop up the pavement with him.

"Well then, you have a nice day then," I said, matching his grin with one of my own.

Baker tilted his head and looked at me, obviously doubting the sincerity of my words.

"Why, thank you," he said, pushing past me.

I politely touched his shoulder. "We've sent pictures of your lovely green accessory to our office in DC. In a day, maybe two, we'll know everything there is to know about it. If it had anything to do with Harrison's death, we'll be back for you, so enjoy what time you have left on the outside."

"The DA will just let me go again," he said smugly.

Mandi, who was watching from the sidelines, chimed in. "We learned from this mistake. You won't be going to the DA. We'll be taking you straight to a Federal prosecutor, one who specializes in magic-based crimes."

"I didn't cross state lines," said Baker.

"To do what?" I tried. He didn't take the bait.

"Absolutely nothing," he replied.

"Using magic in the commission of a felony automatically makes it a federal offense," said Mandi.

"Don't leave town or try to get rid of the amulet," I said. "Not that it'll matter. This arrest already established you had it in your possession. Destroying evidence will only add to the charges against you," I said. "So, like I said, have a nice day. It may be your last."

Clutching the amulet to his chest, Baker turned and stormed off. We watched him go and again there was howling in the distance. Baker walked faster.

"Better ask the Sheriff to put a tail on him," said Mandi. I nodded. She flipped open her department issued cell. "Let's see if Spyder found out anything."

◆　　◆　　◆

We spent the next two days doing more grunt work, tracking down anyone Harrison had recently had contact with. Several museums and private collectors of questionable repute were moderately forthcoming in answering our questions. Many of them had bid on artifacts recently, but none had even heard of the Jade Hound, let alone been offered the opportunity to buy it. Mandi felt that all of them were being truthful on that point, although from past experience we'd learned that a sociopath can have such tight controls over their emotions that Mandi's empathic abilities were neutered. Unfortunately, it was hard to tell if any of those we questioned fell into that category.

According to the deputies assigned to Baker, he hadn't left the house except to get groceries or work out.

We were back in town on our way to question one of Harrison's neighbors who had allegedly been out of town for a week, when our cell phones rang. The ring tone was a punk version of "My County Tis Of Thee", which was the default for a call from Spyder. He's a good kid, even if he's a little on the wild side. When I say kid, I mean it. Spyder was a master class hacker who messed with magic and ended up being transformed into an electronic life form. He generally lives on the net and calls himself the World Wide Spyder. When all that happened, he was all of eleven.

I flipped open the phone. The view screen showed his current avatar face, a blue-faced alien Elvis, complete with antennae. "Hey Spyder, you got anything on the Jade Hound?"

"That's why I was calling. Jana in records found a series of murders tied to it over the last several decades, most scattered around Europe. Harrison was the first on US soil. And guess who just got back from London?"

"Harrison and Baker," I said.

The screen exploded in electronic fireworks and the words We Have A Winner flashed across it.

"How does it work?" I asked.

"Apparently, Baker may not be the perp. As near as Jana can figure, the Jade Hound was dug up back in the 1920's in the Netherlands from the grave of a man who ironically himself was a grave robber. The first deaths happened in England soon after. There have been more killings sporadically over the years. There seems to be a connection to having the amulet stolen and it has been stolen a lot. When it ends up in a private collection via a will, nothing happens. When it's stolen, all hell breaks loose. No offense," said Spyder.

"None taken. So we can safely assume Harrison stole it and Baker took it from him," I said. "Probably came by, saw what had happened and used the situation to his advantage."

"That'd be my guess," said Spyder.

"Any specs on the hound?" Mandi said, looking over my shoulder.

"Neither Jana or I could find much, outside of a couple of old stories. Nobody's been able to take the thing down or as near as we can tell, even tried. It likes to stalk its victims. It can stay unseen and has some association with bats. And it plays mind games, letting its prey know its there. Want to guess how?"

Mandi and I exchanged a look. "It howls."

"Got it in one," said Spyder.

Mandi's cell rang and she stepped away to answer it.

"What's Jana's best guess on how to kill it?" I asked.

"Major body damage, but how to do that is anybody's guess," said Spyder. "You'd better take Baker into protective custody."

I frowned. Okay, maybe he wasn't guilty of murder, but that didn't mean I liked the guy. I mean, who climbs over the still warm remains of a buddy to rip him off. Still protecting people was part of the job, regardless of what I felt their scumbag status was. "Will do. First we'll have to find him."

Mandi shut the lid of her flip phone. "Already done. That was Sheriff Weeks. Baker ran into the police station, trembling and sweating, demanding protection. The howling followed him and is getting louder. John didn't know what to do, so he called us."

"We need to get him and his men to evacuate the area," I said.

"Already taken care of. Spyder, we'll need armored airborne transport ASAP and a safehouse," said Mandi.

"Nearest safehouse is in Maine, about five hours by car from your current location," said Spyder.

"Which is why we asked for airborne," said Mandi.

"There's a little bug in the KY," said Spyder. "We only have two classified to be able to withstand an attack by something as powerful as the Jade hound. One's in the shop following an attack last week."

"Last week? What's the problem?" I said.

"Plating got torn apart. That stuff is custom made to resist missiles to monsters to mystic attack and it's on back order," said Spyder.

"And the other one?" asked Mandi.

"Sarge and Mox are using it to transport a prisoner to Eastern State Penitentiary," he said.

The Quakers built that prison over two hundred years ago and they knew a thing or two about holding inmates, arcane and otherwise. In 1971 it was converted fully to a maximum security facility for mysticly inclined criminals. The place looks like a castle.

"ESP is in Philadelphia. They could be here in less than an hour," I said. Plus the pair of them had enough firepower between them to fry almost anything.

"They could if they hadn't started out in New Mexico," said Spyder.

"Great," I griped.

"I'll have our esteemed Deputy Director and resident fire demi-goddess on route to you ASAP," said Spyder.

With my luck, it wouldn't be soon enough.

We made haste to the police station and had to flash our badges to get past a police manned barricade.

"You think a block away is enough?" I said to Mandi.

"I suggested three, but John's manpower is limited."

I nodded. The fact that he took Mandi at her word put us a step above the usual situation.

A sharpshooter with a high-powered riffle was positioned on the station roof, but it made me feel only marginally better.

Weeks met us at the door. "Glad you're here. Ever since Baker showed up, the damned baying hasn't stopped. What the Hell is going on?"

We gave him the short version.

"Our best bet is to get him out of town to protect any innocent bystanders. John, could you get a hold of an armored car?" asked Mandi.

"Yeah, I should be able to. Give me half an hour," said John, moving toward the phone on his desk and pointing us toward Baker.

"I guess you didn't listen to me," I said.

"What?" asked Baker.

"I told you to have a nice day. But I guess anyone stupid enough to steal an amulet with a death curse ain't exactly bright enough to take good advice," I said.

"We should get him into a cell," said Mandi.

"I didn't do nothing," Baker said.

I grabbed him by the shoulder and yanked him to his feet. "Shut up and move. We're here to try and prevent that monster hound from pureeing you like it did your buddy. A cell will make that a little bit harder for this thing."

Just then there was another howl and it sounded close. Shots rang out from the roof.

"I guess it figured that subtle wasn't going to work if we got him to a safehouse," said Mandi.

The upper half of the front wall of the station was all windows and they shattered inward, glass rocketing everywhere. A piece caught me above the eye and pretty soon I was seeing red.

The hound had a face even a mother would abandon in a well and bury under a ton of cement. The thing was hovering in the air. Fortunately the ceiling wasn't very high, which forced it to land. I'll take a grounded monster over a flying one any day of the week.

Mandi held out her hand to Baker. "Give me the Jade Hound."

"Gladly," said Baker before I could tell my partner no.

"Everyone get into the cells and lock the doors," ordered Mandi. Baker sprinted, but the cops stood firm, their revolvers drawn. An incredibly brave and stupid thing to do. If we survived this, I was buying every one of them a drink.

Mandi was trying to get the hound to chase her, but it was ignoring her in favor of the retreating Baker.

"This isn't working," she said and put the amulet in a wastepaper basket. Mandi pulled her automatic out and fired a shot at the Jade Hound. The amulet was unharmed, but it did get the monster's attention. It stopped and turned its head to glare at Mandi, but continued to move toward the cells.

Mandi picked it out of the garbage. "This isn't working."

No it wasn't and I figured out why. I ran over to my partner and pilfered the Jade Hound out of her hand.

"Karver, what are you doing?" she said, but there wasn't time to answer. My partner would figure it out momentarily.

The hound stopped and turned around to see who the latest idiot was to have stolen its jewelry and saw me. The key word being stole. Baker gave it to Mandi. I waved, aimed my gun at its left eye and fired. The bullet made it go splat, but we have very special ammo at the DMA. The load has everything from iron to silver to holy water and the kitchen sink mixed in. Never know what you'll be facing down.

The blood poured out and congealed into something that resembled a bat, if Salvador Dali got to design it while on crack. I fired a second shot and the bat returned to blood and had the secondary effect of hitting the beast in its shoulder. I had the hound's attention, but it looked like the eye was already starting to heal. I had to get it away from the cops. I leapt out the gaping hole in the front wall and the monster followed.

I'm not a powerhouse like some in the DMA. I can't cast spells or bench press a semi or shoot energy blasts out of my chest. The demon that possessed me did some tuning up of my body. I was stronger and faster than a normal person and had some enhanced senses and perceptions. I can sense a demon at over a half mile and have an unexplainable love for polka music and yodeling, as if the memories of what it made me do weren't bad enough.

I knew the hound wasn't from Hell, but I wouldn't mind figuring out a way to send it there. At the moment, I was just trying to get away. There was a motorcycle out front which I set out to hot wire before the beastie got outside. The cops and Mandi were helping me by distracting it with gunfire. The locals' bullets were only annoying it. Mandi's ammo was taking chunks out, but even that was only slowing it down and making more bats. Fortunately the regular ammo seemed to work fine on them.

The hog roared to life as the hound's head cleared the jagged glass of the remaining window shards. I raced away seconds ahead of winged death, infinitely grateful for the remnant skills of a misspent youth.

Without looking behind me I turned the accelerator to the max. I felt rather than saw the hound dive bombing me and made a sudden turn around a corner, leaning into it. I got low enough for the hound to pass over me, but I ended up spilling the bike in the process. Ignoring the case of road rash, I got to my feet and spun around, searching the town skies for a flying killer.

I saw a dot outlined against the sun, which probably would have gone unnoticed by someone with normal eyesight. I limped over to the bike, my gun in hand. I stood over the cycle, waiting. Once it was at about three stories, I leapt backwards and started running in reverse in the opposite direction of its dive. I managed to leap onto the hood of a parked car.

I shot as the hound pulled out of its dive and was almost on top of the bike. My shot hit its target and the gas tank exploded, engulfing the winged monster in a fireball. I had thrown myself behind the car and slowly lifted my head to look.

Flames were licking the sky and devouring blood bats. Smoke obscured my view, but I could make out a smoldering carcass mixed in among the remains of the motorcycle.

I wasn't dumb enough to approach the hound, but I did stand up to get a better look.

"That wasn't so bad," I said, but instantly regretted it. That horror of a face lifted up and looked at me. It wasn't made any prettier for having been charbroiled. It started baying and the sound made my blood run cold. I did the thing that you're never supposed to do when facing a predator. I ran away down the street, my gun pointing and firing behind me.

The hound got up slowly. I had hurt it, but not enough to keep it down, but maybe enough to keep it grounded. The skin on both of its wings was bubbling and blistering. One appeared torn part way through. The hound started running after me instead of taking to the air, which if I overlooked the fact that I was being hunted at all, would be considered a good thing.

I headed back toward the police station in hopes that Mandi had come up with something. My partner didn't disappoint. As I rounded the corner, an armored car smashed into the hound, crushing it between the grill and a brick wall. Again it was stunned. Mandi was at the wheel and threw the vehicle into reverse. Spinning it around, she pulled alongside me and waved, then sped ahead. I could hear the hound shedding bricks as it got back to it's feet.

The rear door of the armored car opened and I jumped in. In the front of the rear compartment there was a bulletproof glass window that allowed the driver to see the guard in the back. Mandi had it open.

"Go, go, go!" I shouted when I looked behind us and saw the hound gaining.

"Not part of the plan," she said.

"We have a plan? I must have missed the memo," I said.

"Paperwork's not your strong suit. Wait for the hound to get inside with you," Mandi said.

"Have I been that bad a partner?" I screamed. The monster was getting closer.

"No. As soon as its in, crawl through to the cab. I'll hit this switch and the back doors will shut . . ."

"Trapping the hound," I said, finishing her sentence.

"See, I knew you'd catch on," she said as the front paws of the hound scratched and scurried their way inside the armored car.

◆ ◆ ◆

By the time the third leg was in, I was halfway through the window. It was a tight squeeze. "I guess it's a good thing I skipped dessert at lunch."

Mandi grabbed me by the back of my suit and pulled. I saw her eyes go wide as she looked behind me and then slammed the brakes. The sudden stop threw me into the cab and onto the dashboard, a split-second ahead of the hound's jaws clamping down on the air occupying the empty space where my legs had just been. The momentum also shut the doors part way, so by the time Mandi hit the button, there wasn't far for them to go to lock shut. The hound spun and realized it was trapped.

I started to slam the window shut, but Mandi motioned for me to hold and tossed a tear gas grenade in and shut it herself.

Mandi smiled and shrugged her shoulders. "It couldn't hurt."

I nodded and collapsed on the seat.

"You okay?" she asked.

"I will be," I answered as the entire armored car started to shake as the hound tried to claw its way out. It was a high tech armored car with extra thick metal and it was holding. Sheriff Weeks popped up at the driver's side window.

"Everything okay in there?" he asked.

"John, you should know better," I said, wagging a finger at him. The man was one of those who didn't run when the hound came in. That earned my respect, so I honored his request to use his first name.

"What are you talking about, Karver?"

"You shouldn't come a-knocking if the car is a a-rocking," I said.

"In your dreams," said Mandi. Turning to John she said, "He's fine, but we better get this vehicle to a deserted location just in case."

"You don't think it'll hold the thing?" John asked, his face losing all color.

"Not sure, but I don't want to take the chance," said Mandi. "According to Spyder, our backups' ETA is in forty minutes."

Spyder had told Sarge what had happened and he and Mox made it in twenty-nine minutes.

We were in a ballfield on the edge of town when the armored Crete class helicopter touched down.

Sarge disembarked while the helicopter was still fifty feet off the ground. He landed as easily as I would have jumped down four stairs. Not bad for a guy who was drafted back in WWI. As a soldier, Sarge Winston's unit came across a summoning of something old and threw himself on the jewel that was the catalyst for the spell. The thing bonded to his chest with the summonee trapped inside. They have a curious relationship, but it makes Sarge hard to hurt.

"Heard you had some fun, Karver," said Sarge, shaking my hand, then Mandi's

"Yeah, you missed the party," I said. I pointed my thumb over my shoulder at the still rattling armored car. "Mandi saved you a party favor."

The helicopter had touched down at this point and Mox nodded at us. Her hair was blond this week, which went surprisingly well with her Polynesian features. Spyder had brought her up to speed.

Mox went halfway into the cab and opened the window. The hound tried to come at her and got a face full of fire for his trouble. She had her shoes off and one bare foot on the ground. A moment later the lawn seemed to disappear and red hot lava poured out of her hands to fill the back of the armored car. Inside the baying of the hound got louder and sounded like a cry of pain, but it was a natural born killer so I didn't have any pity for it. Once the magma was up to the ceiling, Mox reached inside and touched the sizzling lava to draw out the heat. It slowly cooled to hardened ash.

When she stepped out, the armored car was in a crater over ten feet deep. The raw material to create all that magma had to come from somewhere.

Sarge opened the back door and a red beam shot out from the crimson stone in his chest, carving a box-shaped stone of the ashy mess. The Assistant Director reached in and dragged it over to the copter and loaded it in the back.

We made sure the hound was put in a secure containment area, but where is one of the few things we do keep secret.

I got a half-hearted lecture from Sarge the next day about taking unnecessary risks.

"You don't have to always put your life on the chopping block," he said.

"If it could save someone else, yes I do," I said.

Sarge's lecture was based on department policy, but the smile I got showed his true feelings on the matter.

We even managed to have Don Baker charged with taking evidence from a crime scene and not reporting a murder. The penalty was only three years and he could have got less if he plea bargained, but he didn't. Of course, the fact that we didn't tell him the hound had been captured until after the fact may have had something to do with it. Plus we managed to take his house and property away to pay for the clean up of the town using a little known provision of the Rico Act.

That just about wrapped things up, except for the fact that the Jade Hound disappeared from the evidence lockup a few months later and is presumed stolen.

# The Prying Investigations of Edwin M. Lillibridge
## Robert M. Price

The recent recovery of the final remains of *Providence Evening Telegram* reporter Edwin M. Lillibridge, long resting uneasily as if coveting a friendlier refuge, has occasioned much speculation as to the means of the newsman's passing from this world, as the condition of the bones speaks volumes, albeit in an unknown tongue. His disappearance as long ago as 1983 caused some comment at the time, but in those days any mysterious doings connected with the shunned Free Will Baptist church on Federal Hill were deemed best left alone. Besides, Mr. Lillibridge had been a bachelor with no surviving family, and, with the eventual expiration of his sponsoring newspaper, there seemed no one left with a vested interest in discovering his fate. It was, as is well known, only the recent exploration of the old church ruin preparatory to its ordered demolition that led to the fortuitous discovery of Lillibridge's troubled bones. And when the coroner disclosed their singular condition, including the odd *charring* and in some cases acidic *dissolution* of some of them, it was quite naturally deemed a case better left closed, if only by time and ignorance.

An unexpected discovery of my own has now led to the disclosure of the odd facts leading to the vanishing of the lost reporter, and I feel it incumbent to share the information thus recovered with any whose curiosity about Lillibridge's life and work may still linger.

◆　◆　◆

In his cramped office in the *Telegram* building, Edwin M. Lillibridge fanned himself to ward off the early autumn heat. He listened with growing interest to a set of local parents who had much more serious preoccupations than the temperature. The man and woman, as Lillibridge could easily tell, had been through their story many times already, and without the satisfaction they sought. There had been in recent years a subtle but disturbing increase in the rate of missing children incidents, and it was a matter of persistent ill-rumour in the old town that the disappearance had something to do with the theosophical sect nested in an old Baptist church building crouching atop Federal Hill. When the couple's young son failed to return home after school detention, they took the matter to the local constabulary but were surprised to meet with a combination of unease and indifference, as if the stance represented a studied but regretted policy of the department. Mr. and Mrs. Alsop, for that was their name, soon gathered from wider but informal inquiries that the police had their own reasons for taking such reports less than seriously. The bereaved parents took this to mean the police were being paid for their lack of curiosity, probably by the well-endowed Starry Wisdom Church. The congregation's wealth was rumoured to be very great, stemming from the mysterious discoveries of their pastor, the Reverend Doctor Enoch Bowen.

This clergyman had himself been affiliated with the Free Will Baptist denomination until a sabbatical trip to the Near East, on which he aimed to pursue a hobby in amateur archaeology, had issued in the chance discovery of a horde of antique treasure somehow hitherto unmolested by the local Arabs. It had been shortly after his return to Providence, curiously reticent to discuss the nature of his find, or indeed even to verify the report of it, that Dr. Bowen had returned his ordination credentials to his denominational office and instituted a new regimen of theology and worship at the familiar building, with the full backing of the then-dwindling congregation. That his discovery had at least included some modicum of the legendary wealth of the Pharaohs seemed certain from the sudden campaign of building renovation that gave the old pile a new lease on life. It was at that time, for instance, that the older stained-glass windows with their conventional themes had been replaced by subtly different religious symbols and cameos, some of them mystifying and a few downright disturbing to pious neighbors not belonging to the new sect. Dr. Bowen himself, a man of abstemious habits, did not change them in any outward respect, continuing his Spartan lifestyle to all appearances. No one accused him of enriching himself, and this, plus some strategic charitable giving to the neighborhood poor, served to deflect suspicions from the unorthodox Church of Starry Wisdom. After all, it was a time of religious fermentation all across New England and New York, and the appearance of one more new brand on the metaphysical shelf occasioned gossip for only a short time till more titillating topics soon replaced it.

There was certainly nothing sinister about the reputation of Pastor Bowen, a bookish man whose repute for counseling the distraught was well-deserved. If anything, his new theology only enhanced his reputation as a local Swedenborg or Quimby. Thus it had been no difficult decision for Mr. and Mrs. Alsop to pursue their inquiry with the man himself. They found it hard to credit any implication of involvement in their tragedy on the clergyman's part, and, if anything, any ill-considered accusations of Starry Wisdom's role in the child-snatching must fire their minister with a zeal to get to the bottom of the whole wretched business. Or so the couple had hoped. In the event, they found the silver-haired Dr. Bowen quite forthcoming with his trained listening ear, ready to extend well-worded sympathies, but oddly reticent to lend any practical aid. Then again, he proposed, prayer was a mighty weapon, and he should be sure to wield it in their case. The couple left with a feeling like that which they now inspired in the reporter: that Dr. Bowen's words were well-rehearsed, a script familiar from repeated performances. There had, after all, been those numerous other disappearances.

Lillibridge listened patiently until it was his own turn to repeat himself, for he had more than once found himself listening to very much the identical story. He had already tried to dig into the mystery, but to no avail. The chief impediment to his investigations, investigations which the police, not he, should be pursuing, was the surprising development that not long after confiding in the reporter, most of the affected parents had quietly *joined the Starry Wisdom Church* and were henceforth reluctant either to maintain any inquiry or to cooperate in it. Of course, all said it had been the compassion of Enoch Bowen in their hour of need that had attracted them to Starry Wisdom. It sounded reasonable after a fashion, but Lillibridge could not help thinking it odd.

He saw them out, wishing them well and assuring them of further news should he find any, and then made his way down the block where he hoped an old friend, Officer Shaunessy, might be found. Lillibridge and the policeman had more than once traded tips that came in handy. Besides, the doughty Irishman was too upstanding a man to take part easily in any departmental corruption, and Lillibridge decided he must now ask his help, hitherto reluctant for fear of raising a dangerous subject: an honest policeman in a corrupt department walked a narrow line, and Lillibridge did not want to give him a shove into personal danger. But now he knew he must do something, and he decided Officer Shaunessy could surely take care of himself.

Sure that he saw the tall, broad form of the man he sought a pair of blocks ahead of him, Lillibridge quickened his step until he reached the great Irishman and tapped him on the shoulder. The larger man spun about with reflexes surprising for one possessing his stature and weight.

As soon as he beheld the familiar features of the reporter, the constable relaxed, his red face lit by a widening smile. "Eddie, me b'y! Tis good t' see ya! It's off duty I am, and I'd be pleased if y' were to join me for some refreshment."

Withal, the ill-matched pair continued together for scant further steps before turning into a local tavern, through whose swinging doors they passed. Lillibridge scanned the dim, smoky interior, looking for a booth or table where men might converse with no one eavesdropping. Finding such a redoubt, he waved to the burly policeman, who made his way across the crowded floor balancing a couple of glasses of beer.

"Bill, I wish I were here for a social occasion pure and simple, but I'm afraid I'm seeking you out on business, a bad business. I'm hoping you might have some information to share."

Setting his mug down, the patrolman quickly shed the mood of relaxation he had begun to allow himself. "Aye, there's always bad business o' one sort or t'other to keep us busy in moi loin a' work! What's troublin' ya, Eddie?"

Lillibridge looked around before continuing. "It's a sensitive subject, Bill, in more ways than one. But I have to ask. Today I was talking with another couple who'd lost a son. Here on Federal Hill. The only lead I've got is the Starry Wisdom Church. I know the police have . . . thought it best to deal with Reverend Bowen with kid gloves. But if you know anything you could tell me, I should truly appreciate it. I hardly need to tell you I would keep your name out of it."

Bill Shaunessy had already sat back against the upholstered bench, leaving his beer to drink itself. His genial smile was gone. He did not appear to be angry. What provoked his round, wide-boned face looked more like a sense of dread and pain. One could tell he was trying to decide how to say that he would not be saying anything.

"By the Saints, Eddie. You've brought up a sore point. Not as I blames ye. But there's a lot more to the thing than ye know. I know ye think we're paid t' look t' other way. And some are. That I know. But I know, too, that things could get a lot worse. A *lot* worse. So bad that missin' a few of our dear ones now an' then wouldna seem so great a sacrifice."

Lillibridge turned pale, so pale that the change was visible even in the shaded interior of the saloon. His friend's face remained frozen to stone. The reporter moved his mouth as if to reply, but it hung idly for a moment, then closed again. Shaunessy resumed his low-voiced, reluctant words. "But this oi'll tell ye. There's a man ye might talk with, though not t' quote in the paper. An' don't be after tellin' him Oi sent ye."

If Officer Shaunessy had his beat to pound, so did Edwin M. Lillibridge. He was used to following a story down any dark alley it might take him. This time it took him to one of the oldest and most stately dwellings on College Hill. He had seen the place but had no associations with it. The inhabitant was largely unknown to him, despite the fact that Lillibridge had occasion at least to catalogue name and face of most of the prominent members of the community. This one was only a name and face. He was a successful businessman, involved somehow with shipping, but neither he nor his trade had ever before proven newsworthy. As he rang the bell and was shown in, the reporter was surprised to observe the halls crowded with packing cases, with most of the rest of the sumptuous furnishings draped with blankets and tarpaulins. Plainly, the master of the house was busily engaged in leaving town, from the looks of it, for good. Lillibridge wondered, only half-seriously, if the sudden instinct to migrate might have anything to do with the matters into which he now found himself looking.

Harold R. Collins III made his appearance with hand extended, though apparently in no welcoming mood. He was quite evidently preoccupied. He bade his visitor to state his business and come to his point. Not wanting to be rude, he nonetheless had much on his mind.

"As I do, Mr. Collins. So I appreciate all the more you're seeing me on such short notice — and apparently just in time!" The other man looked a bit nonplussed, as if something in Lillibridge's words had obliquely suggested danger to him.

"I mean, I wouldn't have wanted to miss you. Mr. Collins, I am told you have lately resigned your membership in the Starry Wisdom Church in Federal Hill."

"*You're* not a member, are you?"

"Oh, no! No, sir, I'm not. Nor a detractor. I am merely curious to get to the bottom of certain rumours that have raised their heads again of late. I'm not really looking for a story. I think public interest in Starry Wisdom peaked some years back. I'm more interested in the welfare of some friends, and they told me that Starry Wisdom . . . might be . . . of help."

"Then I should say you have come to the wrong man, sir. As you say, I have strayed from that particular flock. Whatever concerns *it* no longer concerns *me*."

"But, there you are! That is just the perspective I'm looking for, Mr. Collins. I am hoping that perhaps you will know certain things that you will no longer feel honor-bound to keep secret, if you know what I mean."

"You are clever, my good man, but surely one is all the more bound by honor to keep vows made to those in whose debt one no longer stands. How does scripture put it? 'He sweareth to his own hurt and changeth not.'"

"Indeed, sir, one of the Psalms, as I recall. My mother used to quote it. But it is a matter of danger . . ."

"I should say that it is! And I don't mind telling you, it is not merely honor which compels my silence."

"Just as it is not mere wanderlust that motivates your impending departure, no?"

"As I say, Mr. Lillibridge, you are clever. But I am afraid I can be no help to you." And yet, with these words, Collins reached out to take the reporter's hand and silently placed something cold into his palm, closing the other man's fingers around it. "Now I fear I must return to my preparations. You can show yourself out?"

That is what Edwin Lillibridge did, and he waited, in case eyes should be following him, till he got back to his office before opening his hand. For a second he thought he might have held a coin, but then he realized it had to be a key. Lillibridge now sat there, gazing at the thing. He hoped it might prove indeed to be the solution to the puzzle facing him. And he thought he knew where the key would fit. But it was nonetheless puzzling, since the same place was open to the prying eyes of the public.

And so Lillibridge decided he must next do something he had not done for a good many years, before journalism became his religion. He would attire himself in his Sunday best and attend the services at the Starry Wisdom Church of Providence. He felt no particular foreboding at the decision. He was undaunted at the prospect of attending the meeting of an eccentric sect. Any city that took pride in housing the Mother Church of the Christian Science denomination of Mary Baker Eddy could hardly flinch at the presence of the Starry Wisdom sect.

Lillibridge sat himself down in a sturdy pew about halfway down the nave and scrutinized the place during the service preliminaries. The sanctuary, nearly eighty years old, was in excellent repair. Then he remembered the refurbishing campaign financed by the Reverend Bowen's Egyptian delvings. Of the once-controversial stained-glass designs he could make little, especially since the morning was cloudy and no artificial light source illuminated the windows from behind. All that struck him as being out of the ordinary was one tall window framing what looked like a procession of monks. The artist must have had trouble with full-figure representation: the pacing, robed forms bore odd proportions, almost simian. He knew portrait painters often had difficulty with the rest of the human form when rarely called upon to depict it.

The congregation was surprisingly large, given that the sect had a few years earlier left town under a cloud of suspicion not unlike that which prompted Lillibridge's own investigation. There had never been provable charges; the congregation feared, and not groundlessly, vandalism and lynchings, should some agitator whip the local superstitious Catholic immigrants into a frenzy. Under assurances of police protection, which the department could hardly refuse, Dr. Bowen and a number of his disciples did finally return to the city a few years later to take possession once again of the old Free Will Baptist church into which they had poured so much energy and resources.

But Lillibridge was even more surprised at the strikingly diverse racial composition of the church. For next to stolid Yankees sat squat and swarthy Asians or East Europeans, Lillibridge could not quite tell which. Nor were Negroid and mulatto faces unrepresented. He reflected that this racial tolerance would of itself have been enough to cast a pall of scandal over the congregation in the eyes of society's proper mavens. Lillibridge himself, despite sympathies that had necessarily grown with experience, found himself momentarily taken aback with a mild feeling of distaste and disdain. But then he could not have sworn the origin of it was mere reflexive bias. Something in the general mood of the place disturbed him on a level so subtle it was practically instinctive. But then again, that might as easily be the product of his long alienation from organized religion. No wonder he felt out of place.

For the same reason, he guessed, he felt mildly uncomfortable with the hymns, though the congregation sang them rousingly enough. There were occasional odd references, names he thought sounded vaguely Egyptian, but then again, he had not heard, much less sung, any hymn in years. All of them would have struck him as equally bizarre, especially those of the famous Ira Sankey, which one sometimes read quoted in news reports of Dwight L. Moody, choruses celebrating the blood atonement of the Saviour in almost primitive terms. It all brought back to him what had alienated him from churchgoing so many years ago. And now, here he was back again, albeit as something of a spy.

Now the Reverend Bowen was ascending the hourglass pulpit. Some parishioners moved along the crowded pews from where their position behind the gathered columns, like indoor oaks, had impeded their adoring view of their shepherd. Lillibridge could see the aging clergyman, still visibly hardy like Moses, with undimmed eye and unfailing strength on into advancing years. As the old man's smiling gaze swept the familiar faces of his flock, Lillibridge thought he saw the preacher pause a moment longer on his own upturned visage. But he must not be suspicious. This reaction must be entirely natural for a minister noticing the unaccustomed face of a visitor. The reporter reminded himself to betray no trace of suspicion, but to display only the genuine curiosity he felt.

Dr. Bowen was by this time reading the scriptural text upon which he would expound. Again, it was wholly unfamiliar to the reporter, but he was not a religious man. He would likely fail to recognize a reading from the Bible if someone told him it was Shakespeare.

"A veil is stretched out between world above and the realms that are below. And shadow came into being beneath that veil. And it came to pass that the shadow became matter; and that shadow was projected apart. And it took shape in the matter: like unto an abortus. And it did take on a plastic form molded out of shadow, and it became an arrogant beast resembling a lion. Opening his eyes, he beheld a vast quantity of matter without limit. And he did wax arrogant, saying, 'It is I who am God, nor is there any other apart from Me!' And a voice came forth from above the realm of absolute power, saying, 'You are mistaken, Samael,' which is interpreted, 'God of the Blind.'"

And there was something about the "Urim and Thummim," divination stones through which God had made known his will in ancient Israel.

Lillibridge, who might have been tone-deaf to scripture, at least had a sensitivity to writing and communication, and he could make nothing of these strange words. Even less could he discern the import of the tedious sermon that followed. What the text might have had to do with it was hard enough to determine, but the sermon was principally a tedious mass of specialized jargon of which no sense might be made by the outsider. Even a secretive sect need not close its doors to the public if it so concealed its revelation beneath a thick blanket of theological code. The chorus of *Amen*s made it clear that the faithful had understood the disquisitions of their beloved leader well enough.

A smiling Lillibridge shook hands with a few congregants as the meeting dispersed, but no one was eager to exchange more than bland pleasantries and polite invitations to return for another visit. That was to be expected. It was neither the time nor the place for searching questions. The reporter hoped at least for a direct look in the eyes and a handshake from the pastor, but in this, too, he was disappointed. Unlike most clergy who position themselves at the church door to bid parishioners goodbye, Dr. Bowen had exited the platform through one of the doors flanking the chancel. Either he was not comfortable with crowds or he sought thus to increase his mystique. No one but Lillibridge seemed to mind.

Sitting at a lunch counter, in a row of suit-clad church refugees, Lillibridge fingered the key in his pocket as he looked over the menu. Absent-mindedly, he ordered some sort of sandwich and planned his next move. He now knew why the nervous Mr. Collins had thought the church key, for such it must be, was needful, since the limited access to the truth Starry Wisdom allowed a Sunday visitor was not likely to be worth much. Yet Lillibridge had picked up one choice piece of information. It seemed that services would be suspended for the next month while the greater portion of the congregation embarked upon a long-planned cruise to the Holy Land, with Dr. Bowen as their guide. Through his researches, Bowen must know the region well, and such trips were not uncommon in affluent congregations. Lillibridge knew, as Collins must have, that the temporary absence of the Starry Wisdom faithful would afford him a rare advantage to gain secret entry into the old stone pile atop Federal Hill. It was an opportunity of which he meant to take full advantage.

Edwin Lillibridge had plenty with which to occupy himself, attending to his ordinary reportorial duties, anticlimactic as they might now seem, as he waited for the Starry Wisdom congregation to follow their leader safely out of the country. He laid no special plans for his infiltration of the sanctuary. By the expediency of sham inquiries made to the office, pretending to seek an appointment with church staff for the purpose of demonstrating new office equipment, Lillibridge had ascertained that the staff would be absent during the cruise, those not aboard the ship taking the time off locally. He felt sure there would be night watchmen on duty, but during the day he should be able to venture boldly into the sanctuary through the front door. To any casual passerby it must seem business as usual, as neighbors not attending a particular church seldom bother to keep apprised of its schedule. He expected to have uninhibited access to whatever might lie behind any doors through which his skeleton key might admit him.

The day came, and the reporter made his way to the courtyard which stretched before the elevated plot of ground on which the Gothic Revival bulk of the Starry Wisdom Church stood, as if perching on a platform to come closer to heaven. There was a normal day's foot traffic, as he had expected, and he tried to look his most inconspicuous as he crossed the cobblestone expanse and inserted the key, first, into the iron gate. It swung open cooperatively, and he ascended the stairs, aware of occasional eyes resting on him from the street and reassuring himself that it meant nothing. He did not take the rest of the stairs ahead of him all the way up to the huge sanctuary doors, reminiscent of those of a medieval castle. Instead, he took the sidewalk around to the side, where he thought he remembered the office door being located. The key fit this one, too. He guessed that Mr. Collins must have been some sort of deacon or vestryman to be entrusted with this key. He had managed to retain it upon his departure from the group. Lillibridge wondered how amicable a parting it had been, and he speculated whether representatives of Starry Wisdom might not yet seek to reclaim the key from the man, who after all had appeared to expect some visitation he earnestly hoped to avoid.

He was able to gain access to the church office, but not to the desk drawers or locked files. Nor did he dare to force them. He dreaded leaving any evidence of his visit, much less blatant proof of prowling. So he quit the office and walked softly down the hall. He passed the entrance to the sanctuary for the moment. He felt he had seen what it had to offer when he had visited before. So he continued to the next door, which should lead to the sacristy, the "backstage" area adjacent to the chancel, behind the pulpit and choir loft. It would contain access to the immersion tank traditionally used by Baptist churches, which this had once been. He doubted Starry Wisdom had much use for it these days. But who knew what he might find in the preparation area of the sacristy, which, as he seemed to recall, would have been the room through which the pastor would have made his post-sermonic exit.

The door cracked, then creaked, open, in obvious want of oil. Lillibridge flinched at the noise, hoping he was the only one in earshot. He could not know for certain that he was alone in the building. He was surprised at the size of the room, which seemed to double as the pastor's study. Nearby was a large desk, with a bookcase surmounting it against the wall. He paused here and could not resist scanning some of the exotic titles. He had never heard of any of them nor had the faintest notion of their contents. The *Necronomicon* might be an actuarial compendium for all he knew, if not a collection of death certificates. The language appeared to be Latin, which Lillibridge had never spent a minute studying. Likewise the tongue-twisting *De Vermis Mysteriis*. Two "i's" in a row? He thought perhaps he had once heard of *The Book of Dzyan* in connection with a magazine feature on Madame Blavatsky, but he couldn't be sure. Reluctantly, he replaced the books and looked for any paper scraps that might bear revealing or incriminating notes. Nothing seemed amiss, much less suspicious. Another table, closer to the chancel door, bore a set of neatly stacked and polished vessels, apparently communion dishes, but also other odd-looking tools or liturgical devices whose use he could not guess. All bore exquisite, yet disturbing, workmanship, including delicately stylized representations of marine life forms out of some ancient poet's imagination: he thought of the Norse Kraken and Homer's Scylla — and shuddered. But what did he know of such things? Was not the fish a very ancient Christian symbol? So he turned and saw another, inner door that opened upon the baptismal pool. For some reason, he felt drawn to take a look.

Here was an odd thing. The tank had been made over into a large aquarium. Obviously the rites of Starry Wisdom no longer included baptism by immersion! Lillibridge himself maintained a small aquarium at home. He was fascinated by what he now saw and momentarily sought for the inevitable containers of fish food but decided against feeding the shy denizens of the tank, who hid in the reeds at the bottom of the large structure. He did not want to disturb anything the night watchman, who must be assigned to feed the fish, might notice. But he did allow himself a pleasurable look into the depths of the miniature habitat. The waters were oddly murky. It was difficult to make out more than vague motion inside. But at once, some of the waving seaweed parted, revealing a kind of crustacean, yet octopoid, chimera he had never seen before, even in books. It disappeared as quickly as it had revealed itself, and Lillibridge staggered back from the glass pen with revulsion.

Regaining his composure with a silent self-rebuke, the interloper made for the door, re-entered the uncarpeted hallway and began to ascend a flight of stairs which he calculated must lead to the bell tower. He knew he should likely find nothing there, but it should afford a nice vantage-point for the enchanting panorama of Providence below.

Creaking stairs took him to the door of what he first took for a storeroom built into the capacious shaft of the upthrust tower. He knew he was not high enough in the structure for this to be the level where the church bell hung. It was even a bit low for the ringer to stand and grab hold of a bell-rope. More than likely, a storage room in such an improbable place would house cast-off objects and furniture from the old Baptist days, items for which the present congregation no longer had any use. At any rate, he should have to enter it if he were to find access to the higher levels of the increasingly claustrophobic tower.

The investigator's initial glance seemed to confirm his guesswork, as the first thing he beheld was a group of elegantly upholstered high-back chairs of the kind that line the rear wall of the chancel in old churches for the sanctimonious posteriors of church deacons or some such. Perhaps their style was no longer considered tasteful, or perhaps they were judged too ostentatious and had been retired here. But, no, that would not explain their arrangement, for a second look showed Lillibridge that the thronelike seats were arranged in a perfect circle, some seven of them, surrounding a squat table of unusual design. On closer examination, the reporter saw that the central object was an asymmetrical stone pillar, plainly an ancient artifact, no doubt one of the treasures retrieved from Egypt by the delving Dr. Bowen. Outside the circle of chairs, pushed against the walls, were seven large head sculptures of primitive design, such as could be found on Easter Island, though these looked to be plaster copies, like stage props. This was plainly a ritual space unto itself, the site for celebrations or meditations of a more private type than the public services such as he had lately attended. He knew at once he had found the place where the real business of the Starry Wisdom Church was done. Now — what *was* that business?

The light was poorer up here, and dust augmented the denseness of the shadows, drifting as it seemed from the boards above, the ceiling of this level and the floor of the one above, the interior of the steeple. Once Lillibridge's eyes made the adjustment, he looked more closely at the central altar stone, if that was what it was, and at the object displayed upon it, which he had not noticed at first. There was a polished metal box, open in the manner of a jewelry shop display, and nestled in it — no, held within a peculiar metal band in such a way that none of its facets actually touched the velvety cushions of its container — was a strange, dull gem. Not without a certain witch-fire glow, albeit of the subtlest kind, the polished surface of the stone was cut into the most irregular shape, none of its various faces possessing a right angle to share with its neighbor. It was somehow frustrating, baffling, to look at the thing. And yet one could not look away. Though opaque, the object yet seemed to possess a strange *depth* into which the eye was irresistibly drawn. Abandoning his studied caution, Lillibridge now sat down in one of the great chairs, not moving his gaze from the black, red-streaked gemstone. He brought a finger near the stone but withdrew the digit when he felt a kind of radiant electricity emanating from it.

For a moment his rapidly drifting mind recalled Joseph Smith, the Mormon prophet, as he wondered if it were not such a gem, a "seer stone," that Smith had used to discern his revelations. But at once that thought was lost, crowded out by what he could have only called false memories, vivid, timeless glimpses of a past that seemed to unfurl into an impossible distance, yet all redolent of memory's familiarity. His mind was now in some manner anchored to the stone. Perhaps he was sharing the memory of the stone . . .

Lillibridge's mouth gaped wide and his arms hung limp, crookedly propped on the heavy, carven arms of the great ecclesiastical chair. In such a state he did not, needless to say, hear the soft scuffling sounds emanating from the unseen steeple interior just above him.

In the unnamable world in which his spirit now drifted, Edwin M. Lillibridge confusedly acknowledged the strange feeling of having been *joined* by some unseen companion. Shortly he found his stupor dissipating, as he began to see with a sight that must have imagination as its vehicle. He appeared to be the center of attention for many pairs of eager eyes. But the eyes waved from chitinous stalks. They were very far from being human. But they did seem intelligent. He felt like an infant being held up in the delivery room of a hospital for the mother to behold. One of the odd beings surrounding him in this dream held what appeared to be a sharp-edged tool, though at first it had seemed no more than a further extension of its arachnid anatomy. A chorus of the most peculiar buzzing, as of a summer's wealth of crickets, albeit with some sort of electrical distortions admixed, filled the space they shared. Before long, he felt "joined" again, this time by another presence who seemed to represent the curious spirit of one of the entities.

It seemed to him, again, by a misplaced sense of memory rather than perception, that he was located, not on the fair earth, but on an unspeakable world of impenetrable blackness, a hell of onyx, obsidian, and pitch through whose crevasses slowly oozed rivers of black lava.

But then he knew a different sort of endless blackness, as he seemed to be transported, in company with a great hoard of the crustacean things, through fathomless space. He sensed more of their insane buzzing, though the vacuum of space allowed for no true sound. At length the caravan of beings exchanged dead blackness for blinding white. The vestigial Lillibridge-consciousness understood, with a knowledge to which his sense perception would have been inadequate, that they had arrived at earth's south pole. The time was many thousands of years in the remote past, though recent enough for the all-encompassing ice fields to have smothered all life.

At some unknown time later, there was a great conflict, warfare between the lobster-like invaders and another, already-resident species, one, if possible, even more mind-blastingly alien. For these beings looked like great scaly barrels surmounted by quivering star-fish heads, and with membraned wings sprouting from all sides of their trunks like the leaves of huge vegetables. The two races fought by means of energy beams directed at one another and at their respective citadels. The human part of him assumed the bizarre space-explorers were fighting, as earthmen did, over territory, though he could not imagine what value anyone would see in the sterile ice desert. But then he realized that he himself, that is, the entity contained within the oddly-faceted gem, was the true object of the contest. They were warring over the gem from the steeple tower! It must be a talisman of terrible potency or of some equally great value. And at length one side prevailed: the starfish things exterminated all but a relative few of the things from the black planet who, it seemed, had originally fashioned the jewel of all knowledge. The straggling remnant of the lobster-race abandoned their Antarctican outpost to seek refuge further north where they should in future restrict themselves to curious mining operations, looking for substances unavailable on their own lightless world.

Meantime, the living gem found itself the object of great and elaborate rituals of veneration among the Antarctican creatures, who offered ichor-streaming sacrifices upon oddly-angled altars, seeking to plumb its depths in search of knowledge that might help them secure victory in yet another conflict, this time against certain amorphous entities of their own creation, viscous masses of protoplasm teeming with eyes that moved questingly in every direction, like some real-world counterpart to the Argus of mythology. But from this all they gained was the knowledge of their inevitable defeat beneath the onslaught of the monsters, and Lillibridge shared the vision of the attack of the things, including their eventual overwhelming of the temple of the gem. But the Antarctican vegetable-race had contrived a metal box of curious design to house the thing, for they surmised that darkness such as the inner entity had known on its parent world would unlock its guardian spirit with incalculable power. And in their last extremity, the high-priest of those doomed aliens managed to shut the box! From its lightless interior came the Avatar of Darkness, which Lillibridge's spellbound, purely passive awareness now recognized intuitively as the external form of that consciousness with whom he shared location in the striated gem. An awful mountain of smoky tenebrousness sailing forth on a pair of vaguely defined bat-wings, the god or devil swept its gaze over the ranks of triumphant rebels with its surmounting cycloptic eye, a deadly orb with three overlapping pupils. From it a withering death-ray projected, crisping the flabby masses of the creatures that had overwhelmed their creators and masters. As it returned, like Aladdin's genie, into the narrow confines of its container, the juggernaut left behind it outspread acres of ruined masonry which soon began to be reclaimed by the drifting snow and ice, to await possible discovery by the children of men.

Aeons passed as the Lillibridge-consciousness sank back into dreamless sleep-within-sleep. But then he heard the strange, sibilant chanting of a new race, scarcely less outré than any other he had seen, for these had the form of reptiles that had somehow evolved into near-humanity. Their explorers had unearthed the case containing the mystic gem from its grave amid the dead snow fields and transported it back to their home on an antique continent lost even to the most archaic mythologies of mankind: elder Valusia whence one day King Kull should arise. These crafty beings soon surmised the nature of the treasure they had found and made the sacrifices in cold blood that the Thing inside required as barter for the knowledge that it offered. From it the serpent-race snatched the secret of assuming any shape desired, or of projecting it onto the receptive minds of those among whom they wished silently to pass. And yet in the end they lost their advantage, as envious factions gained access to the gem and begged of it ever superior skills in besting their rivals, until the ensuing intrigues spelled the obliteration of the greater part of their people, only a few managing to linger on in impotence alongside the new race of men in future centuries.

And one of them, having learned no wisdom from the dangers of too much knowledge, carried the box and the gem with it across jungle-garlanded Africa to adjacent Lemuria, where it was lost sight of till the first Cro-Magnons stared dumbly at its pale aurora and erected about it flimsy curtains of mammoth-hide hung from a crude lattice of tusks and antlers. From its hypnotic glow the cave-men received unbidden promises of great boons in hunting and warfare. And they were glad to pay the price in squalling infants and shrieking maidens. And thus was the enhancement of the brain of man accomplished, sparked by an infusion of death-dealing and death-bought wisdom from the Avatar of Darkness. And thus was man's bloody path established forever: the incessant seeking of knowledge and the application of it to ever greater death and destruction.

Sensations were crowding upon him too fast for the human consciousness, who had by now lost track of its own name and identity, to register them all. But at some point he grasped that the immortal gem had found its way from continent to continent, from one civilization to another, in the manner of a deathless *atman* traveling from life to life concealed within the shifting soul of mortal man. And next it seemed he dwelt in Plato's Atlantis, where the champion Kull had caused the stone to be set into the pommel of his broadsword. It gave him victory over all enemies, but when he seized the throne of Valusia and was nearly destroyed by the lingering serpent-race who contrived to regain the gem and with it their dominion from of old, the king had the gem removed and cast into the ocean. But of course that was not the end of this small token which survived where whole continents foundered. Many centuries later the thing was cherished anew, by another mighty king, the tyrannical Pharaoh Nephren-Ka, whose native diabolism enabled him to put the stone to the greatest advantage yet. For from its depths he purchased the knowledge of all the future history of his realm. But the first bit of the future he saw was his own overthrow by his decimated subjects who could stomach no more of his butchery, as a whole generation had perished as the price for his revelations. Henceforth his name was never spoken and was chiseled from all monuments.

And it was in the concealing wreckage of the tomb of Nephren-Ka, a perverse structure with its apex pointed down, dug into the sleeping earth below, that the intrepid Enoch Bowen had lately rediscovered it, drawn by a seeming instinct he could not have disobeyed had he possessed any inclination to do so.

"Lillibridge. Edwin M. Lillibridge." Yes, *that* was the name of his fleeting human consciousness! He remembered! Someone was repeating that name, trying to rouse the shattered man from his stupor of too much knowing. Then the reporter had *not* been alone in the building. But who was it, standing before him now? Pulling himself as erect as he could, Lillibridge squinted, unaccustomed to real, ocular sight. The tall, silver-haired figure carried a lantern to dispel the gloom that enveloped them both — and others. It was night. Hours had passed. But no. The man before him was the Reverend Bowen. He was back from the congregation's cruise trip. This meant Lillibridge had been sitting there, overcome, for long *weeks*. His growing physical enervation had no doubt only made him the more receptive to the nightmare visions that had assaulted him during these terrible days.

The clergyman was replacing Lillibridge's press credentials in the reporter's coat pocket. The exhausted and disoriented man knew he would have a lot of explaining to do. He had violated the sect's Holy of Holies, that was true, but he had done no real harm, taking nothing, leaving virtually no mark to betray his passing — until the minister and six of his elders chanced to discover him as they entered the shrine to perform whatever rites were customary to the secret place. Well, Lillibridge now knew what it was he had come to discover, but he had no evidence that would stand up in any court, unless he could find where the childish bones were buried in the convenient churchyard. But what proof did Bowen have that Lillibridge had done anything of a criminal nature? His presence was proof of his trespassing, true, but then to prosecute Lillibridge must lead to the public exposure of the suspicions against Bowen's sect, and in such a case the discretion of the police would be of no avail. All this passed swiftly through the mind of the reporter, forced to take stock of his indelicate position with the instinctive alertness of a cornered animal. But it shortly developed that Dr. Bowen had no such plans. Plans, though, he did have.

"My dear Mr. Lillibridge. I had expected to make your acquaintance sooner or later. Seeing you in one of our services, I arranged to have you followed, as it turned out, to the house of the backsliding Mr. Collins. He is not good company to keep, Mr. Lillibridge. Mr. Collins is a disciple who looked back while plowing for the kingdom of God. Thus he went off the straight path. And he has led you off the path, too, I regret to say. But rest assured, Collins has been made to see the error of his ways, for all the good it will do him. And I gather from what I see here that you, too, have come to a fuller apprehension of the truth. Indeed, I should say that, given what you have no doubt seen, you walk no longer by faith but by sight, isn't it so?"

"So what is it you plan to do with me? Sacrifice me as you did all those children? Am I worth a few more hallucinations to you and your sycophants?"

"I cannot say as I care for your tone, Mr. Lillibridge, but, yes, essentially that is it." He gave a curt signal to his assistants, two of whom bound the limp and unresisting interloper to the chair arms, following which two more dragged the huge seat back and across the floor until it rested squarely beneath the trapdoor leading to the recess of the steeple. The noises of shifting and knocking were now unmistakable. The Thing up there must have hungered to get at him for weeks now. But its impatience would soon be at an end.

Here it came, dropping through the suddenly gaping portal like a load of reeking tar dumped onto a raw street surface. It enveloped the screaming man, smothering his protests, mercifully cutting off his oxygen and his consciousness before it sent something resembling a hollow horn through the top of his skull to suck at his brain.

But Edwin Lillibridge did not in fact lose consciousness. Instead, he merely found himself displaced, and restored to a state of mind now familiar to him. He found himself again at one with the intelligence within the stone, though the stone no longer housed it. As he directed the billowing Avatar of Darkness to turn its ravenous attentions to the wide-eyed humans trapped in the narrow room with it, the Lillibridge-facet had but a single thought: *I am It, and It is I.*

# THE ROACHES
# IN THE WALLS
## James Chambers

I can never think of Tessa now without remembering those slow-motion minutes in the cold dark, the nightsticks that drummed a whirlwind of pain into my numbing body, the cracked, stone floor in that Red Hook warehouse where I lay curled up and quivering beneath the hardest beating of my life. The physical pain wasn't the worst of it. It almost never is. That night everything in the world changed for me. Funny how it comes back to me best in flashes.

Tessa's luminous, crimson lips dripping my name like crystal bells ringing.

The stink of the old building's acid mustiness.

Wooden crates piled high around us, each one emblazoned with an octopoid corporate logo.

A splinter of moonlight lost to clouds passing beyond grimy windows.

Chemical fumes.

The panicked flurry of a billion tiny legs; the buzz and flutter of millions of pairs of papery wings.

My name is Lou Fine, and it's true I let Tessa lead me on, but before that night she'd been out of my life for more than two years. In that time not a day passed when the sun rose and fell that I didn't think about her, and I spent too many nights in the embrace of a whiskey bottle while the ruckus of the city streets whispered to me with sweet belligerence. Too often I strained through a haze of alcohol and desperation to remember the scent of her hair, the arc of her smile, how her body had felt beside mine. That kind of thing predisposes you to put faith in something you know you shouldn't.

See, Tessa and I hadn't parted friends. Her choice, not mine, but in the rare moments of objectivity that came to me, I saw that maybe she had been right. What business of mine had it been that her brother, a bigwig with the Transit Authority, was taking bribes? I should've let it go rather than let it destroy us. I should've burned the evidence I gave to the police. Except that I would've been burning a part of myself with it, and that's what Tessa never understood.

So when she walked into my office that night sheathed in midnight-blue silk that hinted at everything I longed to have again, I fell for her like I was a boxer on the take and the third round bell was about to ring.

Stupid enough to believe she'd forgiven me and come back — that's me, all right. Slow on the uptake and best taught by means of jackhammer repetition.

At least when it comes to women.

But then maybe that's just because I'm a man.

Tessa wasn't asking for much, though, and the implied reward was out of all proportion to the task, a boon valuable beyond infinite riches in the limited kingdom of my life. But maybe that's not saying much for someone who runs a third-rate security service and makes the books balance by working as a part-time police snitch.

How could I turn her down?

Someone had stolen a shipment of goods from Tessa's employer, Palmer Pacific, an international chemical corporation where she worked in the publicity department. No surprise the cops had turned up nothing. Tessa hoped my street connections might nurture a lead, something to make her look good by way of her bosses. I listened to her story and promised to do my best.

We agreed to meet the next night — at her place.

That's called *motivation*.

This all happened that day the cockroaches started dying. Pictures of chestnut carcasses spread like bread-crumb trails flooded the news, and the sidewalks were littered with clusters of motionless exoskeletons garlanded with curled, chitinous legs. No one knew what was killing them, but in a city that views its battle with cockroaches in nearly Zoroastrian terms, understandably no one did much to stop it. Maybe the endless grind of evolution had decreed that these indestructible little bastards would not, in fact, outlive humanity and survive to crawl through our radioactive wreckage. And if the price of it was a few weeks of bug-strewn pavement and extra-crunchy office carpets, people could live with it.

For my part, I raised an eyebrow and tried not to get too many deceased critters stuck to the soles of my shoes. All I had in mind was turning up something for Tessa.

It was almost too easy, but by the time my fist was splitting its third lip for the day, I felt like I was earning my keep. A few hours more working over the various scumbags I relied on for information, and I came up with the tip Tessa needed. A shipment, a big one, had come into a warehouse in Red Hook the same night Tessa's missing goods disappeared.

Now the city is a massive and labyrinthine place and it could've been coincidence, but I doubted it. The snitch told me the boost had been for chemicals. Hard to see much of a margin for that kind of thing in a black market that preferred dealing in cell phones, sex, and counterfeit Rolexes.

That was red flag numero *uno*, duly ignored by this lovelorn investigator.

Who had time to worry after I gave Tessa the news and she wrapped her arms around my neck? What could make me hesitate when she held me like she had in the days when we were new to each other and our futures held nothing but promise? She kissed me, too, and for the first night in a long string of hard nights that nagging itch to drink myself out the world for a few hours left me and stayed away.

Sometimes you fight your whole life for everything you believe is right and come up the loser for it. What keeps you going is that golden fragment of your past, that fading memory that stokes the last ember of hope glowing in your soul, because when that burns out — which it inevitably will — all that's left is terminal emptiness. For me Tessa was that fragment, and her return to my life much-needed fuel for the fire. Her coming back to me vindicated my existence and all the choices I'd made in the past under a cloud of "doing the right thing."

Has ever a more elastic phrase graced the English language?

My elation wasn't enough, though, to keep me from noticing something dry and coarse in the caress of Tessa's lips, a different taste than the one in my memory. The sensation made me shiver a little. I chalked it off to excitement.

Yeah, that's right: red flag numero *duo*, neatly rationalized by this ordinarily sharp and incisive mind of mine, muddled by the prospect of romance and all its earthly trappings and delights.

Why is it when we're bound for new depths of our personal Hell, we always manage to speed ourselves along?

I told Tessa to go to the cops with my information, but instead she asked me to take her to the warehouse so we could make sure I had the right place. I refused. She pressed. Not hard to guess who won the argument.

Tessa didn't let me past the lobby of her building that night, but she made it clear what would be waiting for me tomorrow after we got back from the warehouse, after I jumped through this last little hoop. We set a time to meet, and then I watched her fade into the dimness of the inner corridor and rise up the stairs. Her body moved like a walking massage.

A day passed. Roaches kept on dying in unprecedented hordes. I slept through the brightness, oblivious to everything except my seething need for Tessa.

When I saw her that night waiting for me outside her apartment building, I couldn't hold back. I grabbed her and kissed her. She trembled against me, and for the second time I experienced that odd flavor bleeding from her mouth and felt my nerves jangling.

We took a cab across the Brooklyn Bridge and had it drop us a few blocks from the warehouse. It wasn't the kind of neighborhood someone like Tessa should've been wandering at night, but she had me to protect her. I led us through the confining shadows, navigating the narrow streets to a side entrance of the warehouse. The road was vacant and still, the surrounding buildings locked and shuttered. The dim sounds of music rose from a tour boat making a circuit of the nearby East River. In the air hung the faint aroma of saltwater and rot.

I threw a stone and shattered the light above the door then swept Tessa into the darkened entryway and went to work on the locks. Her hand shook where it clutched my arm. I glanced up into the fathomless mask of her face. A faraway look filled her eyes, and her gaze darted from my fingers working the lock picks to the blank, steel door as if she could see through it.

Fifteen minutes and three locks later, the door swung inward and I stepped inside. Tessa followed. We moved through the blackness, guided by the faint luminescence of my flashlight. We passed a row of offices and strode into the cavernous storage space. Tessa nudged me aside and then lurched forward before she darted to the right and rushed into the dark. I chased after her and called her name in a whisper as she descended a flight of stairs to the lower level and vanished from sight.

From the blackness below she screamed.

I rushed downward and caught her in my light, threw an arm around her, and then turned to look at what had startled her. Piles of crates filled the lower room, each one emblazoned with the odd logo of Tessa's company. A layer of dead cockroaches blanketed them all.

"This is it," I said.

Tessa kept silent and took my face in her hands to brush her lips over mine. Her soft, warmth peeled back the icy atmosphere.

She pulled away and whispered, "Destroy them for me."

Her dark eyes churned and implored me.

"Burn them," she urged.

"What the hell are you talking about?" I asked.

"Please. Burn them. The chemicals in those crates are poisons. They're the pesticides that have been killing the roaches. It's something revolutionary, a toxin that can be designed to be lethal against only one species. They're already experimenting with it in the city. You've seen the results. I've been waiting years for my chance to stop them from using it, because it's not safe. When it degrades over time it becomes poisonous to humans, but Palmer Pacific won't wait to perfect it. There's too much money to be lost."

"You lied to me," I said.

I shoved Tessa away and backed into the darkness.

"Yes, Lou, I lied. But only because I didn't think you'd find it for me otherwise. Please," Tessa said. "I want us to be together again, but you have to do this for me."

Her eyes darkened and jumped, and I wondered what had happened in the past two years to change Tessa from the obstinately honest and rational woman I had known into a person consumed by obvious obsession. It had been there all along, right out in the open, but I only saw it then — that strange gleam in her expression, that frantic urgency.

I simply hadn't cared to look earlier, and that, of course, marked red flag numero *tres*, noted but dismissed by my overwhelming pride.

Tessa nestled against my chest, lifted her lips to mine, and kissed me. I let her do it and wondered whether or not I was going to burn the place down or slap her and leave her standing alone in the gloom.

That's when I felt two things that reminded me of how simple it was to fall for even the most obvious deceptions when conscience is exchanged for desire.

The first was the abrupt tickle of something probing my lip and the inside of my mouth, a thing that felt like whiskers or a stray hair or an insect's feelers. The second was the smack of hard wood at the base of my spine, igniting a sunspot of pain that sent me to the floor, just the first in a squall of crushing blows.

I struggled back to my feet, lasted nearly a minute shouting and swearing and swinging my clumsy fists, but they drove me down again. It had been enough time, though, to land three solid hits, and at least one of my attackers fell over and didn't get up again. I fought as long as I could, but there were too many of them. Every blow they struck chipped away at my consciousness and sapped my strength.

What did I see in those last minutes of awareness?

That's something I've asked myself as often as I used to wish I had Tessa back at my side. Despite everything I've learned since, I still wonder if I didn't hallucinate at least some of it.

Like the six segmented legs that sprouted from Tessa's waist and the flood of cockroaches that spilled out of her mouth. The way the shell of her body dissolved like melting ice into a stream of dark, scuttling bugs, all unraveling from one massive roach the size of a cat embedded at Tessa's core. How the thing shook little bugs loose from its long, dully glistening legs.

Or the half-dozen or so other enormous roaches that scurried around the room, leading rampaging trails of normal-sized roaches.

Or the men in gray utility clothes who came bustling down the stairs, friends of those playing the steady rhythm against my decidedly non-resonant flesh and bones.

The Tessa-bug crawled by me, paused briefly before one of my attackers cracked a nightstick against its shell and sent it scurrying into the void. It hesitated long enough, though, for me to peer into the shining black bulbs of its micro-faceted eyes. There I saw the vastness that sprawled behind them, an expanse unlike anything I had ever sensed, an orphaned abyss begging for sustenance to feed its eternal hunger. It was a roiling, slick blackness of death and madness cresting and breaking like waves against volcanic rocks. An imprisoned tumult desperate for impossible release.

My gut told me it was real, that the mammoth roach's eyes were windows not organs, that some bit of mesmerism or magic had tricked me into believing the thing and its progeny had been Tessa, and a spike of terror shrieked from the depths of my mind. I held out as long as I could but even as the ceiling lights blazed to life the darkness folded in around me and the rush of footsteps as more men poured into the lower chamber ushered me off to nothingness.

When I opened my eyes the crates were gone. So were the men and all of the roaches both living and dead.

A solitary figure remained, a wiry, gray-haired man dressed in an expensive, pinstripe suit. He looked down at me from his angular face, a visage as severe as that of a feral dog's.

"You're awake. Good," he said. "Then you'll live. You have no idea what you've been playing with here, Mr. Fine, what kind of Hell you'd have unleashed if you'd burned those chemicals and released them into the atmosphere. You ought to leave this kind of thing to the professionals. Be grateful we found you when we did."

"Well, thank you for beating the shit out of me, you sanctimonious old fuck," I replied, my voice a hoarse gargling monstrosity.

The old man laughed a little and smiled.

"Don't feel too bad. You gave us a hell of a fight. Eight against one, and you sent two of my men to the emergency room. Might be I could use a man like you, a man with curiosity and the balls to back it up. Or maybe you're just not smart enough. Could be after this you've learned your lesson about letting your dick lead you around but maybe not," he said.

He reached into his coat, produced a business card, and tossed it at me. It fluttered onto my chest.

"Call me sometime if you want to find out," he said.

I fumbled a hand over the card and clutched it tight before I dipped back into a big blank and the world ceased to be for a little while. When I awoke again, I was on my own.

The roaches stopped dying around the city after that, and being New Yorkers people talked the whole thing into the ground for a day and then promptly forgot all about it by the weekend. After I'd found my way home and slept for eighteen hours, I popped enough painkillers to tame my tenacious full-body ache and then went looking for Tessa.

No one answered her buzzer so I slipped in behind one of the other residents and made my way to her door. I worked the lock and let myself in. The wall of foul air that crashed down on me said everything I needed to know. Tessa waited in the bathtub. Wasn't hard to see she'd been dead longer than three days. I called the police, kept it anonymous, and then left.

Tessa never had come back into my life, not really. It was just an imitation, a fucking cockroach puppet spun of illusion and my complicity.

This kind of shit — it plays with your mind in ways you can't anticipate. It makes you think unnatural things, inhuman things. It makes you acutely aware of the cold brutality the world so gleefully dishes out to us day after day after day.

I had to shake the horror I felt, and that meant I had to understand the thing that had masqueraded as Tessa. I had to know if it had been real or the product of some blossoming madness in my own mind. A little digging revealed that the designer pesticide was just as the Tessa-thing had claimed. A mix instantly lethal to any insect it was engineered to attack, harmless to humans and other animals except when given time to break down and change. Then it did nasty things like cause respiratory diseases and birth defects. Best estimates figured another three years' research to lick that problem.

Don't ask me to explain the chemistry, because I can't. No more than I can explain the giant roach-things or how the filthy little vermin imitated Tessa so perfectly.

Actually, that's a bit of a lie.

An explanation is there for anyone who wants to believe in it. I've investigated it on my own, and I've made up my mind, but I don't ask anyone else to do any more than to make up theirs.

See, eventually I went to visit that old man from the warehouse, Easton Grant, and he spun me a tale of ancient times before humanity existed, eons past when monstrous creatures born under alien suns ruled the cosmos and held the Earth in their grip like a glass bauble. Their enemies aligned and trapped the greatest of them beneath the Pacific where even today it slept and waited for the time when its sepulchral city would rise from the ocean floor, so that its state of death might die, its reign commence anew.

"It can only happen when the universe is in the right configuration," Grant explained. "And there must be enough people on Earth who worship Cthulhu. That's its name. But there is one free to walk the Earth, to prepare the way. That one's called a great many things — the Crawling Chaos, the Messenger of the Old Ones, the Dark Man — Nyarlathotep. Millennia ago he was hobbled when one of his most powerful aspects was captured and imprisoned. Think of the resulting effect as a sort of cosmic lobotomy that diminished his power."

Grant leaned forward in his chair, a sinister scowl making his face seem even narrower than it was.

"And where better to trap a bit of the devil for all eternity than in a prison scattered throughout billions of tiny lives in a species so insidious and hearty that by all accounts it will outlast mankind itself?"

"Roaches," I said.

"Indeed," replied Grant.

"But then why me?" I asked. "Why Tessa?"

The old man shrugged. "Convenience. It connected the dots between you, Tessa, her job, the pesticides, and it played an angle, hoping to escape. Cthulhu's faithful pull the strings at Palmer Pacific. This pesticide was their new great hope, but they couldn't hide it from our extensive network of watchers. And so we stole it away from them. The thing you thought was your old flame hoped to get the chemicals into the air before we stored them somewhere safe, which we have now done."

"Where's that?" I asked.

"You don't need to know," Grant said. "Trust us. No one knows our name, but our organization has been at this work for centuries."

Grant offered me a job then, working with his high-powered research foundation, invited me to walk their marble halls and leather-dressed offices and fight the "primal forces of darkness" or some such bullshit.

I told him his suit looked like crap and walked out.

I work on my own. I don't need Grant or his nightclub-wielding jarheads to help me do what I know is right.

No lie, the roaches are bad for business. They make new clients skittish, scare others away even before they reach my third floor office. Regular bribes to health department officials put an ugly dent in my operating capital, and I worked a lot of sleazy divorce cases to scrape up the cash to buy this entire building.

The place is so infested that at night I hear the roaches scurrying and crawling behind the walls, and during the day they're out and about in plain sight, fearless even in the light.

Residents of the neighboring buildings hate me because I won't have them exterminated. Tough luck for them moving in next door and for having landlords who welcome cash incentives to turn a blind eye as eagerly as city officials do.

Like everyone else I used to hate the damn bugs, used to squash them whenever they showed their ugly, little faces. Now they hardly bother me, a frail ripple of disgust in the interminable dread the Tessa-thing planted in my soul. In fact, I can't sleep at night unless I feel them all around me, scuttling and darting through the dark and the cracks in the walls and the floors, letting me know everything is all right, that at least for now that abomination I saw broiling through the Tessa-roach's eyes hasn't drawn any closer to our world.

Yeah, there's that, but then there's something else.

The roaches remind me of Tessa, the real one, not the Tessa-thing, remind me of why she died and how she looked when I last saw her, and why I've chosen to live like this. She was dead three days at least when I found her, after all, but she wasn't alone. Do I have to draw you a fucking picture?

# To Skin a Dead Man

## Cody Goodfellow

---

**N**uts to you," Bogomil laughed, and died.

Next to him in the backseat of the speeding car, a hard-faced frail named Matilda Blau broke into sobbing and curses, and the two men in the front were likewise overcome by anguish.

"Check him again," demanded Tom Thorpe, the mourner behind the wheel. "He ain't dead 'til I say so."

The passenger, an oafish torpedo called Helix, sat back from leaning out the window, and rested a Thompson submachine gun between his knees. "He's in the hot place, but he's laughing at us." He twisted around and pasted Bogomil in the mouth once, to be sure.

"You yellow bastards!" Matilda Blau shrieked, "You'd never have the guts when he was alive!" The white-gold curtain of her hair hid Bogomil's frozen, bloodied grin. "Frank, no! Come back, please . . . Speak to me . . . tell me . . ."

"Oh, he's gone, doll," Helix giggled. "He's cold as a stone."

"He's no stone," Thorpe snapped, savagely wrenching the machine into a U-turn. "He's a dead cat, and I know how to skin him. Thinks he can take it with him, he's got another think coming."

Helix popped sweat bullets. "Where we going, Thorpe? You can't turn us back into the city!"

"That dirty bird has the key to the loot in his brain, fatty, and I mean to beat the worms to get it out."

They took a truck route back into town, racing through shadowy orange groves at seventy with their lights out. Thorpe steered them into the jumble of warehouses and factories behind Union Station, tracing a labyrinth of nameless streets until he came to a crumbling brick building around which an armada of roadsters and even a few limousines had gathered.

Thorpe climbed out and lifted Matilda off Bogomil's tear-soaked

---

corpse. "Hey, fatty, get our pal's other wing."

"What's your game, Thorpe?"

Thorpe didn't answer as he dragged Bogomil's leaden weight out of the car. Helix took an arm and they shouldered him across the dusty lot with Matilda in tow.

The front doors were a logjam of bodies — swells in tuxedos and silk suits, chumps and toughs and bookies in motley, and a few skirts for color. Thorpe led them around to the back door, where two men holding up a third argued with a neckless bouncer.

"He stinks, boys. Put him back in the ground."

"Ah, but this is Hud Hurley, the Raleigh Railsplitter, undefeated in seventy-nine bareknuckle bouts! When he was still warm, Gentleman Jim wouldn't even get in the ring with him –" The gatecrasher tilted the boxer's head back to catch the light. Maggots spilled out his ears.

"And nobody here will get in the ring with him, either. Dangle."

Thorpe and Helix hauled Bogomil up for inspection. "Fresh as a daisy," Thorpe said, and slid the bouncer a sawbuck.

"The Swede's got a full stable," the bouncer grumbled.

"The Swede knows me."

"The Swede don't know nobody warm."

"I wasn't born this handsome, yegg. Swede used to train me, before that rat-bastard West ruined the sport."

"Huh," the bouncer cracked a gold-plated smile, "Three-Round Thorpe. Didn't recognize you standin' up." He took the bill and stood aside.

The wide, low corridor sloped downward, and funneled the echoing roar of a crowd mad for blood. "Oh no," begged Helix, "you're out of your tree! You can't –"

"All I want," Thorpe sneered, "is to make him tell us where he buried it, fatty. Who wouldn't want to know that?"

Helix buttoned up. They hurried past a line of fighters slouching against the wall, shackled and hooded so the bookies could look them over before the Battle Royal.

At the head of the corridor, the incandescent lights made a white wash of the arena, but Thorpe could see the bars of the big cage over the boxing ring. The crowd made like Niagara Falls as the fighters began to file in.

Thorpe and Helix turned into a locker room. Helix let Bogomil slump over on Thorpe while he threw up into his hand.

The air boiled with the sick-sweet smell of human rot, bolstered by the rancid, reptilian tang of Magnussen's bubbling cauldron, in the back of the room.

Bodies stood chained to the wall or lay still on carts and in the midst of it, like the last meatball surgeon toiling in an Army hospital,

Swede Magnussen tried to wire the jaw back on a fighter without getting mauled by its wildly whipping upper teeth and flapping black tongue. His assistant, a big deaf, dumb kid with a cleft palate, easily held the bulky dead man down on the table with one hand while he tightened the strap on another one that almost got loose. His last assistant wasn't big enough to hold them down, and it cost Magnussen a hand.

"Hey, Swede," Thorpe shouted, "a jolt of snake oil for my friend, here."

Magnussen wiped blood and pus off his goggles. "Nothing doing, we're full up in here"

"This one's no fighter, Swede. We just wanna chat him up a bit, tie up some loose ends."

Magnussen gave up on the jaw and hooded the mangled fighter. He stepped down off a little ladder and shuffled over to inspect Bogomil's corpse. "I don't do walk-ins, anymore. Too messy. I only do it for the sport." He barely came up to their elbows, but his feisty, icy eyes shrank them down to kids inside. "*These* fighters, Thorpe, they never take a dive."

Thorpe's face twisted like barbed wire was sliding around under it. "Come on, Swede. This dirty twist took a big score with him. After, you can use him for gladiator school, or chop him up for bait, and there'll be a bit of scratch on the backside."

"Nothing doing."

"Fine, fine . . . Hey, Swede, how's your apprentice at the old Jesus-game?" Thorpe pointed at the deaf-mute.

The kid got real small inside his sweater, and Magnussen shielded him with his hook. "No way would he raise your friend, if I won't."

"I'm not talking about my friend." He showed his revolver.

Magnussen's cragged little face knitted up tighter. "So, it's like that."

"Sure, Swede, isn't it always?"

Thorpe and Helix dropped Bogomil on a table. The kid strapped him down while Magnussen climbed up on a stool and rummaged in his little black bag. "His artery's all shot away."

"He doesn't have to live forever, Swede, just long enough to talk."

"If he hasn't started to rot, he might still be himself, but he might not want to talk."

"We'll chance it. Helix, go watch the door."

Helix turned, grumbling, but the door flew open and boxed his ear. Blau stopped a man in a trenchcoat and fedora from barging in. They traded whispered barbs and he shrank away like she'd put venom in him. She shut the door and bolted it.

"Make some magic, Swede," Thorpe ordered.

Magnussen packed some plumber's putty into the bullet hole and measured out a hypo filled with a sickly green syrup. The needle was longer than a hatpin. "Here goes," he muttered, and jabbed Bogomil's chest. He drove it in to the hilt, then depressed the plunger, slow and steady, until the last putrid glimmer of the green elixir was pushed into the dead heart.

"That's all there is," Magnussen said, polishing his hook on a bloody rag. "Sometimes, it just don't take, even if they're fresh . . ."

Bogomil howled.

The sound was as far from human as could be, like dry ice squealing against steel; there was nothing of the smug, jocular thug that once wore that body. It was a mechanical sound, the cry of an empty vessel protesting the outrage of living again.

Blau put her hands to her ears and shrieked. Helix jumped out of his skin and drew his gun, but Thorpe had to fight up that awful torrent of inhuman agony to get in Bogomil's face.

"So, where's my meat?" Thorpe asked.

The howl broke into wild galloping laughter. Bogomil's chest kept expanding as he sucked in breath. The arm strap ripped away and he sat bolt upright. Across the room, four other dead men did the same.

Bogomil's hand shot out and caught hold of the soft pipes under the dumb kid's jaw, and pulled. Thorpe reared out of reach and drew his revolver, but Bogomil was faster in death than he ever had been in life. Greased up with the dumb kid's blood, he slithered loose and launched himself off the table in the direction of the door.

Magnussen swung and lodged his hook in Bogomil's shoulder, but the galvanized corpse was not to be thwarted by a dwarf, and dragged him like a kite.

The other dead men got up and liberated each other only to attack them. Bogomil threw himself into the thick of them and tore them apart with his hands to get at the door.

Thorpe couldn't see Helix or Blau for the rampaging dead men, but he saw the door open and heard the redoubled cheers of the crowd, who must be getting their money's worth, by now. The rioting corpses pushed out into the hall, where screaming trainers tried to cudgel them into submission.

Thorpe leapt from table to table to the door, his eye on Bogomil's dapper, oiled hair, and the dangling Swede across his back like a cape. Helix jumped up on a table and snapped shots off at the fighters, who pressed so close that the truly dead ones couldn't fall down. Behind the door, he spied Matilda Blau, cowering, but armed with a little automatic of her own.

Snatching a fire axe off the wall, Thorpe sprang at his erstwhile partner with the axe high above his head and roaring like a berserker, bringing it down just as the arc of his fall gave its weight the greatest force. The red blade clove Bogomil's shoulder down through his solar plexus. Blood, black and thick as pine tar splashed lazily out of the cavity. The dislodged Swede dropped to his knees and rolled out of the fray. Bogomil slashed with his remaining arm at Thorpe, who lost his grip on the trapped axe.

Blood blinded him, and rage deafened him, but he pressed on, because it was all one big mess to be dug through, and his money was on the other side.

Bulling Bogomil up against a wall, Thorpe grabbed a hacksaw off a cart and laid it across the uppity cadaver's throat. While the intact arm battered and clawed at his face and the other flopped against him, Thorpe took what he needed.

A peculiar calm settled on the locker room as he got up to find Magnussen examining his defunct assistant, and his own partners mauled but still upright in the corner. The stampeding dead had all filed out into the livelier stomping grounds of the arena.

"Come on," Thorpe called. He grabbed Magnussen's little black bag and dropped his prize into it. "Always a pleasure, Swede."

They stumbled over hills and valleys of trampled, mutilated bodies in the corridor. The gladiators were raising merry hell in the arena, but most of the audience had already beat a retreat to the exits. Behind them, Bogomil's headless corpse stumbled into the hall and, dragging the gore-festooned fire axe out of its innards, groped off to join the rumpus.

Helix asked, "So, where's the shiny stuff, Thorpe?"

"He was all dummied up from the drug. He had nothing to say, but a lot on his mind." Thorpe had a thought. "Big surprise how he came after you, huh, Helix?"

The big dope blinked a few times, slow-cranking his brain like a Model A on a cold morning. "He was just making for the door, Thorpe." His blobby oleo face melted under Thorpe's blowtorch gaze. He sighed and hung his head. "Anyway, she was right there, too. *She* knows why."

Blau made a claw of one hand and went to rake Helix with it. "You plug-ugly liar! Frank was ten times the man you are. You never knew a thing worth knowing in your whole rotten life, but you know something now, don't you?"

Helix caught her hand and twisted it behind her back. "You watch your mouth, sister! Frank was a fool for you, but not me! I got to the meet the same time as you eggs, and I'm out in the cold, same as you. And the company stinks."

Thorpe pried them apart. "Forget it. I got another idea. We'll get to the bottom of this tonight, or so help m –"

He held up the black leather bag and shook it so they heard Bogomil's teeth chatter. He tossed the bag to Blau, who caught it in the belly, and lost the breath to curse him again.

They got in the car and pulled out of the lot, raced down a narrow alley that fed onto Alameda. Just as they swung out onto the avenue, a trenchcoated pedestrian jumped up on the running board and stuck a gun under Thorpe's nose.

"Let's have the bag, dad," said the gunsel, casually, with no rancor. Thorpe's gun was trapped in his overcoat. Blau gave a little *yeep* and clutched the bag to her bosom. Inside the bag, Bogomil, too, smelled trouble, and tried to chew his way out.

Thorpe stepped down on the gas and reached for the bag. "Do as the nice man says, baby." With his other hand, he unlatched the door and threw it wide open.

The gunsel went out with it, hanging onto the door by his armpits and trying to shoot Thorpe. He squirted two rounds into the roof, one out Blau's open window, and one through the bag. Blau shrieked herself to sleep.

Thorpe batted the gun out of his face and swerved across the centerline. His wheels bucked as they crossed the trolley tracks, and clanging bells drowned out the gunsel's screams.

Thorpe measured twice and cut once, skinning along the side of the oncoming trolley. The corner of the people's chariot smashed his door shut and scraped the gunsel off effortlessly in its rumbling passage, sparks and chrome flying and faces flashing by with their mouths in big O's like a Christmas choir.

Thorpe's ears rang with the gunsel's runaway shooting, so he barely flinched when another shot squeezed off from just over his shoulder. The windscreen starred and shattered. Thorpe ducked and drew his pistol. With one hand more or less on the wheel, he turned on Helix and cocked the hammer. Helix sat there, dumb as a stump, hands up and empty. His eyes twitched at Thorpe, who reached over and found the gunsel's left arm still across the back of his seat, up to the elbow. Its index finger twitched once more on the trigger, and was still.

Thorpe tossed the limb into Helix's lap as they passed a cop in a traffic circle who stinkeyed them out of sight. A daffy notion crossed his mind, making him giggle low in his throat. He wondered if, before night's end, they might not have all the parts to build Bogomil a new body.

He turned it over and over in his mind. When they did the job, a dragnet closed around them and they split up to elude it. Bogomil took the swag, to hide in the hills. As luck would have it, they all got through in the clear, and converged on the meeting place, a cabin in San Fernando. They found Bogomil dying and two of Pork Cleary's goons cold at his feet. He laughed at them as they tried to wheedle the location of the loot out of him, but swore it was safe.

"We'll see how safe," Thorpe growled, and passed the gates of

Shady Glade Cemetery. At the end of the winding mountain road, they stopped before a lonely little bungalow shaded by weeping willows.

Thorpe kicked his door off its surviving hinge and jumped out with the bag, raced across the manicured lawn, rapped on the door like the landlord. Helix ran to catch up, and Matilda Blau staggered in after, still woozy from fainting.

An oily little man in a velvet dressing gown opened the door and prepared to deliver some urbane observation on the lateness of the hour, but Thorpe shoved him aside and went through the house to a book-plated study.

He dropped the bag on the desk and sat down with his revolver out on his lap as their host bustled in with Helix's hand on his shoulder, and Blau nipping from a flask.

"I'm afraid you have me at a disadvantage," the geek squeaked, "but if you will allow me to summon my housekeeper –" His hand went into his pocket, but Helix chopped the arm with his gun-toting fist, and the man sank into a chair with a whimper.

"I know plenty about you, geek," Thorpe said. "You're Aubrey Dubois, and you're an undertaker at yonder cemetery." He looked over his shoulder out the window behind the desk. Beyond a low fieldstone wall, the moonlight made a frigid silver wonderland of the city of headstones and mausoleums that dotted the rolling hills above Hollywood.

"Then you must know it doesn't pay all that well," Dubois said. "I have some savings, which you are welcome to –"

"I know why you do it. You're the outside man for *them*."

Aubrey tried to look dumb, but he loved to play games. "Them?"

"The hyenas: the reason smart birds all get cremated."

"Ah," Dubois replied, "but nobody *really* gets cremated anymore, you know." He licked his lipless chops. His hand inched back to his pocket. "So, what do you want?"

Thorpe unsnapped the bag and upended it on the desk. Bogomil's head rolled out, tracing a lopsided ellipse of blood from mouth and neck. The gunsel's bullet had smashed out his front teeth and exited just below the base of the skull. The mouth gnashed and smacked, struggling to speak, or just to bite. The eyes rolling in the face were just glass buttons, with none of Bogomil's clever sparkle that told you he was going to rob you blind, and you'd come back for more. But what Thorpe needed was still locked up in there. "Do what you do, geek."

Dubois got up and edged closer to the animated head, eyeing it with the distaste of a gourmet at the Automat.

"Perhaps, if . . . I don't suppose there's time to do this properly? I could open a bottle of fine claret . . . Chateau d'Averoigne . . ."

"No time. I've seen your kind do their stuff. They weren't so fussy. Just do it, and start singing."

Dubois went around the desk and sat down. At Thorpe's urging, he daintily tied on a silken bib, then picked up Bogomil's head and looked it over with growing eagerness. He wiped sweat out of the trimmed mustache under his long, canine nose. "Surely you don't expect me to . . . to . . . with you watching?"

"We ain't squeamish. You want a fork?"

Dubois closed his eyes and breathed deeply of the bloody bouquet of Frank Bogomil. "Strong," he murmured, with real squirmy pleasure, "sanguine . . ." He relaxed and settled back with the head, forgetting his audience. "Clever . . . this man has you all dancing on strings . . ."

His nostrils flared and his snaggled yellow teeth flashed. With a pitiful mewl of hunger, he bit off Bogomil's nose.

Blau hissed and raised her gun. Thorpe blocked her and pushed her back. "You don't have to look," he said. Helix backed up against the door with his hand over his mouth again.

Once he broke the skin, Dubois abandoned himself to his appetite. Worrying the cheeks off the bone, he gobbled up tender flesh and straps of muscle like a lawnmower from ear to cauliflower ear, nibbling these but finding the cartilage too tough for his refined palate. All through the meal, Bogomil's jaws snapped at air and wheezed to return the favor until, one by one, the muscles that worked them were shredded up and devoured.

Finally, when he'd stripped most of the meat off the face, Dubois allowed himself the *coup de grace* — at least until he got the vise to crack open the skull. Peeling off the lid first with his teeth, Dubois sucked an eye out of the head, rolling it round on his tongue like a centuried vintage, then crushed it between his teeth with a sickly little pop. He sucked the other one out and let it melt on his tongue. Thorpe leaned closer, horrified but hopeful as he saw what Dubois was becoming.

The lights went out. Black ink filled the room, chewed up by lightning flashes and mechanized thunder. Thorpe rolled across the desk and dropped behind it, where he found Dubois folded over and wet from the waist up.

"He got me again, Thorpe," said a voice that wasn't Dubois at all.

"Bogomil — Frank, where did you hide the score?"

In the dark, Thorpe heard his dead partner chuckle. "What a pack of saps."

Thorpe's skin knitted up in gooseflesh. It was easy to forget that someone was carving up the desk with a big gun. A few feeble pops answered back — Blau, firing from cover somewhere else in the pitch-black room. "Damn you, she-dog!" Helix barked. This couldn't last.

Thorpe took hold of Dubois's lapels and roared in his face, "Who killed you? Who took it? What do I have to do, to get what's mine?"

Bogomil whispered in his ear.

Hot lead smashed through Thorpe's back and into Dubois. Thorpe's right side burned, and blood bubbled up out of his mouth as he shouted, "How long have you been jungled up with Pork Cleary and his gang, Helix?"

A pause, as Helix fumbled in the dark with a new ammo drum for the Thompson. "Even dead, he's a gutless squealer!"

Thorpe popped up from behind the desk and squeezed off a couple rounds, but the muzzle flashes showed him he was aiming at empty air. "Who's gutless, Helix? You came at him with two men, and you let them get plugged. If you're gonna drill me with that chopper, you might as well spill where you put the score." His little speech ended, he coughed up blood and sagged back behind the ruined desk.

"Why'n the hell should you die smiling?" Helix slotted the fresh drum into the gun and sprayed the desk. Thorpe laid down, but a round creased his back. The window shattered and rained down on Dubois, who chuckled once more in Bogomil's voice, then rattled and died in his own.

"You're twice the dope I was, Thorpe. You think, if you bring him back, he'll tell you where he hid it?" Helix cleaved the desk in half and sent Bogomil's head spinning into Thorpe's lap. "He's laughing at us!"

Thorpe reached into Dubois' pocket and found only a little silver dog whistle. He put it to his lips and blew, hearing nothing but his own burning breath coming out of it.

A floorboard creaked to the left of the desk, and Thorpe rolled, saw a pair of size fourteen brogans and shot the ankle off one of them.

Helix cursed and fell backwards. "Ah, damn it, this game's rigged."

"You got a better one," Thorpe said, to keep Helix talking, "I'll play."

"I got nothing from him, Thorpe. Not even when I shot him. He just laughed at me, and said we could share it in Hell."

"So why'd you let the stiffs loose at Magnussen's?"

He scoffed with a wet splatter that showed how good Blau had plugged him. "You dope, I didn't do it! That dip hit me with the door, so I didn't know what was what."

Thorpe started to rise with his revolver up, when he felt the air stir at his back, and heard broken glass crushed against the windowsill above his head. Slowly, he turned and beheld a fearsome silhouette in the blue moonlight.

Yellow eyes glowed dimly in the dark. Guttural chuckling and falsetto meeping made Thorpe want to invite Helix to finish him off. It sprang from the sill to the desktop and more peered in with their blunt canine muzzles dripping coffin-juice and their stomachs rumbling.

Thorpe lay next to Dubois with his empty revolver up, but they took no notice of him. They were watching, and they knew who wanted to dance.

Helix screamed, "Eat it, hyenas!" and squeezed the trigger, but the Thompson was a temperamental gun that often jammed between drums, as it did just now. The ghoul on the desk pounced on Helix and drove him to the floor. The rest of the pack scrambled into the study and tucked into the strange treat of live prey with awful gusto.

Thorpe dusted himself off and took stock. He was lucky; only one lung flat. He grabbed Dubois's unfinished dinner and dropped it in the bag.

The tomb-horde scuttled to Helix and Dubois and dragged them out the window. Incredibly, hamstrung and half-gutted, Helix was still laughing and screaming as they bore him off to the graveyard. "I'll be waiting for my share, Thorpe! In the hot place! I'll be waiting –"

He found Blau out on the lawn, already making for the car. In the light of the moon, her hair sparkled like his one brief glimpse of the score.

"Wait up, baby," Thorpe said. "You weren't gonna leave me here, were you?"

"I've had enough of this. You ever find the loot, keep it, share it with the orphans, I don't give a damn. I'm through."

"We're not licked yet, baby. There's one guy can put this right yet, and I know he'll be anxious to see us."

"Oh God, no, Thorpe. Not –"

"Yeah, baby. We're going back to square one. Let's go see the Professor."

He watched her long, curvy legs trying to bolt out from under, saw ghosts whisper in her ear and flash across her white velvet face. Her icy blue eyes measured him, as cold and inscrutable as the hyenas', but every bit as hungry. He noticed just now that one of them was puffy and bruised under her makeup.

"Get in the car," he said, his hand restless in his pocket, "and drive."

Going down Sunset with the bag between them on the seat, Thorpe bandaged himself and stuffed rags into the hole through his chest. "I guess you fell pretty hard for Frank, didn't you, baby?"

She worked the wheel one-handed and rolled a cigarette with the other. "He didn't have me around just to look at. I drove the getaway car. I got us out of the dragnet. I –"

"You got wound up like a tin toy, but you were smart enough to hate yourself for it."

She reached out and touched his knee. "Why are you trying to wreck everything? We don't have to go through with this. We could find it ourselves –"

"It's not about the score anymore, and you know it."

"You're cracked! You were lucky to get away the first time. You go back, and he'll see right through you –"

Thorpe swatted her hand away and rested his arm on the bag. Inside, Bogomil's head twitched. "Nobody holds out on me, baby. Nobody winds me up, and gets away with it."

They turned north up the Coast Road as a dreary rain splattered on the windscreen.

The nice thing about Von Hohenheim's estate, was you could make all the noise you wanted. The roar of the ocean and the thick fog drowned all but the loudest screams, and the nearest neighbors were a quarter mile way, and almost as depraved as the man they were going to see.

They stopped in front of the big iron gates. Blau swigged from her flask and rolled another cigarette. "You want to sneak around the back and climb over the wall again?"

He started to shake his head, when the gates swung open. He lit her cig, and she burned his hand with it while she turned the machine up the crushed gravel drive. "Your funeral."

They got out and walked up to the porch, where a giant double door groaned open. Butterscotch lamplight bathed them and blurred the outline of a little man who bowed to them and nodded for them to enter.

He stood only up to Thorpe's waist, and had no arms, but Thorpe figured he broke even, because his short little legs ended in hands. His sad, saggy fish-face and hangdog eyes reminded Thorpe of portraits of Spanish nobility, but he couldn't put his finger on the itch of familiarity behind it.

They followed the butler across a vast red plain of Spanish tile that stretched out into perfect darkness. He heard no music, but Thorpe thought he saw gray shades clasping each other and shuffling in the black void — hundreds of them.

The Spaniard ushered them out to a patio overlooking the ocean. A fat, white-haired man in an impeccable white suit stood under the awning, smoking a fat green cigar and swirling a fishbowl of brandy under his bony nose. He smiled and drained the brandy, crowed, "Mister Thorpe, such a delightful surprise!"

"I don't know you, Mister, but I've heard things, and maybe we might have some business."

Von Hohenheim set down the snifter and puffed his cigar. "I am always willing to entertain an amusing proposition. At my age, diversions are so few and far between. Carlos, take the gentleman's bag."

"I'll hold it," Thorpe said, but when he looked down at the up-turned face of the Spaniard, his tongue turned to a turd in his mouth.

Carlos *was* familiar — but last time, he was taller. Helix cut the butler in half with the Thompson when he'd caught them upstairs, and came after them with a sword.

"Mr. Thorpe, do you like my servant? He was known as Carlos the Bewitched, when he was a king of Spain."

Thorpe resisted an urge to step on the ugly little Spaniard, with his granulated gray skin like pressed ashes, and his mismatched limbs. But worst of all were his eyes, those dry white eggs that regarded him without blinking. Swede's stiffs were machines, and Dubois's hyena playmates were beasts, but this cheap little statue of a man had a real live, suffering soul bottled up in it, and every atom of it silently screamed for release. "I like him fine, but I don't want to buy him. I got something I need handled."

"What, pray tell?"

He didn't know Von Hohenheim like he knew the Swede, and couldn't shake him down like he did Dubois. Diplomacy wasn't Thorpe's long suit. "A dear friend of mine met an untimely end, and I hope he can be . . . revived for a time, to settle his affairs."

Von Hohenheim threw his arms wide in a gesture of bewilderment. Far out to sea, lightning struck. "Wherever did you hear that I was capable of such things?"

Thorpe tried not to stare at the hard evidence lurking at his feet. "Will you do it, or not?"

"Such procedures are not simple, or cheap. I am, however," this last with a piggish wink at Matilda Blau, "flexible with regard to payment."

"No dice, prof. You can have his share of the . . . estate, soon as it's liquidated." Thorpe felt walls of dead gray flesh closing in, though he could not see them at the edge of the lighted shelter, or hear their shuffling feet.

He believed he had a thread of cover to hide behind, because he and Bogomil and Helix wore hoods on their last visit, and the fat man was out. Maybe it didn't matter if Von Hohenheim had him pegged, or not. Nobody got this rich by playing on the level.

"Then we have little to offer each other," the fat man sounded like a baby denied a treat, but then the twinkle in his eye came back bright as ever. "But maybe this will be worth it, just for the doing, eh, Mr. Thorpe?"

Von Hohenheim took the bag down to a cellar that, by the echoes of incantations and machinery, must have been at least as spacious as the house. Thorpe and Blau waited in a plush lounge. Thorpe sat stock-still, watching the low, round doorway and twitching at each strange sound, while Blau pillaged the liquor cabinet. "Your boyfriend better not rat us out," he growled.

"I think the fat man already knows," Blau shot back, voice husky and slurred with whiskey. "I just don't think he cares."

"Aw, you're nuts."

"Show me a rich old freak who ain't! I think he gets a kick out of seeing how crossed up we got, over his loot –" Blau went white and pointed. Thorpe shot up and whirled, his gun out.

Von Hohenheim stood in a doorway Thorpe hadn't spotted before, beaming like the cat who swallowed God. "There wasn't much to work with, you know. The successful resurrection of the deceased from its essential salts is foolproof only with the lion's share of the vital organs intact, but I've learned to cheat on the ingredients, as you can see."

Something squeezed past the fat man and into the room. At first, Thorpe's eyes told him he saw a dog, because it ran low and fast at him, but as they adjusted to the impossible sight, he gave up trying to give it a name.

It was made of hands.

Some kind of body must have been at the center of it, but it could only be a hub for the countless, spoke-like arms sprouting from it in all directions, a hundred swarthy and pale and callused and smooth and scarred and tattooed hands, padding across the tiled floor and groping the air and reaching out for his revolver.

He stepped back and cocked the hammer, and Blau screamed, "What did you do to him?"

Von Hohenheim's belly shook with shotgun guffaws. "That's not your partner, Madame. Hector is an amalgam of all the men who've tried to steal from me in recent years . . . or at least the parts that did the stealing. Are you versed in the classics, Mr. Thorpe?"

Thorpe, dumbstruck, shook his head. Right before his eyes, Hector's busy hands snatched the revolver from his grip without him getting a shot off.

"Then you've never heard of the hecatanotheres, the servants of Hephaestus, or Vulcan, to the Romans. No matter . . . if you'll follow me downstairs, you may speak with Mr. Bogomil."

Looking sidewise at each other, Thorpe and Blau followed the fat man down a wide staircase and into a natural grotto filled with big machines and junk that made their hair stand on end. Von Hohenheim led them to a table in the midst of a jungle of crackling electrical gewgaws. A big steel bell cover sat on something restless, barely keeping it contained.

The fat old man laid a hand on the bell cover and soaked up the drama. "Now, his appearance may alarm you, as the remains were not enough to bind his essence, and corrupted with a vulgar reptilian-derived reanimation agent. Mr. Bogomil's salts had to be leavened with the salts of unborn human specimens. But I assure you that the creature under this cover is your friend, in body and spirit. I can compel him to speak the truth, but I warn you: The dead do not lie."

He lifted the cover.

They saw Bogomil's head, big as life and twice as smug, but beyond it, the resemblance went haywire. It looked like Von Hohenheim had tried four or more times to shape a body out of the mess, but gave up trying to make sense of the tangle of snakes and babies that wriggled and reached for them from that insipidly grinning thing.

But Thorpe restrained himself, because there, in those eyes, was that gleaming, scheming ghost they'd been chasing all night, the one that got away laughing at them. *Almost got away*, he thought, with a loud, last laugh trapped in his throat.

"You may ask him anything," Von Hohenheim said, "but be succinct. He may expire at any time."

"You mind giving us some privacy, prof?" Thorpe asked.

"Oh, you have no secrets from me, Mr. Thorpe. Go on, this promises to be the jape of the season."

Thorpe had all he could take from the fat man, but he had nothing good to give back. "Where's the loot from the last score, Frank? Where did you hide it?"

Bogomil's mouth worked, spewing milky fluid. His snaky limbs uncoiled and beckoned Thorpe closer. "You kids," he whispered. "Can't find your candy . . . Daddy . . ."

"Frank, you've got no right! You're dead, and Helix paid for it in spades."

Bogomil clucked his tongue, which slid out of his mouth and hissed, baring tiny fangs. "I laid down . . . got rolled . . ."

"Don't play me for a sap, Frank! You didn't lay down for Helix. That's something that . . . I always admired about you, Frank, you never laid down for nobody . . . but you have to know you can't take it with you. You can't take it away from me –"

Bogomil mouthed breathless sounds. Thorpe leaned closer.

A muted bang cut his legs out from under him. He clung to the table. Bogomil whispered in his ear.

Blau shot him again, dead-center. If Thorpe had been born with a bigger heart, he would've died instantly. Still hanging onto the table, he moaned, "Where is the score, Matilda?"

She came around to look him in the eye, or not to look at Bogomil. "He said he loved me, and to hell with you eggs, and fine, said I. But he treated me like his meat, and nobody does me like that, and doesn't get bit!" She popped off a shot at Bogomil, but it splashed through him like mud and took a divot out of Thorpe's hat.

In the lurid light of the grotto, Blau's white-gold hair looked like bleached seaweed. "I slipped him knockout drops and stashed the score where none of you punchy dopes would ever find it."

"But then you . . . came back." Thorpe saw boiling white spots in one eye and blood in the other, which was a welcome change from the scenery of Bogomil's smile. "You had to try to prove you had claws, before you'd kiss him, but Helix queered your crazy little game, didn't he?"

Blau snarled and aimed shakily at Thorpe's face.

He felt a second — or last — wind in his sails, and talked fast. "Try this one on: Bogomil tried to talk in the car, but your screaming and pawing covered it up, because he wasn't dying fast enough for you, was he?"

"Liar!"

"Gum in the works, all the way down the line! You let the stiffs loose at Magnussen's. And that gunsel who tried to barge into the locker room was some other dope you had on the string, wasn't he? You wound him up so good, he had to show off by trying to hijack us, just to kill the head."

The barrel of the little automatic stopped shaking. To Thorpe, it was big enough to block out the sun. "Say another word, palooka, but make it a good, long one."

"He rooked you best of all, baby. He knew he couldn't trust you not to poison him if he ate you, so he switched the boxes. You took a trunkful of brass."

Blau snarled and pulled the trigger.

The gun clicked.

Von Hohenheim's laughter stirred bats from the stalactites. "Ah, by Gorgo's balls, what larks!"

Blau clawed Bogomil's head, trying to find something to strangle. Deformed and dying as he was, yet he was far from helpless. His tongue bit her hand and tiny, twisted limbs wrapped round her wrist, so when she staggered back with his venom already stilling her heart, he went with her.

Thorpe watched with fading eyes as she stumbled into a crackling Jacob's ladder. The climbing rungs of lightning enfolded her and her dance partner in a fiery blue cape. Blau's eyes and lungs exploded as she jolted and tried to shake Bogomil loose and hold him to her breast until it looked like there were two of her; but when he looked around, Thorpe saw two of everything, though only dimly.

Von Hohenheim went over and threw the switch on the machinery. "Well, I suppose that's it, then," he sighed. "I thought it would be more sport simply to let myself be robbed once in a while, but if this is as good as it gets –"

"Wait," Thorpe croaked. "You can raise . . . the dead . . ."

"Oh, Mr. Thorpe," Von Hohenheim tutted, genuinely sorry, "I have all the cannon-fodder I could ever possibly need. And there's not enough of Mr. Bogomil left to feed a fly."

Thorpe laid down on the floor and dragged Magnussen's bag over. "I don't mean me or him, fatty . . . I mean her."

Von Hohenheim turned and regarded the charred remains of Matilda Blau while Thorpe rummaged desperately in the bag.

"I lied," Thorpe gasped, "about the score . . . being . . . fake. She had the goods all along, but she only trusted him to cheat her. She only hoped we could bring him back, so he'd kill us and they could elope."

Von Hohenheim could hardly restrain himself. At a wave of his hand, Hector ambled over and swept Matilda Blau into a dustpan. "I suppose it could be amusing . . ."

Thorpe jabbed a syringe of the Swede's snake oil into his throat and rested the plunger on his knee, where his head would drive it home when he died. "Tom Thorpe . . . never . . . takes a dive . . . for nobody. If she thinks she's taking what's mine with her, she's . . . got . . . another . . . think . . ."

Von Hohenheim suppressed a giggle as he mixed Matilda Blau's ashes with the salts of aborted fetuses and less pleasant ingredients. He hoped Mr. Thorpe would be coherent enough to appreciate the cream of the jest, when he came back, and pondered how best to phrase it. For, though he enjoyed a good housebreaking as much as the next four hundred year-old alchemist, he wasn't about to throw away hard-won gold for the pleasure; all that glittered in his house was not brass, but cut glass and gold-plated lead.

*No*, Von Hohenheim decided, as he traced the sigil of the Ascending Dragon over the urn, and Thorpe's screams invented a whole new language just for cursing, *Best if he finds out for himself.*

# UNFINISHED BUSINESS

## Ron Shiflet

Wade Kearney sipped his whiskey from the glass, nodding with approval. He grinned broadly at the proprietor of Brennan's Bookstore and said, "Now this stuff is *damn* good. Not like the cheap swill I've been poisoning myself with."

Joe Brennan, the bespectacled owner, grinned. "My cousin in Kentucky sent me a case of this, last week. I'll never get through it all."

Draining the contents of the glass, Kearney said, "That's why it's important to have friends. I wouldn't dream of leaving you in the lurch."

Brennan finished his drink and sat the bourbon under the counter, beneath the cash register. "Well, old friend, I hate to be rude but I must get these books shelved. Feel free to make yourself at home."

"In a bookstore?" Kearney asked. "You must have me confused with someone else. Your sister won't be in today will she?"

Brennan laughed, opening a carton of books. "You afraid of her?"

Sighing, Kearney said, "Let's just say I'm not on her hit parade. I don't think she bought my explanation about what went down during the Satterwhite case. I'll admit, my actions seemed pretty hinky but it wasn't no ordinary case."

Placing a book on the shelf, Brennan said, "Well, she and her associates at Miskatonic are in a constant state of paranoia, seeing conspiracies behind every door. There's some brilliant minds at that place but most have been somewhat sheltered from the realities of the street. At least that's my take on them."

"I sure didn't win them over. Did she talk much about what happened?"

"Not really," said Brennan, "she's not much for confiding in me. I would be happy to hear your version of events anytime you wish to discuss them."

"I appreciate the offer," Kearney replied, "but I wouldn't know where to start. The whole affair is so screwy that my head's still spinning."

Brennan continued shelving books, stopping long enough to look over his shoulder and say, "Just start at the beginning and don't worry about how crazy it sounds. Even in this business, I've heard some incredible stories."

"Mind if I smoke?" Kearney asked, reaching into his shirt pocket.

"Go ahead," Brennan answered. "Now, about that case . . ."

The bell above the shop's door interrupted the statement, causing both men to glance that way. "Looks like you got a customer," Kearney said.

"I could use one," Brennan replied. "It's been a slow week."

A tall thin man with a narrow face entered the bookstore, blinking rapidly until his eyes adjusted to the difference in illumination from the bright day outside. Slowly making his way to the counter, he pulled a small notebook from his coat pocket and double-checked something written in it.

"Good afternoon, sir," Brennan said, greeting the man with a smile. "How may I assist you?"

"I'm looking for a book," said the man.

"No shit," muttered Kearny, rolling his eyes.

"By a particular author?" Brennan asked.

"No, by subject. I'm looking for any books on Richard Upton Pickman or his work . . . you wouldn't believe my lack of success up to this point."

Brennan frowned. "Yes, I would. His work inspired controversy in its day but most folks were eager to forget about him, following his disappearance."

Kearney followed the conversation with interest, trying to recall what he had once heard about Richard Upton Pickman. "Wasn't he that Boston artist?"

"Some say he came from there," Brennan answered. "Others claim from a far different realm."

"Different realm, what the hell's that mean?"

The customer, walked by, stopped and said, "Are you at all familiar with Pickman?"

"Only vaguely," Kearney said. "I'm a PI, not a scholar."

The man smiled. "That must be an interesting profession."

"It has its moments," Kearney replied.

"Do you have a card?" The man asked. "I might have use for a man of your abilities in the near future."

Brennan arched his eyebrows, grinning at Kearney. Kearney grunted, reached into his pocket and fished out a stack of business cards, bound together by a rubber band. Sliding the top one from the stack, he handed it to the man. "My name's on the card. What's yours?"

"Time enough for that later," the man said. Then, without skipping a beat, he turned to Brennan and asked, "Do you have anything on Pickman or not?"

Stifling a retort, Brennan said, "I think so. Allow me to check and I'll be right back."

The customer turned to Kearney and said, "Strange sort of fellow, isn't he?"

*Now if that ain't the pot calling the kettle black.* "He's okay," Kearney replied. "When it comes to books, there's none better."

"Oh, are you a bibliophile, Mr. Kearney?" Kearney thought for a moment, relieved to see Brennan returning to the counter. "Maybe he found something for you," he said, avoiding the man's question. Using Brennan's return as an excuse to make himself scarce, he went to the back of the store and began to rifle through a stack of pulp magazines. *Desert Adventures #27! There's one I haven't read. And this one has a new Rip Hanson yarn.* Thumbing through the pages, Kearney listened to Brennan and the customer, wondering if the man's possible need for an investigator had anything to do with his search for a book on Pickman. He sighed, remembering the occasion he had been hired to find a missing book. *That* had been a total fiasco and the last thing he wanted was a repeat performance.

"I was hoping for something a little more substantial," said the customer, to Brennan.

"I'm sorry Mr. Balmer," Brennan replied. "But that's the only book on Pickman that we have in stock . . . and I'm damn surprised that we have it."

*So the man's name is Balmer.*

"Does it contain any color plates of his work?" Balmer asked.

"No, I'm afraid not," Brennan answered. "You need to under-stand, Mr. Balmer, most people wanted to forget the man."

Balmer frowned. "I'll take it, though I really need to locate some-thing that contains examples of his work."

"Then you've never seen his work?"

"No," Balmer said, "I've only read descriptions. It's important that I see examples."

"Morbid curiosity?"

"Not at all," Balmer replied. "No, it could be important finan-cially."

Interested, Kearney ambled to the front of the bookstore to better eavesdrop. Listening, he heard Balmer explain — after swearing Brennan to secrecy — that he had acquired some paintings as part of goods purchased at an estate auction and believed it was possible that they might be Pickman originals.

"I don't know," Brennan said, looking skeptical. "The odds of that occurring are pretty slim, though stranger things have happened."

"That's what I thought," said Balmer. "Then I began to do some research after being appalled by the artist's subject matter. I soon discovered that Richard Pickman was the only artist of note that had made a name — infamous though it was — by focusing exclusively on such tasteless and unwholesome material."

Kearney moved closer, detecting the gleam of intense interest in Brennan's eyes. He thumbed through a popular novel of little merit, interested in the turn of the conversation. *Does he want me to help him find something on Pickman?*

"Well," said Balmer, "what I really need is to see some original Pickman art, or at least some good prints. Only then will I know for certain if there's a chance that I might have stumbled upon some."

Brennan smiled. "Either that or find someone who has seen the originals and who is astute enough to make a sound judgment on the matter."

"The few experts I've consulted have either never seen his work or had no inclination to do so."

Brennan scratched his head. "That seems to be a rather narrow approach to art. But then Pickman's work did provoke a visceral loathing in most people."

"Maybe so," Balmer replied, "but it still doesn't solve my problem, though you almost act as if you knew the man."

Grinning, Brennan said, "Only briefly."

Balmer grew excited, barely able to contain himself. "Then you've seen his work as well?"

"Yes," Brennan answered. "I had the dubious pleasure on one occasion. I was a much younger man back then but I'm pretty sure I would recognize an authentic Pickman if I saw another. The man's work didn't easily lend itself to imitation. Only someone as tormented as he could provoke such strong reactions in the viewer."

Kearney moved even closer, thinking he might need to catch Balmer. He looked like one of those dames who are always on the verge of swooning. Instead, he stepped forward, clutching at Balmer's arm. He watched Balmer push it away and say, "Then you've got to help me! I'll pay you well for your trouble . . . tell me how much you want."

"Now hold on," Brennan replied, extricating himself from the man's grasp. "It isn't a question of money."

"What then?" Balmer asked, looking crestfallen.

The smile vanished from Brennan's face, replaced by a somberness that Kearney had never seen before. "I'm an old man, perhaps having only a few short years remaining. Would you have me spending my final days in the throes of nightmare?"

Stunned by the words, Kearney stared at Brennan. He'd never heard him speak in such a manner and was worried by its implications. Suddenly, Brennan burst out laughing and said, "Of course I'll look at your paintings. I wouldn't miss it for the world! And please excuse my pseudo-histrionics. I'm afraid I've been over-indulging my taste for pulp fiction. I couldn't resist hamming it up a bit."

Both Balmer and Kearney were relieved but for different reasons. "Pulp fiction?" Kearney asked. "That sounded more like Monogram movie dialog to me. I thought you were losing your marbles there for a minute."

"Ha, ha," Balmer said, clearly unamused. Then, remembering that he needed Brennan, said, "Please forgive me. I'm not normally such a stick in the mud but the acquisition of those paintings has made me rather tense. I'm anxious to know if I truly own some original Pickmans."

Brennan patted his shoulder, saying, "That's quite all right. I don't blame you for being anxious. I'm more than eager to take a look at them."

"Oh thank you!" Balmer exclaimed. "I'll see that you're more than compensated for your time." Then turning to Kearney, he said, "And if this pans out, there will be profit in it for you as well."

Kearney grinned. "Profit, now there's one of my favorite words."

Balmer's smile vanished, not amused by Kearney's comment. Not wanting to wear out his welcome, Kearney left after making up an excuse about returning to his office to wrap up a case in its final stages. He knew Brennan would fill him in later if he didn't hear from Balmer first.

It was several days before Kearney heard from Balmer or Brennan. He had been unexpectedly called out of town to assist another PI that he had once worked with at the Pinkerton Agency. It had been a damn slow morning and he kept looking at the top right-hand drawer of the desk where he kept a bottle of Old Crow. It was strictly for medicinal purposes, or so he would have one believe. He used it when needing a little pick-me-up after a particularly hard night, the hair of the dog and all that. Almost succumbing to temptation, he looked up as the door opened and Balmer walked in. Kearney had taken an immediate dislike of the man when first meeting him at Brennan's. Still, he was willing to overlook that if Balmer had a decent paying job for him. *Lord knows he's no worse than most of my clients.*

"Hello Balmer," he said. Kearney immediately noticed that the man was less than impressed with the décor. Unable to resist needling him, Kearney asked, "Did you and Brennan look at the pretty pictures?"

Looking like he'd bitten into a lemon, Balmer said, "Mr. Brennan warned me about you, so I'll not let you get my goat."

"That's okay," Kearney answered, "I've already got one."

Ignoring the joke, Balmer said, "Mr. Brennan tells me that you're good at what you do. I suppose I can live with your sledgehammer wit."

*Good old Joe. He put in a good word for me, even after hearing about how I botched the Satterwhite affair. I'll definitely spring for lunch the next time I see him.*

Balmer looked around the office, sour expression still in place. Kearney watched him, finally saying, "It's served me well."

"I beg your pardon?" Balmer asked, wondering what the hell Kearney meant.

"My sledgehammer wit, it's served me well."

Balmer smiled. "Oh yes indeed, I can see that it has."

Grinning, Kearney said, "Have a seat and tell me what I can do for you."

Balmer sat, getting right to the point. "Have you ever done any security work? I'm in the market for such a man."

Lighting a smoke, Kearney asked, "You looking for a bodyguard or something else?"

"No, not a bodyguard," he replied. "I need someone to guard the Pickmans that I'm soon going to exhibit." His satisfied smile ranked up there with the best of them.

"Oh, so Brennan gave you the good word, eh? Congratulations."

Rising from his seat, Balmer said, "Not only *that* but he put me in contact with an expert who confirmed his judgment!" He paced excitedly, continuing to speak. "I plan to exhibit the paintings for one week only and will then place them up for auction. I expect to make a tidy sum from their sale."

Exhaling a plume of smoke, Kearney said, "So you want to hire me to guard these pictures . . ."

"Paintings!" Balmer exclaimed.

"Okay, *paintings*," Kearney said. "That sounds easy enough providing the price is right."

"What do you mean if the price is right?" Balmer asked. "Don't you have a standard fee?"

"Normally, but I enjoy gouging you big city art-types."

Balmer's face reddened and Kearney quickly said, "It's a joke! I thought Brennan warned you about me."

"Fine," said Balmer. "But please try to remain serious until this exhibit is over."

Kearney named the price of his fee, resisting the urge to raise it. He was pleased that Balmer didn't beef about it, giving him a nice retainer along with detailed instructions on what his duties would entail. Kearney offered him a drink but it was refused by his new client with a tactless expression of disgust. Watching Balmer leave, he took out the Old Crow and had a celebratory drink alone.

One month later, Kearney found himself in a small building off of Arkham's Main Street. He was staring at two of the most grotesque paintings he had ever seen. *I'm not an art buff but I figure ninety-nine percent of the population would give these works a big thumbs down. I don't even want to consider the other one percent who might appreciate such garbage.* The fact that Balmer expected to make a fortune from them only served to confirm Kearney's opinion of the "art crowd." The two paintings in question had been sent to Boston for cleaning prior to their exhibition in Arkham. *I don't know what that entails but the kind of cleaning they need is with elbow grease and extra-coarse grain sandpaper.* Kearney believed they were sickening examples of a deranged mind and didn't consider himself squeamish by any stretch of the imagination.

Balmer approached him, noting the look of disgust on his face. "What's troubling you Kearney, don't you appreciate art?"

Grunting, Kearney replied, "Is that what this is? I have a couple of other names for it."

Smiling thinly, Balmer said, "You don't have to like them, just see that they remain safe."

"From who, the taste police?"

"Regardless of your personal feelings, they're extremely valuable."

"Have you insured them?" Kearney asked.

Balmer grinned, saying, "Why do you think I hired you?"

"For my witty repartee?"

"Not hardly," Balmer replied. "I'm getting ready to leave for the evening. I'll lock the doors and I don't want you unlocking them until I arrive in the morning. Your job is simple, just remain here with the paintings and allow no one else inside. Use your gun if necessary."

Irked, Kearney sighed. "Hey friend, I know my job. So please don't climb up on your high-horse with me."

Balmer walked to the front door, turned and smiled. "My apologies, Mr. Kearney. See that you put that anger to good use if someone attempts to steal my paintings."

Waving him off, Kearney locked the front door. Balmer had originally wanted to exhibit the paintings in one of the local galleries but couldn't find one willing. Pickman's work was still considered blasphemous and no gallery director in Arkham was willing to take the heat that such an exhibit would engender. Because of this, Blamer had been forced to rent an empty storefront just off Main Street. Kearney thought it was a lot of dough for a week but Balmer figured it would pay off in the long run. *Truth is, Balmer's got the place looking pretty swanky.*

Kearney walked to a small desk near the front entrance, finding his thermos of coffee. He thought that the greatest danger facing him on the eve of the opening was falling asleep. Shaking his head, he tried to understand why anyone would want to hang the paintings on their walls — the artist maybe — but not the paintings. They were in a part of the room partitioned off from the rest of the building. *That suits me fine because the less I see of them, the better. That one called "Taking Communion" is still knocking around in my mind. God, how someone could paint something like that is beyond me!*

According to Balmer, the work was the kind of subject matter that had provoked such public outrage against the artist. It had been deemed too blasphemous in its day and had never been exhibited, even briefly. It was done in the artist's typical photo-realistic style, portraying an incredible scene of horror within an unspecified church. The painting showed a parish priest hanging upside down, his throat having been torn out. A score of shaggy dog-like creatures with partially-hooved feet and rubbery skin circled the priest while reaching for a golden goblet that caught his blood. Pickman — in his madness — had even included himself in the painting. Standing before an altar, he preached from a moldy old book to the congregation of horrors. The letters N E C R O N O M were clear but the remaining ones were obscured.

Shuddering, Kearney tried to think about something else. *Those creatures remind me of dogs but they walk upright like men and appear almost human in spite of their deformities. It's damn hard to get that scene out of my mind.* He took a swallow of coffee, feeling better and hoping the night would pass quickly.

Shortly before two A.M., he dozed off. He woke in the chair with a stiff neck and foggy mind. Looking around blearily, he saw no sign of trouble but heard a noise at the door leading from the gallery and into the alley. Shaking his head to clear the cobwebs, he got to his feet, pulling his .45 automatic. He walked silently to the rear of the building and listened. Hearing something gouging into the wooden door, he yelled a warning. "There's guards inside and the cops have been called!"

The noise stopped briefly but started again after a few seconds. Thinking fast, he ran to the front of the gallery, unlocked the door and went outside to circle around the building and surprise the intruder. *Of course if I had really been thinking fast, I would've called the cops before going outside.* A dense fog had settled over Arkham and he was almost upon the burglar before realizing it. Seeing a large bulky shape through the fog, he yelled, "Hands up, asshole! Step away from the door!"

Before he could react, a big steel garbage can was sailing toward his head. Dodging the object, he cursed in pain as it connected with his shoulder. Now sprawling on the damp pavement, he peered through the mist and saw the shape approaching him. Aiming the gun, he fired. The gunshot echoed through the silent streets, followed by an animalistic grunt. Preparing to shoot again, he held his fire as the figure turned and loped down the alley, disappearing into the night.

◆　◆　◆

Kearney sighed, muttering, "At least I wasn't the only one having a bad night." After calling the cops, he phoned Balmer who was already in quite a state.

Balmer rushed to the gallery, relieved at finding the paintings intact. Frowning at Kearney, he said, "You smell like garbage. What the hell happened?"

Kearney related to him the story he had told the police. Balmer looked worried, saying, "This isn't good at all."

Smiling, Kearney said, "The cops say it was probably only a wino, trying to find a dry place to flop."

"Perhaps," Balmer said, "but I don't think it was a wino who called me repeatedly throughout the night."

"What are you talking about?"

Pursing his lips, Balmer said, "I received numerous phone calls last night, all with the same message."

"And?"

"The message was, destroy the paintings or pay the price."

Kearney sipped his coffee. "I assume you told this to the cops."

"No," Balmer replied. "I suspect it's the work of some deranged religious fanatic . . . Pickman was hounded by them in his day."

"Whatever happened to him?" Kearney asked. "I've only heard bits and pieces."

"No one is certain," Balmer answered. "Brennan claims to have met a man with some interesting theories on that."

"Such as?"

"The entire thing is insane . . . not really anything to be taken seriously. This fellow Brennan spoke with was extremely drunk so that should tell you something."

"I'd still like to hear it," Kearney said.

"Okay," Balmer replied. "Those creatures in the paintings are supposed to be ghouls."

"I figured that much."

"Well, according to Brennan's drunk, Pickman painted these things from photographs and personal experience . . . with the implication being that he was in fact, one of the things."

"I see we're in the middle of that insane part of the story you mentioned."

"I told you," Balmer snapped. "According to him, Pickman was a changeling . . . a ghoul-spawn switched at birth with a human child."

Kearney rolled his eyes. "So what happened to him?"

"He was supposedly taken to the ghoul underworld or some such nonsense, in order to silence him. Apparently these *ghouls* weren't happy that he was drawing attention to their presence."

Laughing, Kearney said, "Maybe it was ghouls that phoned you last night."

Instead of laughing, Balmer asked, "Did you take a close look at the back door this morning?"

"Just cursory," Kearney answered.

"And you didn't think those gouges on it looked strangely like claw-marks?"

"I see what you mean," said Kearney, "but what sort of thing has claws like that?"

Looking pointedly at the painting behind the PI, Balmer said, "I couldn't say. But certainly not a wino."

Kearney stared at the painting and shuddered. "It could've been a damn big wino," he countered, not believing it for a minute.

Sighing, Balmer said, "We can certainly hope so."

The next two days passed in a flurry of activity. Sizeable crowds passed through the gallery and several Poobahs of the art world had put in appearances. Kearney hadn't been present much during the day, having been relieved by an off-duty cop needing some extra money. Balmer was primarily worried about something being pulled at night, insisting that Kearney remain fresh for the night shift. Balmer was happy with the attention but Kearney could tell that the man was under a lot of strain. Nothing further had occurred during Kearney's two shifts but the late night phone calls to Balmer had increased in frequency. The gallery was closing for the evening when Balmer turned to Kearney and said, "I believe that I'll stay here this evening."

Surprised, Kearney said, "Can't get enough of my company?"

"I welcome it tonight," Balmer replied.

"Okay, what's up?" Kearney asked, sensing that something was amiss.

Balmer turned pale. "Last night, someone tried entering my house. I called the police but they found no evidence of it. Following that, I left and checked into a hotel. Frankly, I'm now afraid to stay there. Perhaps in the morning you can accompany me there to get a few items?"

"Sure," Kearney said, "no problem. But why stay here tonight? The hotel would be more comfortable."

Balmer blushed. "The truth is I'm short on funds . . . at least until these paintings are sold. So you see it's in your interest to ensure that no harm comes to me."

"That's just swell," Kearney said. "But what's to stop me from quitting here and now?"

Balmer smiled, saying, "The fat bonus you're to receive once the paintings are sold?"

"Okay," growled Kearney. "Why not? Besides, I like to see a job through to the end."

Relieved, Balmer said, "Thank you," and then retired to the musty basement to ready an Army cot for the night. Once things were in order, he returned upstairs, spending a couple of hours talking to Kearney. *He's really not such a bad egg once he drops the haughty attitude. He's scared shitless and not about to be high-hatting anyone for a while.*

Around three A.M., Kearney heard a noise at the back door. Hoping it was a stray mutt, he crept to the back room, listening intently. Turning to go wake Balmer, he stopped as a mournful baying emanated from the end of the alley, causing the hair on his neck to stand on end. It was quickly answered by another, and then to his shock, came the sound of hooved feet clattering on the pavement.

Running to the stairs, he yelled for Balmer and rushed to the phone. He picked up the receiver but it was dead. No dial tone, nothing. "Shit," he mumbled, reaching for his automatic. Racing to the back of the gallery, he heard Balmer yell from the basement. "Kearney, what's happening?"

"Just get your ass up here!" Kearney answered.

Returning his attention to the door, he yelled, "Come through that door and your ass is mine!" It sounded tough but wasn't at all how he felt. Sensing that no ordinary burglar was on the other side of the door, he struggled to hold the gun steady. He couldn't help but think about Brennan's drunken acquaintance. *These ghouls weren't happy that he was drawing attention to them.* "Get a grip, Kearney," he mumbled.

Balmer suddenly screamed, sending Kearney rushing for the stairs. "I'm coming!" he yelled, hearing the sound of struggle and boxes being overturned.

"Oh god, help me!" Balmer screamed.

Halfway down the stairs, Kearney saw the ghouls. He didn't want to believe his eyes but there was no mistaking them. "Pickman's models," he whispered, developing a great deal more respect for Brennan's drunken source.

At least five of the creatures had burst through the basement floor. Firing three quick shots, he hit one of the things twice and missed another. The creature he hit was relatively unaffected by the shots, though a grayish liquid — like what had been found in the alley — oozed from the wounds. "Help me!" Balmer pleaded, his eyes bulging in stark raving terror. A ghoul held him securely while the others ignored Kearney's weapon and bounded toward the PI.

Kearney heard the gallery's back door explode inward just moments prior to the ghouls' charge. *They're all over the building!* Emptying his firearm, Kearney turned to flee. He hadn't gone two steps when it felt like he was struck in the back by a bus. Stunned, he was picked up roughly and hurled against the basement wall where he fell to the floor. Barely conscious, he heard Balmer pleading for his life. Struggling to rise, Kearney was again knocked nearly senseless by one of the crouching, dog-like beasts. Trying to focus, he stared into the bloodshot eyes of the mould-caked, flat-nosed monster and shuddered. Grabbing a piece of discarded pipe, he swung at the ghoul's face but the blow was deflected by a large scaly claw. The creature whacked Kearney with the steel object, cracking two of the detective's ribs.

Moaning, Kearney lay on the floor, listening to the horrified cries of Balmer. A short time passed and he became aware of figures descending the stairs. Two ghouls clutched the shredded remnants of the gallery's prized exhibits. They were followed by a third figure that Kearney recognized immediately. *His physical appearance may have changed drastically since painting himself into "Taking Communion" but there's no doubt that I'm staring into the eyes of Richard Upton Pickman . . . or what he's become!*

Pickman looked to the corner where Balmer was mindlessly gibbering. "They're real . . . they're real . . . my God, they're real!"

The former artist made a few guttural sounds. The tone was commanding and immediately acted upon by the ghoul holding Balmer. With lightning speed, Balmer's neck snapped and lolled crazily. Pickman nodded his approval, pointing to the hole in the basement floor.

Balmer's slayer, still clutching the corpse, shambled toward the hole as his monstrous companions followed. Pickman and the other two creatures remained. "Crap," whispered Kearney, figuring that his number was up. Staring at Pickman, he said, "All this for a couple of damned paintings?"

Pickman smiled, if one could call it that, and in a raspy voice said, "Unfinished business."

Kearney watched the grotesque trio approach, trying to summon his courage. Glaring at Pickman, he whispered, "Go to hell."

Stepping forward, Pickman's facial muscles tensed and then relaxed. That damnable smile returned and he laughed. Then ignoring Kearney, he motioned for the creatures to follow and disappeared through the gaping hole in the basement floor.

◆  ◆  ◆

Balmer was never found by the cops, not exactly a surprise considering what Kearney knew to be true. They went through the motions of putting out an APB and instructed Kearney to wait for a ransom note though nothing ever came of it.

Kearney sat in his dingy office, pondering the end of the strange case.

*Hell, the abductors had already taken everything of value and monetary concerns never entered into the equation. The cops bought my cooked up story — at least 90% of it — and I'm not under suspicion as far as the abduction goes. They didn't believe a man would allow himself to be beaten so severely to establish an alibi. Well, they were damn right about that. I ain't no fan of pain. The fact that I practically crawled to my office didn't sit too well with them, considering there was a working phone-box on the street outside the gallery. Yeah, the reason for that was simple enough.*

*After regaining consciousness in the wreckage of the gallery, I chanced to find a small framed pencil sketch that had tumbled out of a box during the melee. Hurting though I was, something compelled me to turn it over and take a look. The setting was a fairly well known cemetery though there was nothing of the macabre about the work. It was a rather bustling daylight scene of people sightseeing and paying their respects to friends or family. But in the background — apart from the other activity — was a large brooding crypt. In front of this structure stood the saddest-looking boy I think I've ever seen. Near his feet, barely visible, was a single word in a style identical to the signature on the Pickman canvasses. It asked a simple and apparently important question — at least for the one who had written it. It simply asked, "Why?"*

*I took the sketch, feeling an unexplained need to keep it. As for why, that's a question I expect I'll be asking myself for many years to come.*

# THE WATCHER FROM THE GRAVE

## J.F. Gonzalez

### I

*Now about the "terrible and forbidden books"— I am forced to say
that most of them are purely legendary. There never was any Abdul
Alhazred or* Necronomicon, *for I invented these names myself.*
—H. P. Lovecraft, Letter to Willis Conover,
dated July 29, 1936.

Justin Grave was lucky that the house he finally landed had such
a cheap rental rate. It was situated at the end of a long, narrow
road in Reamstown, Pennsylvania, a lonely two story rambling
farmhouse situated on ten acres of land. His closest neighbor was half
a mile up the road. He could work well into the night with the phono-
graph playing loud and it wouldn't pose a problem.

The rental agent had informed him that the previous occupant of
the house had kept late hours too, and that most of the neighbors had
hardly known he was around. She seemed to think he was a student,
pre-med maybe, who was on a brief sabbatical from University. In
either case, acquiring the house took a load off of Justin's mind. The
rent was affordable, the location bearable, and the space gigantic compared to his apartment in town. He already decided where the study
*and* the library were going to be. All he had to do was settle in.

He moved in right after Christmas. The holidays were bitter cold,
and on New Years Eve greater Lancaster County, Pennsylvania received a foot of snow that covered everything from barns to downtown
city streets. Justin moved in three days before the storm.

The storm lasted four days, unleashing a cold front brought along by
a fierce wind that blew in from Canada. It was a good thing he'd moved in
and unpacked before it hit. What better place to be in a howling storm
than snug in your own warm study with the fireplace blazing?

---

The storm brought no relief. Justin sat by the radio on the second day of the storm, listening to a weather broadcast. The forecasters were predicting a Nor'easter to pummel much of the New England and Mid-Atlantic region. Bad weather. The rest of the month was going to be shot as far as neighborhood exploration went.

This became apparent two weeks later. He had just finished another Rex Bates tale for *Adventure Magazine* when he suddenly realized it had been six months since he'd worked on anything horrific. His last appearance in the land of the weird had been " . . . When the Bells Toll" which had appeared in the December issue of *Weird Tales*. That story had been written at the commencement of the previous summer. The six-month time lag had been spent writing two science-fiction novels to be serialized in *Amazing Stories* and *Astounding* respectively, along with the usual work. As a writer of pulp fiction, Justin Grave could turn out romance novellas for *Romance Stories* and *Love Stories*; detective stories for *Black Mask* and *Detective Fiction*, adventure serials for *Popular Fiction Magazine*, and weird-menace tales for *Spicy Mystery Stories*, *Thrilling Mystery Dime Mystery Magazine*, *Terror Tales*, and *Horror Stories*. Thank God for pseudonyms.

But the itch to churn out a couple of horror stories gnawed at him. His first sale had been to a small circulation pulp (a rag actually) titled *Tales of Terror*, in the summer of 1928 when he'd graduated from high school. His first appearance in *Weird Tales* saw print six months later. In the ten years that followed he had probably published well over five hundred stories and a few serialized novels in every pulp magazine on the stands. By the time he graduated to writing full time, his name was being advertised on the covers of the horror pulps along with H.P. Lovecraft and Clark Ashton Smith, as well as in most of the adventure and detective fiction pulps. Even some of the pen names he used for the romance pulps began to make cover status after a few years. Half of the stuff he churned out was pulp for the masses, with a guaranteed life of one month on the racks in whatever pulp magazine it appeared in, only to be gone by the next month's issue. Forever.

At least it paid the bills.

The storm outside was providing the perfect atmosphere to get back into the horror mode. The house in general seemed to emanate a sense of foreboding. He noticed it when he first settled in. It was as if the very air was weighted, leaden. The elements seemed to churn and change in different rooms. It was probably his imagination — his mind had been turning to horrific themes for story ideas — but he still couldn't shake the feeling off. It felt the strongest in three rooms; the kitchen, the bathroom, and the master bedroom. It was worse in the master bedroom. He would lie in bed, eyes wide open, faint murmurings fluttering through his mind. The silence of the house seemed to whisper to him and he got up a few times to investigate, thinking he really *was* hearing something moving stealthily in the house. He never found anything.

Which was why he wanted to start on another horror tale. Channel the nightmares out of his mind and put them on paper. That method had always worked before. It would work again.

A couple of feeble attempts at starting a new tale were undertaken in negative results. Writer's block had set in after six months away from the creepy crawlies that he normally enjoyed dealing with. After his fifth attempt, he tore the page out of the typewriter and tossed the crumpled ball into the wastebasket. The storm showed no sign of abating and cabin fever had set in, making an afternoon walk a no-go. He had to clean out his mind, carve out the clutter that was occupying his brain-pan.

He decided to explore the rest of the house. The attic and the basement hadn't been explored yet, and now the urge to examine them blossomed. He left his work area and donned a jacket to make the trip downstairs.

The rental agent had steered clear of the basement during his initial tour. She'd simply pointed to the door of the basement, which was set by the kitchen. The key was in place on top of the heater. He scooped it up and fumbled it into the lock. The lock turned with a creak of protest, and he eased the door open slowly. Light from the kitchen stabbed feebly down into a yawning pit of darkness. The steps descended for about three feet and were swallowed by blackness.

And the dark, pulsing, foreboding feeling ebbed out from the basement, washing over him. Stronger than ever before.

His heart thumped hard in his chest as he grabbed a flashlight from the kitchen counter and flicked it on. The beam stabbed into the darkness, making the downward trek less hazardous.

He descended slowly, the ominous feeling growing heavier and heavier on his shoulders. He couldn't shake the feeling that there was something *wrong* with this house, with the basement. And despite that feeling, he denied that it had anything to do with the supernatural. He wrote about it, dealt with it in his fiction, but he had never believed in it. He refused to believe in it now.

He tried to deny that there was something wrong. But his heart told him otherwise.

He explored the basement that afternoon with the nervousness and fear of a child in an amusement park house of horrors. The feeling dwindled as the beam from his light began flashing on normal looking objects, and it soon subsided. A stack of boxes in the corner yielded moldering, ancient Penny Dreadfuls and turn of the century pulps. Another crate revealed back issues of *Harper's* and *Blackwood's Maga-zine*, more gems.

Justin spent that afternoon leafing through them, transferring them to a pile on the floor to be taken upstairs for cataloguing into his own collection. When he was finished, he cast the beam of light around the shabby basement. There were a few chairs, a makeshift table with a layer of dust on it, an ancient stone fireplace that sat cold and empty, and a door set against the far wall. It was locked.

Justin trundled his catch of the day up the stairs to his library. He spent the rest of the evening sorting through the ancient pulps. He couldn't help but think of the day his wanderings through the closets of the house the week before yielded a similar find. Beneath a pile of old blankets in his study closet was a box of vintage pulps; early copies of *Weird Tales* (some with his own published work!), *Strange Tales*, and other pulps. There was Arthur Machen's *The House of Souls*, Robert W. Chambers *The King in Yellow*, the infernal book of Magic and Supernatural *The Golden Bough*, and a book he had never heard of, *From Beyond* by James Smith Long. He flipped open the cover of the latter; a collection of short fiction by a forgotten writer.

Stacked in a heap with the pulps and books were notebooks filled with spidery handwriting. Justin had dragged the stuff out and spent the afternoon sifting through it. Most of the notes were scholarly in nature, depicting thematic structure and symbolism of the fiction in Long's book, but there was a good deal of personal criticism as well. One of the journal entries stated "... *am getting closer to what they're hinting at. Even the newer crop of writers like Lovecraft hint at the same thing, yet I'm not so sure. Either way, I know I must do more research before I am absolutely sure of my theory.*" Other books found in the stack were volumes on psychology, astronomy, anthropology, philosophy, history, theology, the occult, and archeology. There weren't enough hours in the day to sift through all of them, so Justin gave up after a few hours and called it a night.

And now he had found more of the former occupant's belongings. And things were getting weirder by the minute. He didn't know much of anything about the former occupant, just that he had simply "disappeared" after not paying the rent for the last two months. The landlord came to collect the rent last month and found that he'd simply left, with no forewarning. The landlord cleared out the furniture and put the residence up for lease again.

The following day brought no new lightning bolt revelations for story ideas, so he trumped down the stairs to investigate the basement further.

He stood in the center of the room, trying to figure out what to hit next. A box of magazines sat by the far wall and he inspected them. He pulled the top magazine off the pile and flipped it open. His eyes widened in shock at the vile, perverted images. He had seen pornography once on a trip to visit his agent in New York, and the graphic images had shocked him. They shocked him now, and he flung the periodical to the floor in disgust.

He sifted through the rest of the magazines with bated breath. They were all of the same ilk; their sexual perversions spiked through his brain, creating images that were sickening and repulsive. He moved the stack to the center of the room, making a mental note to burn them in the fireplace that evening.

Now his curiosity was more piqued than ever. He still couldn't shake his mind of the images. What kind of person could keep such perverted literature and photos in his home? It was obvious that who-ever possessed them had enjoyed them by evidence of their condition, which showed a sign of careful handling. It was this which turned his attention to the locked door set against the far wall.

He tried the knob again; it was locked firmly. He began hunting around the basement until he found a crowbar on top of a pile of tools and debris by the fireplace. He hefted the tool in his hand and inserted its slim end into the crack of the door. Heaving with all his strength, he began prying the door open with the strain and groan of splintering wood.

When the lock snapped, the door flew open and banged against the wall. Justin stood panting in the cold basement, his nostrils suddenly tracking a damp smell that issued from the tiny room he had just unearthed. He stabbed the beam of his flashlight in the room, revealing a dusty piece of string that hung from the ceiling. A light fixture.

He reached inside the room and clicked on the light.

The room was bathed instantly in light and Justin blinked. Black spots danced in his vision and he blinked them away as his eyes ad-justed. When he finally saw what was displayed against the far wall of the room he had to put his hand to his mouth to hold back the scream that threatened to issue forth. As it was, the shock of the gruesome sight pitched him on his butt while the back of his head thunked softly against the wall. The pain from the bump failed to supersede the shock of what he was seeing.

What looked to be a makeshift altar stood at the far end of the little room. It was constructed of what appeared to be large blocks of stone, about six feet by three feet. Running along both sides were what ap-peared to be gutters with drains that fed into two funnels that dripped into two buckets. The smell that came from the room was one of death and blood. Heart thumping hard in his chest, Justin took a step closer and peered into the buckets. They were empty, but it was obvious what they had once contained judging by the dried crimson that stained their steel surface.

Justin felt his gorge rise as he looked around the tiny room. Above the makeshift altar was a strange symbol, part pentagram, part some other hieroglyph that he didn't recognize. It appeared to have been drawn in blood. Dusty black, white, and red candles sat at various positions around the altar, and on his right, sitting on a makeshift ledge, was what appeared to be a human skull. Heart beating harder now, Justin approached the loathsome object for a closer inspection. It *was* a skull! But it looked strangely . . . *unhuman.*

He didn't know how long he sat there staring numbly at the scene. But when he finally came to his senses he heard the dull chimes of the grandfather clock upstairs in the entry hall tolling six p.m. His eyes widened in surprise. Five hours had elapsed since he trekked downstairs to investigate the basement. He shook his head to clear the shock and cobwebs from his mind. Where had his mind gone in that time?

As if in answer to his question a vision rose in his mind, as if he were remembering a dream. It was a vision of an endless plane, a wide gulf beyond time and space. He felt himself floating in this dream, drifting among various shaped objects and shadowy figures. He heard droning, monotone voices calling out and he closed his eyes and drifted through the flow. He drifted onward through the vast gulf of this curious dimension, and then before he knew it he was back in the little cellar room and the clock was tolling.

His mind was racing with a million questions and thoughts. He looked at the blood-stained altar, dismissing the dream as mere fantasy brought on by exhaustion. The important thing was dealing with what he had found in his basement. The blood-stained altar only meant one thing: a crime had once been committed at this house, maybe the very same crime that had led to the disappearance of the former tenant of this house. He needed to find more evidence before he decided what to do next.

It was obvious that Justin had stumbled upon an amazing discovery. He was standing in what was very likely a private ritual chamber. The vile pornographic literature in the box outside had probably been the former resident's, as well as the books and magazines upstairs. The maroon stains on the makeshift altar, and in the buckets, were now easily explainable, as were the strange symbols drawn on the walls. All of which explained the weird feeling he got when he first set foot inside.

There were other items scattered about the small room. A two-by-three foot cedar chest lay in a corner, padlocked shut. More notebooks slid in the shelves like books. Weird, symmetrical drawings and patterns were drawn with what looked like blood on one of the walls. He reached for the crowbar he had left in the doorway of the room, and turned its blunt edge to the padlock on the cedar chest. Three hard blows snapped the lock, and he flipped the lid of the chest open.

All that was inside the chest was an old leather bound book.

He was barely aware he was holding his breath as he bent down and picked the book up gingerly. The leather was old and cracked. Actually, it didn't feel like leather at all, at least not the leather he was used to. This leather was smooth, thinner than normal, and had a distinct look to it. He examined the back and front covers, noting the thickness of the volume–it was at least 900 pages–then he flipped open the cover and stared at the title page. *The Necronomicon.*

That weird hieroglyph symbol again. And then the name of the author.

Abdul Alhazred.

Now Justin began to smile. Surely this had to be a fake! Howard himself had revealed to him in a letter that he'd invented the name *The Necronomicon* and Abdul Alhazred many years ago, when he was a mere child. Howard had been amused by the fans that had written in to *Weird Tales* asking where they could find a copy of the famed book of black magic that was apparently kept under lock and key at the Miskatonic University Library in the town of Arkham, Massachusetts. Yet another phony town and a phony university that so many gullible fans thought were real. They were all props to aid in Howard's and others' stories of a cosmic race of monsters known as "The Old Ones" who were waiting to once again reclaim the earth. Justin had written three similar stories himself, all of which had been very well received by *Weird Tales* readers. Howard had praised one of them, "The Whispering Thing in the Cellar," as a fine piece of work.

But if the *Necronomicon* and everything that went with it were fake, how did that explain the book he now held in his hands?

He examined it more carefully. It was carefully bound, as if by hand. The pages were old and felt like parchment. Almost like papyrus. The writing in the book was obviously English, and appeared to have been hand-written directly on the pages. He turned the book over and examined the cover, his fingers skimming across the surface. The binding was smooth and dry, grayish in color. There were splotches of pink in it here and there, and some of the gray appeared mottled. There also appeared to be tiny hairs jutting out of it, and –

Justin took a closer look and promptly dropped the book on the floor, his hair standing on end.

*The book was bound in human skin!*

That decided it. Now he was calling the authorities. The book itself, while odd, wouldn't catch the attention of law enforcement, but the evidence of homicide in the room would interest them plenty.

Justin pulled himself away from the grisly scene and turned to move out of the room. He got no further than the threshold when a wet, rotted hand gripped his arm.

His heart flew in his throat and he choked back a scream. The thing standing beside the doorway was emaciated, scarecrow-like in its visage. It held Justin's upper arm in one bony grasp, its grinning caricature leering at him through broken, rotting teeth. Twin orbs burned insanely in hollowed eye sockets. Wild, white hair sprouted from the skullcap like honey suckle blowing in the wind. It took a shambling step forward, its other arm reaching out to grab Justin by the throat, when he suddenly broke free and started running toward the stairs.

Blind fear raced through him as he stumbled over the box of pornographic magazines in the center of the room. He hit the ground on his hands and knees and was back on his feet in a flash, racing towards the stairs. Behind him he could hear the thing that had grabbed his arm giving pursuit. Its labored breath wheezed behind him. Justin banged into a bookcase as he rounded a corner of the basement, nearly stumbled over a chair, and was almost to the stairs when he tripped over something else that pitched him forward. The bridge of his nose smacked the fifth stair with a hearty *crack*. He yelped at the impact, blood spattering the stairs and the front of his shirt. Fogginess clouded his brain and he pulled himself up only to be pushed down by the thing, which was now leering over him. Justin felt his bladder give way. It was the last thing he remembered before the thing flipped him over and moved its hungry mouth toward his blood-ravaged face.

## II

The latest issue of *Nightshades* magazine was at the printer when its owner and Editor-in-Chief David Corban received a call from his editor at the monthly trade publication *Horror Scene*. "Justin Grave just passed away this morning," Mike Ashbury's tired voice issued over the phone. "Heart attack. Sorry about springing bad news on you like this."

David had been expecting the news. Justin had fallen ill in recent years, and informed David only two weeks ago that he wanted him to be his literary executor. David cradled the receiver on his shoulder and kicked his feet up on the window ledge overlooking Raymond Avenue. "Thanks for telling me. You're the only guy I know that can bring bad news and still manage to keep me in a cheery mood."

"Well, I'm not trying to make his death sound like it's good news," Mike said. "Justin lived the kind of life I hope to someday live. He lived his life to the fullest."

David snorted. "You can say that again. The guy was almost ninety years old!"

"And he was still writing up until the time of his illness," Mike interjected. "Mythos Books is putting out the last two novels he turned in to them, and if you were smart you'd get a collection out of his recent short stories."

"We had been talking about it before he got ill," David said. "I suppose now that I'm his literary executor I can issue the stuff to myself for free."

The conversation drifted a bit and eventually came back to Justin Grave's short fiction again. "You really might want to consider a collection of his recent stuff," Mike reiterated.

"Mythos put out a volume last year," David said, musing the subject over. "It was a sixty year retrospective. Come to think of it, it didn't include that much of his recent fiction."

"There you go then," Mike said. "At the very least you should consider an omnibus or something."

David laughed. "It would take five volumes to showcase Justin Grave's horror and dark fiction in an omnibus." Still, Mike was thinking in the right direction. A collection of Grave's horror, mystery, suspense, and dark fantasy fiction — most of it long out of print — could kick start Nightshades Publishing back into high gear. Presently there were two volumes of Grave's short fiction in print from Mythos: *Death Cry in the Night*, a collection of weird menace stories from the shudder pulps of the 1930's, and *In the Depths*, the retrospective that contained work from the late 20's through the 90's. David owned the seminal *Cloak of Darkness and Others*, which had been published in 1977 by a noted small press. It largely contained the more well known of his horror stories from the pulp era and beyond, and was now a highly sought after collectors item. With the recent trend in horror fiction toward the extreme end and the noir, Justin Grave's work was receiving an almost rediscovered flavor. Anthologists were mining his work from the pulps for a wider audience, and most of the novels he wrote when he came out of retirement in 1973 were now being reissued. David leaned back in his chair, eyeing the late afternoon traffic along Raymond Avenue. "It's a great idea. I just wish there was something we could mine that's really rare . . . you know, something nobody has collected yet."

"Have you thought about tracking down *The Watcher from the Grave* for reprint rights?"

The title drew a blank in David's mind. Mike was a literary bibliophile, one of the three most well read people David knew. David's interest was piqued. "I've never heard of it. What is it?"

"I've never read it," Mike admitted. "From what I understand, it was published in late 1939 and early 1940 in serialized form in *Shudder Magazine*. It supposedly started some kind of controversy when it appeared."

Now David's interest was really piqued. "That's pretty amazing. You wouldn't happen to know what kind of controversy? "

"No. I really don't know anymore more about it." Mike added a short pregnant pause. "If you could dig it up somewhere, I'd love to see what it was that caused folks in rural America to heave their cookies."

"Well, I'll try to track it down." The conversation ended with a promise for David to get the bi-monthly column he wrote for *Horror Scene* in to Mike by the first of the week. David hung up the phone, his gaze still trained out the window. Justin had placed no less than ten stories with *Nightshades Magazine* during the magazine's eighteen-year history, the last one presently at the printer to appear in the latest issue. The new story was sure to go over big with *Nightshades* readers. The tale concerned the rumor of a ghoul-like god that feasted on the flesh of the living. A small, yet fanatical cult devoted to the ghoul devotes itself to appeasing the god. Extreme sexual favors in the form of succubi and incubi are the return for devotion. It was a story that straddled the traditional mode of the Cthulhu Mythos with the new erotic noir of Lucy Taylor and Edward Lee. Pure pulp for the masses.

David grinned as he leaned back in his chair. Justin Grave's first posthumous piece was going to be his epitaph; his small, but fanatical audience was surely going to love it.

## III

David made a trip to The Hollywood Book and Magazine Store that evening after closing down business for the day.

David's favorite clerk, Brian Eaton, was seated on a chair, leafing through a recent issue of *Fangoria*. Brian was medium built, in his late twenties. The sides of his head were shaved down to the skull, wild hair sprouting from the top to cascade down to his shoulders. His left ear was pierced with six earrings. He played bass guitar in a local alternative band called Evil Offspring, and was a walking encyclopedia when it came to pulp trivia. The Hollywood Book and Magazine store itself was the kind of place that pulp fans in the Los Angeles area flocked to. The entire second floor of the place was devoted entirely to pulps — everything from *Famous Fantastic Mysteries* and *Amazing Stories*, to rare pulps like *Strange Tales*. David heard that the owners of the store sold the extremely rare second issue of *Weird Tales* a few months back for a tad over ten grand to a collector who had been searching for it for the past five years.

Brian looked up from his early evening reading and grinned as David walked in. "Yo, Dave. New issue at the printer?"

"You bet." Dave sidled up to the counter as Brian put the magazine down and approached, grinning wide.

"So what can I do for you this evening?"

"You know anything about a pulp magazine called *Shudder*?"

Brian nodded. "Sure do. It came out right around the time *Un-*

*known* made its debut. It didn't last long though. Why?"

"Well, I'm looking for a novel that was serialized in *Shudder*. A Justin Grave piece. *The Watcher from the Grave.*" He waited to see if recognition set in. It did.

Brian's face lit up, excitement in his eyes. "Yeah, I know what you're talking about. That's the story that caused some major editorial freak out. There were even Senate subcommittee hearings over the contents of pulp magazines being too damaging for kids."

Wow! Pre-McCarthyism thirteen years before the infamous Congressman set up the witch hunt that ultimately killed EC Comics and black-listed several Hollywood screenwriters and actors for their supposed communist ties. "Tell me about it," David asked.

Brian shrugged. "Not much to tell. *Shudder* only published seven issues, with *The Watcher from the Grave* appearing in serialized form in each issue. It caused an uproar by the third installment and by issue five the shit had hit the fan. The hearings were already in place. Ironically, the novel concluded in issue seven, the same issue the publisher decided to abort his publishing career by killing off the magazine. He ultimately sued Grave for an unspecific amount of damages and eventually went bankrupt."

This was all news to David. "What was it that freaked everybody out so bad?"

"The story itself," Brian explained, not breaking stride as the history lesson continued. "It had something to do with cult killings, was Lovecraftian in nature but incredibly sexual as well, way ahead of its time. It combined the cosmos of Lovecraft with a hint of Clark Ashton Smith, along with the ghoulishness of Hugh B. Cave and Robert Bloch. It had monsters, sex, death, and a race of monsters that wait in the outer spheres of space and time, ready to plunder the human race. Like I said, it was kinda Lovecraftian in theme and tone — it talked about another sphere where the gods came from, spoke of R'lyeh and Shub-Nigguroth, but then at the same time it wasn't." He chuckled. "Justin Grave was something of a trendsetter anyway — I mean, some of the stuff he was doing in the early thirties makes some of the stuff that's out now tame by comparison. Know what I mean?"

David nodded. Grave was downplayed as a hack writer for much of his career, and was ultimately forgotten in the field of horror for thirty years until an enterprising small press publisher issued *Cloak of Darkness and Others* in hardcover. The collection went on to win several awards, and a year later Grave's first horror novel in over thirty-years, *The Ritual*, appeared in paperback from Lion Books. It still took ten years after that for his work to be taken seriously as important contributions to fantasy literature.

"The story never appeared anywhere else," Brian continued. "During the commotion, an aspiring film maker optioned it from Grave, but nothing happened. Ten years later another producer bought the rights and made it into a low budget feature starring Bela Lugosi."

David's eyebrows shot up. *He* was supposed to be the film buff. "I never knew that!"

"Don't feel so bad," Brian said. "It was one of the endless stream of low budget films Lugosi did toward the end of his career. The film itself was largely confined to art houses and special midnight screenings in a few major cities. It came and disappeared and now it's one of Lugosi's lost films."

David's entrepreneurial mind was racing. If he could secure reprint rights for Watcher and resurrect the film on video (that is, if he could *find* it) he could make a small fortune. "Do you have any copies of *Shudder* in stock?"

David grinned wide. "You've come to the right place. I've got all seven issues in very good condition. They're pricey, though."

"How much?"

Brian named the price and David winced. It was enough to meet his monthly living expenses. David pulled his daytimer out of his black leather satchel and opened it up to his vast array of plastic. He pulled out an American Express card. No revolving debt.

"Couldn't you just see if you can get a copy of the original manuscript from Justin himself?" Brian had just returned from the storeroom where he laid out all seven issues of *Shudder* in their protective plastic covers on the counter. David examined them carefully.

"I would, but the man passed away this morning," David said.

Brian looked bummed. "I'm sorry to hear that."

David relayed his conversation with Mike Asbury earlier that afternoon. Brian listened intently. "Justin told me once that back in the sixties, a fire broke out in his house and he lost everything. Every pulp he had ever appeared in, along with the original manuscripts to all his published works. He's been able to get copies of some of the pulps through the years, but he never did get all of them. I'm not sure he had any copies of *Shudder*." David looked into Brian's pensive features. "So, I don't think that would work. Besides, I want these *now*. It'll make a great tax-write off as well." He grinned.

Brian rang the transaction up. "Not only that, but you will be the proud owner of a sought after collectors item. Now that he's passed, these are going to be worth a lot more money. Count yourself lucky."

"I do." David placed the fragile pulps in his satchel and bade Brian goodbye as he left the shop. His excitement and adrenaline spurred him on to what he knew he had to do in order to break his mini-publishing empire wide open.

# IV

The hardcover first edition of *The Watcher from the Grave* sold out in two weeks.

David was prepared for the reaction to the advertising he put out, and he quickly ordered a second printing before the ink dried on the first. Six months later, *The Watcher from the Grave* had gone through four printings and a bidding war had started between four major paperback houses for reprint rights. Justin Grave's literary agent, and Nightshades Publishing, had set up an estate for the deceased writer which was going to reap huge financial rewards in the months to come.

During the book's production, David was able to scare up the original print of the cinematic version of *The Watcher from the Grave*. It was found moldering away in a warehouse near downtown Los Angeles. Hard detective work had uncovered the print and once viewed, David realized he had to scare up some investors and do some legal checking to make sure the marketing rights to the film were clear. His main concern was that Lugosi's estate would holler blue murder when word leaked out about the print. A referral through a mutual business associate put him in touch with a legal shark by the name of Daniel Walters, of Walters, Lowell and Zuckerman. Daniel navigated the choppy legal seas, and within two months the contracts were signed, sealed and delivered. Lugosi had signed a one-shot deal with the producer of *Watcher* for a flat fee of two thousand dollars. His biographers surely hadn't been able to point out why Lugosi allowed himself to be ripped off. Different theories had been tossed out in explanation, but they were useless to David; the forty-eight year old document between the actors and the producer/holders of the film guaranteed no future royalties to Lugosi's estate should the film ever be resurrected. Thus guaranteeing the future of Nightshade Publishing.

There was no problem in rounding up investors for the fifty grand needed for the post-production, distribution, and marketing of *Watcher* onto video. Return on investment was expected within three months of release. The moola came in a month and a half early. So much for forecasting.

What David didn't expect from all the hoopla surrounding the resurrection of Justin Grave's lost novel was the offer to pen the deceased writer's biography for another enterprising small publishing house. The advance was small, but David jumped at the chance anyway. The travelling required to research the book would provide a much needed working vacation.

Unfortunately, things turned out differently.

# V

David Corban was a week into researching Justin Grave's life for the biography when Nightshades Publishing received a letter in shaky handwriting. It was postmarked Lancaster, Pennsylvania.

July 6, 2000

Dear Mr. Corban,

I note with great interest that you have published Justin Grave's long lost novel *The Watcher from the Grave* in an attractive deluxe edition, and have undertaken to resurrect and distribute the film based on the book later this year on video. While I applaud your keen business mind in tackling such an endeavor, I wanted to share with you some insights I have on the background of the story, and the later film adaptation.

I became acquainted with Justin in 1919, when we were both in grammar school. We became friends in 1925 when we were both high school freshmen. We remained friendly correspondents over the decades. Justin and I shared similar interests, mainly a love for the macabre, and the strange and bizarre. It had always been Justin's goal to create a piece of fiction that would out-do anything being published at the time. We were both avid followers of the great pulps, and while I was never a correspondent or member of the now infamous "Lovecraft Circle," we both shared a deep admiration for the gentleman from Providence. Justin published only a few Cthulhu Mythos stories, his most famous being the one which also ultimately destroyed his career in the early forties — *The Watcher from the Grave.*

Of course, *Watcher* touches on much more than simple deities from outlying cosmos struggling to gain their hold on our world, a world they once ruled. In addition, the work of Dr. John Dee was also a big influence on *Watcher*, as well as research into the ancient civilizations of Mesopotamia, the fabled lost city of Atlantis, and the ancient civilizations of South America. He had a theory, you see, about these "lost" civilizations that he wanted to answer in his novel. Ultimately he failed with mass America, but others before had tried to confront similar themes masked in mystery and fantasy. Lovecraft and Clark Ashton Smith have flirted with such themes for years, but never in such *grotesque* detail that Grave managed to accomplish in a single story. Grave's contemporaries, too, seemed unwilling or unable to grapple with the anthropological aspect the ideas expounded in such themes. The two who came closest, Lovecraft and Robert E. Howard, died rather tragically at the height of their careers. The third, Clark Ashton Smith, virtually abandoned writing in 1937 and produced no more of his strange, dark fantasies. Who knows what light these gentlemen would have shed on such things if they hadn't suddenly died or abandoned their careers?

I've been keeping up with the world of fantasy ever since, and while I admire those who have come after Lovecraft and copped his style — namely Brian Lumley and Ramsey Campbell — none have come close to dealing with what these gentlemen were trying to accomplish. Even Lovecraft himself opted for devising his fictional towns of Innsmouth and Arkham, and casting devilish, tentacled creatures from the deep seas as integral parts of his tales, using them to obscure the *true facts*.

Have you ever read anything by James Smith Long? Don't worry if the name doesn't seem recognizable. Long's work is largely forgotten now, but he published a steady stream of work from the 1840's through the 1870's in England, appearing in many of the Penny Dreadfuls and the Dime Novels of that time. Long died tragically in 1878 in a flat in London (and by strange coincidence, the very same *room* where Mary Ann Kelly was later found eviscerated beyond recognition by Jack the Ripper in 1888). Sadly, Long's work has been out of print for over a hundred years, but his work is astonishing to compare to that of his literary descendants — there's no doubt that Grave must have read Long's work at one point, for Long talks of the same dreaded *book* that is so evident in *Watcher*. Yes, hard to believe, but Long makes reference to Lovecraft's famed *Necronomicon* throughout the stories in his lone collection, a volume titled *From Beyond* (I do not have a copy, but I remember Justin had an old, weather beaten copy. From what I recall from the fly leaf, it was issued in the year of Long's death by a small publisher in London in an edition of 250 copies, of which most were ordered destroyed by Parliament for "blasphemy." The book is virtually impossible to find today. I imagine copies that survived destruction by the pillars of British Society were destroyed during the blitzkrieg of London during World War II). Despite what Lovecraft's biographers say, (and Lovecraft himself, rather contradictorily in his letters), I tend to believe Lovecraft must have come in contact with Long's work at some point. How else could he have heard about the *Necronomicon*?

I am incredibly anxious to view *The Watcher from the Grave* on video when it is released. I remember seeing it in the fall of 1953 at a theatre in downtown Philadelphia. The film version moved me in a way the novel hadn't; reading the novel for the first time gave me those unexpected tingles of gooseflesh one is accustomed to getting when reading great horror fiction (not to mention the three weeks of nightmares afterward; no novel has affected me since then. Not even the work of Stephen King, who I simply adore). The film raised those levels two-fold. Having read the novel in *Shudder*, those in my party wanted to bolt from their seats during those integral parts of the story. You know what parts I'm talking about; the parts when that ghoulish wraith walks out of the cellar and –

(Here the handwriting is illegible, and then it resumes after two lines of white space)

– we refrained though, and upon visiting the theatre the next week, in the accompaniment of more friends and colleagues, I was amazed to see the film was gone from the marquee. I never saw it advertised on a theatre marquee since.     In closing, I would like to commend you on a job well done in both resurrecting such a classic novel, as well as preserving the integrity of a man we all knew well and loved.

Yours Respectively,
Mr. Calvin A. Smyth

David read the letter twice with bemused interest. What did Dr. John Dee have to do with the seeds of *Watcher*? He couldn't understand where Mr. Smyth was coming from in relation to *that*. While Grave's story *was* relenting and literally scared the living shit out of you, it was pretty much a straight-forward horror story with Lovecraftian over-tones that basked in the gruesome: a writer of the macabre vacationing in a fictional town along the Pennsylvania Dutch Country discovers a sacrificial altar in the basement of his home. It turns out the former owner was the follower of a secret cult, one that worshipped "The Watchers," a group of demonic angels sent to watch over the Earth, who later descended and took themselves wives and beget monstrous offspring. They passed forbidden knowledge to mankind and were banished to the outer spheres for their crimes. Like most mythos stories, they are still seeking a channel into our plane of existence.

Further exploration of the house finds that the former occupant had abducted people for sacrifice in strange rites, offering the bodies to a creature described in great detail as "a leering, grinning emaciated scarecrow of a beast with a jaw full of broken, rotted teeth and rank breath that stank of the pit." This creature is revealed to be one of the offspring of the Watchers, who had managed to remain in hiding when the other Watchers were banished to the outer spheres. In order to live, the offspring requires fresh blood from sacrificial victims. The more sacrifices made to the Watcher, the stronger he becomes. In return, he seduces his followers by showering them with succubi and incubi. Vari-ous idols and fetishes are utilized in rituals, some seeming to borrow heavily from Lovecraft's Mythos: several of the mini-deities and fe-tishes grouped under the umbrella of the Watcher cult are amphibious in nature, some half reptilian and half mammal. The cult's total pur-pose on earth was now established: to await for the proper sacrifice, a human being whom the offspring could inhabit, allowing him to open the flood gates into the dimensions from which The Watchers had sprung from, giving reign of the earth to those who had been banished to the outer stars.

Upon discovery of the evidence at his home, the protagonist is caught in a whirlwind of sexual perversion and bloody rituals as he struggles to retain his sanity and his life. The mystery darkens when two young girls are found murdered, their bodies curiously drained of blood, and evidence to the murders lead law enforcement to him. A musty old tome is found in the house — the *Necronomicon* — and the authorities shudder at the sight of it. It contains a virtual pre-history of a world now gone, and a world that will soon become reality again "when the stars are righ.t." Unfortunately they are too late. The protagonist has already used the book to do the Black God's bidding and realized, too late, what the intentions of the cult really are: that *he* is to be the vessel that will bring the Watchers back, allowing the Outer Gods to take hold on this world again. He doesn't realize this until the end, when a young woman who has become his love interest early on in the novel, lures him into the basement of his home and seduces him. Before he is aware of it, the basement is filled with people, some he recognizes, others he doesn't. The offspring is among them, a wraith-like figure emaciated and shambling as it is led to him to take communion of his blood, thus giving the dark god new life which will help to throw open the gates.

The Lovecraft inspired Cthulhu Mythos had nothing to do with this tender tale of a boy and his corpse-like friend. Still, Mr. Smyth's letter raised some interesting observations, and David made a note in his day timer calendar to pay the gentleman a visit during his trip to Lancaster, Pennsylvania, which he was scheduled to partake in a week.

# VI

From the *Los Angeles Times* — July 6, 2000

SIGNIFIGANT ARCHEOLOGICAL FIND IN SOUTH AMERICA STUNS SCIENTISTS
(AP) No longer will geologists refer to the Americas as the "New World" if the carbon dating performed on the artifacts found among the ruins of a newly discovered lost temple are any indication to prove reliable. According to legitimate sources, the initial results from carbon dating on the objects prove to be somewhere in the neighborhood of 35,000–75,000 years old. "This is nothing short of astonishing," Dr. Edward Danzig, Professor of Anthropology and Ancient Civilizations at The University of California said yesterday. "We have reliably placed Homo

Sapiens on this earth 30,000 years ago. To see the evidence such as this, that demonstrate modern man was creating things of this magnitude over 30,000 years before most scientists believe he was on this earth, much less in this part of the world, is incredible."

Dr. Edward Danzig is referring to the statues found in the pyramid-like structure uncovered deep in the heart of the Amazon jungle in Brazil. The statues, all carved from stone, and all measuring twenty feet high, five feet wide at a weight of two tons apiece, depict a strange, hideous beast that can only be described as – " (Continued page 34)

## VII

Calvin Smyth didn't leave a phone number with his return address. David Corban squeezed his eyes shut to alleviate the pain of a raging headache that was rocking his brainpan. He had gulped two Excedrin with his last swallow of United Airline's complimentary soft drink, but the headache persisted. The commuter flight from Philadelphia's International Airport to the tiny Lancaster airport had been made bumpy by rough tail winds. The pilot announced that they were preparing for landing. David settled down in his seat to battle the headache away as the plane prepared to touch down on the runway.

The headache was gone by the time he made it through the terminal gates. After collecting his luggage, snaring a rental car, and driving to his hotel in town and checking in, he retrieved Calvin Smyth's address again. He lived on 1982 N. West End Avenue. The meager street map in the Lancaster Directory was no help. David drifted downstairs to the hotel lobby and ended up parting with three dollars and fifty cents for a more detailed Lancaster Street map.

He went to his car, unfolded the map and found North West End Avenue easily, it was near Franklin and Marshall College, about a five minute drive through town. David started the car and set off down the highway to pay a visit to Mr. Smyth.

Rousing Mr. Smyth proved to be not difficult at all. He answered David's knock with a curious, warm look. His features grew friendly when David introduced himself. The old man's eyes lit up as if he was seeing an old friend for the first time in half a century. At eighty-nine years old, Calvin Smyth was in remarkably good shape for a man his age. Stooped with age, his eyes were lively, his movements smooth. He had a nervous tic along his right side from Parkinson's disease, but other than that he looked healthier than a lot of people David's own age. He opened the door of his modest Victorian home and bade David to come in and make himself comfy. After serving his young guest a cup of coffee, the two men sat down in the living room, where David began trying to steer the conversation toward a comfortable position for which to hurl questions at the older gentleman.

Mr. Smyth grew immediately interested when David mentioned the biography he was researching on Justin Grave. He leaned forward in his chair, his bright blue eyes dancing with delight. "I suppose that's why you paid me a visit then?

"In a way, yes," David said, stepping carefully to the main question. "You don't mind if we talk a little about Justin, do you?"

"Oh no, not at all."

David produced a mini-cassette recorder from his black leather satchel and began recording. Calvin related the usual litany; he had known Justin since the second grade, they had become friends when they were fourteen and he confessed to the many boyhood activities they had done together. David nodded at the appropriate times and coaxed the story along by asking key questions. Justin had been an only child, and both parents had passed on in the early forties. Calvin thought there *might* have been an uncle in Ohio somewhere that had a big family, which would be the deceased writer's only living heirs, but he wasn't sure (David made a mental note to himself to look into this further since Justin's royalties were currently held in trust). "Justin's folks were pretty solitary people. If they had relatives, they surely never mentioned them."

While Calvin never aspired to be a writer, he loved reading ghost and horror stories, something his childhood friend shared. Only Justin had the story-telling bug in him as well, which eventually led to their not spending as much time together once Justin's writing began to take off. "A writer is a solitary person," Calvin said. "And Justin was no exception. All he did was write. He had no time for family or friends, much less girls. The few girlfriends he had were, pardon the expression, 'easy-pickings', if you know what I mean."

But Calvin had noticed a change in his old friend right around the beginning of 1939. He had moved into a home out in the outskirts of the city, and quickly became a recluse. "Justin got that place easy and quickly. Maybe *too* easy. It was almost as if some unseen force had guided him there. I knew that those kind of living conditions weren't to his liking; he had always liked the bustle of a community, with restaurants and theatres within walking distance. Something simple, but modest. So when that place came up for rent, I was surprised he took it. It was a good six months after he moved in that I saw him."

Did Calvin ever visit him there? "Justin always gave me an excuse for me not to come over," Calvin recalled. He sipped his coffee languidly. "Either the place was always a mess, or he wasn't going to be in, or he was asleep or *something*. The one time I did go there, he had already finished *Watcher* and he looked bad." Calvin's face grew somber at the memory. "He looked over his shoulder as if someone was watching him. And he spoke very carefully, as if he was being careful of what he said." Calvin frowned. "It also looked like he had broken his nose at one point and never got it fixed. He had a noticeable bump right here." He rubbed the bridge of his own honker. "I asked him what had happened, and he said he'd gotten drunk and fallen down the stairs. I asked if he'd seen a doctor about fixing it and he said he couldn't afford it. And then he changed the subject and wouldn't talk about it again."

Calvin related Justin's state of mind during the hearings and the lawsuit filed against him by *Shudder's* publisher. "He hit the bottle real hard, becoming a real alcoholic. Most magazines wouldn't take his work anymore, and he started writing under pen names again. He looked bad, the worst he ever looked in his life, and I told him that maybe he should see a psychiatrist. He refused, and six months later he joined the army and was shipped overseas to fight Hitler and his SS."

The talk continued for nearly three hours. Calvin related what eventually happened to *Shudder's* publisher: he was found dead of multiple stab wounds in a New York City brownstone. The film producer who turned *Watcher* into celluloid was killed in a car accident on the Pacific Coast Highway in Malibu, and the film's director eventually landed a spot in the Atascadero loony bin. He committed suicide two years later by gouging out his own eyeballs. David found all this extremely fascinating. What became of the actors who starred in the film? Lugosi's story was a matter of public record, and the other actors had been little known. Calvin had done his homework years ago. "All of them were dead by the mid-fifties," he stated matter-of-factly. "The actress that played opposite Shane Towers, the lead actor, was murdered by a jealous boyfriend. Shane himself died of a drug overdose shortly after the film was shot, and two others died of heart attacks a few years later."

"Kind of reminds me of what happened to *Poltergeist's* alumni," David murmured. Calvin got the hint and nodded. Four of the actors from that film had passed away mysteriously, or been murdered. Strange, but surely coincidental.

After the war, Justin moved to Los Angeles and tried to remain anonymous. He found work as a foreman in a factory, and tried moving back to his hometown in 1950. It didn't last long. He took off for Florida six months later and lived on the streets of Miami for two years. After several stints in jail and alcohol rehabilitation centers, he saw the light and found Jesus. His sudden conversion to Christianity came as a surprise to Calvin, who revealed to David that Justin had always been an atheist. But his friend was glad Justin wasn't "finding salvation in the bottle anymore". Justin picked himself up with the meager cash from the sale of *Watcher* to film, and never made a cent beyond the initial advance. He married a girl from his church two years later, and the couple moved to Tampa Bay where they opened a hotel.

"He eased up on the religion stuff as the years went on," Calvin said. He had brewed more coffee and they sat in the living room with fresh, steaming mugs. "And he started writing again in the sixties under the old name again, mainly for the mystery magazines. Nobody seemed to notice he was publishing fiction again. He'd been forgotten entirely, but it didn't bother him."

Eventually an enterprising young fan would discover that the Justin Grave writing cozy mysteries for *Alfred Hitchcock's, Ellery Queen's* and *Mike Shayne's Mystery Magazines* was the same writer that wrote all those grisly horror stories for the pulps. The fan contacted Justin via one of the magazines, and a correspondence ensued. The fan persuaded Grave to return to the horror field. Grave's first published horror story in almost thirty-five years, "Sleep No More," appeared in *Whispers* three years later. More stories followed in a revived *Weird Tales*, and in another little magazine called *Weirdbook*. *Cloak of Darkness & Others* appeared two years later, and once again Grave was back writing what he loved the most.

David knew the rest of the narrative by heart, having read Grave's recent work and meeting the writer himself at various conventions. What he'd been unaware of was Grave's past and the circumstances surrounding *The Watcher from the Grave.*

Now David popped the question that had been on his mind since he'd gotten Calvin's letter. "You mentioned in your letter to me that part of the inspiration for Watcher was a Dr. John Dee, as well as the myth of several lost civilizations. Can you tell me a little more about that?"

Calvin heaved a big sigh. He seemed to be choosing his words carefully. "Are you familiar with ritual magic at all? Aliester Crowley, the Order of the Golden Dawn and the like?"

David shook his head. "Not really."

"What about ancient Jewish myth, or biblical mythology?"

"Only what was pounded into me in Catholic school." David grinned.

Calvin sighed again and leaned forward. He managed a smile. "I take it you are pretty familiar with Lovecraft?"

"I am," David said, his next question popping out of his mouth automatically. "And that's the other thing I wanted to ask you about. You mention in your letter that the *Necronomicon* is actually referred to in a piece of fiction over fifty years before Lovecraft began using it in his work. What do you know about this?"

"It all ties in together, trust me," Calvin said, taking a sip of coffee. "To give you the short version, the *Necronomicon*, according to Lovecraft, does not exist. However, the *Necronomicon* according to Dr. John Dee *does* exist."

David blinked. "Say again?"

Calvin leaned forward. "The *Necronomicon* is not a myth. It is very much real. But the *Necronomicon* that you know of, that Lovecraft wrote about, is far from the real thing. I have my suspicions that Lovecraft heard about some of the particulars from his wife, Sonia Greene, back in 1921 or so, but then – "

"Wait, wait, wait," David said, his heart beating hard. "Are you telling me all this Cthulhu Mythos stuff is real?"

Calvin smiled. "Not at all. Why don't I start at the beginning?"

Which he did.

It was a fascinating tale, one that David found hard to believe. But the more Calvin spun the story out, the more it all began to make sense. After all, don't all myths and legends have some kind of basis in facts?

"Let me begin with Lovecraft," Calvin said, reclining in his chair and addressing David like a professor addressing a student. "But first, some brief back story. Aliester Crowley was a student, and some say, a master of the occult. One of the things that no doubt happened is that Crowley read Dee's translation of the *Necronomicon*. I say this because it was Crowley who later translated and adopted Dee's Enochian Keys into his own Law of Thelema. He probably read the *Necronomicon* while researching Dee's manuscripts, because there are too many passages in his Book of the Law that read like a transcription of passages in that translation. Anyway, Crowley himself never mentioned the *Necronomicon* in his works. I suspect it was an embarrassment to him when he realized the extent which he had unconsciously incorporated passages from the *Necronomicon* into his own Book of the Law.

"But in any event, Crowley was in New York in 1918, where he was trying to establish a literary career. He was contributing to *Vanity Fair* and other magazines, and it was at a lecture when he first encountered Sonia Greene, who had literary ambitions of her own. Crowley described her as one of the most beautiful women he had ever met. As we know from Crowley's reputation with women, he wasted no time with her. They saw each other on an irregular basis for some months.

"In 1921 Sonia Greene met Lovecraft and it was in that same year that Lovecraft wrote 'The Nameless City', where he first mentions Abdul Alhazred. The following year he mentions the *Necronomicon* in 'The Hound'. In 1924 he and Sonia married."

David interrupted the narrative with a question. "So he found out about the *Necronomicon* from Sonia?"

"That's what is believed," Calvin answered. "We don't know exactly what Crowley told Sonia Greene when they were seeing each other, and we don't know what *she* told Lovecraft. But knowing that Sonia and Howard connected in so many ways philosophically, and in ways relating to literature and such, it's only too easy to picture them talking one night and Sonia mentions some of the ideas she learned from Crowley. She wouldn't even have to mention Crowley by name; she might have simply mentioned that she had heard of this book called the *Necronomicon*, made mention of some of what it contained, and Lovecraft's imagination could have come up with the rest."

David nodded. From what he knew about Lovecraft it was very possible. Lovecraft would write that he had invented the name Abdul Alhazred when he was five years old, but he could have simply confused the name with the intense dreams of the Arabian Nights that he'd had at that early age.

"So the long and short end of it is that Lovecraft's fictitious *Necronomicon* is based on a real book called the *Necronomicon*." David mused.

"That is correct," Calvin said, his blue eyes dancing with amusement. "Not much is known of its author, Abdul Alhazred, who Lovecraft later dubbed 'the Mad Arab" for his tales. Abdul wasn't mad, at least as far as we'll know, but he was probably rather eccentric. Also, unlike what Lovecraft wrote in his mythos stories, the *Necronomicon* was *not* a book of spells, or a grimoire of ancient black arts. It was conceived as a history, and hence, a book of things now dead and gone. An alternative meaning of its name means literally 'the book of the customs of the dead.'"

"Wow," David said, leaning forward in his chair. This was really interesting.

Calvin continued. "The book was written in Damascus in 730 A.D., by Abdul Alhazred. No Arabic manuscript is known to exist. A Latin translation was made in 1487 by a Dominican priest named Olaus Wormius, who was a secretary to the Spanish Grand Inquisitor Tomas de Torquemada. It's likely the original Arabic manuscript of the *Necronomicon* came into his possession during the persecution of the Spanish Moors.

"Anyway, it must have been incredibly risky for Wormius to translate and print the *Necronomicon* during that time. It must have held an obsessive fascination for him, because he was finally charged with heresy and burned after sending a copy of the book to Johann Tritheim, Abbot of Spanheim. The accompanying letter contained a detailed and blasphemous interpretation of certain passages of the Book of Genesis. All of Wormius's translations were seized and burned with him, although I suspect that at least one copy must have found its way into the Vatican Library."

David stroked his chin, nodding. "I've heard they keep tons of old manuscripts and stuff there. That they keep secrets in there they don't want the world to know."

"Exactly!" Calvin said. "If they revealed them it would crumble the hold they have on the world."

Calvin paused for a moment to take a sip of coffee, then continued. "About one hundred years later, in 1586 I believe, a copy of Wormius's Latin translation surfaced in Prague. Dr. John Dee was a famous English magician at the time, and he and his assistant Edward Kelly were at the court of the Emperor Rudolph II to discuss plans for making alchemical gold. Kelly brought the copy from the so-called Black Rabbi, the Kabbalist and alchemist Jacob Eliezer, who had fled to Prague from Italy after accusations of necromancy.

"The *Necronomicon* appears to have had a vast influence on both men. The character of Kelly's scrying changed, which struck horror into the Dee household."

"Scrying?" David was puzzled.

"Forgive me," Calvin said. "The systems of magick now known as Enochian magick derive from the work of Dee and his seer Edward Kelly. Dee had a passion for discovering lost knowledge and spiritual truths. The method employed for these works was fairly standard for the time. Dee would act as the orator, directing fervent prayers to God and the archangels for 15 minutes to an hour. Then a scrying stone would be placed on a prepared table, and the angels were called to manifest a visible appearance. Kelly would watch the stone and report everything he saw and heard; Dee would sit at another table nearby and record everything that occurred. Kelly's scrying technique changed when the two gained possession of the Latin translation of the *Necronomicon*."

"How so?" David asked.

Calvin shrugged. "Kelly's technique became more . . . hideous . . . monstrous in its nature. Crowley interpreted this as an abortive first attempt of an extra-human entity communicating the Thelemic Book of the Law. Very shortly afterward Kelly left Dee, who translated the *Necronomicon* to English. Contrary to Lovecraft, this translation was never printed. The manuscript passed into the collection of the great collector Elias Ashmole, and later to the Bodleian Library in Oxford."

David perked up. "Does it still exist?"

Calvin shook his head. "I'm afraid Dee's translation disappeared following a break-in in the spring of 1934. The British Museum suffered several burglaries and the Wormius edition was deleted from the catalogue and removed to an undergound repository in a converted slate mine in Wales. Other libraries lost their copies, and today there is no library with a genuine catalogue entry for the *Necronomicon*. In the mid 1930's the few known copies of the *Necronomicon* just simply disappeared. It is believed that someone in the German SS government took an interest in obscure occult literature and began to obtain copies by fair means and foul." He smiled ghoulishly. "It is believed there is a large wartime cache of occult and magickal documents in the mountains of Osterhorn near Salzburg that contains a copy of the *Necronomicon*. This may be connected to the rumor of a copy bound in the skin of concentration camp victims."

David let this sink in. "You mentioned that the *Necronomicon* is supposed to be a history. What history is it supposed to be of?"

"Alhazred appears to have had access to many sources now lost, and events which are only hinted at in Genesis, or the Book of Enoch. Many of the legends he had access to are disguised as mythology in other sources, but are explained in great detail in the *Necronomicon*. It is also believed that Alhazred used magical techniques to clarify the past. Essentially, he believed that many species besides the human race had inhabited the Earth, and that much knowledge was passed to mankind in encounters with beings from 'beyond the spheres'. He shared with some Neoplatonists the belief that the stars are similar to our sun, and have their own unseen planets with their own life forms, but elaborated this belief with a good deal of metaphysical speculation in which these beings were part of a cosmic hierarchy of spiritual evolution. He was also convinced that he had contacted beings he called the 'Old Ones' using magical invocations, and warned of terrible powers waiting to return to re-claim the earth. He interpreted this belief in the light of the Apocalypse of St. John, but reversed the ending so that the Beast triumphs after a great war in which the earth is laid to waste."

"The Old Ones sound very Lovecraftian," David said, nodding. "You're sure Lovecraft never read the book himself?"

"Quite sure. I'm even pretty sure he wasn't familiar with James Smith Long's work at all. And you're right, the similarities are uncanny. They parallel each other tremendously. It is clear that Alhazred elaborated upon existing traditions of the Old Ones. According to Alhazred, the Old Ones were beings from 'beyond the spheres', presumably the spheres of the planets, and in the cosmography of that period this would imply the region of the fixed stars or beyond. They were superhuman and extrahuman. They mated with humans and begat monstrous offspring. They passed forbidden knowledge to humankind, and they were forever seeking channel into our plane of existence. And do you know something else?"

"What?"

"This is virtually identical to the Jewish tradition of the Nephilim, the giants mentioned in Genesis. The word Nephilim literally means 'fallen ones'. The story in Genesis is really only a fragment of a larger tradition, another piece that can be found in the Book of Enoch, which was never canonized in the Bible. According to this source, a group of angels sent to watch over the Earth saw the daughters of men and lusted after them. Unwilling to act individually, they swore an oath and bound themselves together, and two hundred of these 'Watchers' descended to earth and took themselves wives. The wives bore giant off-spring, who then turned against nature and began to 'sin against the birds and beasts and reptiles and fish, and to devour one another's flesh and drink the blood'. The fallen angels taught how to make weapons of war and cosmetics and enchantments, and astrology and other secrets. These separate legends are elaborated in later Jewish sources such as the Talmud, which makes it clear that Enoch and Genesis refer to the same tradition. The great flood described in Genesis was a direct response to the evil caused by humankind's commerce with fallen angels, who were cast out and bound."

David said nothing. He was letting this sink in. It was so overwhelming. "In Lovecraft's fiction, cults are formed in an attempt to summon the Old Ones. Is this . . . is this possible for what we're talking about?"

Calvin nodded. "Of course. The *Necronomicon* strongly hints that there is a cult, or group of cults, that worships the Old Ones and seeks to aid them gain control of this planet. One of the tactics attempted by this cult is to breed human and Old One offspring that will then multiply and ingress into terrestrial life until the Old Ones return to their pre-ordained position."

David was silent, letting this sink in. Calvin continued: "It is now generally believed by occult scholars that the Enochian system of magic Dee and Kelly came up with was directly inspired by those sections of the *Necronomicon* that deal with Alhazred's techniques for evoking the Old Ones. Remember, the *Necronomicon* was primarily intended as a history, and while it *does* provide some practical details and formulae, it is hardly a step-by-step beginner's guide to summoning demons from beyond the gulfs of space and time. Dee and Kelly had to fill in many details themselves. It is believed that the scrying technique that Kelly used was under the influence of the Old Ones. The very name of their system — Enochian — is a clue; it was inspired by the age-old traditions recorded in the Book of Enoch, and it was obviously Dee and Kelly's intention to contact the Nephilim, or the Watchers. The manuscript of The Book of Enoch was lost until the late 17th century, so Dee would have had access to only a few fragments quoted in other manuscripts. Alhazred most likely had access to the Book of Enoch, as it was current throughout the Middle East in the ninth century."

"This Enochian stuff," David said, "is it very common now?"

Calvin nodded. "Crowley translated the Enochian system in the early part of this century. He includes it in his Book of the Law. Others have attempted their own translations as well. Anton La Vey, the late founder of the Church of Satan, included a translation in his book the Satanic Bible, which can be found in any Borders bookstore." Calvin smiled. "Hardly typical of what is supposed to be a system of forbidden magic, eh?"

"What is the difference between this James Smith Long's work and that of Lovecraft?" David asked.

"Long utilizes the *Necronomicon* in its original meaning," Calvin said, choosing his words carefully. "It isn't mentioned very often, but in the one definitive book on the *Necronomicon*, Long's work is quoted quite significantly. Obviously the author of the piece had gotten a hold of a copy of *From Beyond*, because he was able to describe the stories from it quite vividly. From what I could tell, the work is vastly different. Lovecraft merely hypothesizes the *Necronomicon*, and comes quite close to its contents. His Cthulhu Mythos is pure invention, whereas Long's work is based on truth. As is *The Watcher from the Grave.*"

David posed the next question, which had been on his mind since the interview commenced. "It's a wild theory. And I can see why it has been . . . suppressed for so long. It certainly goes against much modern Christian and Jewish myth. The question is why have they been suppressed?"

"Your guess is as good as mine. It has been hypothesized that our present civilization is not the first time that man has risen through the ranks to become the most dominant animal species," Calvin said, speaking slowly and carefully. "In fact, there is now ample proof that the earth is far older than scientists have originally thought. Modern science pegs the earth at 6 billion years old. But new theories estimate earth at being twice that age, with a prior civilization of man occupying much of the world seventy thousand years ago, a full fifty thousand years before most anthropologists believed the first Homo Sapiens appeared. This civilization had a completely different language and custom, their own mathematical system, their own government, their own science. And they all spoke of beings that came from beyond the spheres, beings who gave them wisdom, beings who ruled over them and were later banished to the outlying cosmos." He grew quiet. "And that they are waiting for the right moment, when the stars are right, for the appropriate vessel — a man — to throw open the gates and allow them entry back into this world. Where they will once again rule."

David eyed Calvin curiously. "You've researched this?"

Calvin nodded. "A little. Besides the Aztec and Mayan civilizations, which show ample proof to have been erected well before the Aztecs even showed up, there were the lost civilizations of Mesopotamia, Easter Island, and Atlantis. One thing I forgot to mention is that the original Arabic translation of the *Necronomicon* comprised of seven volumes and that the Latin translation ran to nine hundred pages. Much of the history contained in its pages was of this older world. It discussed the legend of the Old Ones, as well as the history and times of the people who existed before the great flood, which some archeologists have now

attributed to a cataclysmic event that happened due to the lunar align-
ment of the planets. It was this havoc which destroyed those older
civilizations. According to the *Necronomicon,* the world was destroyed
by the force of the Old Ones being banished to the outer cosmos. It
suggests that upon their return that the world will once again be laid to
waste as they swoop in for their rule. Of course Genesis and other
books in the Bible paint the picture of an angry God destroying the
world due to his anger at man or the Nephilim."

"So why should I believe this?" David asked, still struggling with his
thoughts. He was under the impression that Calvin believed every word
of it, but he had never known Justin Grave to believe anything as wacky as
*this*. The man had always come across as being a very normal elderly
man. A voice whispered in the back of his mind: *but normalcy is a great
front for concealing secrets.* "There's no hard, solid proof of any of this.
Everything you've presented to me is all speculation. You say yourself that
by all accounts the real *Necronomicon* is lost. But even if it is truly lost,
and has been lost since the 1930's, surely there are survivors of those who
had seen it, or been involved with a cult that may have used it. Are there
any diaries or statements from former cult members? The only thing
anybody who investigates this angle has to go on is pure speculation
based on the writings of two or three men who are now not only dead, but
who wrote *horror fiction* for a living."

Calvin nodded. "You're quite right. But then, people believed Whitley
Strieber's account of his alien abduction. And *he* was known as a writer of
the fantastic before that supposedly happened to him."

Calvin continued after draining the rest of his coffee. "If it's bizarre
and out of the ordinary and steeped in some kind of historical fact,
people will believe it. Pure speculation presented with facts or evidence
to support that speculation often results in bona fide belief. Take the
common myths and superstitions of the world; the Loch Ness Monster, witchcraft rituals, hauntings. People will want to believe that Jack
the Ripper was Queen Victoria's grandson. Or that Amelia Earhart is
still alive somewhere on the Fiji Islands."

"Or that Elvis is still alive." What a joke.

"Exactly! Elvis Presley was already larger than life before he passed
on. Keeping him alive by reputed sightings only adds to the intrigue to
the point where we *want* to believe he's still alive."

David's eyes narrowed at the older man sitting across from him.
"Okay, granted weird things happen, and I don't doubt that they do.
But even if a singular cult like the one you're talking about *did* exist, and
James Smith Long dug up some facts and fictionalized it, only to influ-
ence Lovecraft and a slew of others, why . . ." He grasped at the ques-
tion. "Why would any of it matter now?"

"Suppose the work of James Smith Long wasn't entirely fiction?"

Calvin posed. "Suppose he was trying to . . . *warn us* of what was to come?"

"Which would be what?"

"Long's fiction describes portions of the *Necronomicon* that Justin's work barely scratches the surface on. Primarily the pre-history of earth, but also history of the outlying cosmos. Like Lovecraft's fiction, it suggests that when the stars are right, when everything is in balance in the universe, that the lone Watcher and its followers will be able to summon up the occult power to throw open the gates. And that in order for this to happen, there must be a sacrifice from a willing victim, a victim who goes to the cult of their own free will. In Justin's novel the protagonist does exactly that. When he begins uncovering the truth he is led into his own basement by his lover who, unbeknown to him, is a cult member. He is taken in sacrifice by the cult members and the Watcher at the appropriate date and time. And what follows is widespread chaos."

"And if Justin's novel resembles Long's fiction, there are cult members somewhere in this world devoted to the emergence of what you call the Watchers?"

Calvin shrugged. "Something like that."

Dave was silent for a moment, taking it all in. He finally put forth the second question that had been nagging at him, the one that, if the answer to his first question was true, was even scarier. "Do you think Justin Grave may have discovered something like this?"

Calvin sighed. He set his empty coffee cup down. "I've asked myself that question for the past fifty years or more. Justin never wanted me to see the inside of that house he lived in. And when I did visit him he was very skittish. Squeamish, almost. He steered me away from certain rooms and he just seemed *jumpy*. *Watcher* had already been published and I thought that its writing had terrified him in some way. After the chain of events that led to Justin's downfall, I began to speculate more and more about his behavior during that afternoon visit. Maybe he *had* discovered something and *Watcher* held the key to all of it." He broke off and chuckled slightly, his eyes lighting with some new memory. "He surely downgraded Lovecraft and others after that. Said that their stuff was too watered down, and that they were afraid to face the truth, that they devised all these stupid monsters to bury what he described as *the truth*. He surely appeared to be always on the run from his pulp past, especially *The Watcher From the Grave*. When *Cloak of Darkness* was in production, the publisher wanted to include the novel in the book, but Justin refused. He never wanted that novel in print ever again, and he never mentioned it in bibliographies after that. It was almost as if he were trying to distance himself from that work, as if he were trying to escape its influence. I sometimes got the impression that . . . he was worried that there really *was* a cult out there, and that they were on to him. That by keeping a low profile, moving around a lot, would keep them off his trail." Calvin shook his head. "If I had only known."

David let this sink in. He was very intrigued by what Calvin had just told him, but a part of him was still skeptical. David didn't believe in speculation and rumor; he needed the pure, hard facts to lean toward the angle Calvin was edging at.

Calvin shook his head. "I know it sounds hard to believe. But it's what Justin told me the whole genesis of his story was based on. I only came up with what I've told you through investigation and my own theories."

"Still it *is* an interesting theory, even for entertainment purposes. It's still kind of wild though. The only thing different about it is that the Old Ones, or whatever, lack an organized following today."

"Oh, but according to Long's work there *is* a cult." Calvin said. "They're not as obvious as Lovecraft's Mythos cult; they're not some half-breed mulattos speaking broken English and chanting in weird tongues around a fire in some swamp. Far from it. Why, you remember what happens in Justin's story at the end, don't you?"

David nodded. It had slipped his mind and now it all came back to him. The protagonist's love interest seduces him one night in his basement where he found evidence of the cult, and the place is suddenly swarming with strange shapes which later materialize as people . . . and strange beings. His lover holds him down and he knows now that he is in the hands of the cult. His death guarantees the gate to the other side will be thrown open, allowing the Watchers entry into this world.

Calvin rose and took David's empty coffee cup, prompting David to start making his exit. He gathered his belongings, turned off the recorder and followed Calvin to the kitchen. "Do you think you could tell me where the house was that Justin lived in here in Lancaster County?"

Calvin looked at him with a mystifying expression. "I wish I could, but you're about forty years too late. The place burned down one night and is nothing but an empty field now."

Thus eliminating any chance for David to dig deeper into Justin's life for the book, or the answers to the questions that were now gnawing at his mind.

# VIII

Lancaster, Pennsylvania didn't provide the clues David wanted now that his curiosity was piqued regarding the *Watcher* theory. He had drained all the information he could get out of Calvin Smyth and opted to make his next move: Seattle, Washington, home of rainy weather, stout beers, Ted Bundy, alternative-grunge music, and one deceased writer and a mystery that gnawed at David's brain.

He touched down at Sea-Tac airport five days later and checked into a hotel. Most of his material on Grave was on one large legal pad and five micro-cassettes of interviews with whatever former colleagues and friends in Lancaster he could find that were still alive; one tape was of his afternoon with Smyth.

Once checked into his room he put the DO NOT DISTURB sign on the door and crashed. He slept for twelve hours.

The following afternoon he drove a rental car to the house that was in the Nightshades business rolodex. Justin Grave's former residence before he bit-the-big-one was situated in a quiet tree-lined street at the foothills of green, rolling hills. Low clouds hung over the trees, shrouding them in fogs of intrigue. David parked in front of the ranch-style house and noted the FOR SALE sign erected on the lawn. The executor of Justin's estate wasn't wasting time in carrying things out.

A pleasant looking middle-aged woman met him at the door. Her smile downplayed the age lines on her face. She was dressed immaculately and professionally in a snug, gray burgundy suit and knee-length skirt with a white blouse and tan pumps. Her legs were shapely. Her once-blonde hair was turning a rapid gray, yet her eyes still sparkled with a youthful boisterousness. She had a full hourglass figure that was attractive. The sign outside stated that the sale of the house was being handled by Geri Sheller Realtors. David smiled as he approached the door. "Hi. You must be Ms. Sheller?"

"At your service." She held out a hand in greeting and David took it. "Coming to take a look, or –"

"Actually, I'm a friend and associate of the former owner of the house," David said. "I've just been named his literary executor, and I came by in the hopes of extracting whatever manuscripts or private papers he might have left behind."

Geri nodded. She motioned for David to come inside. David followed her into the house, noting her figure. The woman looked almost old enough to be his mother but she hadn't lost her attractiveness, or her sex appeal. She reminded David of an Ann Margaret or a Raquel Welch.

"The moving crew took everything out last week," she said as she led him to the kitchen. The interior was stripped of furniture and knick-knacks. "Mr. Grave's attorney arranged for his personal belongings to be stored at A-1 Storage. I'll give you the address." She reached a table in the kitchen where she was headquartered and jotted down a number on a piece of stationary. She handed it to David, who made a mental note of it before putting it into his shirt pocket.

David was just about to ask if he could have a look around the house, but was interrupted by the sound of the front door opening and a hollow, "hello". Geri whirled. "Duty calls," she said, moving to the living room to greet a potential buyer. David checked his watch; it was two o'clock, which gave him time to swing by Justin's physician, as well as pay a visit to the storage area. He let himself out of the house, making a mental note to come back and try to get a feel for the place at a later time. Right now he had other matters to attend to.

## IX

He exited Dr. William Johnson's clinic an hour later, more puzzled and frightened than when he had talked to Calvin Smyth five days ago. Johnson was very adamant about Calvin's health up to the time of his death. At eighty-nine years old, Justin was in better physical shape and health than most men half his age. His cholesterol level was normal, his blood pressure controlled by medication, his heart strong and fine. He had no respiratory problems, no back or joint ailments and normal bowel movements. *Well then, what had been the cause of his death?* David had asked.

A massive heart attack, was Dr. Johnson's reply. It was as if a hand had reached into his ribcage and squeezed the muscle until it burst. The news was shocking, but what bounced off David's mind even more were Johnson's final words. *You should have seen the look on his face when the coroner brought him in. He had such a horrified look on him that you would have sworn he had just seen something . . . that defines fear as we know it, before he passed on.*

## X

The clerk at the storage area unlocked the rental space for David and then let him get down to business. The rental space was the size of a one car garage. It was crammed to the hilt with furniture, framed pictures, boxes, and two large spring mattresses. David maneuvered around the stuff until he came upon some boxes. Then he set to work in locating some of Justin Grave's manuscripts, memorabilia, and anything else that he could use for the biography.

And he was also keeping his eye peeled for anything that looked out of the ordinary.

His search yielded two boxes of manuscripts consisting of Justin Grave's published work from 1975 onward. Short stories, essays, and novels. All forty-one of them. Justin had proven to be extremely prolific in the eighties, at one point twelve of his novels seeing print as paperback originals in a two-year period alone. Most of them consisted of those which he referred to as "the foil embossed evil-skeleton-children" cover variety. Once the books started selling on the basis of their actual content than the stupid covers his publishers chose to adorn them in, the cover artwork actually improved.

He put those findings aside. They would be dealt with later.

Rummaging further, he turned up five of Justin's notebooks with story ideas. He flipped through them eagerly and scanned the pages. Story ideas, dream synopses, and general observations and notes. Nothing revealing about *Watcher*, or the horrors the story was said to allege.

Two hours later he stumbled on something in a crumpled, dusty box in the rear of the storage space. He sneezed as dust swirled around. He pulled the box to the center of the room where the light was better. He opened it and gasped down at the contents.

The big leather bound book was old. Musty and cracked, it looked as old as God. It was bound in a pinkish gray leather that resembled skin. The spine was bound by two large steel clasps bolted into the leather. David opened the cover and glanced at the title page: *Necronomicon.*

The idea that it was a fake flashed through his mind. But how does one fake a disheveled, musty, old appearance? The *Necronomicon* looked ready to fall apart.

Beneath the book was another notebook, this one more frayed and weathered. He opened it. The spidery handwriting was unfamiliar, but the contents were shocking. David drew a sharp intake of breath as he read a few paragraphs.

Five minutes later he was racing out of the storage area grounds with the *Necronomicon* and the notebook under his arm.

# XI

He decided to spin by Justin Grave's former residence on a whim. The daylight was fading fast, and in another thirty minutes it would be dark. The house was on his way to the hotel in downtown Seattle. David hit interstate 5 and zoomed toward the house.

The notebook and the ancient book were the proof he wanted but never thought he would get. David's heart raced with excitement as the realization of what he had just discovered thumped through his head. Occult scholars had long debated the existence of an accursed book as described by Lovecraft and others, but now David had the proof.

David hadn't read much of the notebook, but what he'd perused was enough to convince him that something weird had been happening for decades, perhaps even centuries. The notebook was most likely written by a deranged cult follower. The author describes the *unholy power* the book has over him, and his *own weakness to the pleasures* that the Watcher showers upon him. *My very will has evaporated since* the discovery of that cursed book. I no longer have control over myself. Every time the Watcher visits me, I am compelled to commit unspeakable acts all in the name of my pleasure, and his demand that I bow down to him upon my relief. Another line further down: With each victim he grows stronger, more physical in his strength. His thirst for blood is unstoppable! And further down: Oh God, why did I even research this? My curiosity to the writings of James Long have proven to be disastrous! The man had discovered what had been sleeping for centuries: the demon of the undead himself!

David had flipped ahead to the rear of the notebook and found the last entry. His heart raced madly in his chest as he remembered the passage. I can no longer contain myself; these horrible murders must stop. The only way I can warn others is to make this story public and step out of the shadows I have sprung from. I now know the true reason behind Long's death, and the tragic lives of his later contemporaries. It is good for those that came after Long and have tried to emulate him have never discovered the true secret –

But wait! The damp odor of rot invades my nostrils. They've found out what my plans are! I don't know how, but they've found –

It is there that the journal ends.

And it was that which sent David racing to his car, the ancient book and journal in hand. His mind pieced together the events by pure speculation. Justin moved into the house outside of Lancaster in January of 1939, a month after the former resident suddenly disappeared. Was it possible he had moved into the home of a curious researcher delving into the dark secrets of the *Necronomicon*, a researcher who had gotten too close to the truth and was silenced, *only to discover the same ancient book and become possessed by the Watcher himself?*

It was this thought that rose in his mind as he drove through town. Justin obviously intended *The Watcher from the Grave* to be a warning, and his enlisting in the armed services was obviously an attempt at escaping the horrors in that rambling farmhouse. Likewise, his moving around the country, his degeneration into alcoholism, were all results of the madness of the secrets he now knew what the Watcher had in store for earth. Dr. Johnson's words rang in his mind. Was it possible that upon his death that Justin had received some sort of revelation? Could it have been that which sent his heart into complete arrest?

He parked in front of Justin Grave's former home. A single light glowed from the porch, along with a light from the kitchen. A tan BMW was parked in the driveway; it looked like the real estate agent was still there.

David strode up to the front door, his mind already formulating a story to pitch to Geri about his sudden return. The door opened immediately after he knocked, and Geri's face smiled up at him. "Hi! Surprised to see you back in this neck of the woods."

David stepped hesitantly inside. "I was just wondering if I could take a look around the place," he said. "Get a feel for what Justin lived in . . . you know."

Geri nodded. "I understand. Help yourself."

David nodded, relieved that she wasn't putting up resistance. He moved into the barren living room with its large stone fireplace as Geri retreated to the kitchen. He could feel the cold mist of the night seeking its way inside the comfiness of the house. David stood and closed his eyes briefly, trying to get a feel for the room. He took a deep breath. He could imagine Justin living out his last days in this house, harboring the dark secrets that had plummeted him to depression and alcoholism, hiding the secrets that held the very fabric of sanity together. David exhaled and opened his eyes, taking a step toward the oak-paneled study off the living room. The room gave off a warm vibe, expelling the weird thoughts that had just clouded his mind. The hominess settled into his system, beckoning him to relax.

The sound of clicking heels on the bare floor caught his attention and he whirled around. Geri stood in the threshold of the study, a smoky silhouette that gained form and substance as she stepped into the room. "I was kind of hoping you'd come back," she said, stepping into the room. David forced out a smile as she stepped into the light of the waning moon filtering through the trees outside and shining through the large French windows of the study. The top two buttons of her blouse were unbuttoned, exposing the creamy top of her luscious cleavage. Her lips were moist and slightly parted, her eyes holding a feral secret. She stood in front of him, smiling wantonly.

"Yeah, well, I'm kinda glad I came back, too," David said. He thought that maybe after he checked the house out he would ask her to dinner or something, but she beat him to it.

She stepped closer to him, her hands reaching up to touch his chest lightly. "I was attracted to you the minute I saw you," she whispered. David's adrenaline surged, the breathing space in his jeans becoming uncomfortably tight. His mind fumbled for something else to say, like *well, I think you're attractive, too. Why don't we split and have a drink,* when his thoughts were obliterated by her kiss. He returned the kiss in surprise as her body melted into his. Before he knew it, her hands were roaming all over his body and his mind screamed for something rational to say.

As if reading his mind, she said, "It's okay baby, nobody will disturb us." Her fingers fumbled on the buttons of his cotton shirt as her lips kissed his chest. David was filled with the insane feeling that was beginning to make him feel a little stupid. *Don't you think we'd have the patience and maturity to wait till we get to her place, or my hotel room, before we begin commencing the bone dance?* But proper sexual etiquette seemed the farthest thing from Geri's mind as she undid his jeans and took him hungrily in her mouth.

David groaned and a moment later they were both nude on the floor. Geri straddled him, riding him furiously. David cupped and kneaded her large breasts as he moved inside her, not caring anymore about what was proper anymore, just going with the natural flow of sexual adrenaline. Geri moaned and bucked more frantically, impaling herself on him as they raced toward climax, spurning his orgasm on until sweet release came.

She collapsed on top of him in a heap, her face buried in the hollow of his shoulder. He held her, still inside her, his breath coming in ragged gasps. The sudden coolness of the night air pricked his skin, raising it to gooseflesh. The sudden change in the atmosphere raised a warning of awareness as Geri kissed his neck and raised herself up.

There were shadows materializing in the study.

David raised his head at the sudden intrusion, an icy stab of fear penetrating his gut as Geri pushed him down, the expression on her face changed to an icy, cold mask. The shadowy shapes moved forward and David's eyes grew wide with fright as he saw what had entered the room.

Most of them were living, breathing human beings. But they were silent, unemotional and rigid. They stood staring down at him as a lone figure stepped forward from the circle. David's mind reeled as recognition set in. His throat locked in a sudden scream.

Justin Grave's rotting visage peered down at him with a leering grin. Twin orbs of blazing light from beyond the stars shined from the hollow eye sockets of his skull. The black suit he had been buried in was dirt ridden and crusty with mold and white squirming things. He smelled of ripe, rotting flesh. A silent hiss escaped from his parted jaws. David's mind reeled as his body tried to scramble to his feet. Geri slipped off him and pinned him down with her knees as two others moved in to assist her. A rag was stuffed in his mouth and David writhed and kicked at his attackers. The rotting remnants of Justin Grave hunkered down before him.

"The same thing almost happened to Justin fifty years ago," Geri said, her voice dead to emotion. "Lucky for him, he chose to later embrace us rather than expose us. James Long wasn't so lucky."

David squirmed in his captor's grip as the rest of the congregation moved forward. Geri's regal features hovered over David, a grinning parody of evil. "When you become one with us, you become immortal. All it takes is the willingness to serve the Master."

David squirmed more frantically as Geri moved aside to allow Justin Grave's rotting corpse to shamble over him. It lowered its pasty, stinking bulk over him, its lichen gray hands grasping David firmly. David's skin recoiled from their damp, sticky touch. His stomach lurched like a tilt 'o wheel, threatening to upheave its contents.

"And now," Geri whispered, now standing nude with the others who had formed a rough semi-circle around David's prostrate body struggling on the ground, "Justin Grave will make his sacrifice that will throw open the gates from beyond the spheres."

Another muffled scream was launched out of David's parched throat as Justin lowered his head to David's throat. But it wasn't Justin's gaping jaws that made him scream, rather it was the sudden sense of recognition that flooded his senses. For the insane light that burned in the hollows of Justin Grave's eye sockets had been described in *The Watcher from the Grave* and they were the *livid, burning evil of the Watcher himself!*

The last thing David felt was Justin sinking his rotting, yellow teeth into the tender meat of his throat as he began to feed.

# DREEMZ.BIZ

# Richard A. Lupoff

f you're getting this e-mail it's because you're very special to me. A close relative, former lover, dear friend, or esteemed co-worker. Believe me, it's not spam and I'm not sending it to any huge mailing list I stole off somebody's database or bought from a marketing house.

I know what that's like, I've been annoyed by spam and spoofs for years and I wouldn't do that to you. Truthfully, I couldn't live with myself if I did that. I really couldn't. I get mad when junk email turns up in my computer, too.

Danged if I can figure out how the heck they get through. I've got a firewall, spam-blocker, anti-spyware, anti-adware, and they still get through. Every day I get offers to buy knock-off jeweled wristwatches indistinguishable from Rolex or Cartier except for the fifteen-cent mechanism inside, certified drugs from Canada or Iceland or Cambodia, or pills guaranteed to enlarge my penis, breasts, or other organs and make my partner ecstatically happy. Oh, stock tips galore, don't forget the stock tips. And my favorite, of course, pleadingly illiterate letters from the impoverished widows of Liberian millionaires offering to share their fortunes with me if I'll just kindly send 'em my bank account information and PIN numbers purely as evidence of good faith of course. Of course.

Here's what I do with these. I hit the "forward" button, type abuse@myinternetserver.net in the address box, and send 'em off to the oblivion they well deserve.

Then there are the chain letters. Two dozen rules for having a happy life or half a dozen photos of cute children, cute dogs, cute cats, or cute children hugging cute dogs or cute dogs hugging cute cats or fuzzy ducklings or whatever, or a soppy poem that somebody dug out of a 1946 issue of *Good Housekeeping*, or a joke that you thought was really hilarious when you heard it in the bathroom at your junior high school thirty years ago. Whatever it is, just send it on to your fifteen dearest friends within thirty minutes and *something good will happen to you today — this is absolutely guaranteed!*

Right.

The free offers can be tempting. You've probably got some of these yourself. You've won a free digital camera, a flat-panel giant TV set, a brand new laptop computer loaded with hi-tech features, a shiny late-model automobile or a lovingly restored classic '55 Chevy Bel-Air or '32 Ford roadster, or a free weekend getaway to the Bahamas for two, transportation included. All you have to do is click here and you're a guaranteed winner.

I asked my guru about these. I mean, just click here and I'm a guaranteed winner, right? I'm not greedy. The great car or the Bahamas vacation for two would be terrific. I can think of one special person I'd love to take for a spin in a Little Deuce Coupe or romance beneath the Caribbean stars. But, hey, I'd settle happily for the camera or the laptop.

My guru says, "If you want the camera or the laptop that much, save your money and then buy one. You'll have less grief, far less grief, than if you start jumping through hoops for some on-line sharpster."

Still, the offers do manage to get through and when I see a particularly attractive one it takes all my will power not to click where indicated.

But I do resist the temptation.

Always.

Almost always.

We all do slip once in a while or we wouldn't be human, would we?

When an email came through from Dreems.biz with a subject line of *Dreems 4 Sale* it caught my attention. I've always been fascinated by dreams. I don't think we know nearly everything there is to know about them, and I think all the so-called "sleep labs" at research universities are going about their work the wrong way. They study brainwaves and eye movements and skin temperatures and respiration rates. Okay, that's fine as far as it goes. But the physiology of sleeping, particularly of dreaming, is only one aspect of the subject.

What about the dreams themselves? What do people dream, and why do they dream what they dream, and for that matter what *is* a dream? That's one of those questions that seems simple enough, the answer should be obvious enough, until you start to think seriously about it. Then it gets very tricky, surprisingly complicated and evasive and ambiguous.

Okay, so I received this e-mail titled *Dreems 4 Sale* and I thought, yes, the fact that it was about dreams was at least slightly interesting. The "4" was also a nice touch. Very postmodern, very hip, very with-it.

I suppose anybody who still uses phrases like postmodern, hip, or with-it is by definition square, dorky, and obsolete.

Oh, well.

I did like the word "Sale." It's honest, you see? Everybody who advertises on the Internet or television these days offers something absolutely free of charge and without obligation and you get a free gift just for trying our product. Nobody ever says, "I want to sell you something," but that's all that any of them want to do.

So one point for *dreems*, one point for *4*, one point for *sale*. I figured I had nothing to lose by just opening the letter. I know you can get a virus that way, but I'm paying good dollars for protection from viruses. Let the antivirus software company earn its money for once.

<g>

That sign, BTW, the "g" inside the funny angle marks, is computerese for "grin." And BTW stands for By the Way. BTW.

The email is from a company called Dreems.biz. I've never heard of them before but obviously they've heard of me. The letter is addressed to me by name, c/o the email address I use for my home office. I don't know how the heck I got onto Dreems.biz's mailing list, but there I am. Here's what the letter says. I saved it to my hard drive and I'll give you a link to it. Here we go:

Dear Webster Sloat,
The average person spends one-third of his or her life sleeping. For most of us, the other two-third of our lives are divided roughly in half. Half the time is spent working. That leaves just one-third of your lifetime for everything else, and that includes necessities like washing, dressing and undressing, traveling to and from our jobs, preparing meals, folding laundry, and countless other tasks.

How many hours a day are your own? Really your own, to use however you choose? University studies show that for the average person, the answer is barely more than one hour a day!

By joining *Dreems.biz* you can get back the one-third of your life that you spend asleep. By ordering *dreems* from our huge catalog you can *live* those eight hours every night. You need not rely on random chance to determine the contents of your dreams. You can choose anything you want. Be anyone you want. Experience adventure, romance, excitement. Explore outer space. Win an athletic championship. Have a rich, rewarding relationship with the person of your choice. Or use our DreemLearning™ experiences to learn a new language, complete courses in physics, chemistry, sociology. Learn anatomy, mechanics, accounting. Prepare yourself for a new career!

*Dreems.biz* offers a choice of over 10,000 *dreems* in our ever-expanding catalog. Or tell us *your* dream and for a modest additional fee we'll create a custom *dreem* just for you. Our *Dreems* are fully interactive and participatory. This feature is unique, and I'm sure you'll love it once you try it out.

For a free sample membership in *Dreems.biz* just go to the URL below and fill out a simple application. We here at *Dreems.biz* are sure that you'll want to become a full member once you've tried our *Dreems*. If you have any questions, feel free to write to me personally c/o the *Dreems.biz* website. Every letter receives my prompt and personal attention.

Yours truly,
Carter Thurston Hull

Maybe I was a fool to follow up on that one, but I figured there was nothing to lose by just writing to Mr. Carter Thurston Hull. I wasn't joining Dreems.biz, I wasn't even signing up for their free trial offer. All I did was send them a simple question in an email one line long. It was this:

How did you get my name, business identification, and email address?

I figured they'd bought a mailing list somewhere. Or — ah, this was the answer! — I'd filled out a little questionnaire at the electronics store down at the plaza when I took my daughter there to pick out her birthday present. I'd long since given up trying to choose anything that would please her, not even a brand of breakfast cereal, but giving your own pre-pubescent offspring cash for her birthday seemed pretty cold to me. So we compromised. She could pick the store. She could pick the gift. I would hover at a distance and pretend not to know her until it was time to pony up the moolah, then the gift would go on my plastic not hers.

Mr. Hull actually replied, and he was impressively candid as well as prompt. He acknowledged that Dreems.biz purchased mailing lists, and that they'd got my information from the electronics outlet where I'd filled out the questionnaire.

Was there anything else I'd like to know? If so, Mr. Carter Thurston Hull would be happy to furnish the information. In any case, he would be delighted if I would accept that free trial membership in his organization, but of course he would not try to pressure me and I was still, he emphasized, under no obligation whatever.

In fact I had a couple more questions for Mr. Hull. I sent him another email:

What do you mean by "fully interactive and participatory?" Sounds like one of those role-playing games that my daughter buys at the software store. What's so special about your product? And, BTW, why do you spell Dreems.biz that way? Why not Dreams.com?

I thought Hull would be annoyed by that, but he played it straight and I kind of liked his answer:

By "fully interactive and participatory" I mean that our Dreems are *your* Dreems. When you enter one of our Dreems you won't just be an observer—not unless you want to be, and that's a choice you can make. But if your Dreem is, let's say, *Washington Crossing the Delaware*, you won't just see our First President in action, you can be one of the soldiers in his Continental Army. You can be right there in the boat with him, that cold December night. If you choose, you can *be* General Washington. It's up to you!

You can be Babe Ruth or Humphrey Bogart, Marilyn Monroe or Eleanor Roosevelt or Madame Curie or Rosa Parks. You can be anyone you choose, for the duration of your Dreem. And when you wake up, you'll be yourself again, but very likely you'll be a happier and maybe a wiser self.

You'll find that our Dreems are as different from any role-playing Game and provide as much better an experience as a full symphony orchestra is from a child playing a tin whistle!

Please — give us a try!

Yours truly,
Carter Thurston Hull

PS — We call ourselves Dreems.biz because somebody else already has the domain name Dreams.com.

Of course, I might merely have been tapping into an automated FAQ routine that produced those seemingly personalized answers. Or there might have been some low-paid computer science major working at an entry-level job, picking canned answers out of a catalog and assembling replies. But I didn't think so. These answers really seemed, if you'll excuse my saying so, real. And I liked the candor of the "PS."

Carter Thurston Hull and Dreems.biz seemed to be on the up-and-up, don't you agree? I even got ahold of my guru and invited her over to the house for a sandwich and a glass of beer, which my daughter watched us consume with undisguised scorn. I showed my guru print-outs of our emails, and she reluctantly conceded that the catch, if there was one, was so well concealed that she couldn't find it.

After she left I took a second beer with me into my study. I booted up the computer, clicked on my ISP's icon, and shortly found myself in cyberspace. I went back to Mr. Hull's first email and clicked on the URL at the bottom of the screen.

The application that popped up was pretty simple and definitely nonthreatening. It asked for some personal data but not for my credit card number or driver's license number or Social Security number, so

I figured this wasn't an identity theft racket. It asked me to create a user ID for myself. I picked Dudley Batson after a minor comic book character of my childhood. It asked me to create a password of six characters minimum and I keyed in ******.

Next came a screen that said I'd need some software to participate in Dreems.biz. I muttered, *Ahah! At last! Here comes the pitch. How much are they going to want for this?*

But there was no pitch. I could either download the software or they'd send it to me on a CD. My option. No charge either way. And in either case they recommended that I save it on my hard drive for future reference.

And my selected dreems would be sent to me the same way — via download or on CDs, as I preferred. They offered any three chosen from their on-line catalog. Once I'd used them I could order more. I didn't have to return the used dreems, they were mine to keep.

I clicked on CDs — see, that's more of my luddism coming out, I still like things I can see and touch, not just invisible electrons that come whirring along wires or out of the ether.

Finally Dreems.biz provided a link to their catalog. It was as big as Carter Thurston Hull had said. My first choice was easy.

I'd always been a rock and roll fan, and when the Beatles played San Francisco in 1966 I was frantic to attend their concert.

Wouldn't you know, I was at school that day and started feeling queasy over my sloppy joe and soda at lunchtime. I tried to keep going but my friends said I was literally turning green before their eyes. They dragged me to the nurse's office and an hour later I was in SF General having my appendix yanked.

It was a routine operation. The doc told me later that if I'd tried to go the concert I would never have made it. My appendix would have burst and then I would have been in *real* trouble. But as it was, I was out of the hospital in two days and back to school in a week.

And the Beatles had played at Candlestick Park and I'd missed the show.

I still have my unused ticket. Could probably sell it on ebay for a king's ransom.

I clicked on the little box and a check mark appeared.

What was my second choice?

I was starting to feel slightly more ambitious. I've always loved history and wished I could have witnessed the events that decided the course mankind would take. The Manhattan Project fascinates me, the dramatic events, Albert Einstein's famous letter to President Roosevelt, the development and testing process, Robert Oppenheimer, Leslie Groves, Klaus Fuchs.

Would Dreems.biz have a file on the original test, the world's first nuclear explosion? I scrolled through the on-line catalog with my fingers crossed and there it was. Trinity, White Sands, New Mexico, July 16, 1945.

Click.

Check.

And what would my third free sample be?

Right then I was sitting at the computer, filling out the form. I swung around in my chair and scanned the walls of my study. The room was lined with bookcases, the books arranged by category. One bookcase was devoted to computer manuals and user's guides. One was filled with reference books — almanacs, dictionaries, atlases, collections of quotations and records and trivia of every sort. And one was filled with my relaxation reading, my guilty pleasures, what my favorite literary critic calls lurid trash.

I rolled over to the last of those and pulled down a volume of collected stories by H.P.Lovecraft, the eccentric antiquarian pulp author of Providence, Rhode Island. I flipped through the pages reading a striking phrase here, a familiar scene there, in one after another of my favorite stories. There was "The Dunwich Horror," "The Rats in the Walls," "Shadow Over Innsmouth," "The Color Out of Space," "The Shadow Out of Time." I dropped the book on my desk and let it open where it would, and it fell open to "The Call of Cthulhu," probably Lovecraft's most famous story.

With the book lying open on my desk I keyed in my specs for a custom Dreem. I wouldn't Dream "The Call of Cthulhu." I would be there in the room in Providence as Lovecraft wrote the story. I would *be* Howard Phillips Lovecraft.

Once I'd sent off my order to Dreems.biz I experienced buyer's remorse. What was I getting into? Was this some new Internet scheme? Was Carter Thurston Hull a racketeer who would empty my bank account, ruin my credit rating, and destroy my life? Was Dreems.biz a cult? Would a couple of men in black come calling at my door while ominously silent helicopters hovered overhead? I considered logging onto the website again and canceling my order, but I didn't do it. My curiosity was fighting my caution, and curiosity was winning.

A couple of days later a FedEx truck pulled up in front of my house and the driver handed me a package. I'd ordered software this way in the past and the driver was a regular. We exchanged some small talk, then he said, "I've been delivering a lot of these lately. Never heard of Dreems.biz myself."

I told him this was the first time I'd dealt with them and I'd let him know what I thought of their product after I'd tried it out.

You understand, I was still working as a technical editor for a Silicon Valley startup that had barely survived the dotcom bust and was struggling to get back into profit. They let me telecommute part-time and show up at the office the rest of the time. On top of this I was raising a thirteen-year-old girl, which, if you've ever tried it, you know can keep you busy forty-eight hours a day. But eventually I was caught up with my work, or as caught up as I ever managed to get, and my daughter was in bed for the night. I felt I was entitled to relax.

A glass of good Scotch helped, and some fine music cleared my mind and elevated my soul. I'm not a religious man, but Mozart's *Coronation Mass* can almost make me believe there is a God. By eleven o'clock I was ready for sleep. I climbed into my pajamas, performed my ablutions, and was ready to climb into bed when I remembered the disks that had arrived from Dreems.biz.

All right, I thought, I'll give this thing a try.

I slid the first Dreems.biz CD into my computer. It booted up just fine. I found myself answering some more questions about what I wanted to dream — or *dreem* — and hit *enter.* My monitor screen went nuts for about half a minute, with a variety of colors and images swirling around. Then it seemed as if a bolt of light shot out of it and bathed me for a few seconds. It was like the aura that Sri Babaloo-boom-a-lam-bam-boom claims he can see, send $14.95 for his book, only it was *my* aura. I felt a tingling and I think my hair stood on end although I can't swear to that. Then everything went back to normal, except I felt very tired. I shut the thing down and went to bed.

The jet set down at SFO and Astrid and I put down our drinks and peered out the window. It was nice being back in San Francisco, although I had my doubts about playing in a football stadium. Brian got to the door first and made sure everything was copacetic before any of the boys climbed down the stairway.

It was a quick ride to the football stadium and they put us in a smelly locker room where they told us the local baseball team dressed for games. It was August, baseball season in America, and the baseball team shared facilities with the footballers. A couple of the guys had wives or girlfriends with them. I felt lucky that Astrid Kirchherr stuck with me. She's really a mothering type, and I've been having these dreadful headaches since that yobbo in Liverpool let me have it in the noggin with a steel-tipped boot after a show. I should have killed the thug but I was too stunned and nauseous to move.

There was a nice spread of American grub, fried chicken and potatoes and greens, and after the long flight I was ready to pitch in, and I did. Astrid said, "You haff ein schmear uff schmutz on your chin, *liebchen*," and leaned over and licked my chin with her pink little tongue.

We could hear the other performers from the locker room. They weren't very interesting except the Ronettes, but for some reason Ronnie Spector wasn't with them tonight. The other acts finished, I took a big hit off a joint and a slug of tequila, picked up my bass and headed for the runway.

They had to provide bodyguards for us, believe it or not. Some fool preachers had picked up on John's comment about the Beatles being more popular than Jesus Christ and there were a few demonstrators at the show who thought we were Agents of Satan and wanted to skin us alive for the greater glory of the Prince of Peace and the God of Love.

We made it onto the stage and some disk jockey from a local radio station gave us the big build-up which we really didn't need after all, but that was the way it was. There was a big crowd, mostly young girls. Some of them were screaming, some were crying, some were throwing things at us but the platform was set up in the middle of the field, too far for them to reach.

John gave a signal, Ringo started his countdown, and the three guitars rang out. I stayed in the back, near the drum-kit, laying down a bass line. We were playing "Rock and Roll Music." The sound wasn't what you'd call really perfect or even very good, I'm afraid, but it was good and loud and the kids in the stands went nuts.

Brian had told us to keep the numbers short, loud, and fast, and that's the way we played. We wrapped up with "Long Tall Sally" and got off the stage in half an hour, and that was that.

We didn't head back to the airport after the show. They actually put us in an armored car and took us downtown to a posh hotel. It was still early enough to do something else, so Astrid and I showered and dressed again and asked if anybody wanted to head out with us. George was alone on this trip and he said he'd like to, and we managed to sneak out of the hotel without anybody seeing us.

We wound up at a little club called the Keystone Corner. Muddy Waters was playing there. Can you imagine, a genius like Muddy Waters sitting on a rickety wooden stage all alone, McKinley Morganfield sitting in front of a room with maybe seventy-five seats, maybe a hundred seats, playing his guitar and singing that gorgeous blues and probably getting a couple of hundred dollars and a free meal out of it. And the Beatles just finished a show at a football stadium with, I don't know, thirty thousand, fifty thousand, I don't know how many teenaged girls wetting their pants for us.

After the show I went up to Muddy and introduced myself and my girlfriend and George Harrison and told him I was one of the Beatles and I really loved his music.

He said, "I done hoid of the Beatles. I'm pleased to make your acquaintance, Mr. Sutcliffe and Mr. Harrison, Miss Kirchherr."

That was the whole of our conversation. We had a couple of drinks. I offered to buy one for Muddy but he said he was tired and had to go wash up. We caught a cab back to the hotel and went to bed.

That was the high point of my trip to America.

My radio turned itself on with news of the latest political scandal in Washington and the latest war in the Middle East. I climbed out of bed and resumed my life. My name is Webster Sloat and I am a single dad with a thirteen-year-old daughter whom I love madly and who drives me crazy.

So that was the Dreems.biz experience.

And today there was an all-day meeting scheduled at the office. Could I ever have done without that! But the bills don't stop coming, month after month. I think if I'd been alone I would have quit my job, sold my modest house in Sunnyvale for an absurd profit over the price I'd paid when I was married, and moved into a skuzzy apartment in the city. But having a teenager changes everything, and I mean everything.

Somewhere in my Beatles collection was a CD of the Candlestick concert. I put it on the speakers in the Saab. The music was wonderful, early Beatles rock and roll before they got all arty and experimental. But it was all John, Paul, George, and Ringo. Stu Sutcliffe wasn't on the record.

Or was he? I hit the *back* button and listened to one track in particular. "I Wanna Be Your Man." Was there an extra guitar on that track? If there were three guitars, then Paul was the third guitarist and that meant that Stu Sutcliffe was playing bass. I hit *back* again and tried to filter out the instruments and just hear the voices. Was there an extra voice? Was it Stu Sutcliffe? Or was that voice *my* voice?

I didn't want to try any more Dreems.biz experiences after that. Not for a while, anyway. The Candlestick concert might have been only a dream, or a *dreem,* but it was so real to me, I couldn't distinguish my recollection of the dream from a memory of a real event. Was I Webster Sloat or was I Stu Sutcliffe?

Sutcliffe had died in 1962 of a brain hemorrhage, probably caused by that kick in the skull at the Litherland Town Hall. At least, that's what I'd always believed. He wasn't one of the Beatles in 1966, he'd been dead for four years.

But I had a clear memory, a vivid, lifelike memory, of the Candlestick show with Sutcliffe playing bass and McCartney playing guitar.

No more Dreems.biz for me, I decided.

There was no time limit on the three free Dreems, and I went back to my life and tried to forget about them and about Mr. Carter Thurston Hull. I can't say my life was very exciting. Technical editing, reading for pleasure, listening to Mozart and Dvorak and Shostakovich and Locatelli. I don't know whether I'd grown away from rock and roll or it had grown away from me, but somehow the old pull wasn't there any more.

And of course, raising a thirteen-year-old. Sometimes I thought I should remarry just to have a woman in the house for my daughter to relate to, but I didn't think that was a good enough reason to marry. It wouldn't be fair to the woman involved and it wouldn't be fair to me.

One day my daughter came home from school and asked me for help with an assignment. She had reached the age where she knew everything and anyone older than high school age was a total ignoramus, distinctly including her father, so when she asked me to help out I was flattered, to say the least.

"What was Trinity, Dad?"

"You mean the religious concept?"

"No." She shook her head. "It has something to do with history. Something about an explosion."

I pondered. Aha, she meant the Trinity test in 1945. The first A-bomb explosion, in the New Mexico desert, before they used the bomb against Japan. I wasn't born for ten years after that, but I suppose to a thirteen-year-old anybody as ancient as her father had to have known Julius Caesar personally.

"How soon do you need this?" I asked.

"Tomorrow."

That wasn't time for anything except a quick peek at the encyclopedia and an Internet search. Rather than do the work for her, I talked her through the process. There were plenty of sites devoted to the subject. She didn't need any prompting to pick the best sites and print out the documents. We went over them together, highlighting the key names and dates and events, and when we were finished she sat up for the next few hours writing her report.

I read it through and I was totally impressed. No question, this was *A-plus* work.

Of course, there was no convincing her that I didn't remember all the events she was writing about. Still, she actually gave me a good-night kiss before she went to bed. Now I was the one who couldn't get the events of the summer of 1945 out of my head.

The computer was still running so I sat down in front of the monitor and loaded the Dreems.biz disk for the Trinity explosion. There was that display on the screen, colors and shapes swirling and blending, the bolt of light, the feeling that I was surrounded by a glowing aura, and then the return to the usual computer wallpaper and start-up menu. I shut the thing down and went to bed.

It was still dark out and it was cold in the wooden barracks but there was the sergeant walking up and down shaking us by the shoulder, his own uniform crisp and fresh-looking in the feeble incandescent lights. He growled out the same vulgar witticism that he had every morning since we got here, and nobody even bothered to pretend to be amused. We all grabbed our socks and the rest of our summer gear and got ready to face the glorious New Mexico sunrise.

This was going to be the big day, and once we got to work there might not be time for any meal breaks, so a good breakfast was important. Uncle Sam, I thought, is one considerate son of a bitch. He doesn't want his soldier boys to have to work on empty tummies.

What the hell time was it, anyway? The gadget was supposed to be tested at 0400 hours and it would take us an hour to get to the test site. Leaving at 0300 meant breakfast at 0200. Jesus, it was hardly worth the trouble of climbing into the sack, just to climb back out and go to work. But I was Webster Sloat, Corporal, Corps of Engineers, and I did what I was told.

It was raining cats and dogs. There was almost continuous thunder and frequent lightning flashes. I wondered how they could ever hope to get the test off under these conditions, but the big shots running the test must know what they were doing.

We formed up outside the barracks, water pouring off our rain gear, and double-timed it to the mess hall. You'd be amazed how cold the New Mexico desert gets at night, even in July. The mess hall was warm and bright inside. I was hungry and I took everything I could get as I pushed my tray past the serving tables.

Not long into the meal I realized that this was pretty boring. I guess there's nothing that says the *dreems* have to be exciting. My experience as Stu Sutcliffe had been a trip, but as myself, as a corporal eating breakfast in 1945, life could be dull. I tried to change to another persona. Sometimes you can do that in dreams. What was the big boss of the Manhattan Engineering Project doing? Leslie Groves, Major General Leslie Richard Groves. I concentrated my identity into a theoretical point somewhere inside my head and pushed.

To my delight, I found myself rushing up, right through the top of my skull. I was floating over the table. The mess hall full of GI's shoveled scrambled eggs and grilled sausage patties down their throats. The conversation was desultory, the usual GI mix of complaints, boasts, jokes, discussion of movies and of baseball games. The Cards had beat the Browns in the '44 Series but neither team looked likely to repeat. I knew — I *knew* — that in '45 the Tigers would beat the Cubs.

This was amazing. The more I experimented with my trial *dreems* from Dreems.biz, the more impressed I became. I was able to move around, popping instantaneously out of existence at one place and back into existence at another, like one of those theoretical quantum particles that the high-energy physics geniuses write papers about, and ask me to turn into something resembling comprehensible English.

I could also zip into people by directing my, what should I call it, "point of self" into their heads. I tried it on one of the poor KP's in the serving line, then into the mess sergeant. Piece of cake! All right, then, whom should I become?

There was a clock on the wall. It was 0245 hours. My erstwhile buddies would be heading out of the mess hall, forming up and climbing onto two-and-a-half-ton four-by-fours for the jouncing ride to the test site. I didn't bother to travel with them. I headed for the main test site.

There it was, a hundred-foot steel tower, and there was the gadget, already hoisted into position, wired and ready to go. I looked around for another clock and didn't see one, but without benefit of machinery I knew the time. It was 0315 hours. The rain was still falling, but it was not nearly as intense as it had been for most of the night. The thunder and lightning had rolled away and only faint, distant releases flashed now and then.

Nothing much was happening so I tried another experiment. I could jump from person to person and from place to place. Could I time-jump as well? It was 0315, suppose I did my "point-of-self" stunt and jumped forward an hour.

Instantaneously, it was 0415 hours.

The test was fifteen minutes overdue. I knew what had happened. Everything had been held up because of the storm. Some of the scientists had argued for scrubbing the test for twenty-four hours, but General Groves had huddled with Oppy and decided to wait the storm out. Of course, their decision was right. I knew that, even if they were nervous about it.

I became General Groves. Major General Leslie Richard Groves. He was forty-eight, almost forty-nine years old. With a start I realized that he was younger than I was, running this billion-dollar enterprise, commanding thousands of brilliant minds, pushing brains far better than his own to complete the gadget before Stalin's slave-scientists could get one of their own.

The official reason for the Manhattan Engineering Project had been to get the gadget before Hitler did. The Allies were going to use it on Berlin and end the war in Europe, but the Nazis crumbled before the gadget was finished. Some of Oppy's scientists had wanted to quit right then. Mostly Jews, they were, freaked out by Hitler and his policies. Not patriots, not real patriots, they couldn't care less about fighting the Japs, but Dickie Groves had held their feet to the fire and kept them on the job and the gadget was done now, ready for the big test, and if it worked then Dickie would be Harry Truman's fair haired boy and then the sky's the limit!

Time passed while I squirmed through the snakes inside what passed for General Groves's mind.

Groves looked at his watch. It was nearly 0600 hours.

I'd had enough of Groves. I shot through the top of his skull and looked around for somebody more interesting to visit. I spotted a painfully thin, harried looking individual in rumpled civvies. He wore wire-rimmed glasses and paced back and forth, muttering to himself. I couldn't understand what he was saying.

Inside his head I realized that he was thinking and muttering in German and in a flash I was able to understand his thoughts. So this was Emil Julius Klaus Fuchs, one of the great physicists and great spies of his generation. He was only thirty-four years old. He was a genius. He was a Communist who had fled Hitler and wound up in England as a guest of His Majesty's government.

What a time he'd had! The Brits didn't know what to do with him. Once he had his advanced degrees he wound up in an internment camp as an enemy alien — in Quebec, Canada, of all places. But once the Brits got their Tube Alloys program under way, their version of the Manhattan Engineering Project, Fuchs was free again, back in England, working on a gadget for Mister Churchill. And when the Brits combined their program with the Americans, Oppy was delighted to have Fuchs at his side in New Mexico.

Oh, Klaus was like a bear in a honey-tree. The honey he was scooping up was going straight to Harry Gold, and from Gold to Russia, where Comrade Stalin would build a gadget of his own, and face down the capitalist aggressors as he'd faced down the Nazis. It was nervous-making, but it was important work.

Most important work.

Enough. Enough of the mind of Comrade Fuchs. My next stop was obvious. Could I find Oppy himself? Did I have to look for him? Did I have to make myself a point of consciousness and go zooming around Alamogordo like a bee in a meadow?

No, *dreems* didn't work that way. I wanted Oppy, I found Oppy. He looked at his watch, no, I looked at my watch. It was 0620 hours. Ten minutes to go. What was Oppy thinking?

He was leaning against a wall. He looked casual but in fact he was trembling inside, so wrought up by what he was doing that he feared to stand unsupported lest he fall down. He was wearing his famous floppy broad-brimmed hat and held a cold pipe between his teeth.

Was that reality or was it my *dreem*?

He was thinking — I was thinking — of Berkeley, California, of standing in front of a room full of grad students, a blackboard behind him, a piece of chalk in his hand. He'd been outlining a problem, drawing equations on the board. The minds in the room were fine, he could almost see the keen intellects behind those shining eyes. This was the life he wanted, the life of the mind, the life of the disciple of Newton and of Einstein, a life devoted to fathoming out the deepest secrets and the most glorious creations of the mind of God.

I looked at my watch again. 0629, 0629 and ten seconds, 0629 and twenty seconds. How could a minute last so long, so long when the years of Oppy's life had sped so rapidly?

There was a flash.

What had I done? What had I done? The fireball rose, the shockwave, the blast, the flying debris, the heat, the light, what had I done?

*I am become death, the shatterer of worlds.*

He staggered. I staggered. Oh, Ella, Julius, Frank. Oh, Kitty, what have you married, what is the monster I have become?

And yet the fireball expanded and from it rose the column of dust and earth, the mushroom cloud that the world would know forever. I had seen the films uncounted times, the films of Alamogordo, Hiroshima, Nagasaki, Bikini, Eniwetok. Nothing could compare to being here. Edward would be pleased but he would not be satisfied, not until we build the super weapon.

I laid my head in my arms. There was dancing and cheering around me, but I wept.

In my *dreem* could I rewind events, unhappen them, travel into the past and change history? I left Oppy to his grief, shot forward in space, backward in time, climbed the tower like a phantom creature, plunged into the gadget itself. The countdown ended. There was a click, a flare, I thought I might make the gadget fail. This was my *dreem*, wasn't it? Mine! I could make happen what I wanted to happen. But I held back.

The light, the screaming of the universe itself, the tears of God.

The alarm sounded and I sat up in bed, drenched in sweat. What was this hanging from my torso? I staggered to the mirror. My pajamas were in shreds.

*Because thy heart was tender, and thou didst humble thyself before God, when thou heardest His words against this place, and against the inhabitants thereof, and hast humbled thyself before Me, and hast rent thy clothes, and wept before Me; I also have heard thee, saith the Lord.*

Breakfast for my daughter, and off to school she went.

In the Saab I turned on the radio and channel-surfed until I found a religious station. What was I looking for? What comfort was I seeking?

Whatever it was, I did not find it. The hymns were vapid, the preaching worse. I surfed to a music station and listened to a Shostakovich string quartet. The music was stormy and troubling, a match for my mood.

I still had my third sample *dreem* but I didn't use it for weeks. If Carter Thurston Hull was worried about me, he didn't show it. My emails contained the usual mix of business correspondence, baby photos from cousins in Minnesota and Connecticut, jokes and political rants and spam. I answered the business communications, deleted the jokes and rants and spam, and let the photos of new cousins and nephews and nieces tug at my heartstrings. I sent baby presents to Minneapolis and Westport. The proud parents sent thank you messages by email.

At the Fremont office I attended meetings and did my work on autopilot. At home there were no meetings, that was the only difference. Nobody seemed to detect any change in me. What does it mean when you don't show up for work and nobody notices?

My daughter asked if she could spend the weekend with her best friends. I knew the girls involved, knew their parents. They were all solid citizens. I wasn't worried. I let her go.

I sat in the living room the first night she was gone with a bottle of Laphroig and a stack of CDs. I started with Grieg and moved on through Dvorak, Vivaldi, Michael Haydn, Joseph Haydn, Carl Phillip Emanuel Bach, Carl Friedrich Bach, Johann Sebastian Bach, Sibelius and my old friend Dmitri Dmitrievich. I ended with the incomparable Ludwig. I felt that I had no choice. Not his big works, his chamber music. I fell asleep to the music.

The next day I was not hung over. I ate an apple for breakfast and drove out into the country. I spent the day walking in woods, listening to birds, watching clouds. I went home and phoned the house where my daughter was visiting. I spoke with the father of the hostess. The girls were having a grand time being thirteen-year-olds. Did I want to speak to my daughter? I wanted to, desperately, but I told him, No, I don't want to intrude on the girls' party.

For dinner I heated a can of soup and ate half of it. I closed myself in the living room in darkness and silence. Somewhere a dog barked.

The third Dreems.biz disk was on my desk, I knew, next to my computer. It would take me to Providence, to the cramped and cluttered home of Howard Phillips Lovecraft during the brief period of his greatest creativity. I was convinced he was a genius. I had long been intrigued by his strange, dreamlike narratives, his portrayals of the terrors that lurked in every corner of his Id. I had been drawn to him, fascinated by the thought of entering his mind. But my two previous *dreems* now made me wonder.

Was this what I really wanted? In *dreems* I could be anyone, anything I wanted. I could be Abraham Lincoln. I could be Adolf Hitler. I could be Jesus. I could be the Shadow. I could be the Green Lantern. I could be James Bond.

I could be a woman.

I could be an animal.

I could be an extraterrestrial.

What did I really want?

I knew that I would have to write to Carter Thurston Hull, pay whatever fee was involved, become a member of Dreems.biz. But I realized, also, that a danger lurked here. I thought I had as good a grip on reality as most modern men. I had experimented with a few of the more popular drugs when I was in college. I enjoyed them, in a mild way, but they did not excite my enthusiasm and there was certainly no chance that I would become addicted.

Dreems.biz was a lot like drugs. I had tasted a forbidden fruit and now I wanted more. But I was still able, I knew, to distinguish between the experience of *dreems* and that of the real world. In my *dreem*, Stu Sutcliffe had performed at Candlestick Park in 1966. I had *been* Stu Sutcliffe in my *dreem*. But I had not changed reality. When I played the CD of that 1966 concert, Sutcliffe was not on it. When I looked him up on the Internet, Sutcliffe had still died in 1962.

But I wasn't sure. My experience on the freeway, playing that Candlestick Park concert CD, hearing an extra guitar and voice on "I Wanna Be Your Man" was haunting me. Was it all an illusion? Or was my dream – my *dreem* — starting to invade my reality? Or — scariest of all — was my *dreem* affecting not just my personal, subjective reality, but the objective reality of the real, physical world?

In my *dreem* I had been Corporal Webster Sloat, General Leslie Groves, Klaus Fuchs, Oppy, but when I awakened and consulted the history books, there was no change in the Alamogordo test, the Hirsohima and Nagasaki bombings, the experimental explosions at Bikini and Eniwetok.

Dreams did not change reality. But did *dreems?*

I loaded the third CD into my computer and watched the swirling lights and shapes, winced at the flash, and turned off the machine. I put my dirty clothing in the hamper and donned my pajamas, brushed my teeth, gargled with mouthwash, and climbed into bed.

The ceiling above my pillow was not the one I had stared at every night for the past fifteen years. It was another ceiling in another room in another city three thousand miles from Sunnyvale. I pushed myself upright, slid my feet off the bed and into my slippers, and walked to the bathroom. I turned on the light. I stared into the mirror.

A long face, lantern-jawed, surmounted by dark hair a good deal shorter than I usually kept my own, stared back at me. I shuffled back to my bedroom and drew a gray robe around myself. It was chilly in Providence, chilly here on Federal Hill. I knew I was not alone. I did not wish to disturb my aunt, Mrs. Gamwell.

I made my way to my desk and took up my pen and manuscript paper. I had correspondence to catch up with but the larder was empty and my purse was flat. I had revision clients to keep me occupied but somehow I could not bring myself to rewrite the poor specimens of prose that they sent to me.

Perhaps if I let my mind wander some flash of inspiration would come to me. A story for one of the pulps would bring a few dollars, enough money, if I were lucky, to keep the landlord at bay and perhaps even to buy a bag of groceries.

A streetlight shone through my window casting weird shadows on the wall. An errant breeze moved the tree limbs outside. They whispered to me. The shadows on the wall danced and wove, making strange shapes. By studying them I could almost read messages coded into them. I had only to try hard enough, to understand the messages, and I would have my inspiration.

What were the creatures who lurked just beyond the edge of our perception? Could we detect them, should we detect them, what would we learn?

For an instant my room was illuminated to the brilliance of mid-day, then reverted to its former state. I counted seconds, then heard the distant boom of thunder. There came a gust of wind, another whisper of leaves, another flash and another boom of thunder, louder this time and closer, closer, almost as if it were inside my bed chamber.

With a roar the clouds released their contents in a torrent that beat upon my window. I turned in my chair and watched rivulets course down the panes, forming themselves into hieroglyphs that twisted and whirled before my eyes. The messages they spelled out became clear to me.

I reached for the chain that would turn on the lamp on my desk. The paper before me was filled with writing that I recognized as my own. When had I written? What had I written? What had possessed me to create the document that lay before me?

Here was my opportunity to redeem myself. I made an effort to render my mind blank and passive, to give myself over fully to whatever force it was in my subconscious or in the world around me, in the world unseen and unknown but as real, I knew, as an omelet or an aeroplane, that was guiding my pen.

I wrote through the night, having no idea what I was writing, seeking inspiration in the wind and the rain, the shadows of leaves and the booming of thunder. At last I fell, exhausted, upon my narrow bed. The last thing I saw was a vision of something shocking peering at me through the window, rain dripping horridly from it. Its face was a mass of feelers. Its flesh appeared rubbery and its skin scaly. Its hands and feet were like the webbed and claw-tipped extremities of a giant batrachian. Long wings ribbed like those of a bat hung from its shoulders.

With a snap and a gust of foetor the creature spread its wings and rose from the tree limb where it had crouched so terribly. It circled overhead, and I was no longer in my room in Providence but in some black void between the stars — if not beyond them — and the thing was flapping its wings, the feelers that made up its face writhing, its great eyes leering at me in mad and terrible joy.

With a start I realized that I did not have to remain where I was. I fled from the skull I had inhabited but instead of flying freely I was drawn to the thing that wriggled its feelers and flapped its wings. I entered its mind.

Words crowded through my own being, words whose meaning was so vast and so terrible that I wanted to scream but could not. I beat my own hands against my face, trying to wake myself, and at last I succeeded. I sat up in bed, not in Providence but in Sunnyvale, not eighty years ago but in my own time.

A winter wind was blowing outside and rain was falling. A storm had blown in off the Gulf of Alaska, made its way down the coastline and swept inland here in northern California. I could not bring myself to get out of bed, but I reached for the lamp on my night table and switched it on. I looked at my clock. There were hours to go before daylight. I wanted daylight desperately, needed it. Could I survive until the sun rose? I tried to leap forward in time but I was no longer in a *dreem*, I no longer controlled the world.

Carter Thurston Hull.

I thought of the being I had seen, the being Howard Lovecraft had seen.

Carter Thurston Hull.

The words ran together in my brain.

Carter Thurston Hull.

I realized, at last, who he was.

Send this message to fifteen people today and something good will happen to you. I guarantee it.

# About the Authors

JAMES AMBUEHL is a dedicated Cthulhu Mythos collector / bibliographer. He has had / will have stories in the *Ithaqua, Tsathoggua* and *Yig Cycles, Arkham Tales, Lost Worlds of Space and Time, Vol. I* and *Lin Carter's Anton Zarnak*. He also has 2 collections of his fiction out, *From Between the Star-Spaces* and *Correlated Contents*. And he is thrilled to be co-editing anthologies with Bob Price for Chaosium, starting with *The Dagon Cycle* and *Nodens and the Elder Gods* – and, of course, editing anthologies of his own for Elder Signs Press as well. Check out his cache of a dozen or so of his best stories at www.templeofdagon.com (the Featured Writers section) and feel free to email him at: jamesambuehl@webtv.net.

EDWARD P. BERGLUND is a retired U.S. Marine. He edited *The Disciples of Cthulhu* (DAW Books, 1976; Chaosium, Inc., 1996) and *The Disciples of Cthulhu II* (Chaosium, Inc., 2003), with various foreign editions. He compiled the 2nd edition of the *Reader's Guide to the Cthulhu Mythos* (Silver Scarab Press, 1974). He has one collection, *Shards of Darkness* (Mythos Book, 2000). He has had stories in various anthologies: *Song of Cthulhu, Der Cthulhu-Mythos: 1976-2000* (German), *Innsmouth Tales,* and *Kings of the Night,* and coming up in: *Lost Worlds of Space and Time (Vol. 2), Shoggoths!, Charnel Feast, Elementary, My Dear Cthulhu, Perilous Ventures,* and *Tales of the Outre West.*

SIMON BUCHER-JONES gains some respite from the bleak horror of normality by writing. He's written (alone or with others) four novels for, or spunoff from, the official *Doctor Who* book ranges (2 of them have Lovecraftian elements). He's now returned to the moldering corpse of his first love – writing more Mythos stories! Check out www.templeofdagon.com, the Featured Writers section, to read some of those Mythos stories.

JAMES CHAMBERS has been published in *Dark Furies, The Dead Walk, Sick: An Anthology of Illness, Weird Trails* and *Warfear,* the chapbook *Mooncat Jack, Bare Bone,* Allen K's *Inhuman* magazines, and other venues. His short story collection with artist Jason Whitley, *The Midnight Hour: Saint Lawn Hill and Other Tales* was published in 2005. He can be found online at www.jameschambersonline.com.

DAVID CONYERS is the author of several stories appearing in numerous magazines and the anthologies *Horrors Beyond, Arkham Tales,*

*Cthulhu Express* amongst others. A writer and illustrator for the *Call of Cthulhu* role-playing game, his most recent works appeared in Chaosium's *The Spawn of Azathoth*. He lives in Adelaide, Australia. His homepage is www.freewebs.cm/davidconyers/.

TIM CURRAN lives in Michigan and is the author of the novels *Skin Medicine* from Hellbound Books and *Hive* from Elder Signs Press. His short stories have appeared in magazines such as *Flesh and Blood, The Horror Express, City Slab, Space & Time* and *Inhuman,* amongst others. He will also be appearing in the anthology *Shivers 4,* from Cemetery Dance and an upcoming untitled horror/western novella collection with Brian Keene, Tim Lebbon and Steve Vernon also from *Cemetery Dance.*

J. F. GONZALEZ is the critically-acclaimed author of the novels *The Beloved, Survivor, Fetish, Shapeshifter, Conversion, Maternal Instinct,* and *Clickers* (Co-authored with Mark Williams). His short fiction has appeared in numerous magazines and anthologies and is collected in *Old Ghosts and Other Revenants.* His latest novel is *Bully* (Midnight Library). For more information, visit his website at www.jfgonzalez.com.

CODY GOODFELLOW is outwardly a model prisoner, but reliable snitches hint that he has quietly assembled a criminal empire reaching far beyond Cell Block C, and even into the prison administration itself. While incarcerated, he has written two novels, *Radiant Dawn* and *Ravenous Dusk,* and numerous short stories, the meager profits of which have provided scant comfort to his many victims.

C. J. HENDERSON is the creator of the Teddy London supernatural detective series as well as the author of scores of Mythos-related stories starring such diverse characters as Lin Carter's Anton Zarnak and Lovecraft's own Inspector Legrasse. Also like Carter and Lovecraft, he is world famous, dead broke and living in obscurity. To learn more about this tortured bastard, check in at www.cjhenderson.com.

WILLIAM JONES has published fiction in anthologies such as *Darkness Rising 2005, Dark Furies, Thou Shalt Not, Shadowsword, Blood and Devotion,* and several others. His upcoming collection *The Strange Cases of Rudolph Pearson* is to be released in 2006. William is also the editor of *Dark Wisdom* magazine (www.darkwisdom.com). When not writing, he teaches English Literature at a university in Michigan. Visit www.williamjoneswriter.com.

RICHARD A. LUPOFF'S long and varied career has ranged from straightforward journalism to screenwriting. He has achieved the rare distinction of having stories selected for "Best of the Year" anthologies in three fields — science fiction, mystery, and horror. Some of his recent publications are *Quintet: The Cases of Chase and Delacroix* (Crippen & Landru), *Villagio Sogno*, a fantasy, *The Tinpan Tiger Killer*, the concluding volume in his acclaimed "Lindsey and Plum" mystery series, *Terrors*, and the upcoming collection *Visions*.

WILLIE MEIKLE is a 40+ year old Scotsman with five novels published: *Island Life* (vaguely Lovecraftian); *The Watcher Trilogy* (non-Lovecraftian); *The Midnight Eye Files: The Amulet* (Lovecraftian). There are two more novels on the way in 2006.

There's also over 130 stories published in the genre press, both in paper and in online magazines, with work appearing in the UK, Ireland, the USA, India, Greece and Canada. (Very soon, he will rule the world!)

ERIC J. MILLAR was born on July 17, 1981 in Bemidji, Minnesota, where he has lived most of his life. From an early age he has been cursed with an overactive imagination and a drive to tell stories. When he isn't writing, he enjoys cartooning and hunting for obscure books by long forgotten authors. He enjoys the works of Philip K. Dick, Kurt Vonnegut, Michael Moorcock, Alan Moore, Grant Morrison, Warren Ellis and, which should be fairly apparent by his story printed herein, Frank Miller too. You can email him at young_bastard81@yahoo.com.

ROBERT M. PRICE, introduced to the writings of Lovecraft in 1967, when a mere 13 years old, has never managed to exorcise the ghost of the Old Gent, not that he has tried very hard. He edited the fanzine *Crypt of Cthulhu* for 109 issues, then switched over to editing fiction anthologies for Fedogan and Bremer, Chaosium, and others. His own Cthulhu Mythos fiction awaits publication in a Mythos Books collection, *Blasphemies and Revelations*.

JONATHAN SHARP is a mild-mannered English Gentleman, who divides his time between working in a public library, writing background music for television and obsessing over pulp literature. "The White Mountains" is his first published story.

RON SHIFLET is a native Texan whose earliest influences were Lovecraft and Howard. His work has appeared in the well-acclaimed *Horrors Beyond* and *Cold Flesh,* as well as publications such as *The Book of Dark Wisdom* and *Dark Legacy*. He is also the co-author of the newly-released *Wandering Flesh* chapbook with John Hubbard.

STEVEN L. SHREWSBURY, 36, author of *Godforsaken*, has over 350 tales to his credit. His current products are *King of the Bastards* with Brian Keene and *Bedlam Unleashed* with Peter Welmerink, and other novels. His work will soon appear in *Deathgrip: Exit Laughing*, *Barebone*, and *Bladespell*. His website is www.stevenshrewsbury.com.

JOHN SUNSERI flips hamburgers for a living, drinks microbrews as a hobby and never kills more than he can eat, no matter how much he'd like to. He's been published all over the small press and occasionally acts as an avatar for Nyarlathotep when money gets tight. He loves his wife, tolerates his cats, and loathes seafood.

JEFFREY THOMAS is the author of the collections *Punktown*, *Punktown: Shades of Grey*, *Thirteen Specimens*, *AAAIIIEEE!!!*, *Honey is Sweeter Than Blood* and *Terror Incognita*, and of the novels *Monstrocity*, *Everybody Scream!*, *Letters From Hades* and *Boneland*. His books have been translated into German, Chinese and Russian. He lives in Massachusetts.

PATRICK THOMAS has authored over 50 published stories and a dozen books, including the popular fantasy humor series *Murphy's Lore*. He co-created the YA fantasy series *The Wildsidhe Chronicles*, is an editor for *Fantastic Stories of the Imagination*, and writes the syndicated satirical advice column *Dear Cthulhu*. Visit his website at www.murphy's-lore.com or www.dearcthulhu.com.

DAVID WITTEVEEN is a fantasy/horror writer based in Melbourne, Australia. He has been published by *Shadowed Realms*, *Opi8.com* and Pagan Publishing. He also won the Best Flash Fiction award in the Australian Horror Writers Association's 2005 Short Story Competition.